# HELLAWEEN

# MOSS LAWTON

## COLOR BY VICTORIA HARRIS

RAZORBILL

RAZORBILL

An imprint of Penguin Random House LLC, New York

First published in the United States of America by Razorbill, an imprint of Penguin Random House LLC, 2023

Copyright © 2023 by Moss Lawton

Visit us online at penguinrandomhouse.com.

Library of Congress Cataloging-in-Publication Data
Lawton, Moss, author.
Title: Hellaween / Moss Lawton.
Description: New York : Razorbill, 2023. | Audience: Ages 10-14 years. | Summary: Gwen, an aspiring witch, and her two monster best friends try to have a fun-filled Halloween, but must contend with a local kid obsessed with hunting the supernatural.

Identifiers: LCCN 2022051260 (print) | LCCN 2022051261 (ebook) | ISBN 9780593524299 (hardcover) | ISBN 9780593524282 (trade paperback) | ISBN 9780593524312 (nook edition) | ISBN 9780593524305 (kindle edition) | ISBN 9780593524329
Subjects: CYAC: Graphic novels. | Halloween—Fiction. | Witches—Fiction. | Vampires—Fiction. | Werewolves—Fiction. | LCGFT: Graphic novels.
Classification: LCC PZ7.7.L3955 He 2023 (print) | LCC PZ7.7.L3955 (ebook) | DDC 741.5/973—dc23/eng/20220812
LC record available at https://lccn.loc.gov/2022051260
LC ebook record available at https://lccn.loc.gov/2022051261

ISBN 9780593524282 (paperback)
10 9 8 7 6 5 4 3 2 1

ISBN 9780593524299 (hardcover)
10 9 8 7 6 5 4 3 2 1

Manufactured in China

TOPL

Colors by Victoria Harris
Edited by Christopher Hernandez
Design by Danielle Ceccolini

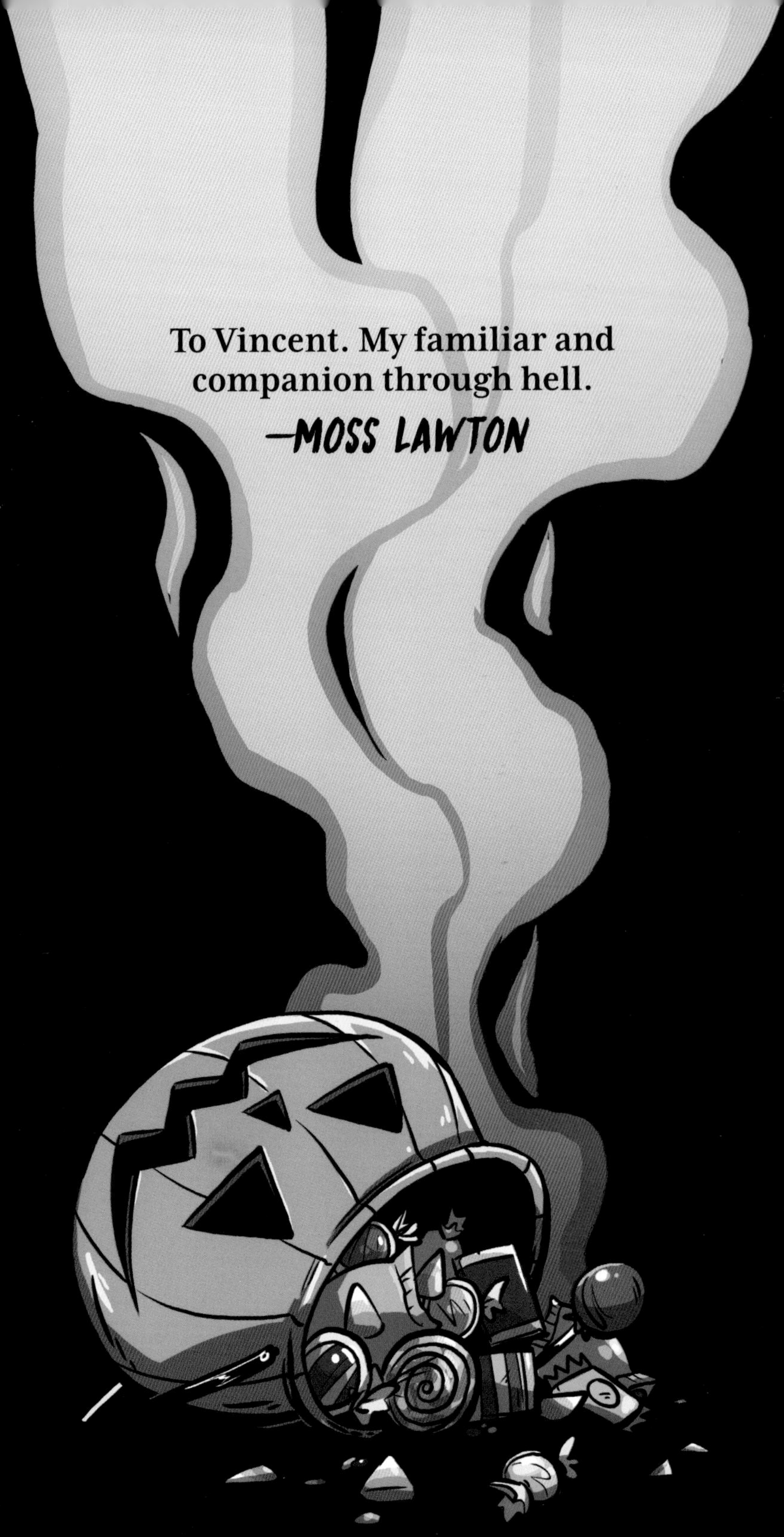

To Vincent. My familiar and companion through hell.

—MOSS LAWTON

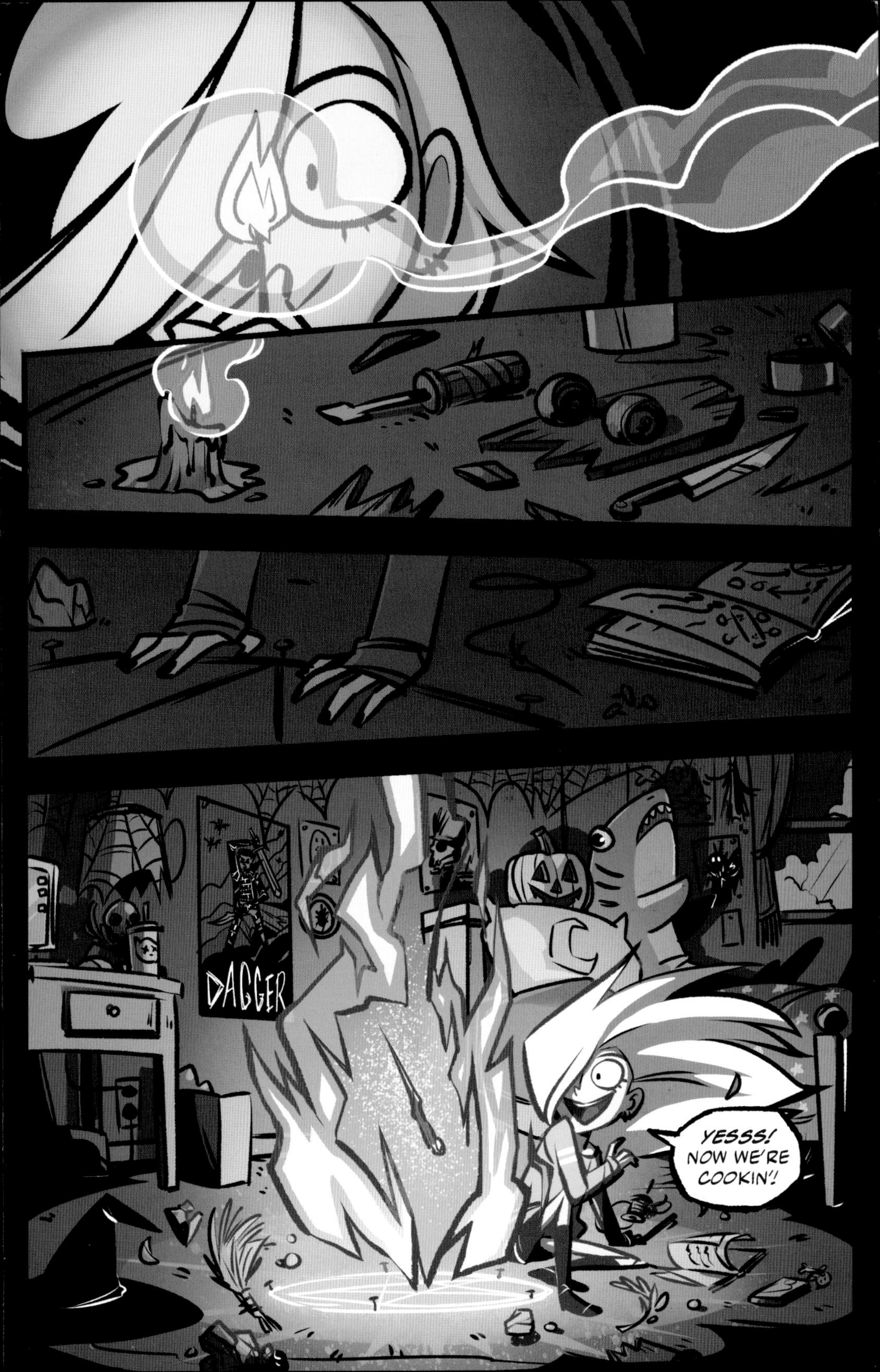
DAGGER
YESSS! NOW WE'RE COOKIN'!

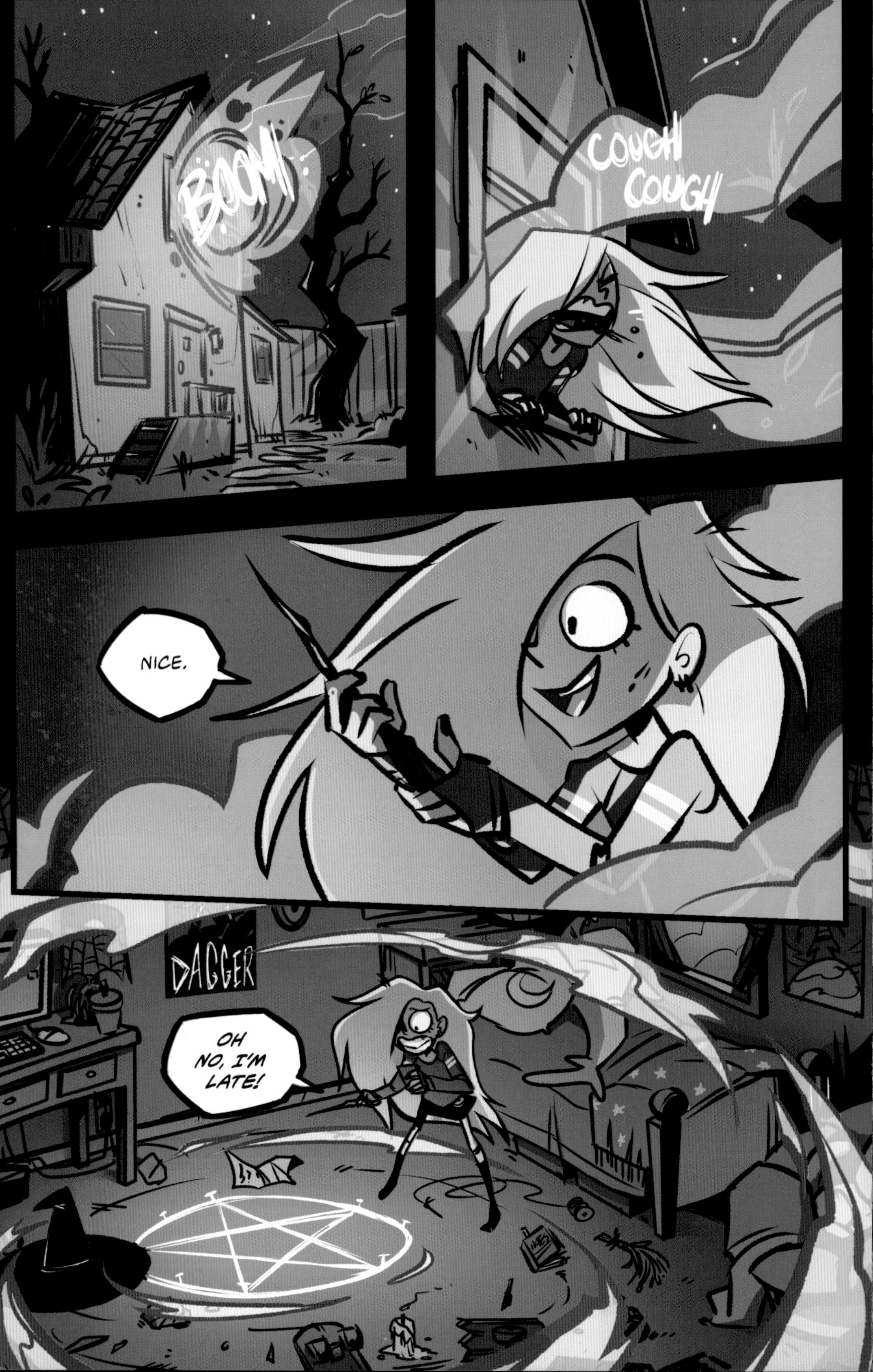
BOOM!
COUGH COUGH
NICE.
DAGGER
OH NO, I'M LATE!

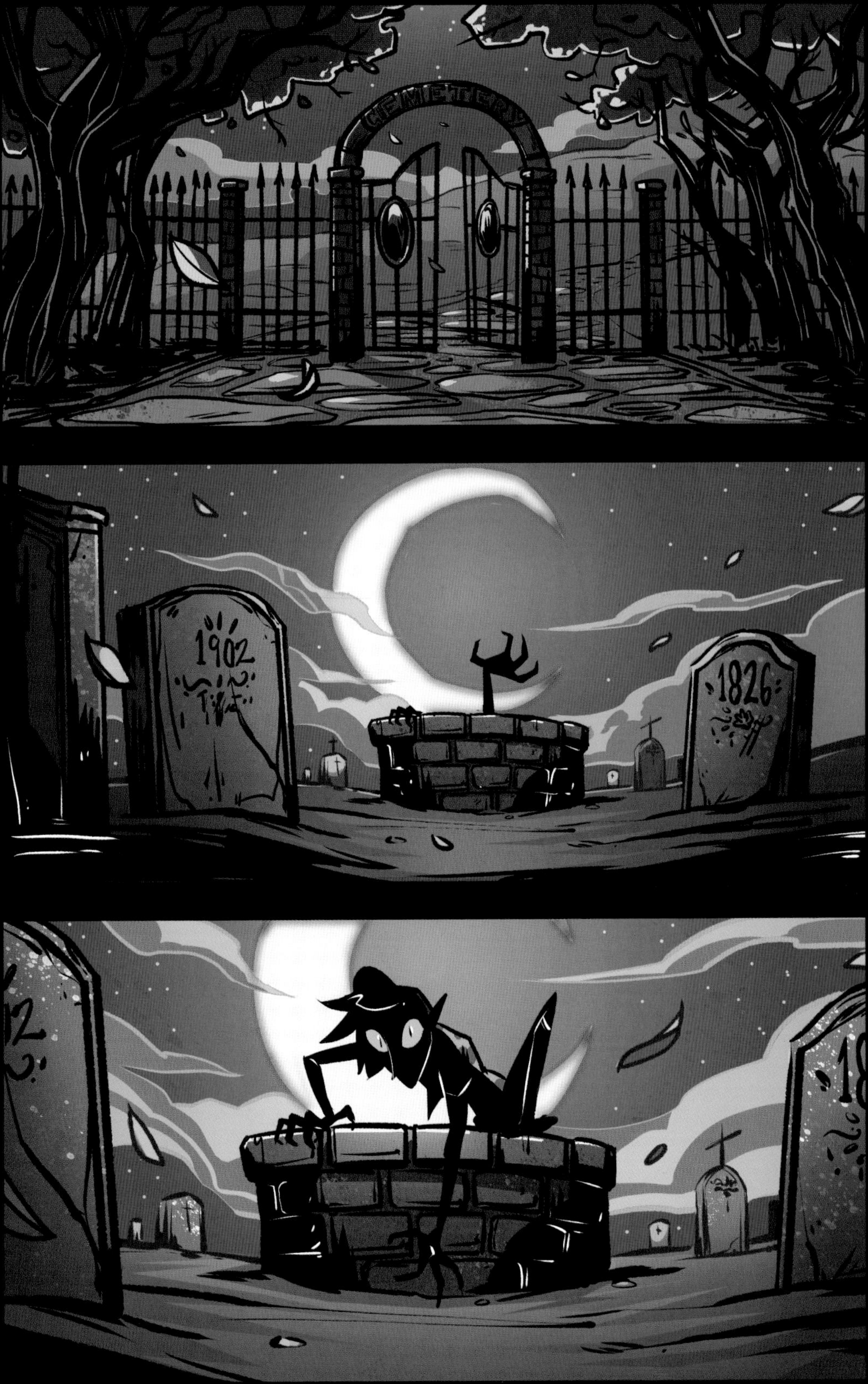
CEMETERY
1902
1826

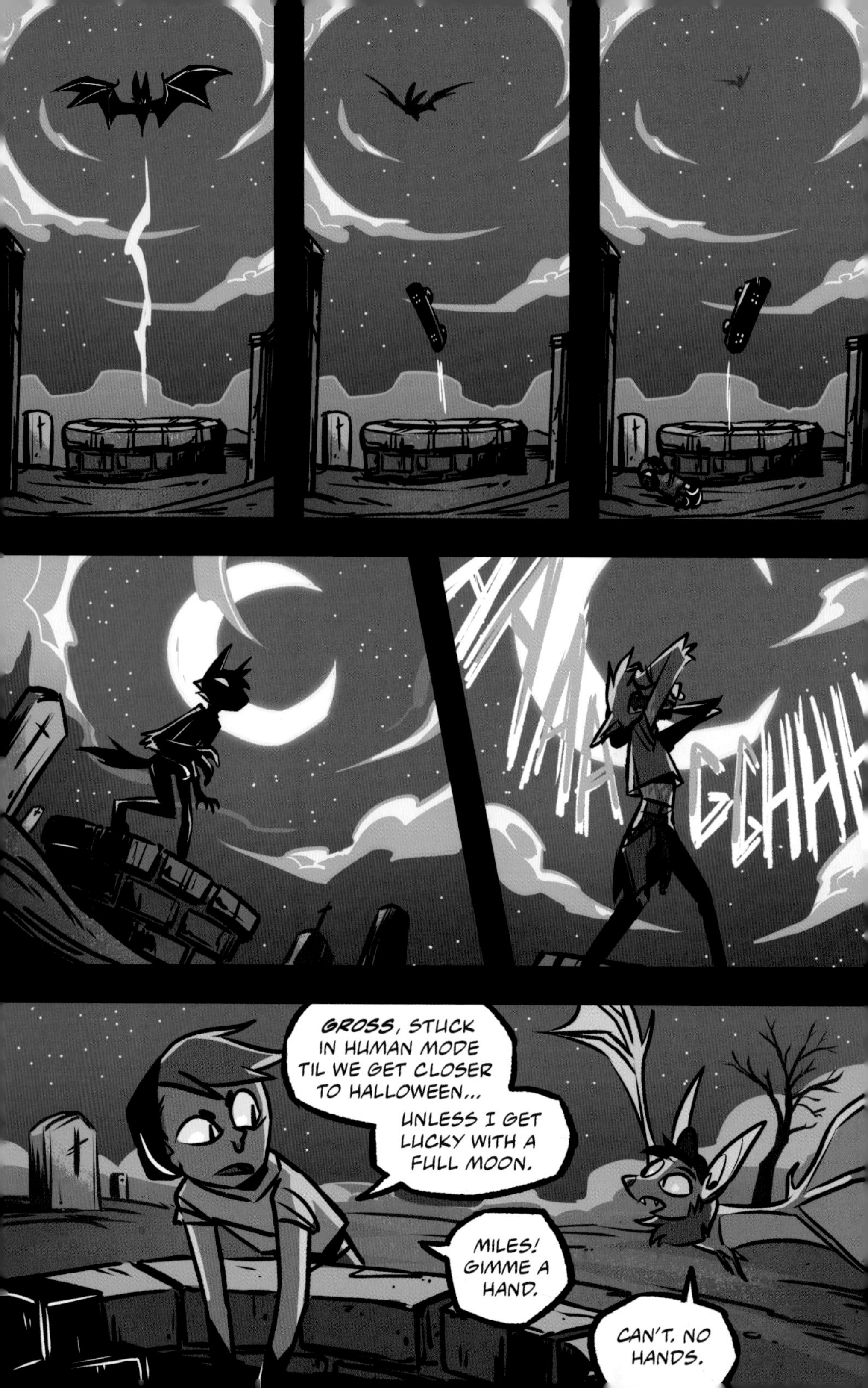
AAAAGCHHH
GROSS, STUCK IN HUMAN MODE TIL WE GET CLOSER TO HALLOWEEN...
UNLESS I GET LUCKY WITH A FULL MOON.
MILES! GIMME A HAND.
CAN'T. NO HANDS.

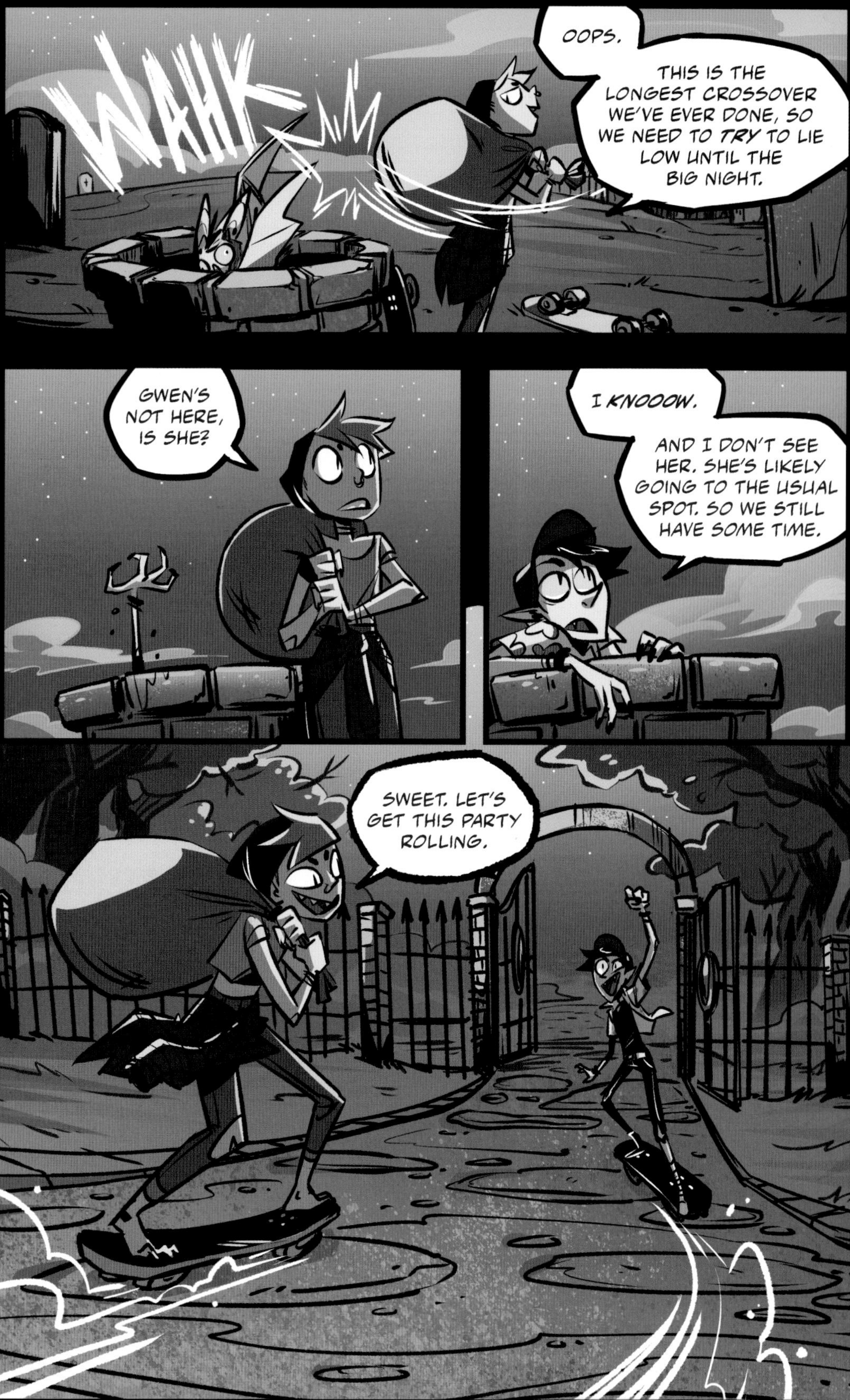
WAHK
OOPS.
THIS IS THE LONGEST CROSSOVER WE'VE EVER DONE, SO WE NEED TO *TRY* TO LIE LOW UNTIL THE BIG NIGHT.
GWEN'S NOT HERE, IS SHE?
I *KNOOOW*.
AND I DON'T SEE HER. SHE'S LIKELY GOING TO THE USUAL SPOT. SO WE STILL HAVE SOME TIME.
SWEET. LET'S GET THIS PARTY ROLLING.

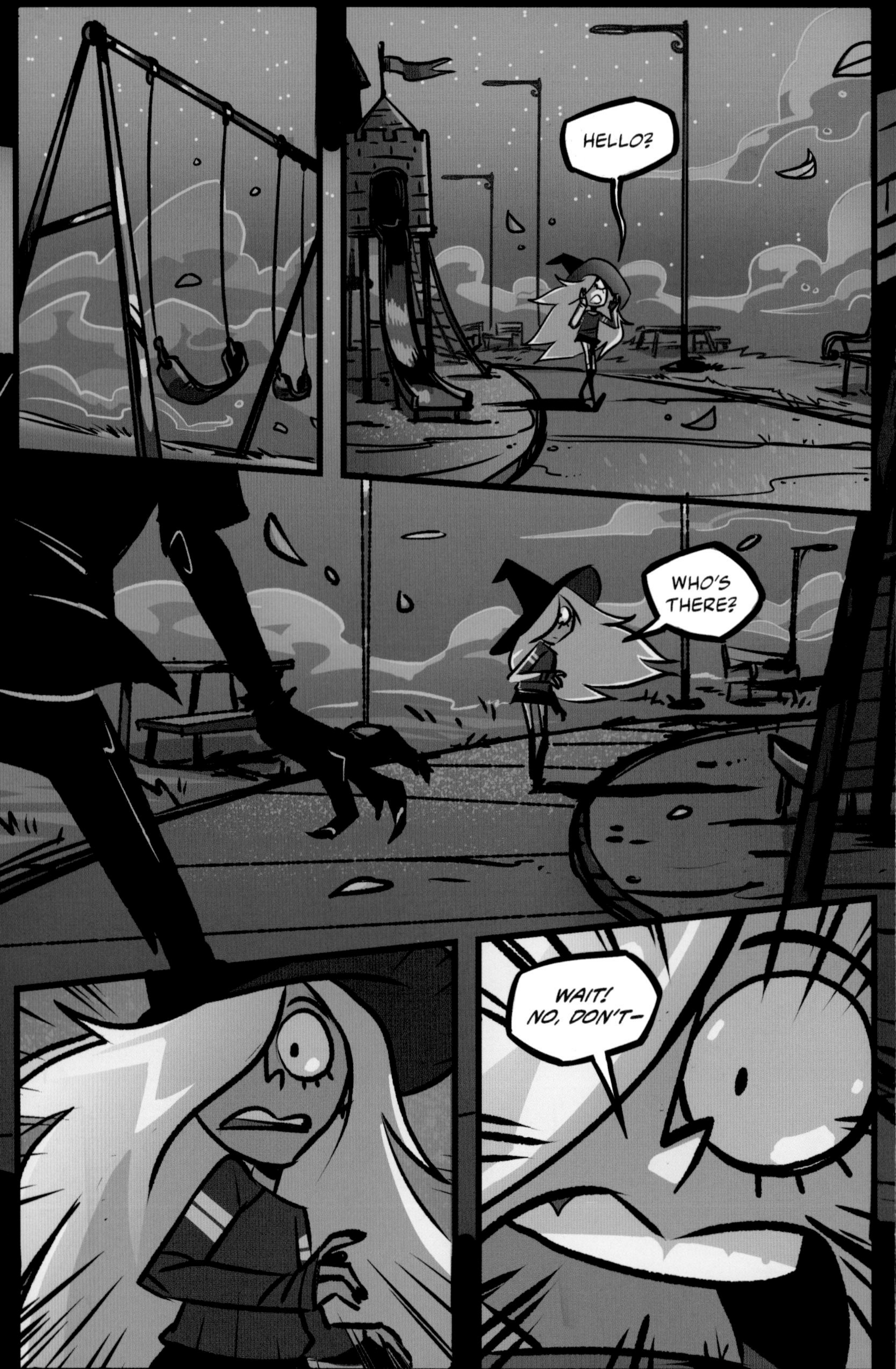
HELLO?
WHO'S THERE?
WAIT! NO, DON'T–

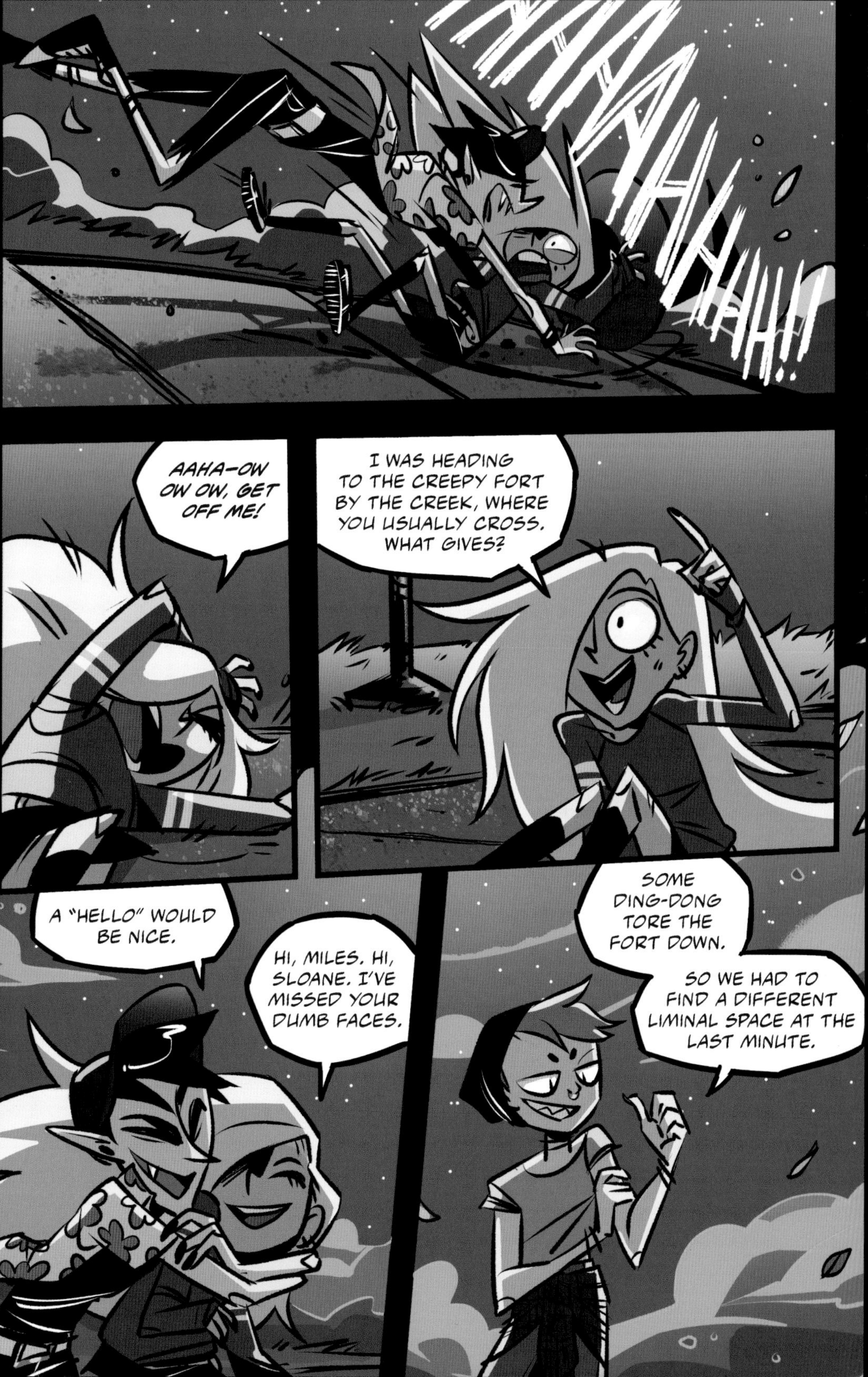
AAAAAHHHHH!!
AAHA-OW OW OW, GET OFF ME!
I WAS HEADING TO THE CREEPY FORT BY THE CREEK, WHERE YOU USUALLY CROSS. WHAT GIVES?
A "HELLO" WOULD BE NICE.
HI, MILES. HI, SLOANE. I'VE MISSED YOUR DUMB FACES.
SOME DING-DONG TORE THE FORT DOWN.
SO WE HAD TO FIND A DIFFERENT LIMINAL SPACE AT THE LAST MINUTE.

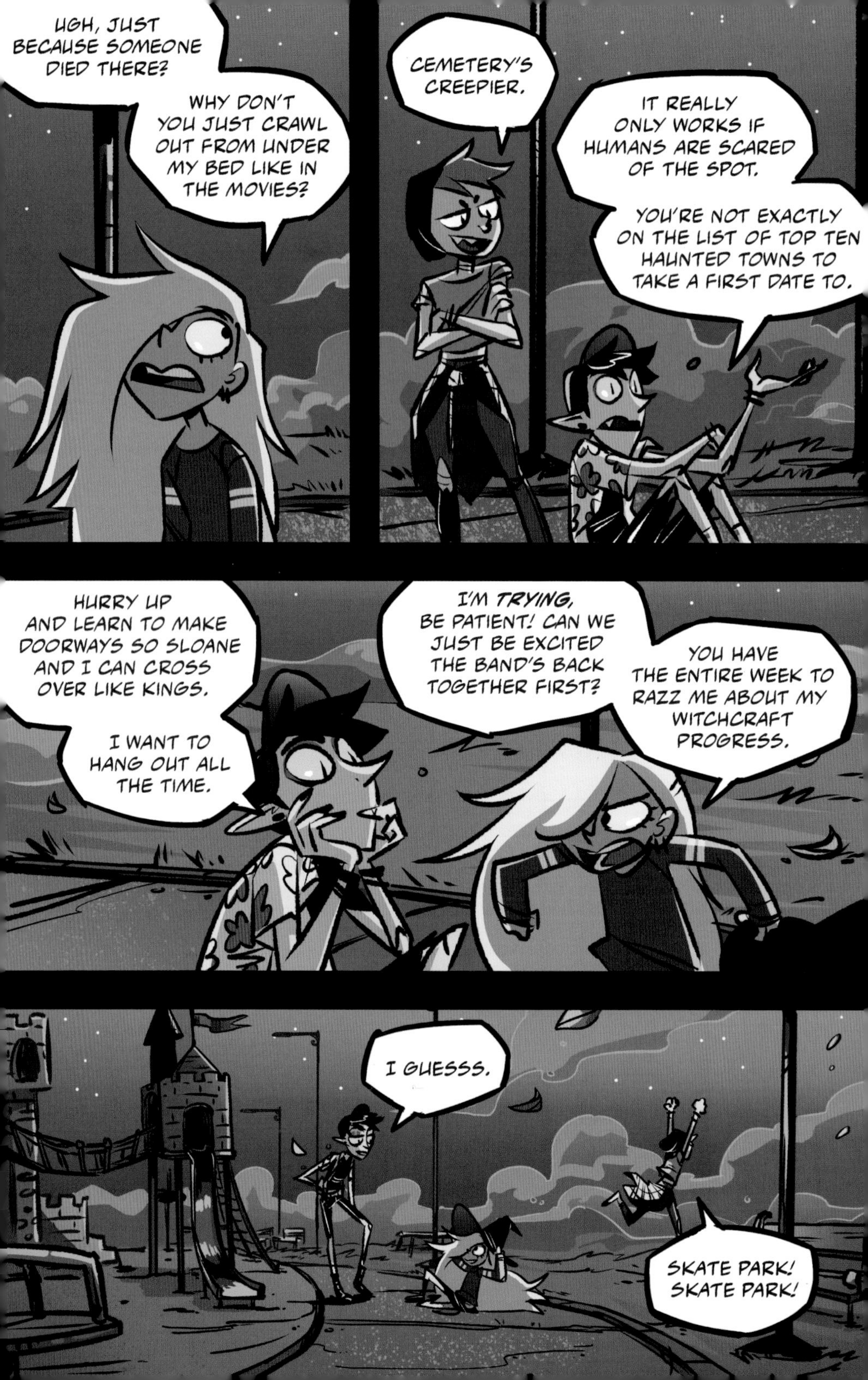
UGH, JUST BECAUSE SOMEONE DIED THERE?
WHY DON'T YOU JUST CRAWL OUT FROM UNDER MY BED LIKE IN THE MOVIES?
CEMETERY'S CREEPIER.
IT REALLY ONLY WORKS IF HUMANS ARE SCARED OF THE SPOT.
YOU'RE NOT EXACTLY ON THE LIST OF TOP TEN HAUNTED TOWNS TO TAKE A FIRST DATE TO.
HURRY UP AND LEARN TO MAKE DOORWAYS SO SLOANE AND I CAN CROSS OVER LIKE KINGS.
I WANT TO HANG OUT ALL THE TIME.
I'M TRYING, BE PATIENT! CAN WE JUST BE EXCITED THE BAND'S BACK TOGETHER FIRST?
YOU HAVE THE ENTIRE WEEK TO RAZZ ME ABOUT MY WITCHCRAFT PROGRESS.
I GUESSS.
SKATE PARK! SKATE PARK!

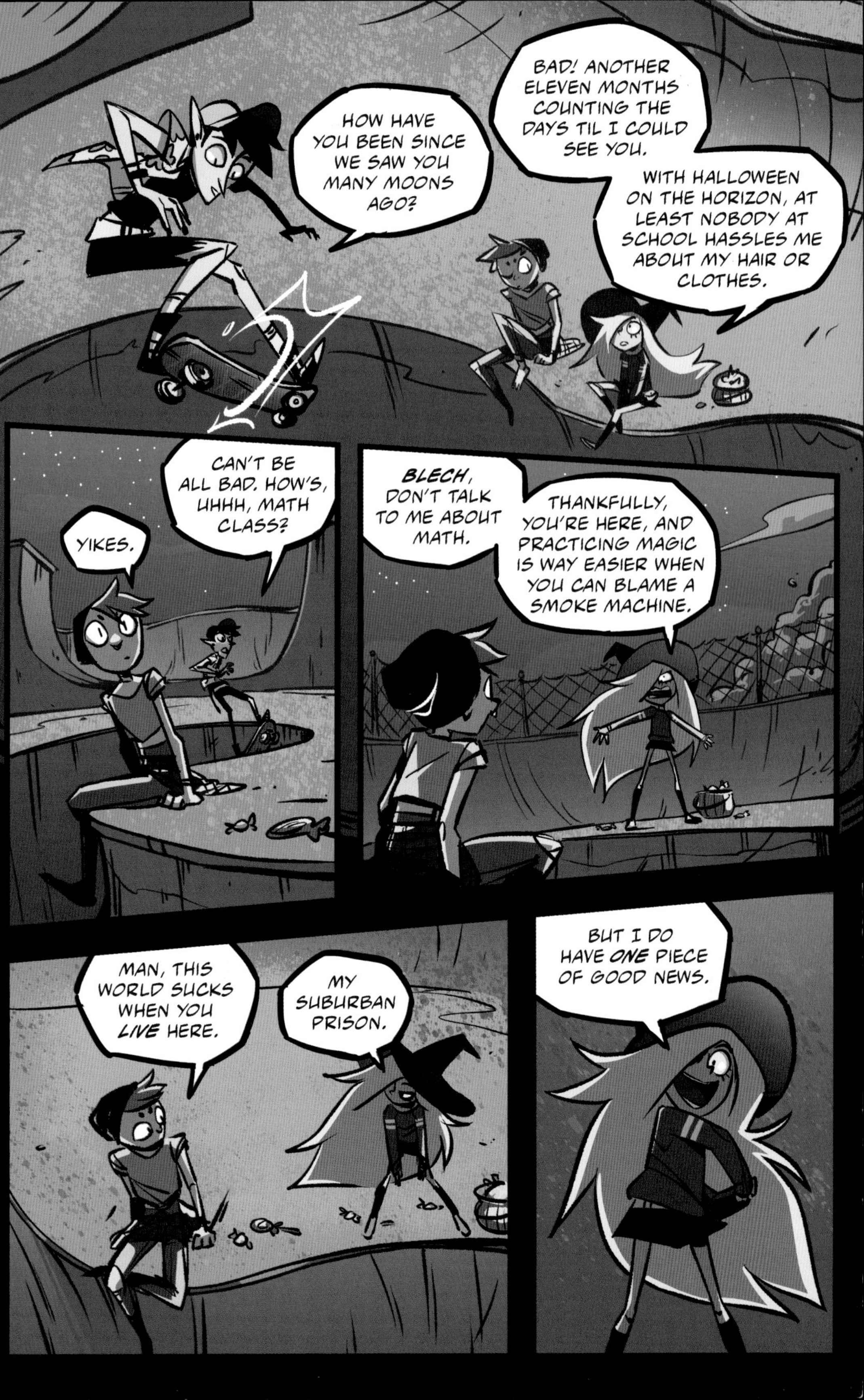
HOW HAVE YOU BEEN SINCE WE SAW YOU MANY MOONS AGO?
BAD! ANOTHER ELEVEN MONTHS COUNTING THE DAYS TIL I COULD SEE YOU.
WITH HALLOWEEN ON THE HORIZON, AT LEAST NOBODY AT SCHOOL HASSLES ME ABOUT MY HAIR OR CLOTHES.
CAN'T BE ALL BAD. HOW'S, UHHH, MATH CLASS?
YIKES.
*BLECH*, DON'T TALK TO ME ABOUT MATH.
THANKFULLY, YOU'RE HERE, AND PRACTICING MAGIC IS WAY EASIER WHEN YOU CAN BLAME A SMOKE MACHINE.
MAN, THIS WORLD SUCKS WHEN YOU *LIVE* HERE.
MY SUBURBAN PRISON.
BUT I DO HAVE *ONE* PIECE OF GOOD NEWS.

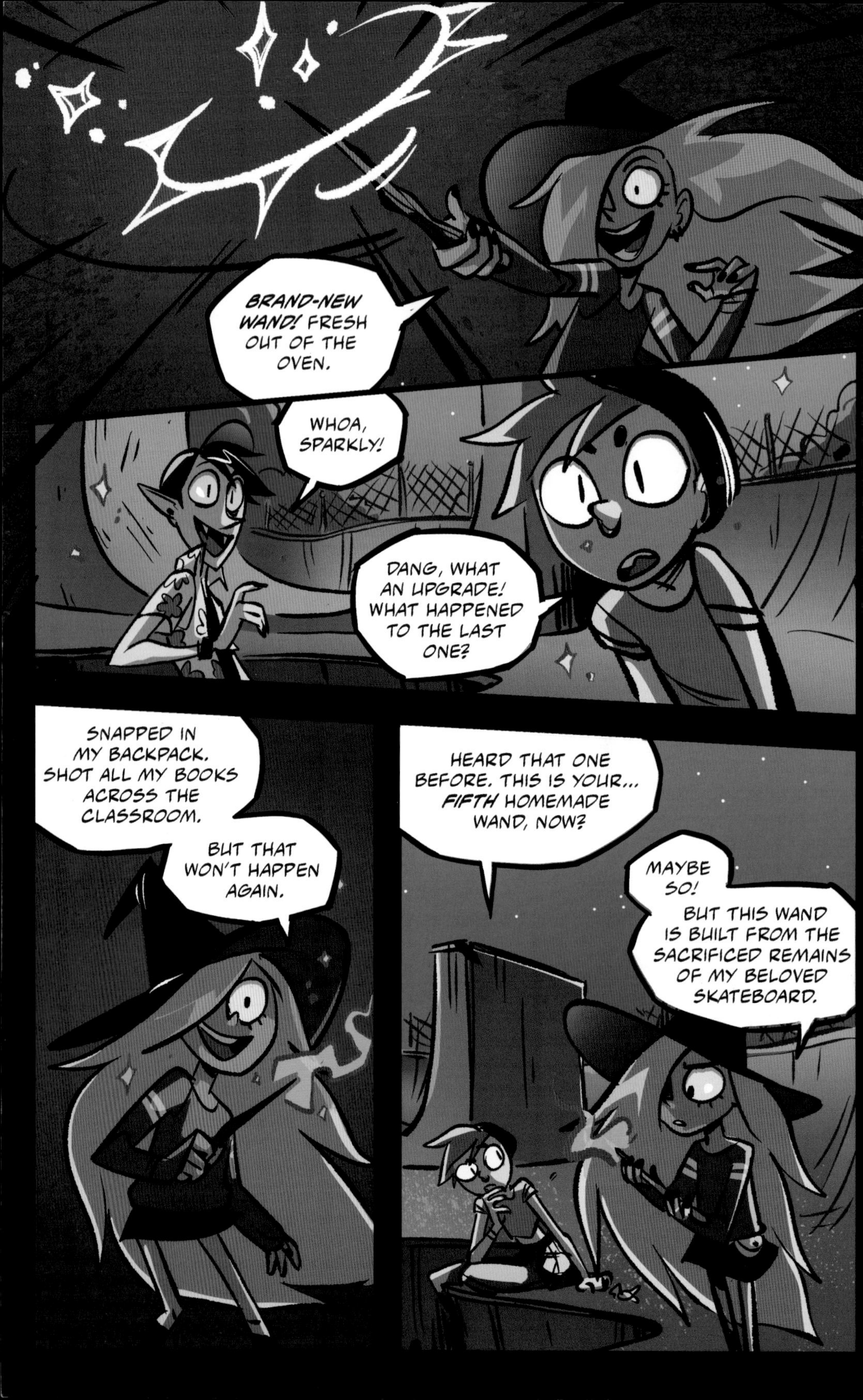
BRAND-NEW WAND! FRESH OUT OF THE OVEN.
WHOA, SPARKLY!
DANG, WHAT AN UPGRADE! WHAT HAPPENED TO THE LAST ONE?
SNAPPED IN MY BACKPACK. SHOT ALL MY BOOKS ACROSS THE CLASSROOM.
BUT THAT WON'T HAPPEN AGAIN.
HEARD THAT ONE BEFORE. THIS IS YOUR... FIFTH HOMEMADE WAND, NOW?
MAYBE SO!
BUT THIS WAND IS BUILT FROM THE SACRIFICED REMAINS OF MY BELOVED SKATEBOARD.

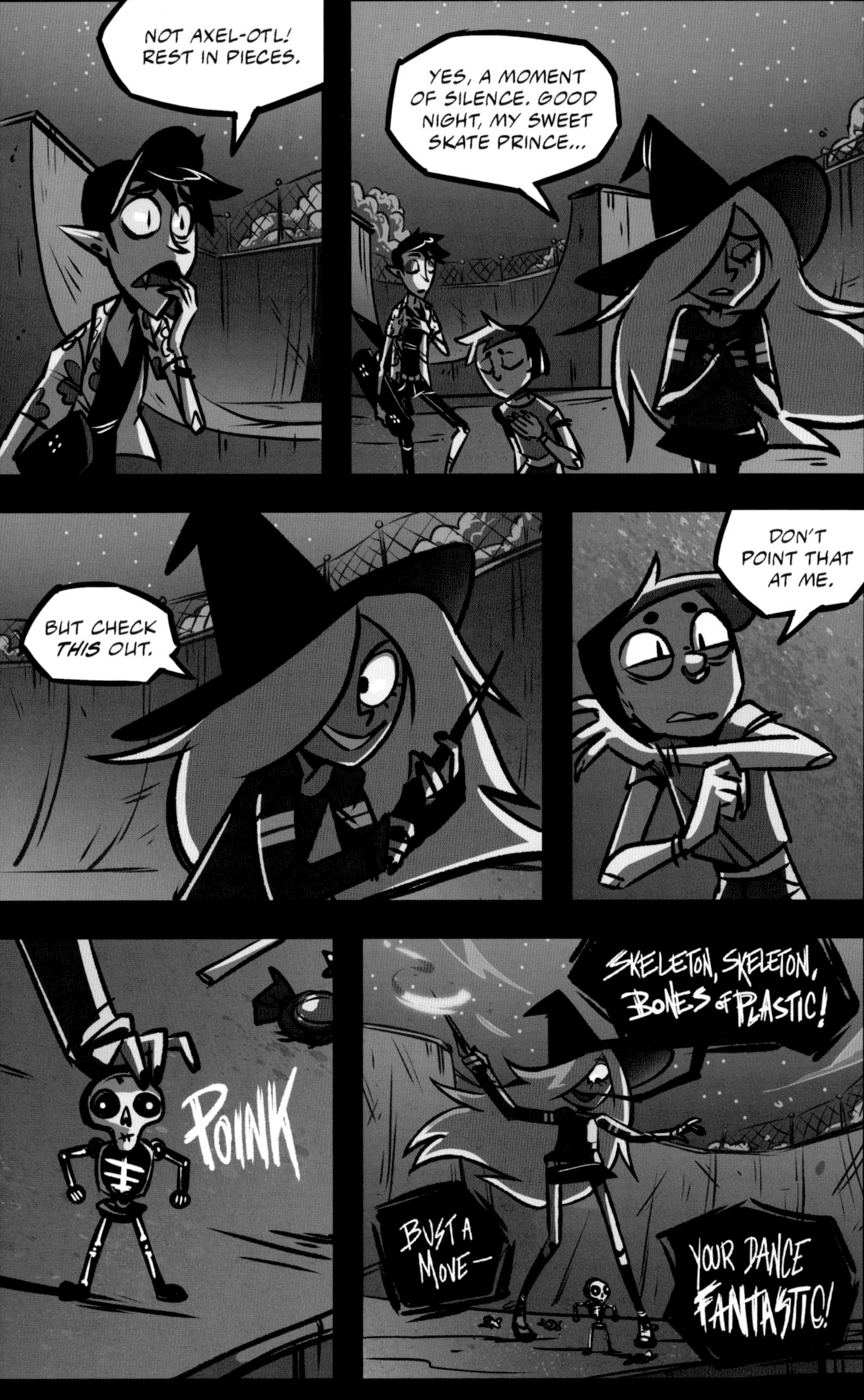
NOT AXEL-OTL! REST IN PIECES.
YES, A MOMENT OF SILENCE. GOOD NIGHT, MY SWEET SKATE PRINCE...
BUT CHECK THIS OUT.
DON'T POINT THAT AT ME.
POINK
SKELETON, SKELETON, BONES OF PLASTIC!
BUST A MOVE—
YOUR DANCE FANTASTIC!

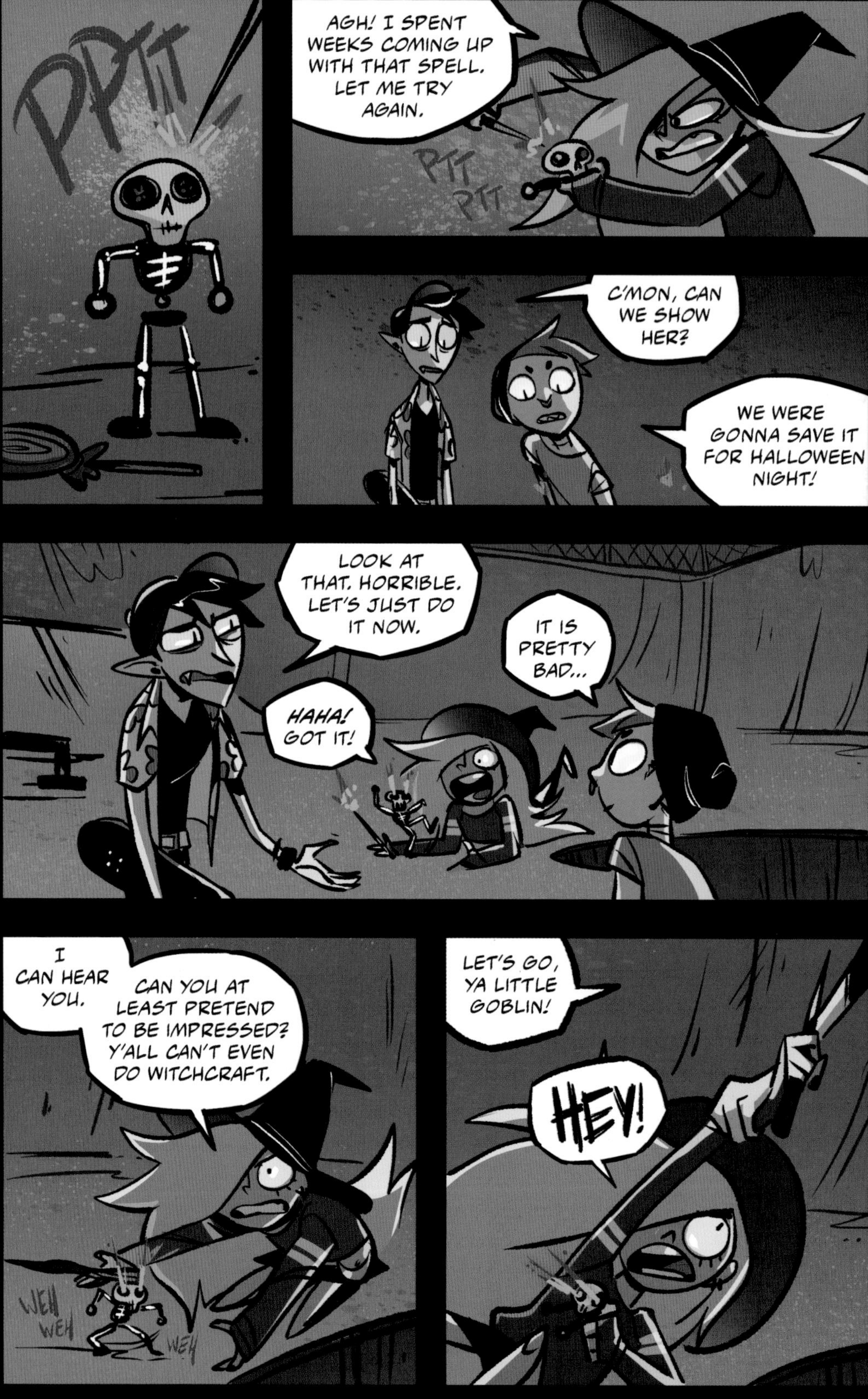
PPTTT
AGH! I SPENT WEEKS COMING UP WITH THAT SPELL. LET ME TRY AGAIN.
PTT PTT
C'MON, CAN WE SHOW HER?
WE WERE GONNA SAVE IT FOR HALLOWEEN NIGHT!
LOOK AT THAT. HORRIBLE. LET'S JUST DO IT NOW.
IT IS PRETTY BAD...
HAHA! GOT IT!
I CAN HEAR YOU.
CAN YOU AT LEAST PRETEND TO BE IMPRESSED? Y'ALL CAN'T EVEN DO WITCHCRAFT.
WEH WEH
WEH
LET'S GO, YA LITTLE GOBLIN!
HEY!

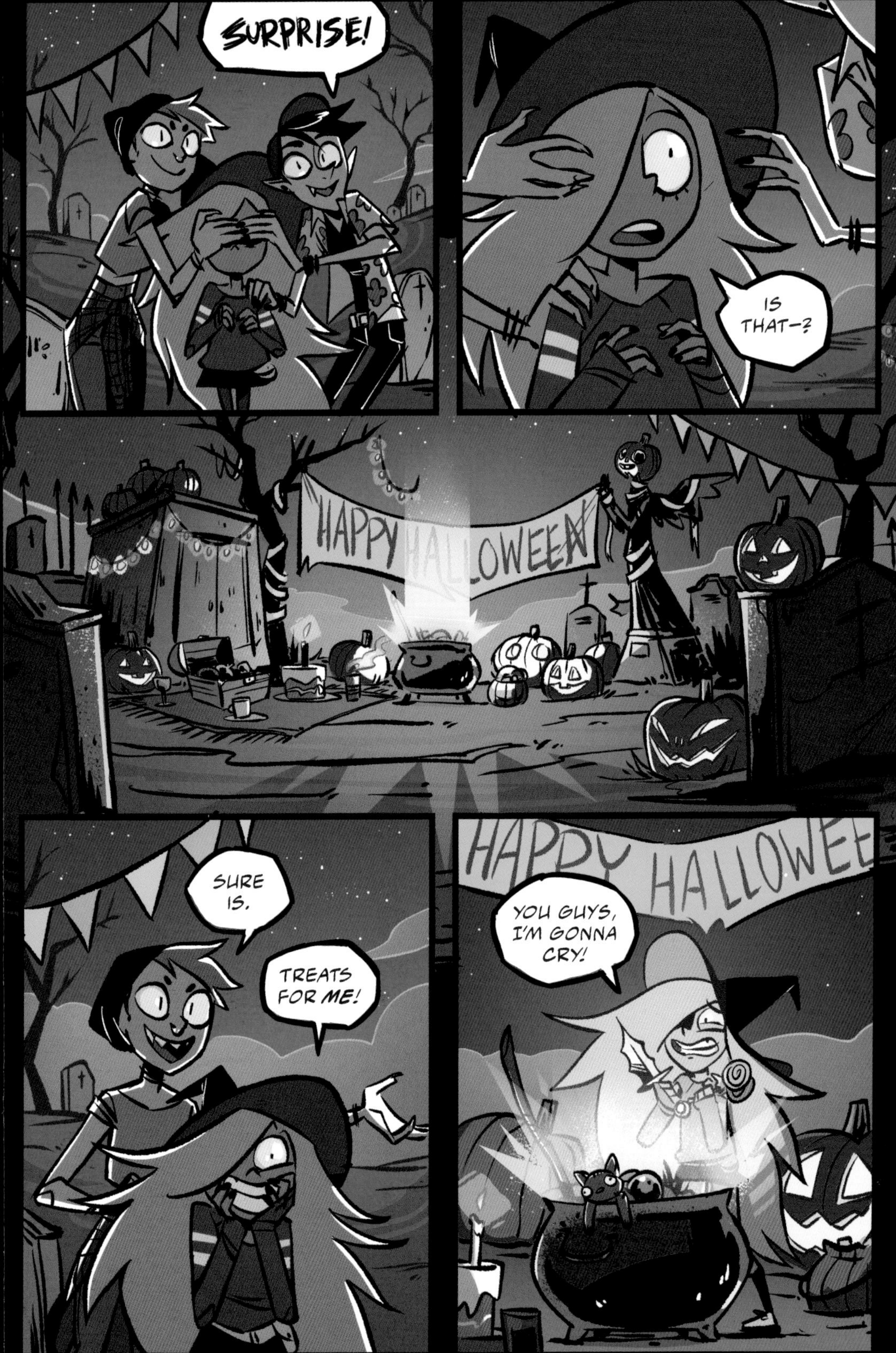
SURPRISE!
IS THAT—?
HAPPY HALLOWEEN
SURE IS.
TREATS FOR ME!
HAPPY HALLOWEE
YOU GUYS, I'M GONNA CRY!

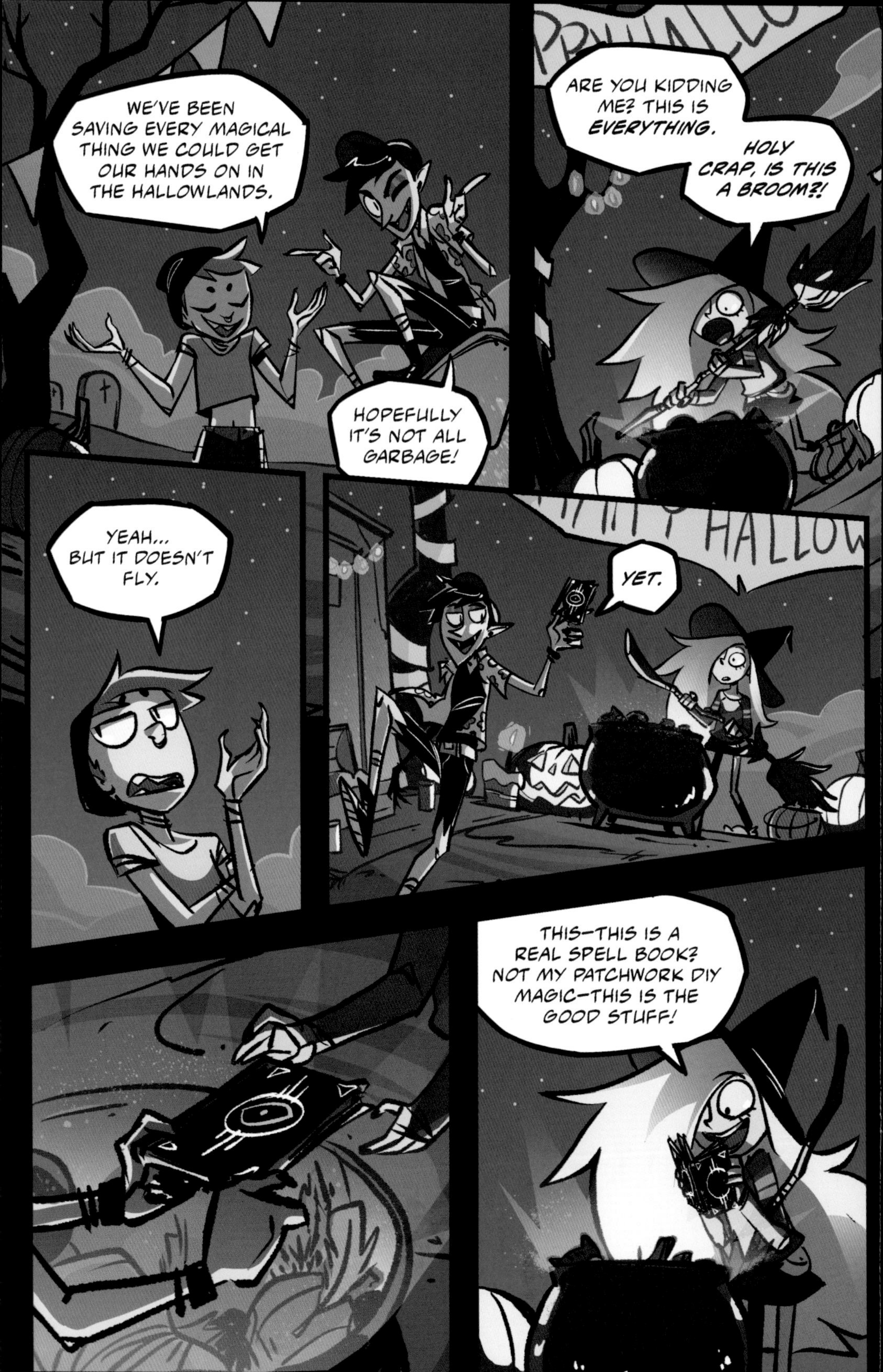
WE'VE BEEN SAVING EVERY MAGICAL THING WE COULD GET OUR HANDS ON IN THE HALLOWLANDS.
HOPEFULLY IT'S NOT ALL GARBAGE!
ARE YOU KIDDING ME? THIS IS EVERYTHING.
HOLY CRAP, IS THIS A BROOM?!
YEAH... BUT IT DOESN'T FLY.
HALLOW
YET.
THIS—THIS IS A REAL SPELL BOOK? NOT MY PATCHWORK DIY MAGIC—THIS IS THE GOOD STUFF!

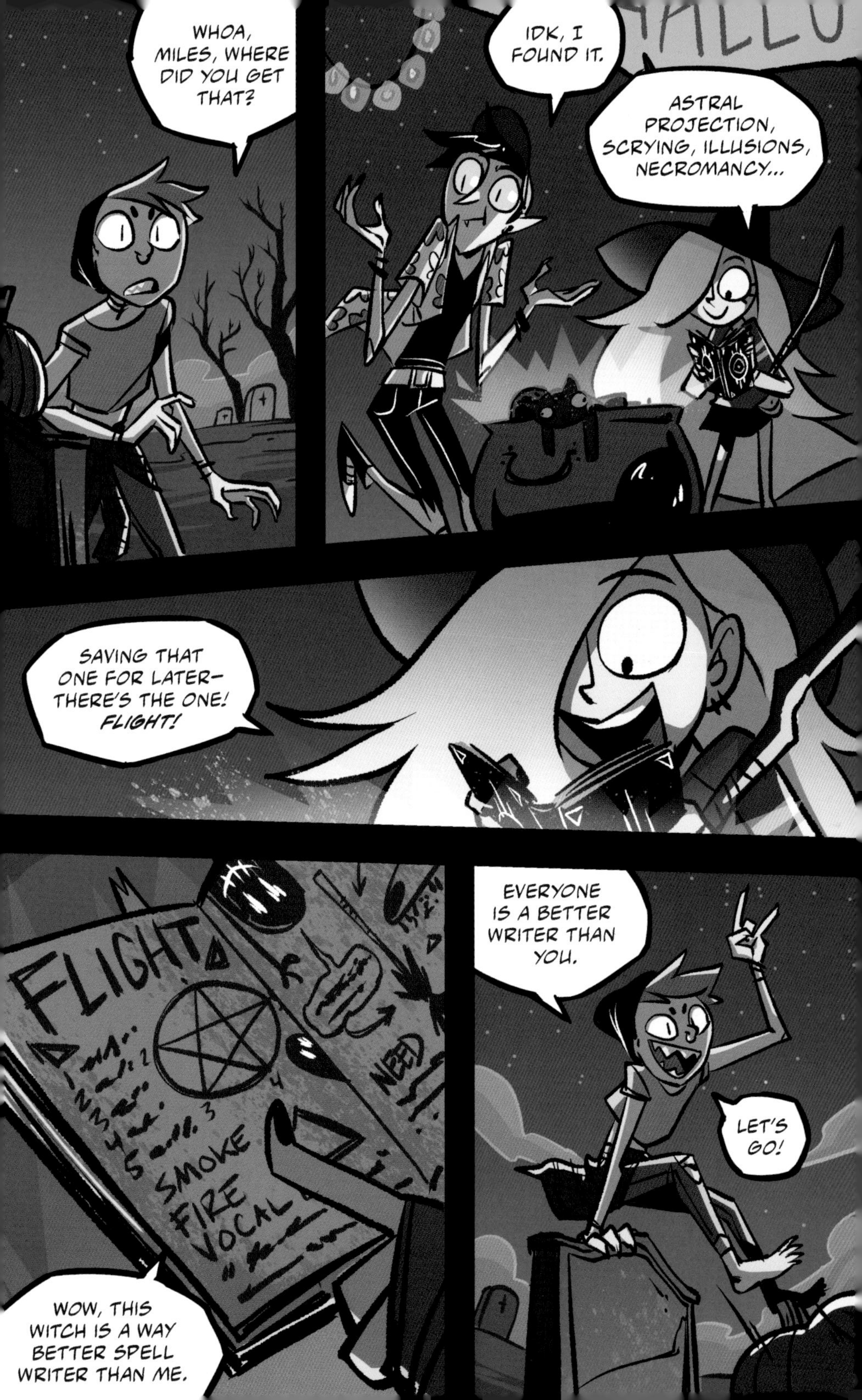
WHOA, MILES, WHERE DID YOU GET THAT?
IDK, I FOUND IT.
ASTRAL PROJECTION, SCRYING, ILLUSIONS, NECROMANCY...
SAVING THAT ONE FOR LATER- THERE'S THE ONE! *FLIGHT!*
FLIGHT
SMOKE
FIRE
VOCAL
NEED
WOW, THIS WITCH IS A WAY BETTER SPELL WRITER THAN ME.
EVERYONE IS A BETTER WRITER THAN YOU.
LET'S GO!

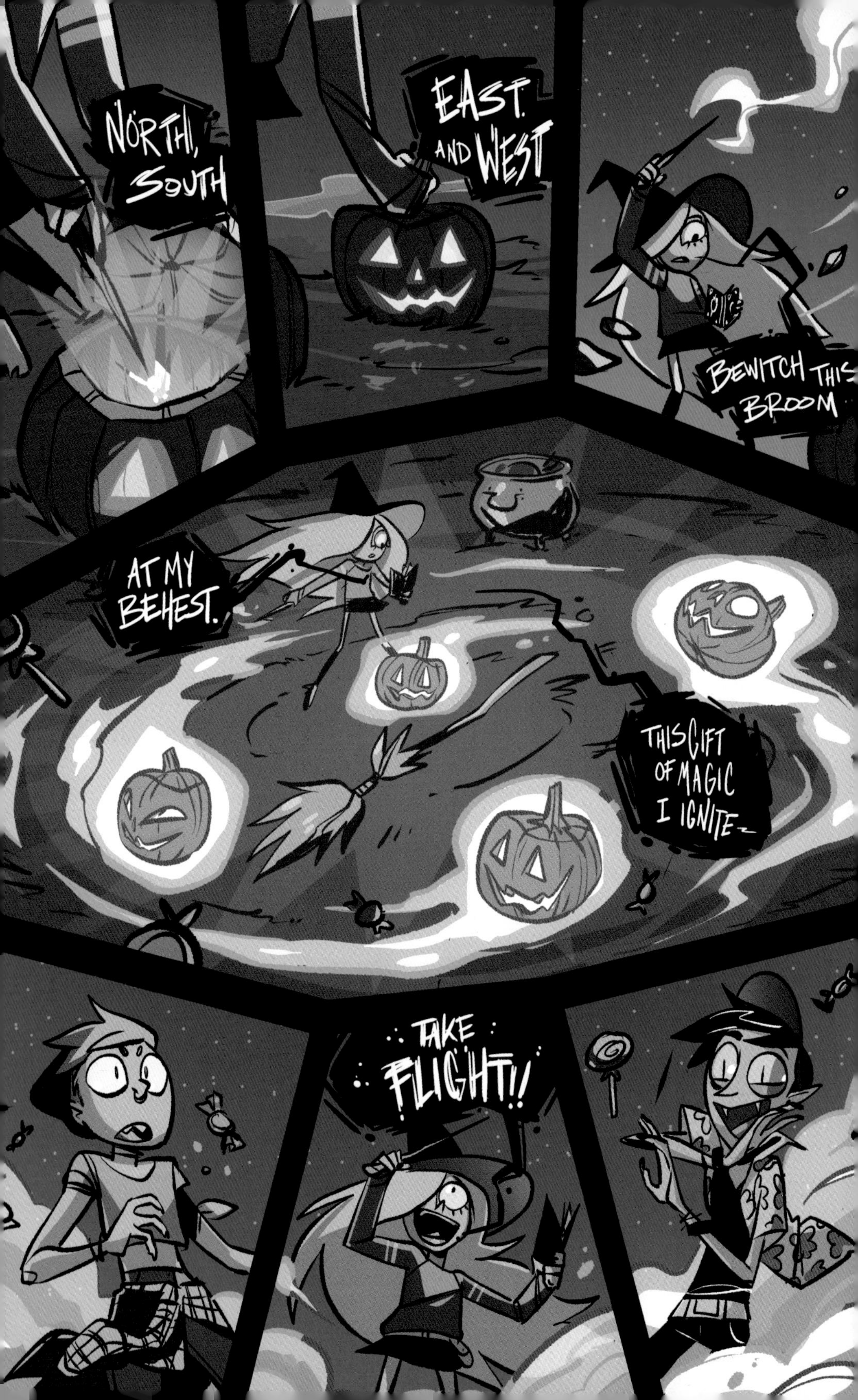
NORTH, SOUTH
EAST AND WEST
BEWITCH THIS BROOM
AT MY BEHEST.
THIS GIFT OF MAGIC I IGNITE—
TAKE FLIGHT!!

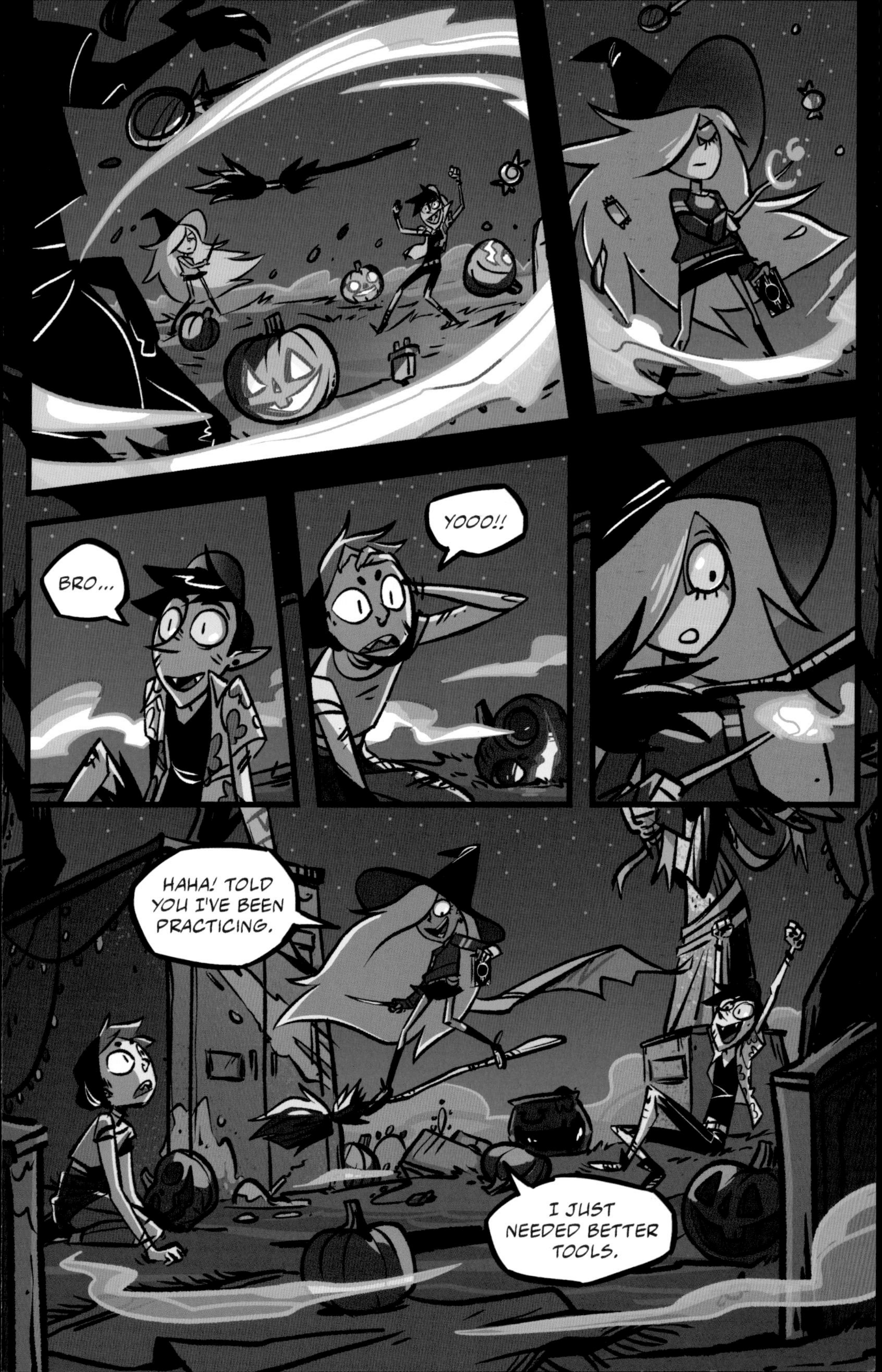
BRO...
YOOO!!
HAHA! TOLD YOU I'VE BEEN PRACTICING.
I JUST NEEDED BETTER TOOLS.

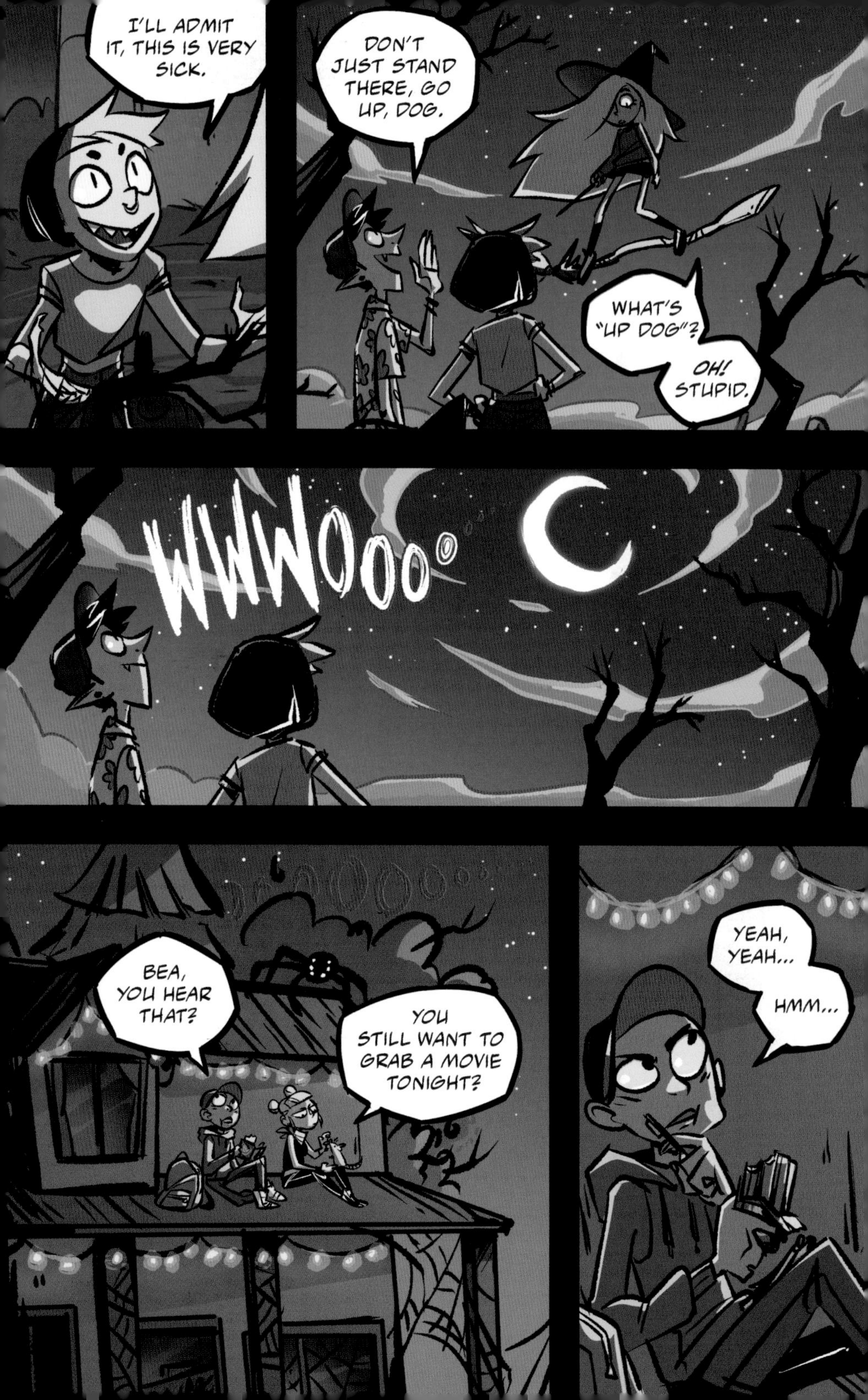
I'LL ADMIT IT, THIS IS VERY SICK.
DON'T JUST STAND THERE, GO UP, DOG.
WHAT'S "UP DOG"?
OH! STUPID.
WWWOOOO
BEA, YOU HEAR THAT?
YOU STILL WANT TO GRAB A MOVIE TONIGHT?
YEAH, YEAH...
HMM...

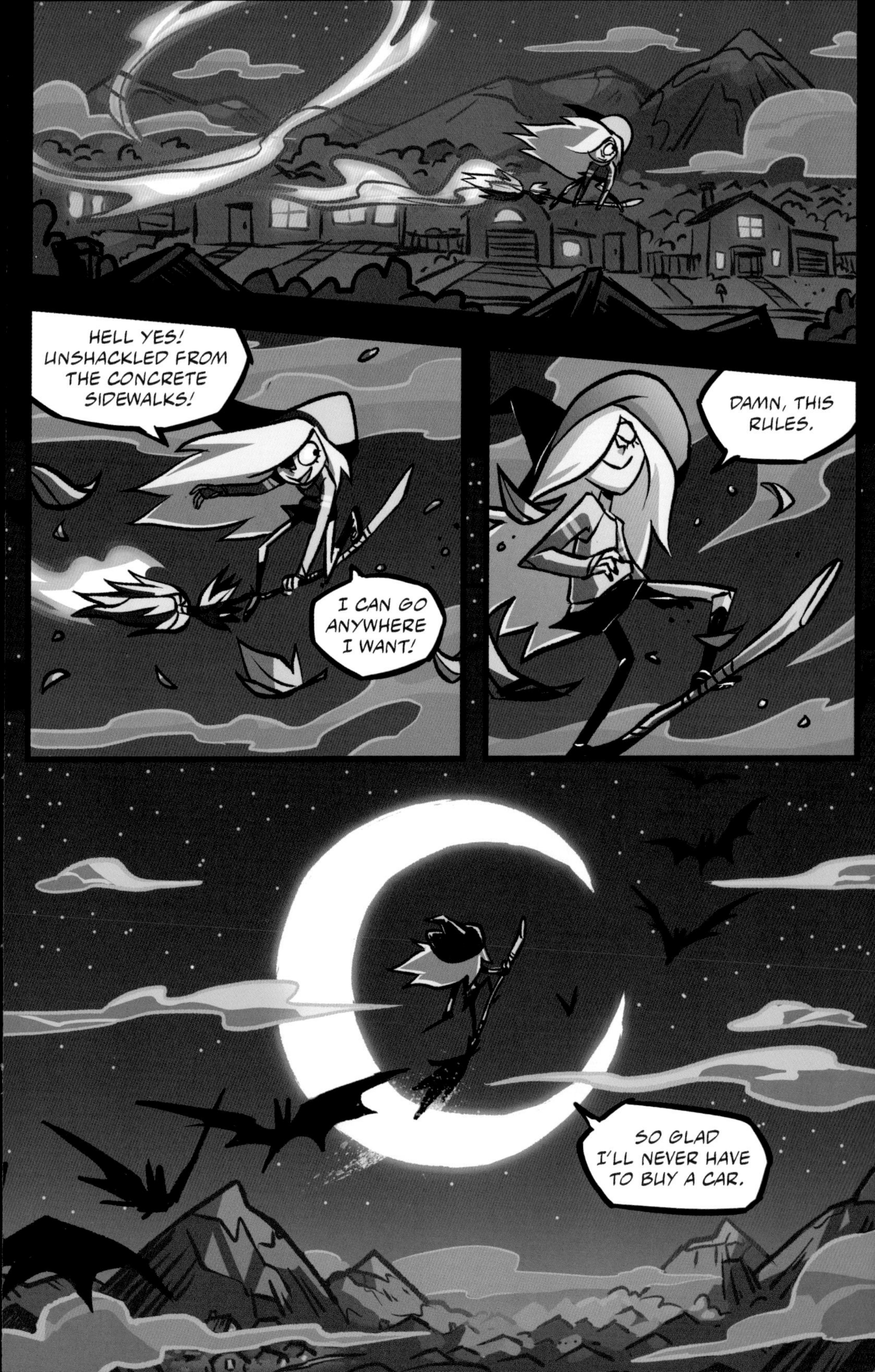
HELL YES! UNSHACKLED FROM THE CONCRETE SIDEWALKS!
I CAN GO ANYWHERE I WANT!
DAMN, THIS RULES.
SO GLAD I'LL NEVER HAVE TO BUY A CAR.

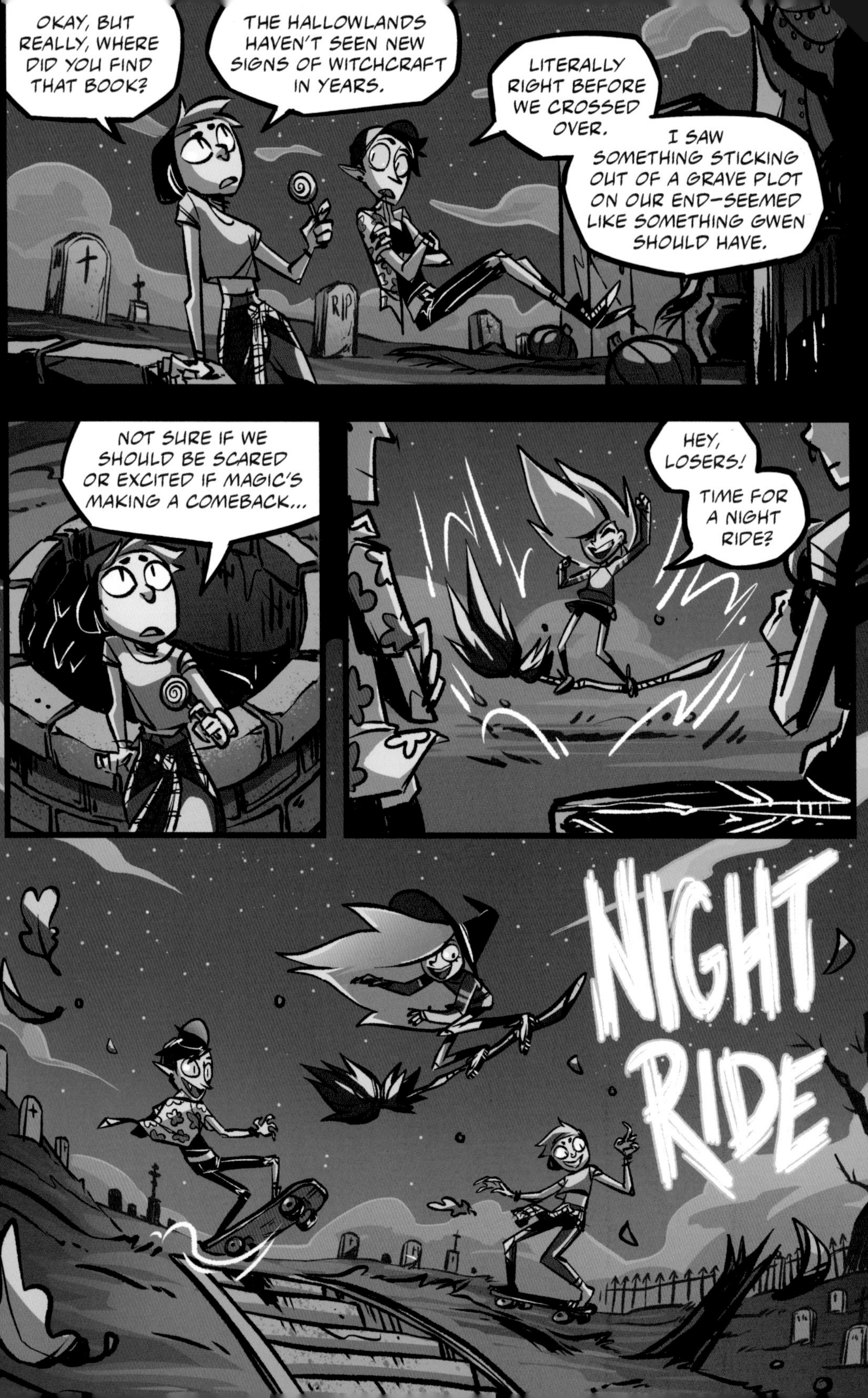
OKAY, BUT REALLY, WHERE DID YOU FIND THAT BOOK?
THE HALLOWLANDS HAVEN'T SEEN NEW SIGNS OF WITCHCRAFT IN YEARS.
LITERALLY RIGHT BEFORE WE CROSSED OVER.
I SAW SOMETHING STICKING OUT OF A GRAVE PLOT ON OUR END—SEEMED LIKE SOMETHING GWEN SHOULD HAVE.
RIP
NOT SURE IF WE SHOULD BE SCARED OR EXCITED IF MAGIC'S MAKING A COMEBACK...
HEY, LOSERS!
TIME FOR A NIGHT RIDE?
NIGHT RIDE

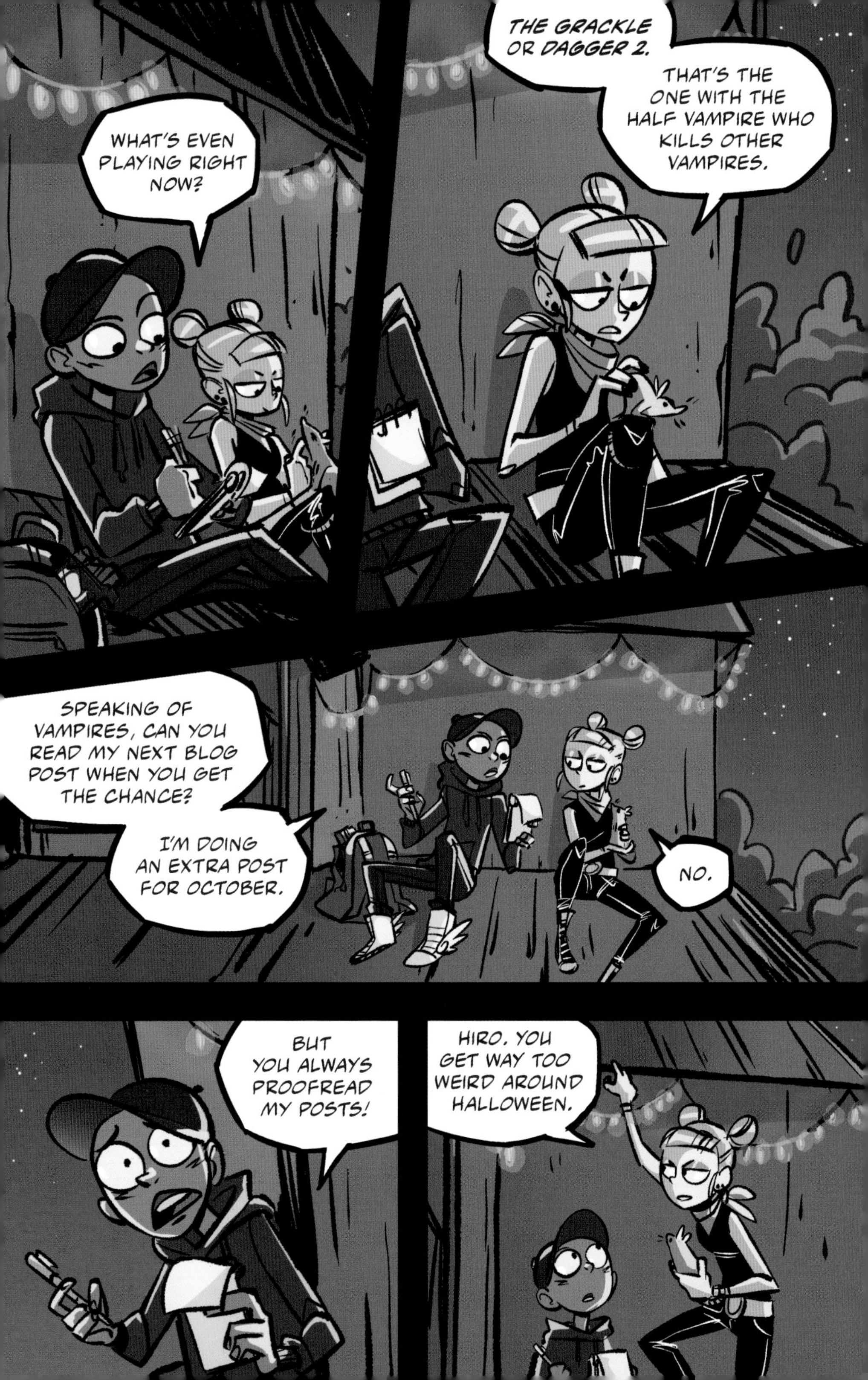
WHAT'S EVEN PLAYING RIGHT NOW?
THE GRACKLE OR DAGGER 2.
THAT'S THE ONE WITH THE HALF VAMPIRE WHO KILLS OTHER VAMPIRES.
SPEAKING OF VAMPIRES, CAN YOU READ MY NEXT BLOG POST WHEN YOU GET THE CHANCE?
I'M DOING AN EXTRA POST FOR OCTOBER.
NO.
BUT YOU ALWAYS PROOFREAD MY POSTS!
HIRO, YOU GET WAY TOO WEIRD AROUND HALLOWEEN.

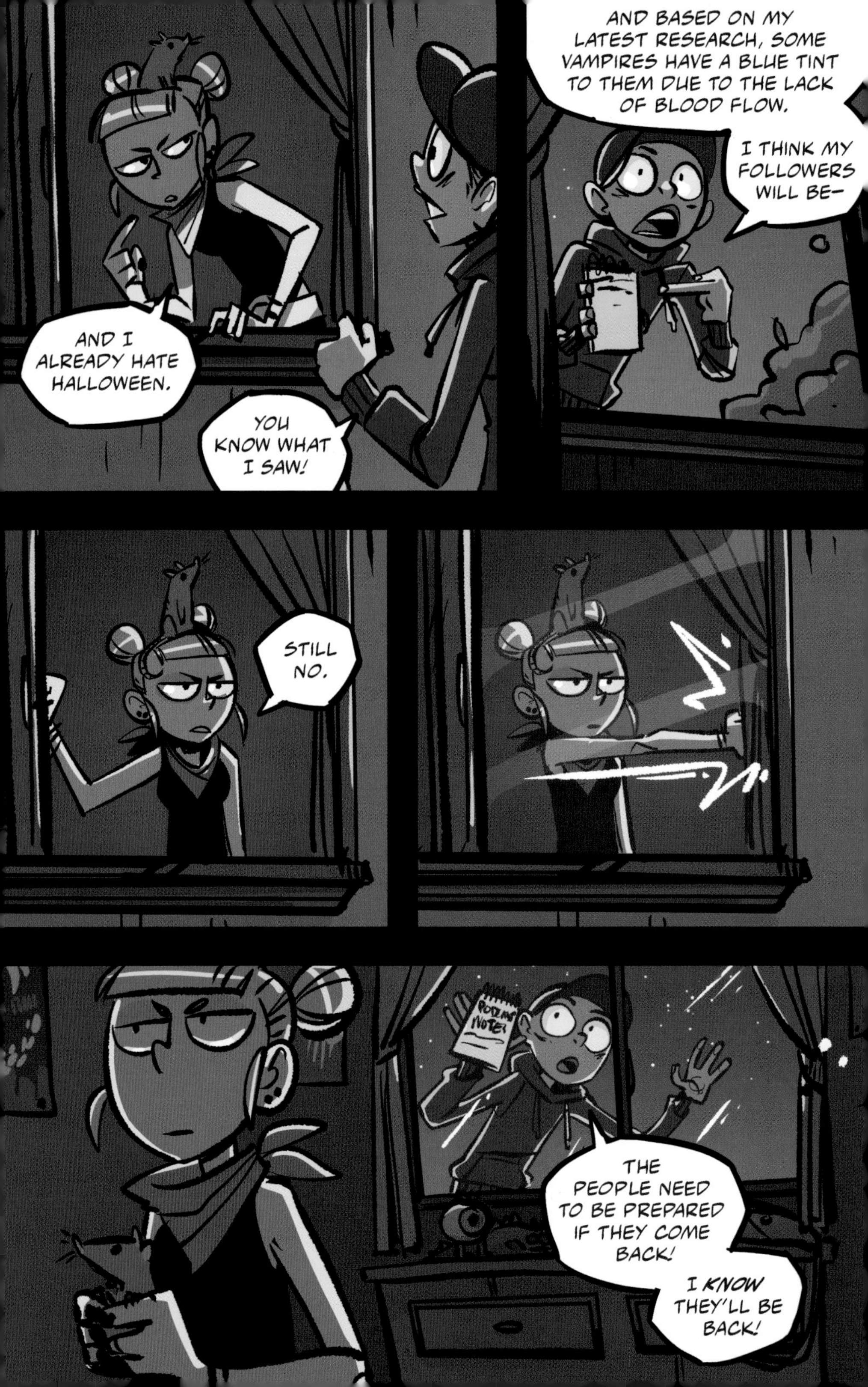
AND I ALREADY HATE HALLOWEEN.
YOU KNOW WHAT I SAW!
AND BASED ON MY LATEST RESEARCH, SOME VAMPIRES HAVE A BLUE TINT TO THEM DUE TO THE LACK OF BLOOD FLOW.
I THINK MY FOLLOWERS WILL BE—
STILL NO.
THE PEOPLE NEED TO BE PREPARED IF THEY COME BACK!
I *KNOW* THEY'LL BE BACK!

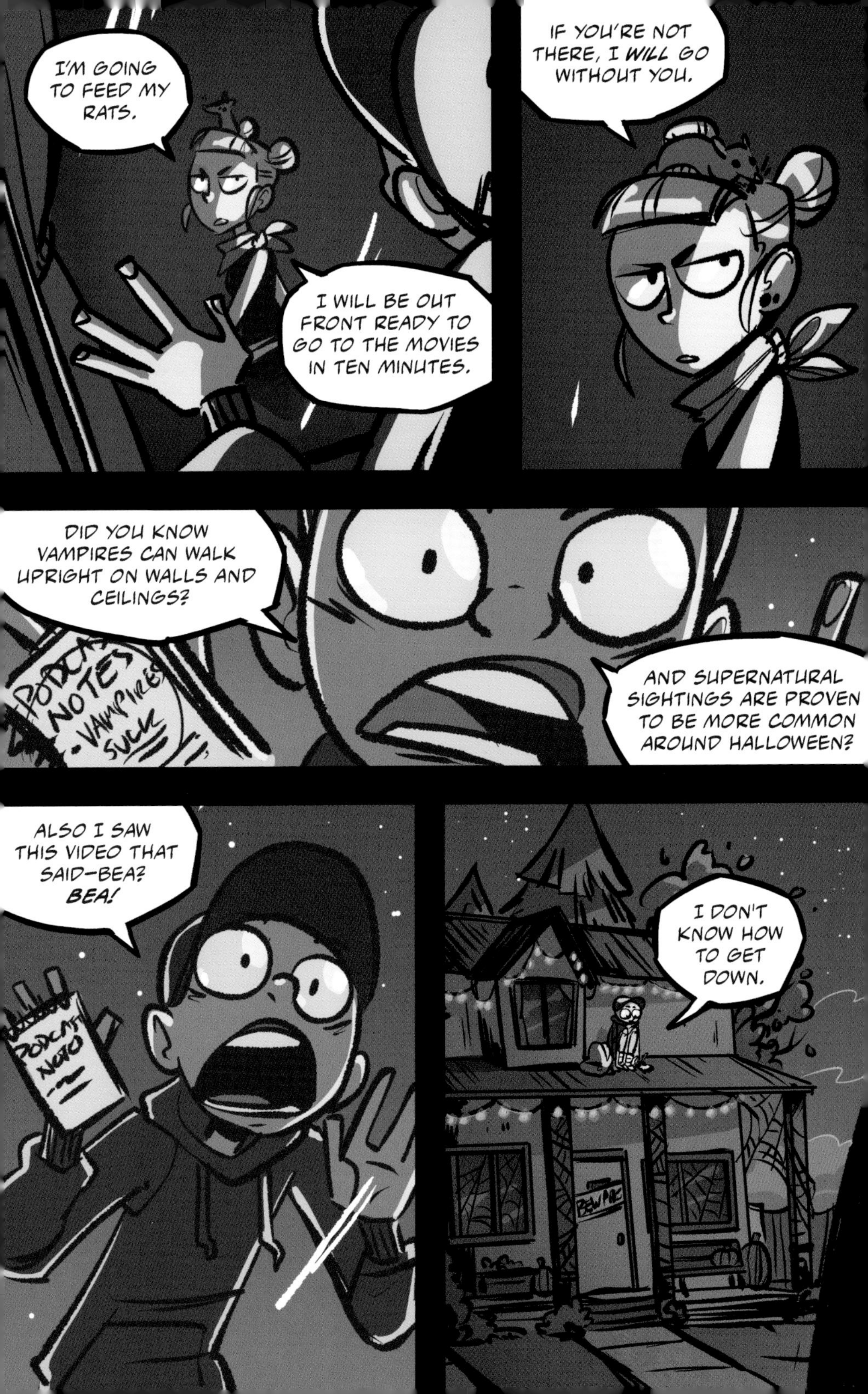
I'M GOING TO FEED MY RATS.
I WILL BE OUT FRONT READY TO GO TO THE MOVIES IN TEN MINUTES.
IF YOU'RE NOT THERE, I *WILL* GO WITHOUT YOU.
DID YOU KNOW VAMPIRES CAN WALK UPRIGHT ON WALLS AND CEILINGS?
PODCAST NOTES
-VAMPIRES
-VAMPIRES SUCK
AND SUPERNATURAL SIGHTINGS ARE PROVEN TO BE MORE COMMON AROUND HALLOWEEN?
ALSO I SAW THIS VIDEO THAT SAID—BEA? *BEA!*
I DON'T KNOW HOW TO GET DOWN.

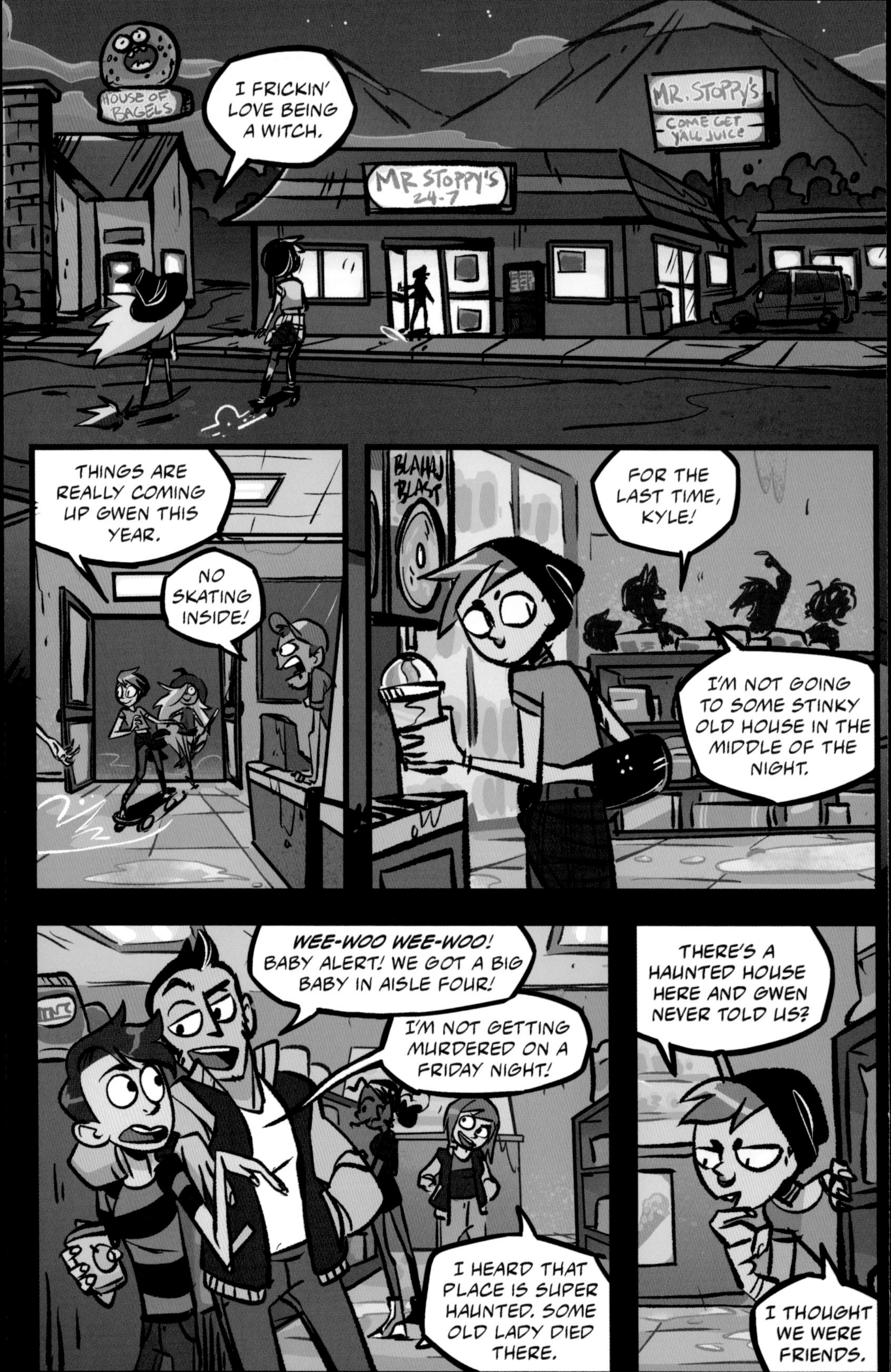
HOUSE OF BAGELS
I FRICKIN' LOVE BEING A WITCH.
MR. STOPPY'S
COME GET YA'LL JUICE
MR STOPPY'S 24-7
THINGS ARE REALLY COMING UP GWEN THIS YEAR.
NO SKATING INSIDE!
BLAHH BLAST
FOR THE LAST TIME, KYLE!
I'M NOT GOING TO SOME STINKY OLD HOUSE IN THE MIDDLE OF THE NIGHT.
*WEE-WOO WEE-WOO!* BABY ALERT! WE GOT A BIG BABY IN AISLE FOUR!
I'M NOT GETTING MURDERED ON A FRIDAY NIGHT!
I HEARD THAT PLACE IS SUPER HAUNTED. SOME OLD LADY DIED THERE.
THERE'S A HAUNTED HOUSE HERE AND GWEN NEVER TOLD US?
I THOUGHT WE WERE FRIENDS.

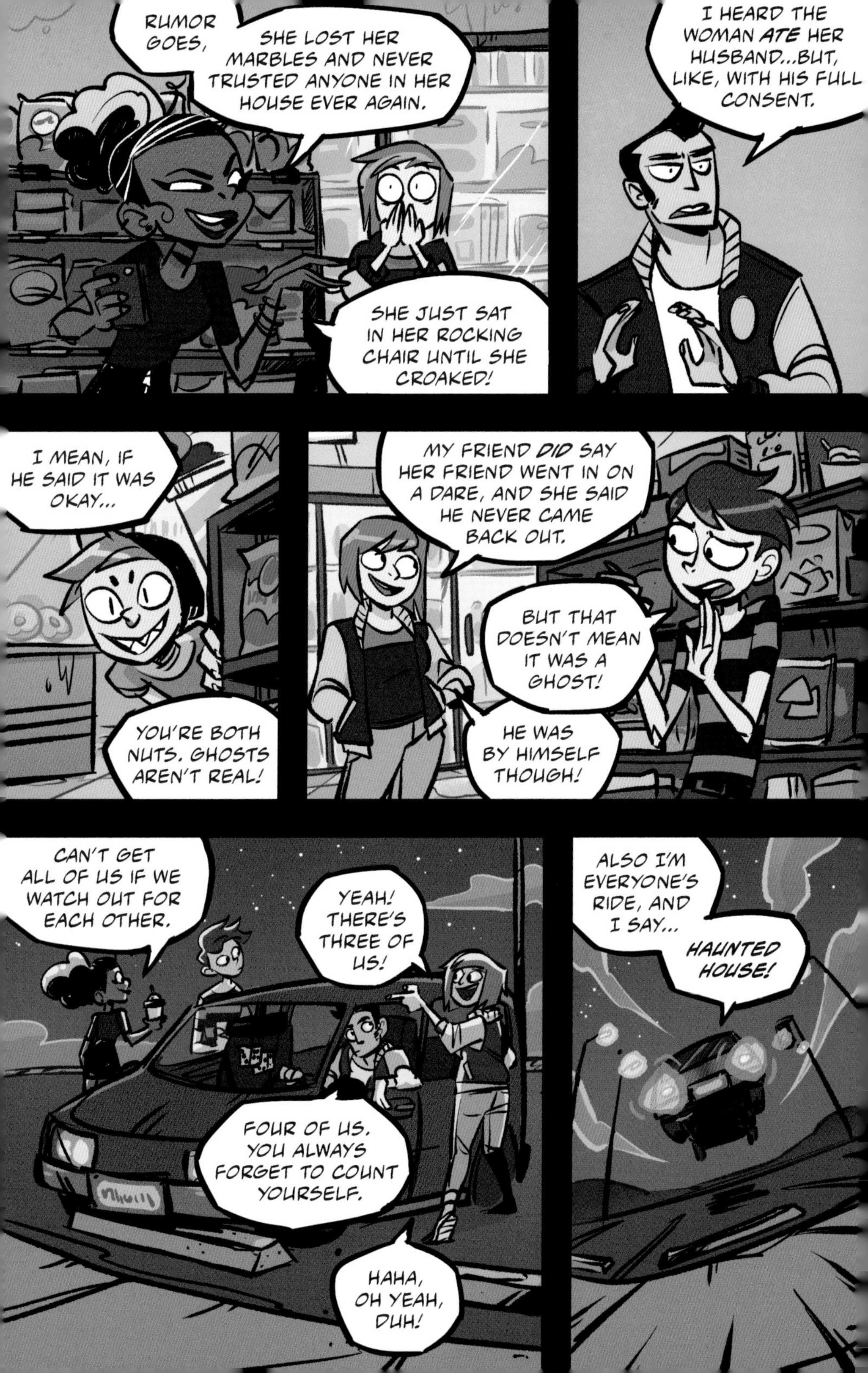
RUMOR GOES,
SHE LOST HER MARBLES AND NEVER TRUSTED ANYONE IN HER HOUSE EVER AGAIN.
SHE JUST SAT IN HER ROCKING CHAIR UNTIL SHE CROAKED!
I HEARD THE WOMAN *ATE* HER HUSBAND...BUT, LIKE, WITH HIS FULL CONSENT.
I MEAN, IF HE SAID IT WAS OKAY...
YOU'RE BOTH NUTS. GHOSTS AREN'T REAL!
MY FRIEND *DID* SAY HER FRIEND WENT IN ON A DARE, AND SHE SAID HE NEVER CAME BACK OUT.
BUT THAT DOESN'T MEAN IT WAS A GHOST!
HE WAS BY HIMSELF THOUGH!
CAN'T GET ALL OF US IF WE WATCH OUT FOR EACH OTHER.
YEAH! THERE'S THREE OF US!
FOUR OF US. YOU ALWAYS FORGET TO COUNT YOURSELF.
HAHA, OH YEAH, DUH!
ALSO I'M EVERYONE'S RIDE, AND I SAY...
*HAUNTED HOUSE!*

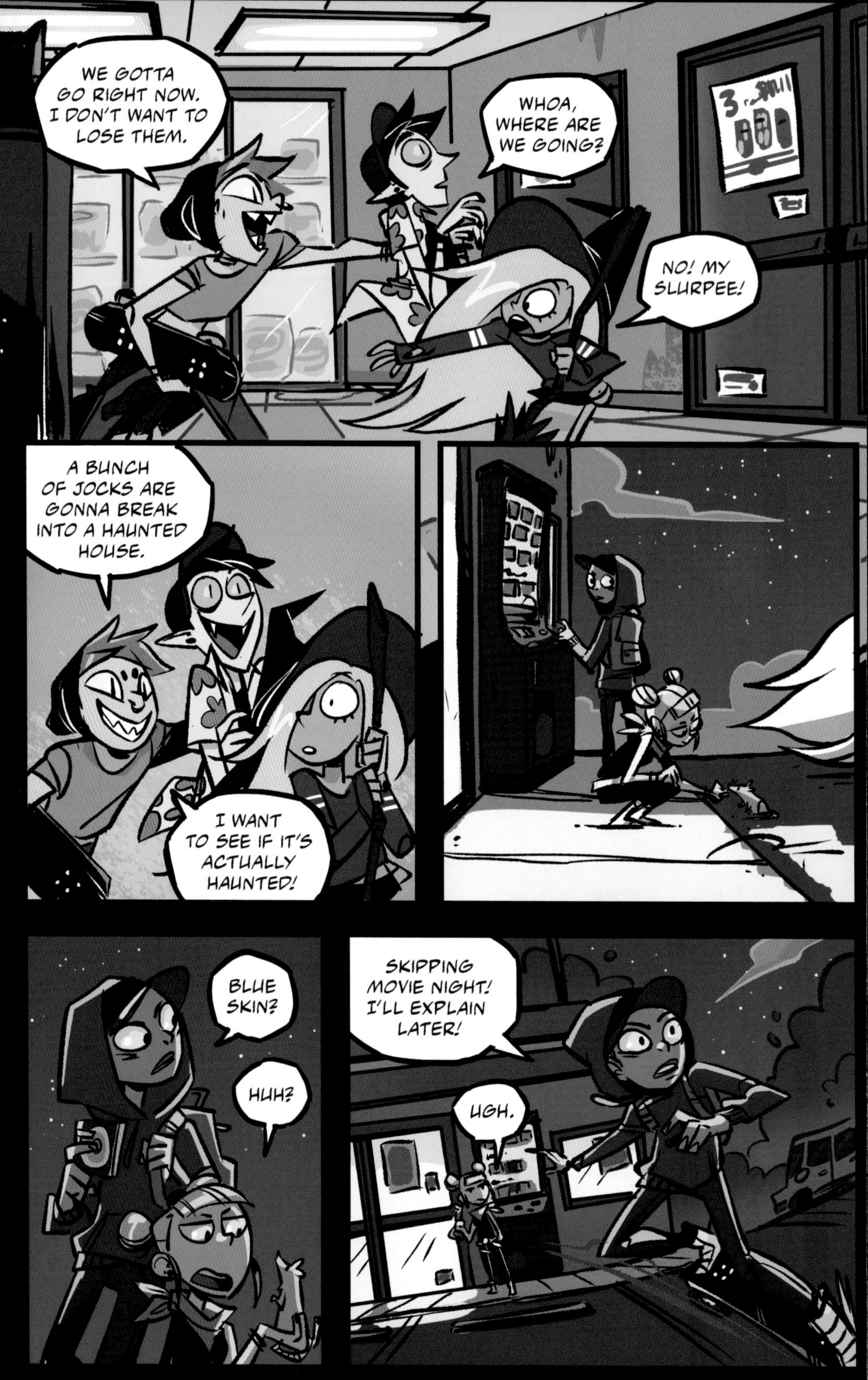
WE GOTTA GO RIGHT NOW. I DON'T WANT TO LOSE THEM.
WHOA, WHERE ARE WE GOING?
NO! MY SLURPEE!
A BUNCH OF JOCKS ARE GONNA BREAK INTO A HAUNTED HOUSE.
I WANT TO SEE IF IT'S ACTUALLY HAUNTED!
BLUE SKIN?
HUH?
SKIPPING MOVIE NIGHT! I'LL EXPLAIN LATER!
UGH.

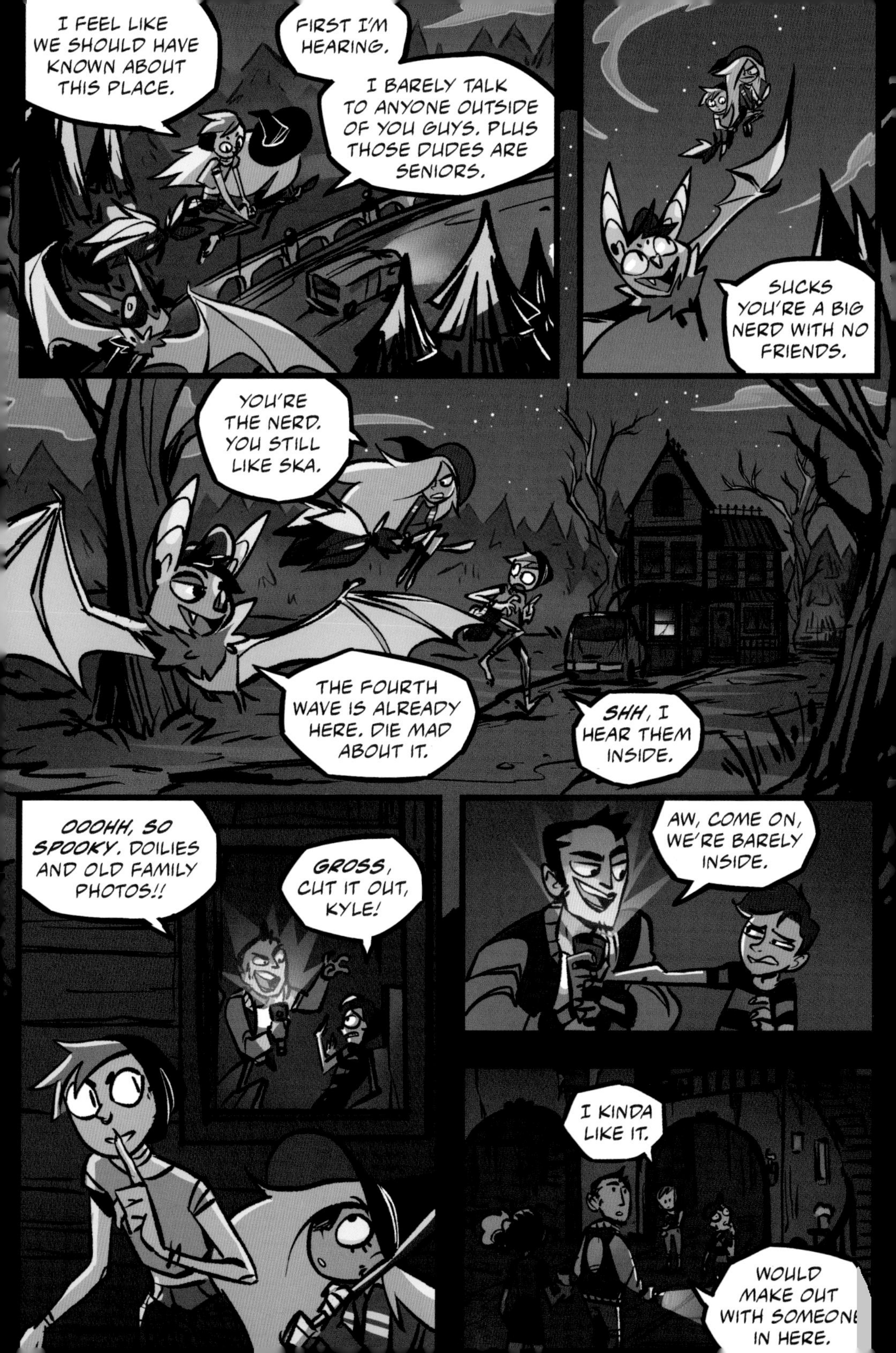
I FEEL LIKE WE SHOULD HAVE KNOWN ABOUT THIS PLACE.
FIRST I'M HEARING.
I BARELY TALK TO ANYONE OUTSIDE OF YOU GUYS. PLUS THOSE DUDES ARE SENIORS.
SUCKS YOU'RE A BIG NERD WITH NO FRIENDS.
YOU'RE THE NERD. YOU STILL LIKE SKA.
THE FOURTH WAVE IS ALREADY HERE. DIE MAD ABOUT IT.
SHH, I HEAR THEM INSIDE.
OOOHH, SO SPOOKY. DOILIES AND OLD FAMILY PHOTOS!!
GROSS, CUT IT OUT, KYLE!
AW, COME ON, WE'RE BARELY INSIDE.
I KINDA LIKE IT.
WOULD MAKE OUT WITH SOMEONE IN HERE.

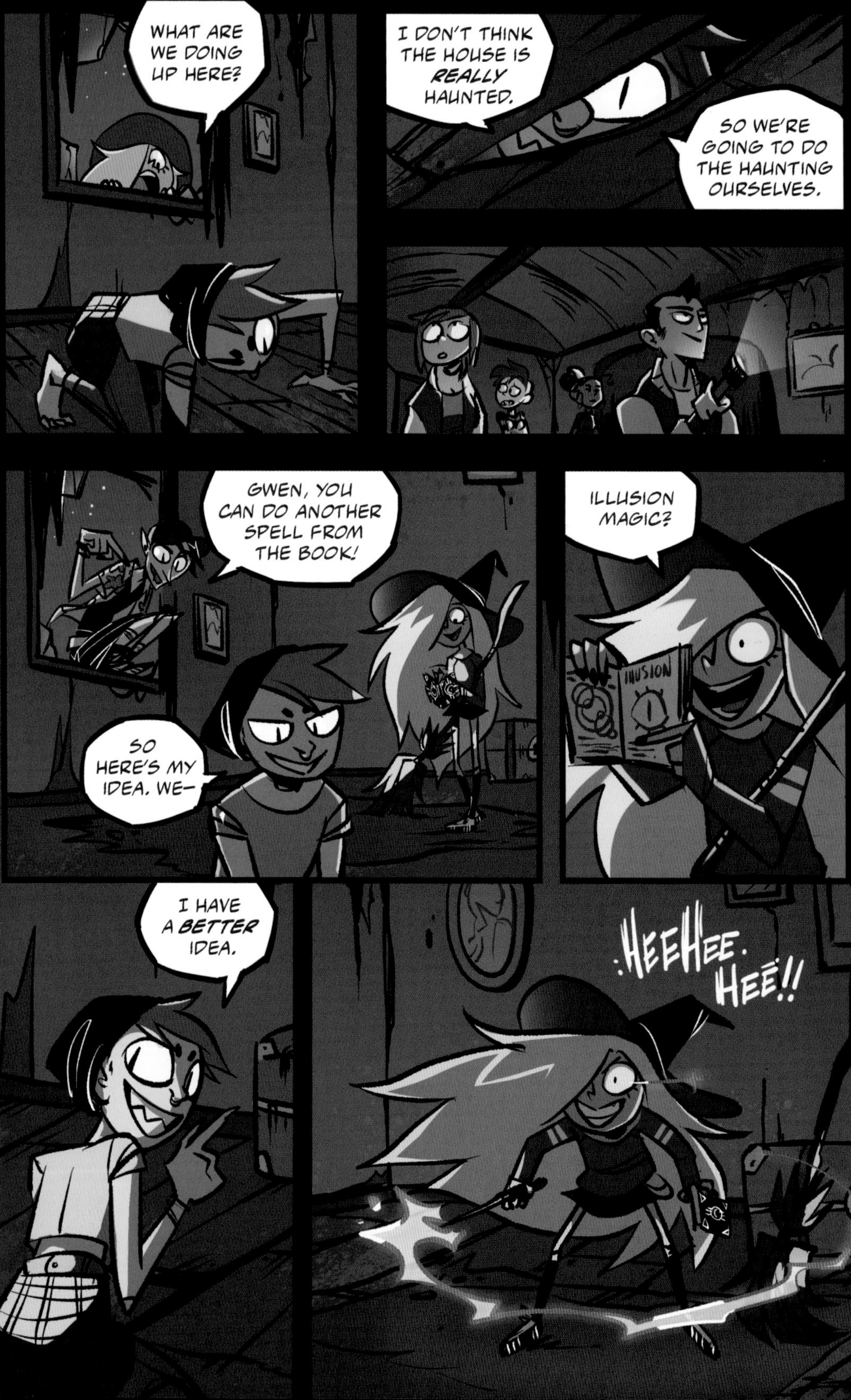
WHAT ARE WE DOING UP HERE?
I DON'T THINK THE HOUSE IS *REALLY* HAUNTED.
SO WE'RE GOING TO DO THE HAUNTING OURSELVES.
GWEN, YOU CAN DO ANOTHER SPELL FROM THE BOOK!
SO HERE'S MY IDEA. WE–
ILLUSION MAGIC?
ILLUSION
I HAVE A *BETTER* IDEA.
HEEHEE. HEE!!

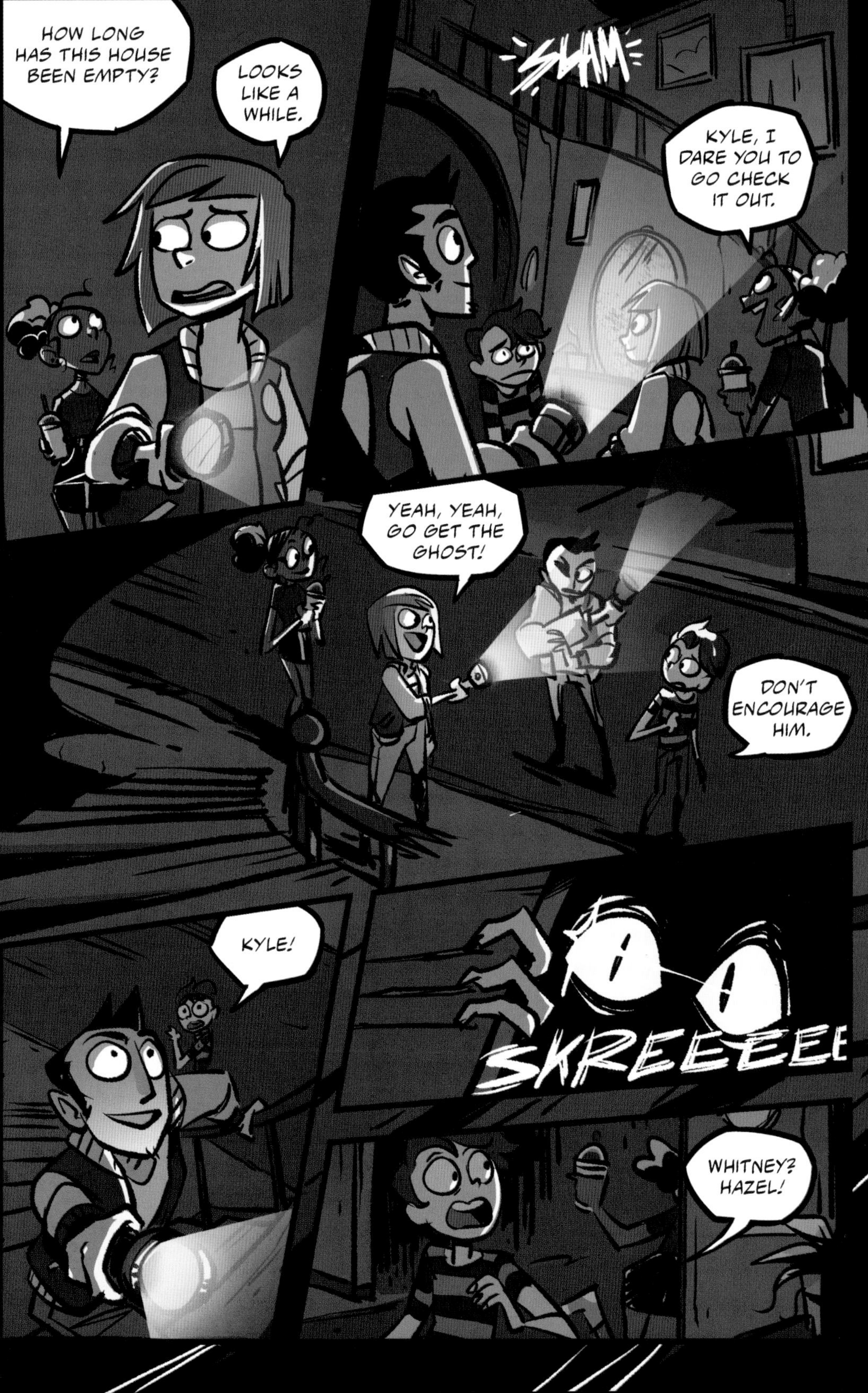
HOW LONG HAS THIS HOUSE BEEN EMPTY?
LOOKS LIKE A WHILE.
SLAM
KYLE, I DARE YOU TO GO CHECK IT OUT.
YEAH, YEAH, GO GET THE GHOST!
DON'T ENCOURAGE HIM.
KYLE!
SKREEEEE
WHITNEY? HAZEL!

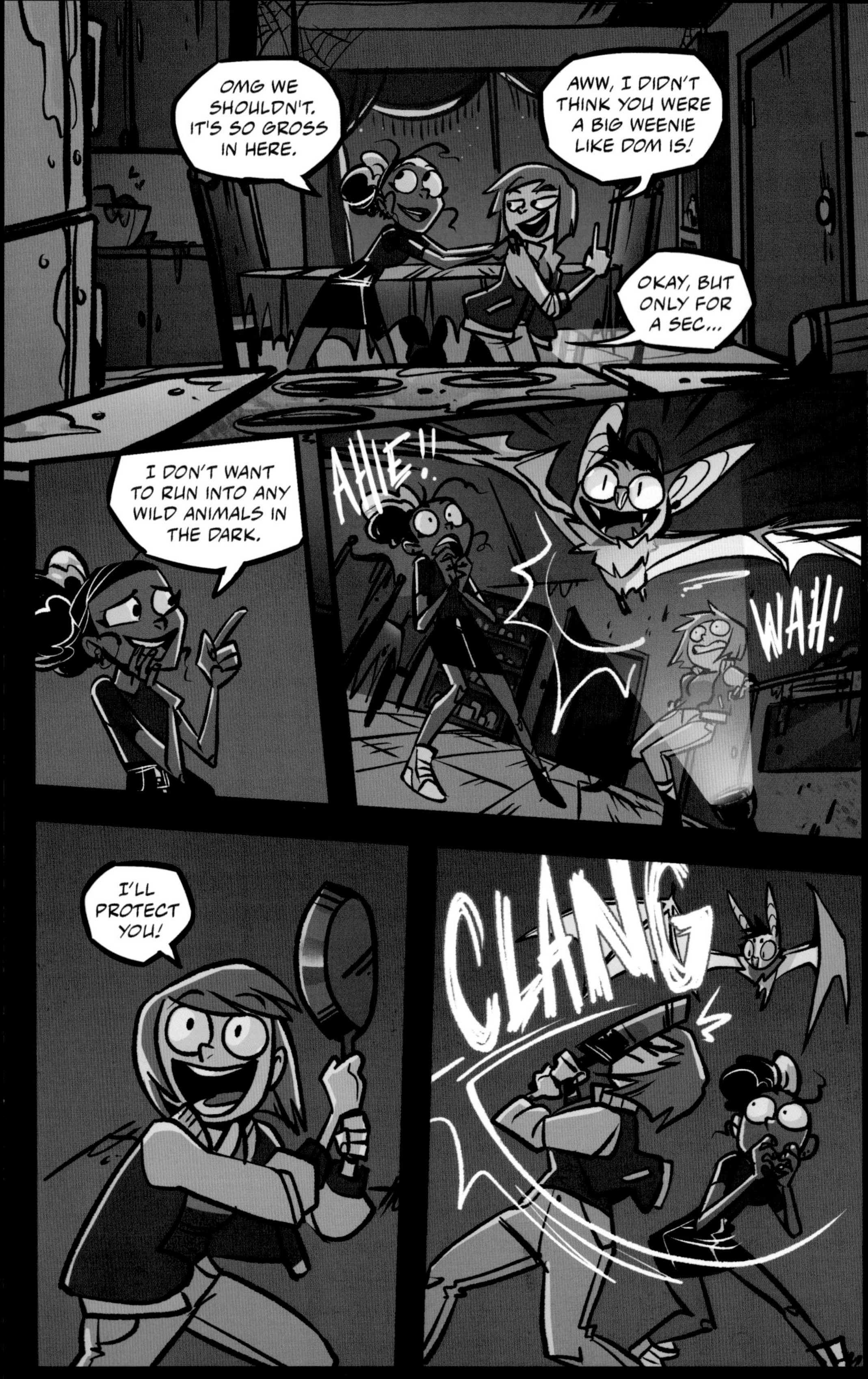
OMG WE SHOULDN'T. IT'S SO GROSS IN HERE.
AWW, I DIDN'T THINK YOU WERE A BIG WEENIE LIKE DOM IS!
OKAY, BUT ONLY FOR A SEC...
I DON'T WANT TO RUN INTO ANY WILD ANIMALS IN THE DARK.
AHIE!!
WAH!
I'LL PROTECT YOU!
CLANG

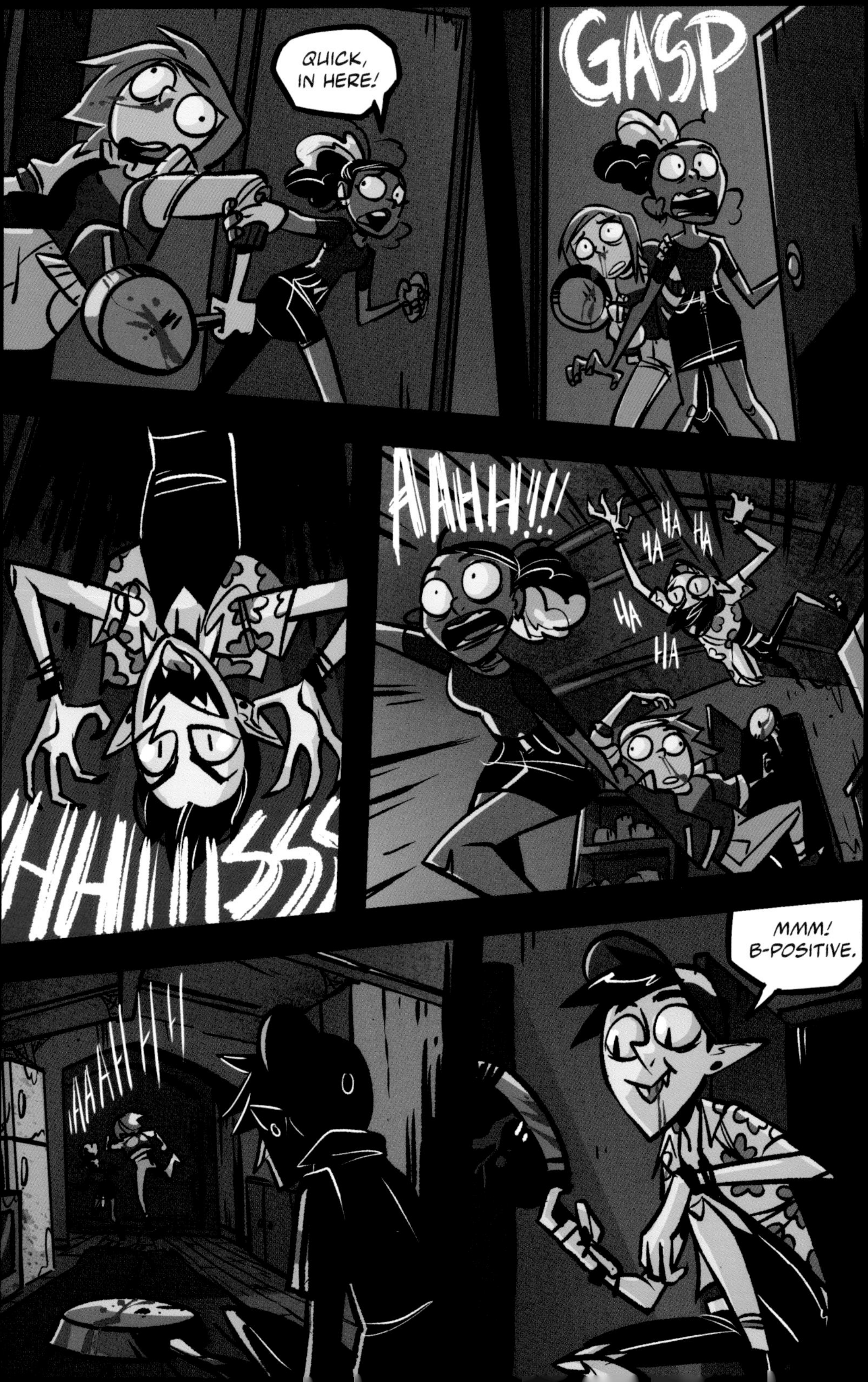
QUICK, IN HERE!
GASP
HHHISSS
AAHH!!!
HA HA HA HA HA HA
AAAHHHH
MMM! B-POSITIVE.

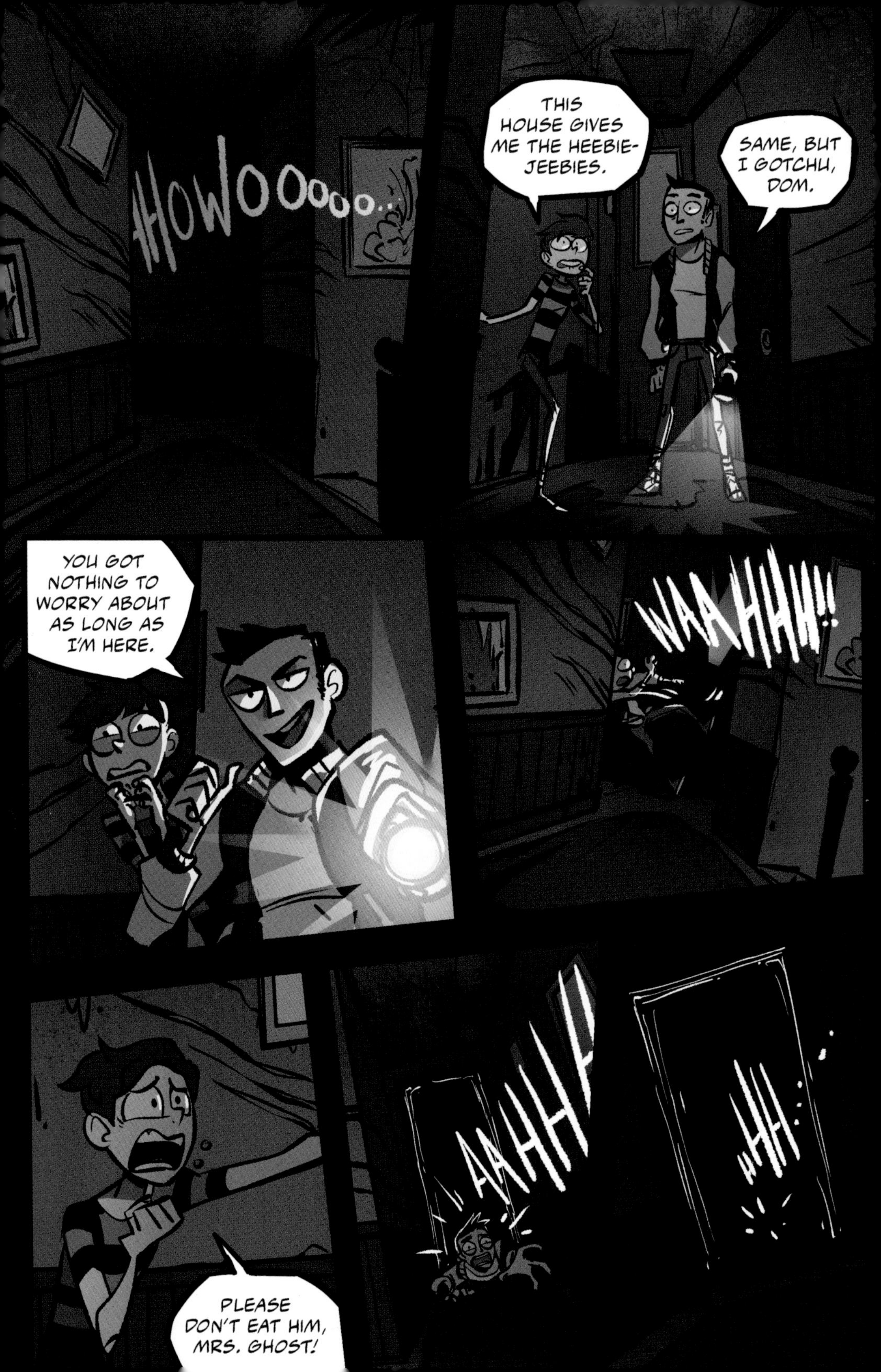
HOWOOooo...
THIS HOUSE GIVES ME THE HEEBIE-JEEBIES.
SAME, BUT I GOTCHU, DOM.
YOU GOT NOTHING TO WORRY ABOUT AS LONG AS I'M HERE.
WAAHHH!!
AAHHHHH...
PLEASE DON'T EAT HIM, MRS. GHOST!

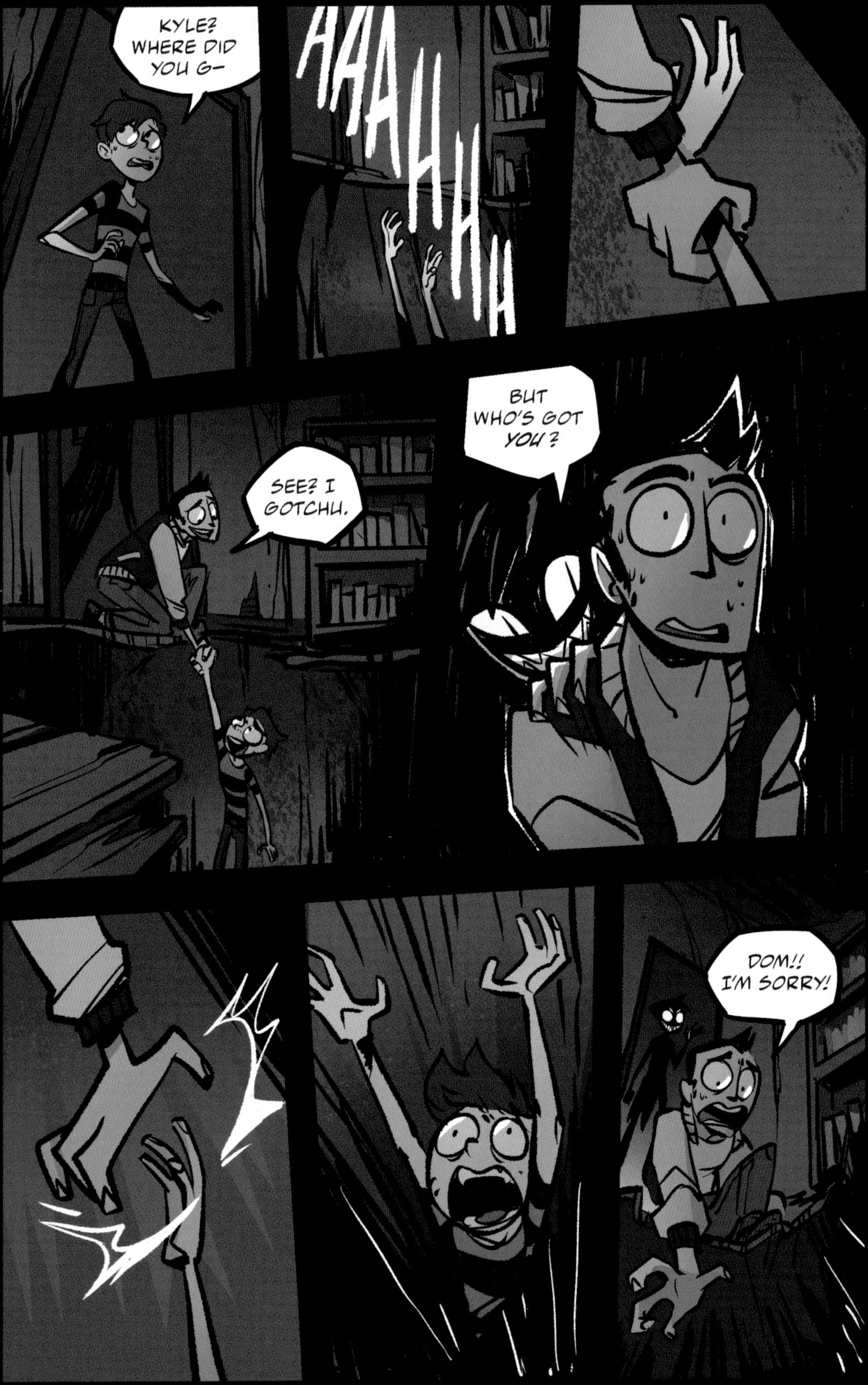
KYLE? WHERE DID YOU G—
AAAAHHHHH
SEE? I GOTCHU.
BUT WHO'S GOT YOU?
DOM!! I'M SORRY!

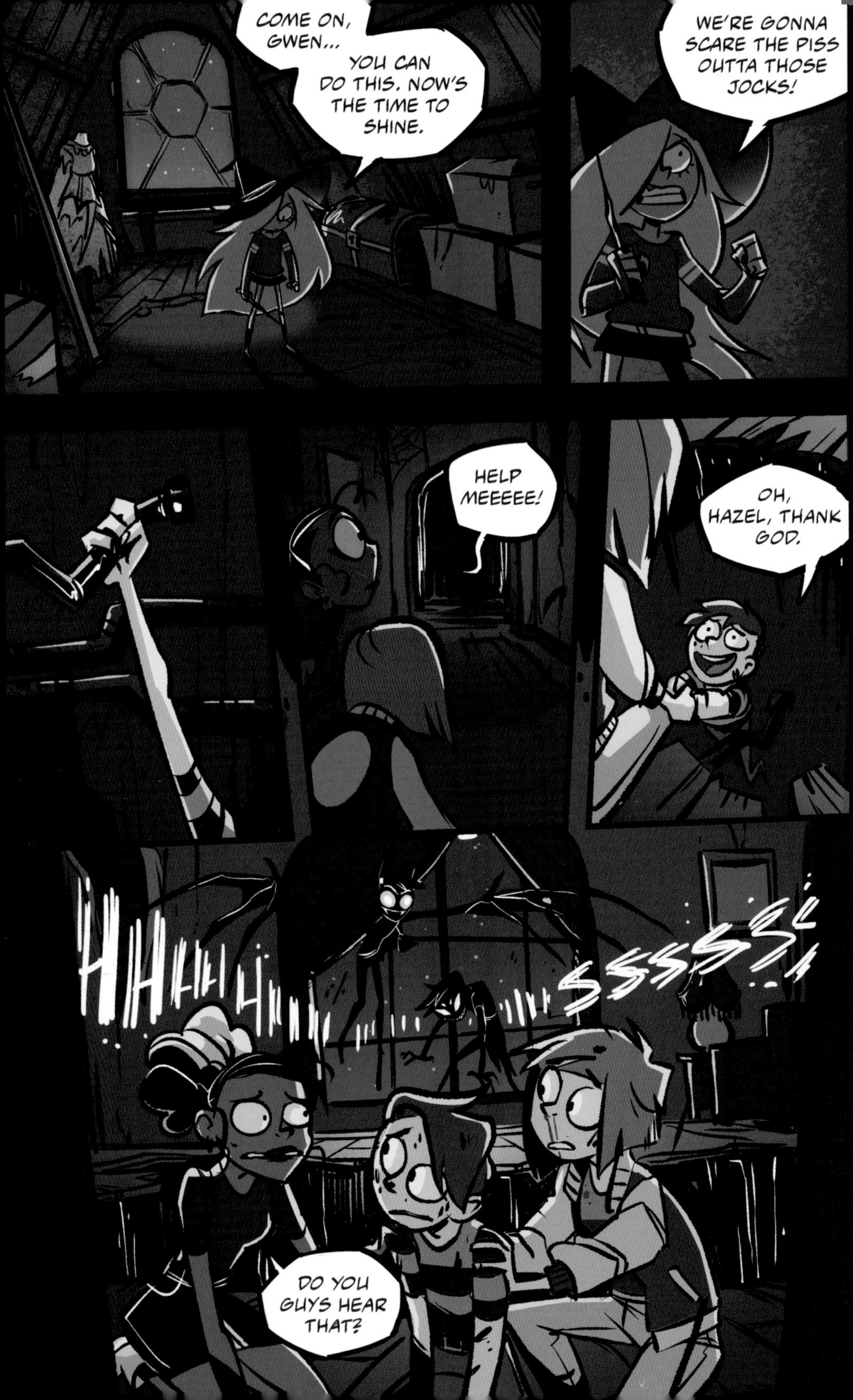
COME ON, GWEN...
YOU CAN DO THIS. NOW'S THE TIME TO SHINE.
WE'RE GONNA SCARE THE PISS OUTTA THOSE JOCKS!
HELP MEEEEE!
OH, HAZEL, THANK GOD.
HHHHHH
SSSSSS
DO YOU GUYS HEAR THAT?

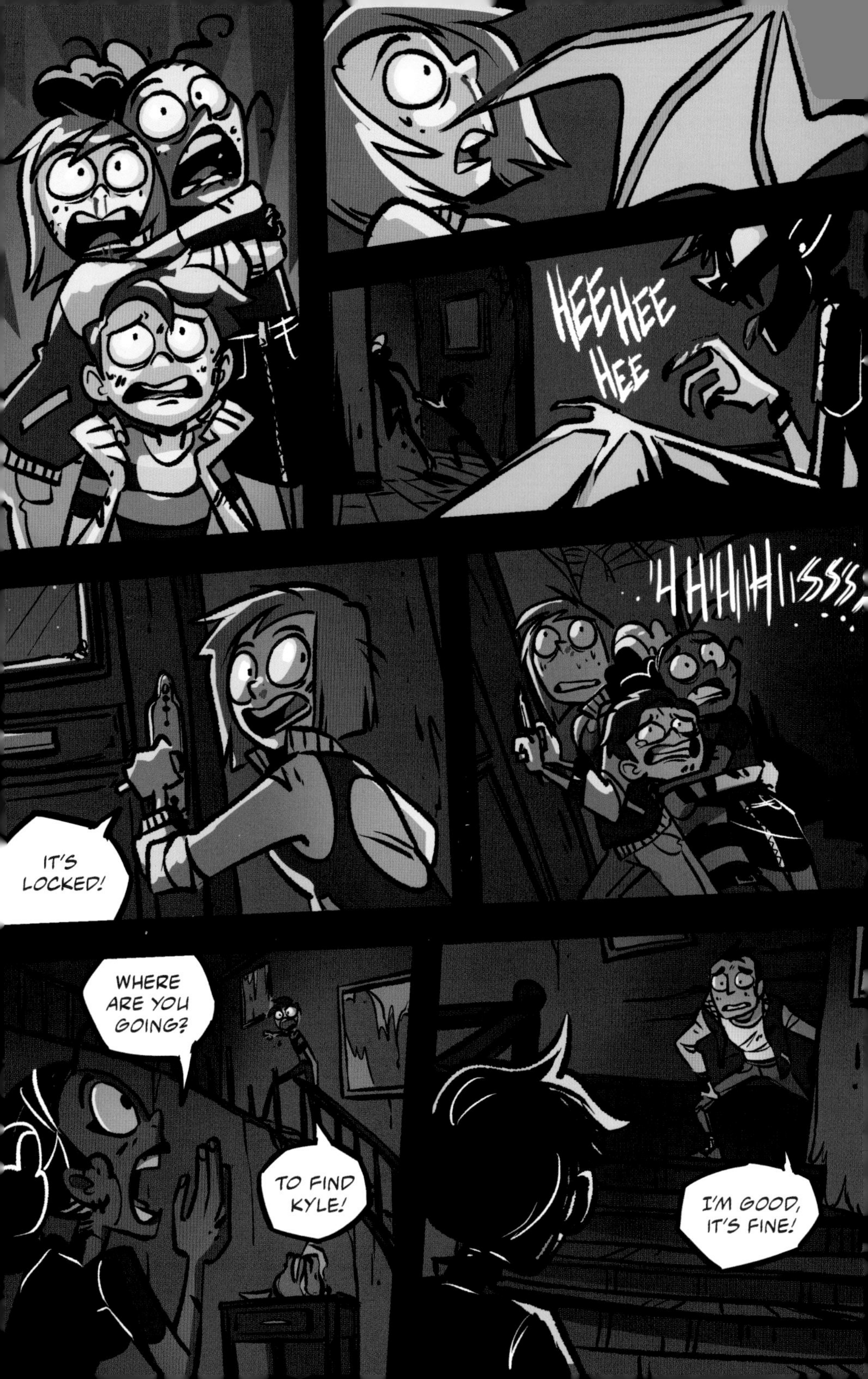
HEE HEE HEE
HHHHHHISSS
IT'S LOCKED!
WHERE ARE YOU GOING?
TO FIND KYLE!
I'M GOOD, IT'S FINE!

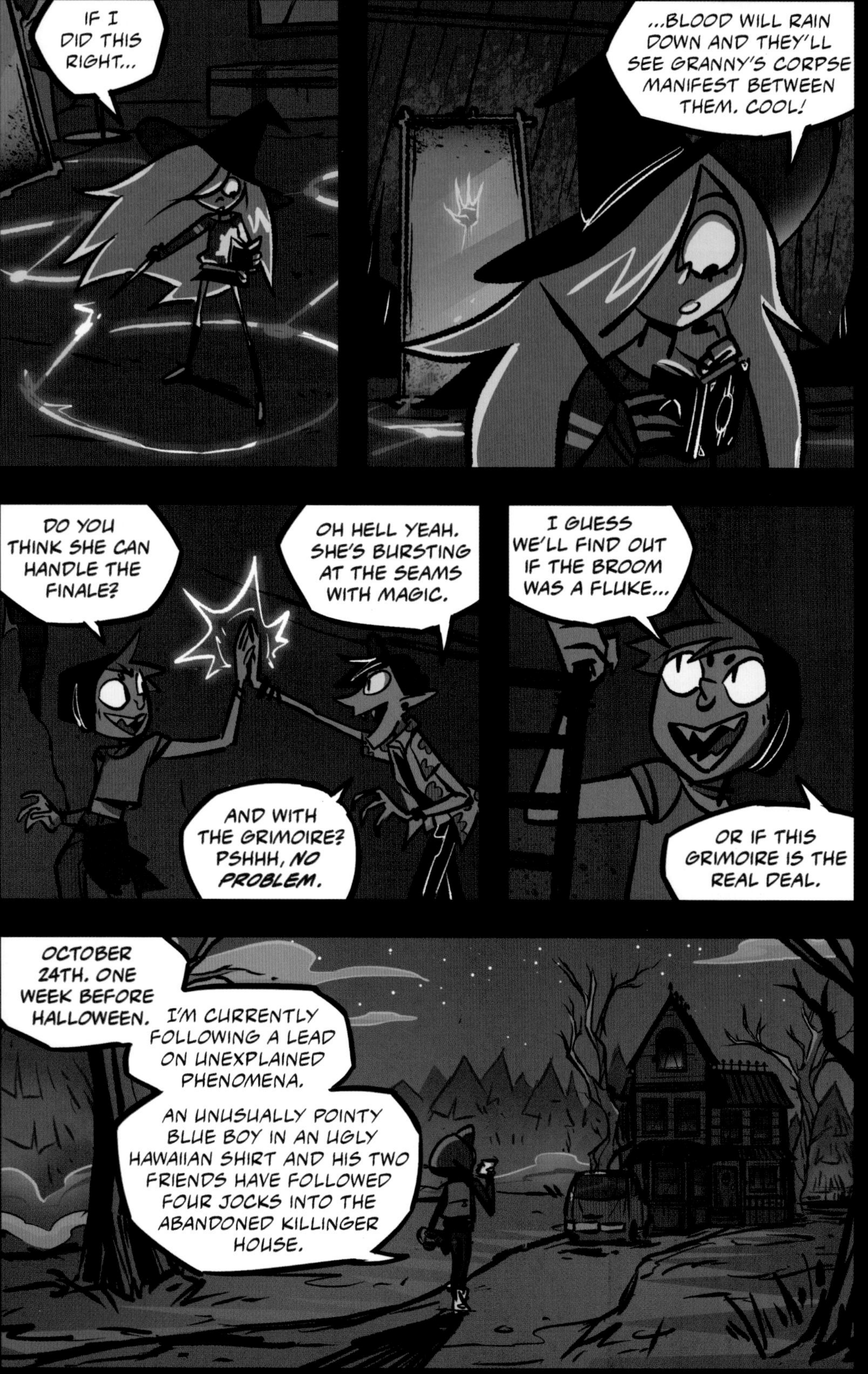
IF I DID THIS RIGHT...
...BLOOD WILL RAIN DOWN AND THEY'LL SEE GRANNY'S CORPSE MANIFEST BETWEEN THEM. COOL!
DO YOU THINK SHE CAN HANDLE THE FINALE?
OH HELL YEAH. SHE'S BURSTING AT THE SEAMS WITH MAGIC.
AND WITH THE GRIMOIRE? PSHHH, *NO PROBLEM*.
I GUESS WE'LL FIND OUT IF THE BROOM WAS A FLUKE...
OR IF THIS GRIMOIRE IS THE REAL DEAL.
OCTOBER 24TH. ONE WEEK BEFORE HALLOWEEN.
I'M CURRENTLY FOLLOWING A LEAD ON UNEXPLAINED PHENOMENA.
AN UNUSUALLY POINTY BLUE BOY IN AN UGLY HAWAIIAN SHIRT AND HIS TWO FRIENDS HAVE FOLLOWED FOUR JOCKS INTO THE ABANDONED KILLINGER HOUSE.

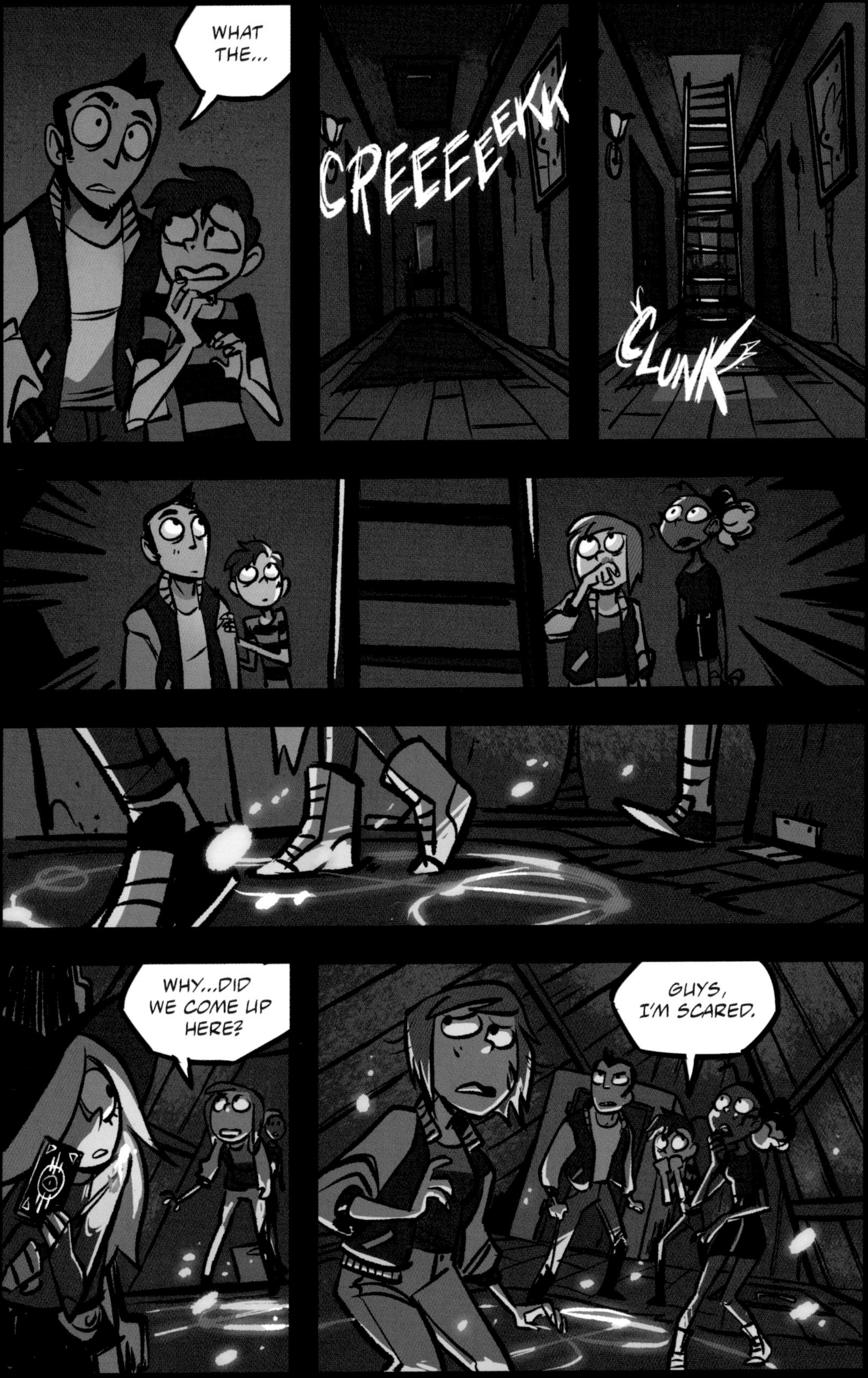
WHAT THE...
CREEEEEEKK
CLUNK
WHY...DID WE COME UP HERE?
GUYS, I'M SCARED.

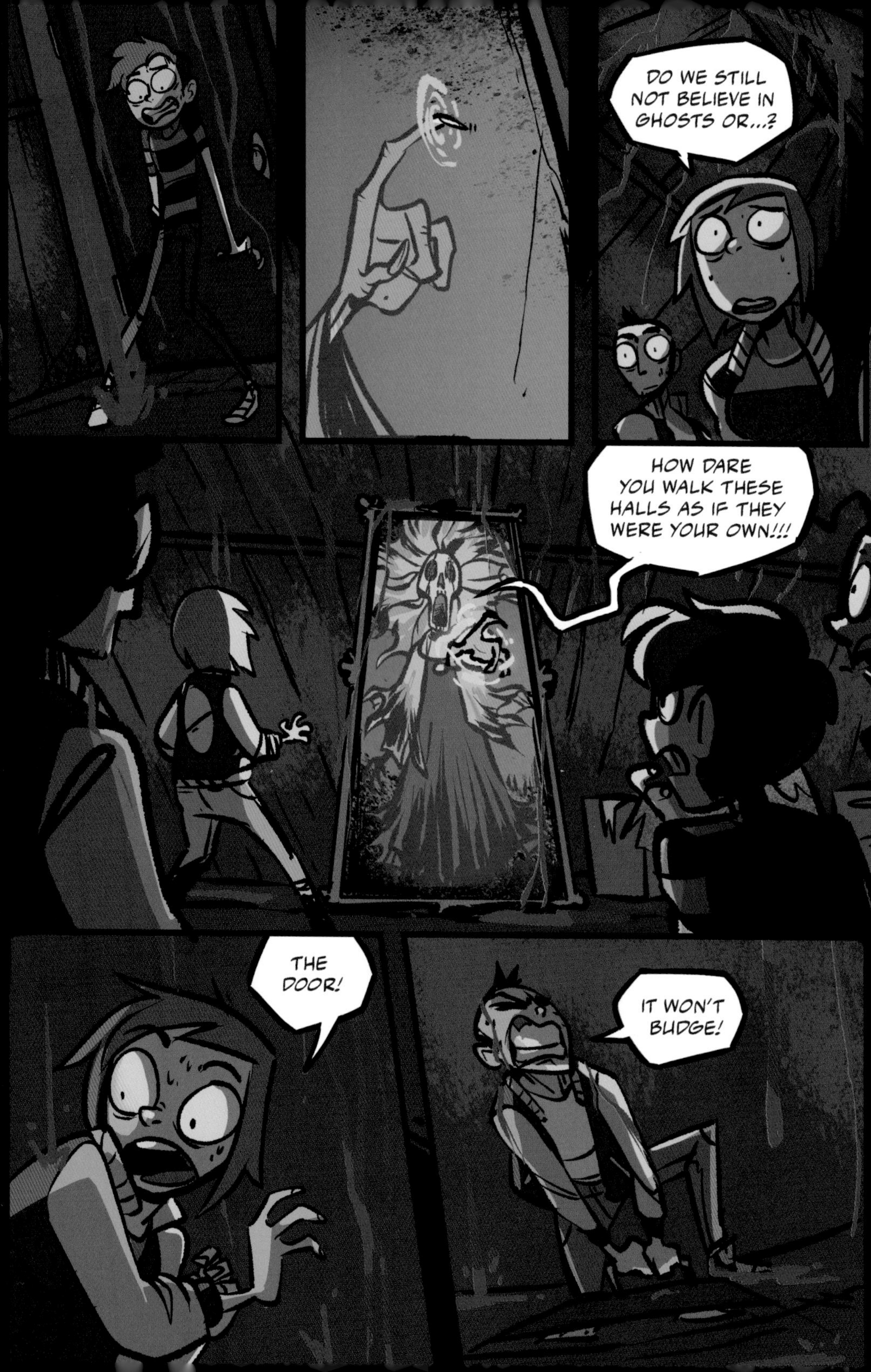
DO WE STILL NOT BELIEVE IN GHOSTS OR...?
HOW DARE YOU WALK THESE HALLS AS IF THEY WERE YOUR OWN!!!
THE DOOR!
IT WON'T BUDGE!

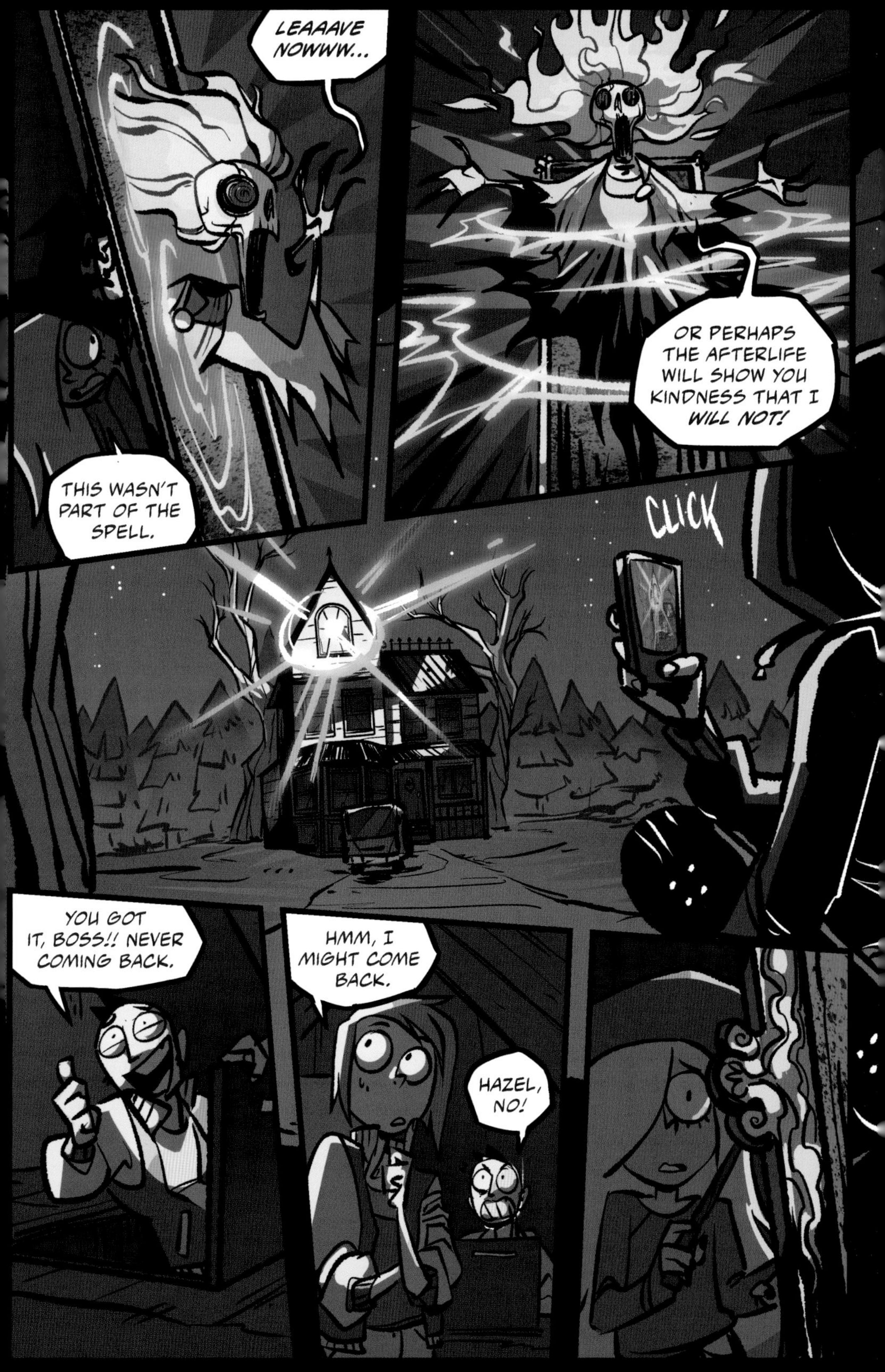
LEAAAVE NOWWW...
OR PERHAPS THE AFTERLIFE WILL SHOW YOU KINDNESS THAT I WILL NOT!
THIS WASN'T PART OF THE SPELL.
CLICK
YOU GOT IT, BOSS!! NEVER COMING BACK.
HMM, I MIGHT COME BACK.
HAZEL, NO!

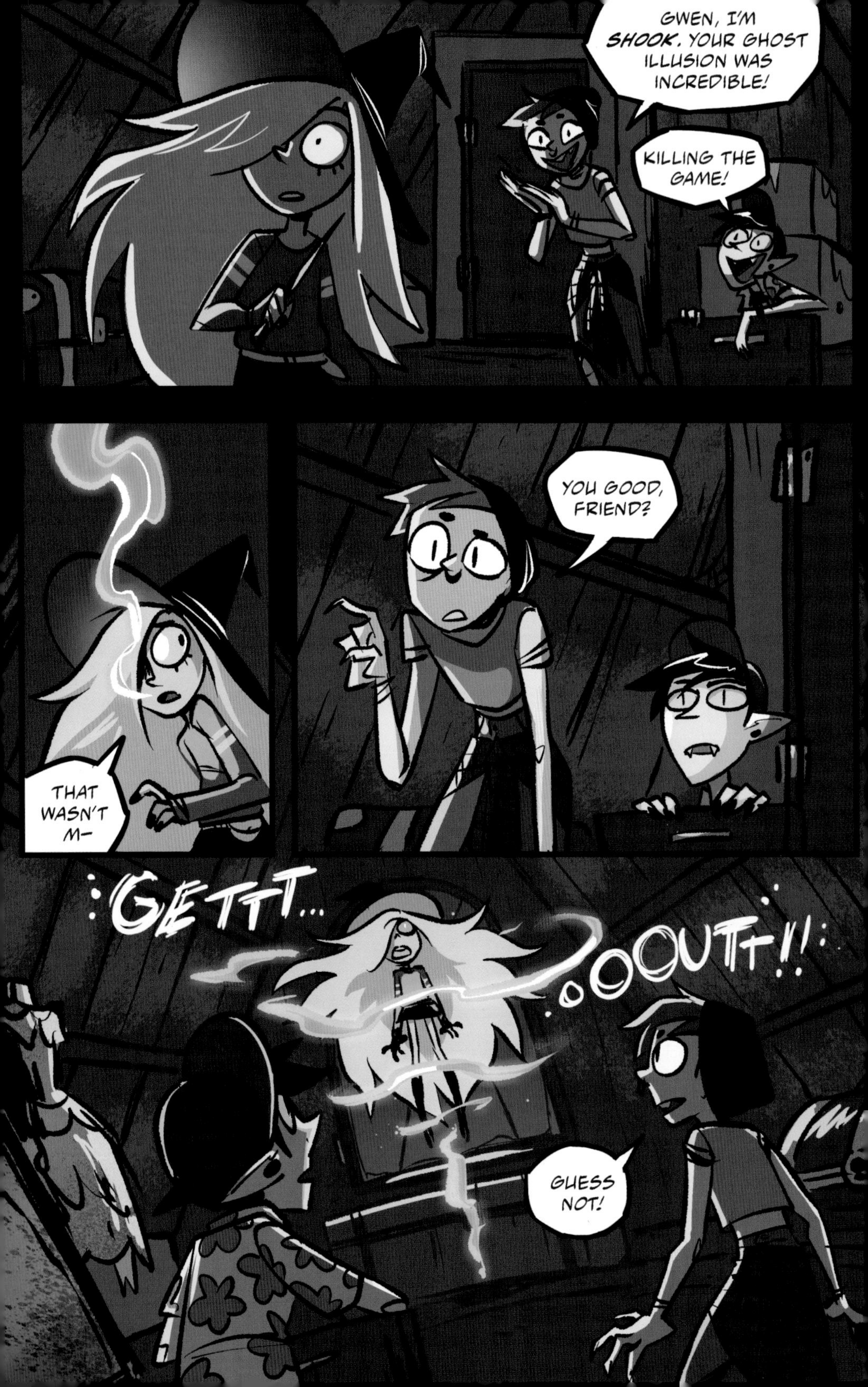
GWEN, I'M **SHOOK**. YOUR GHOST ILLUSION WAS INCREDIBLE!
KILLING THE GAME!
YOU GOOD, FRIEND?
THAT WASN'T M–
GETTT...
OOOUTT!!
GUESS NOT!

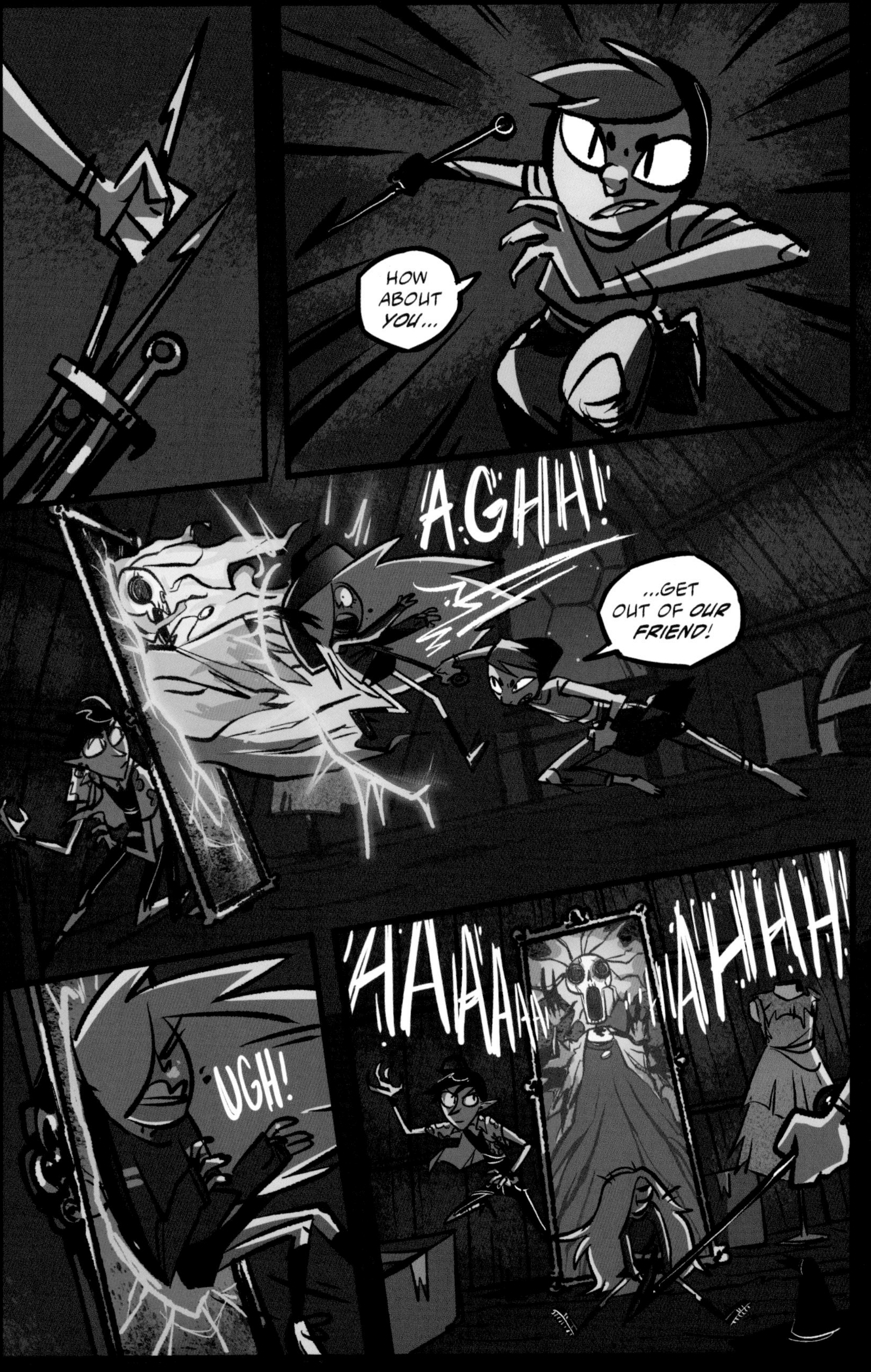
HOW ABOUT YOU...
AGHH!
...GET OUT OF OUR FRIEND!
UGH!
HAAAAAAAAAHHHH!

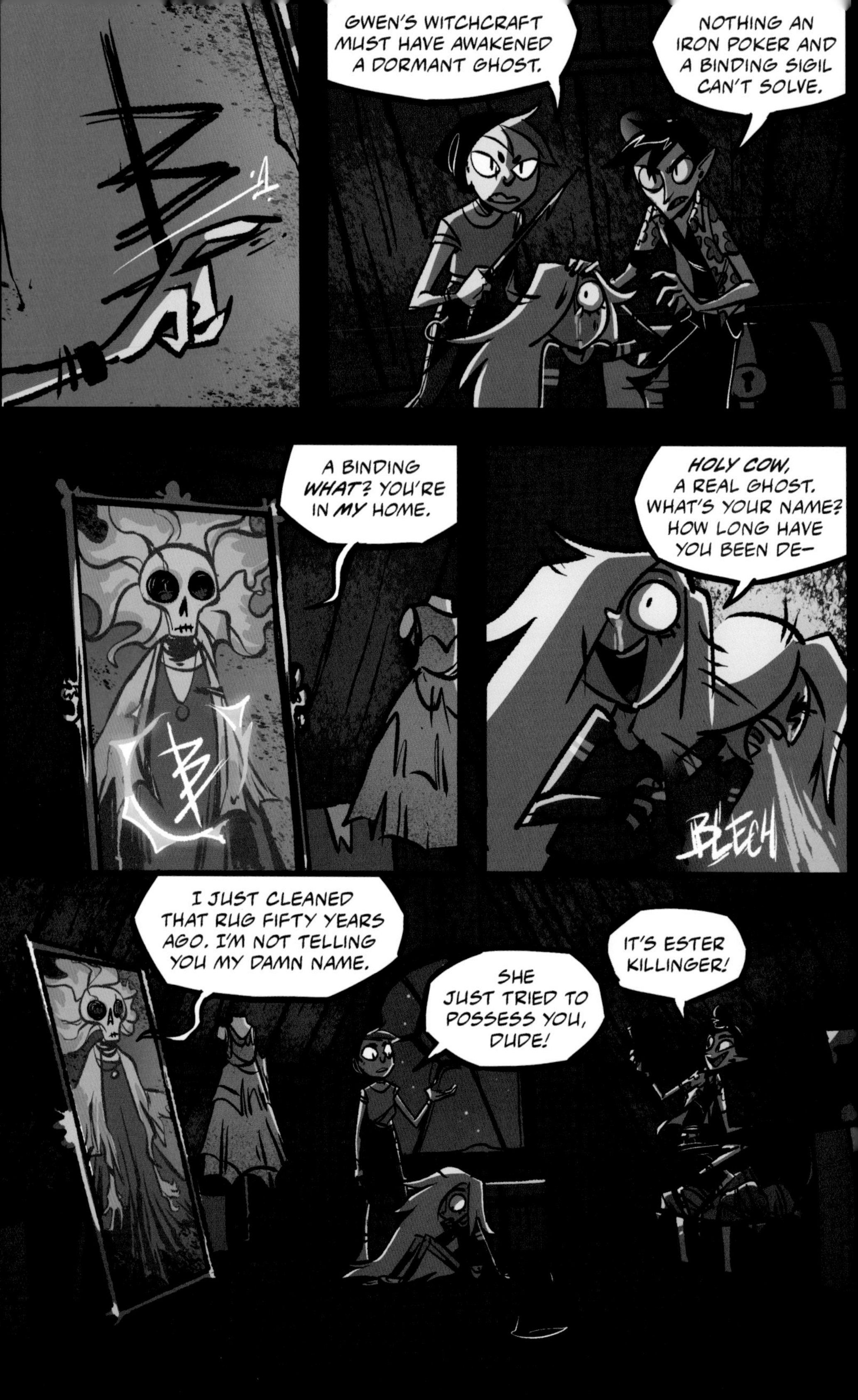
GWEN'S WITCHCRAFT MUST HAVE AWAKENED A DORMANT GHOST.
NOTHING AN IRON POKER AND A BINDING SIGIL CAN'T SOLVE.
A BINDING *WHAT?* YOU'RE IN *MY* HOME.
*HOLY COW,* A REAL GHOST. WHAT'S YOUR NAME? HOW LONG HAVE YOU BEEN DE—
BLECH
I JUST CLEANED THAT RUG FIFTY YEARS AGO. I'M NOT TELLING YOU MY DAMN NAME.
SHE JUST TRIED TO POSSESS YOU, DUDE!
IT'S ESTER KILLINGER!

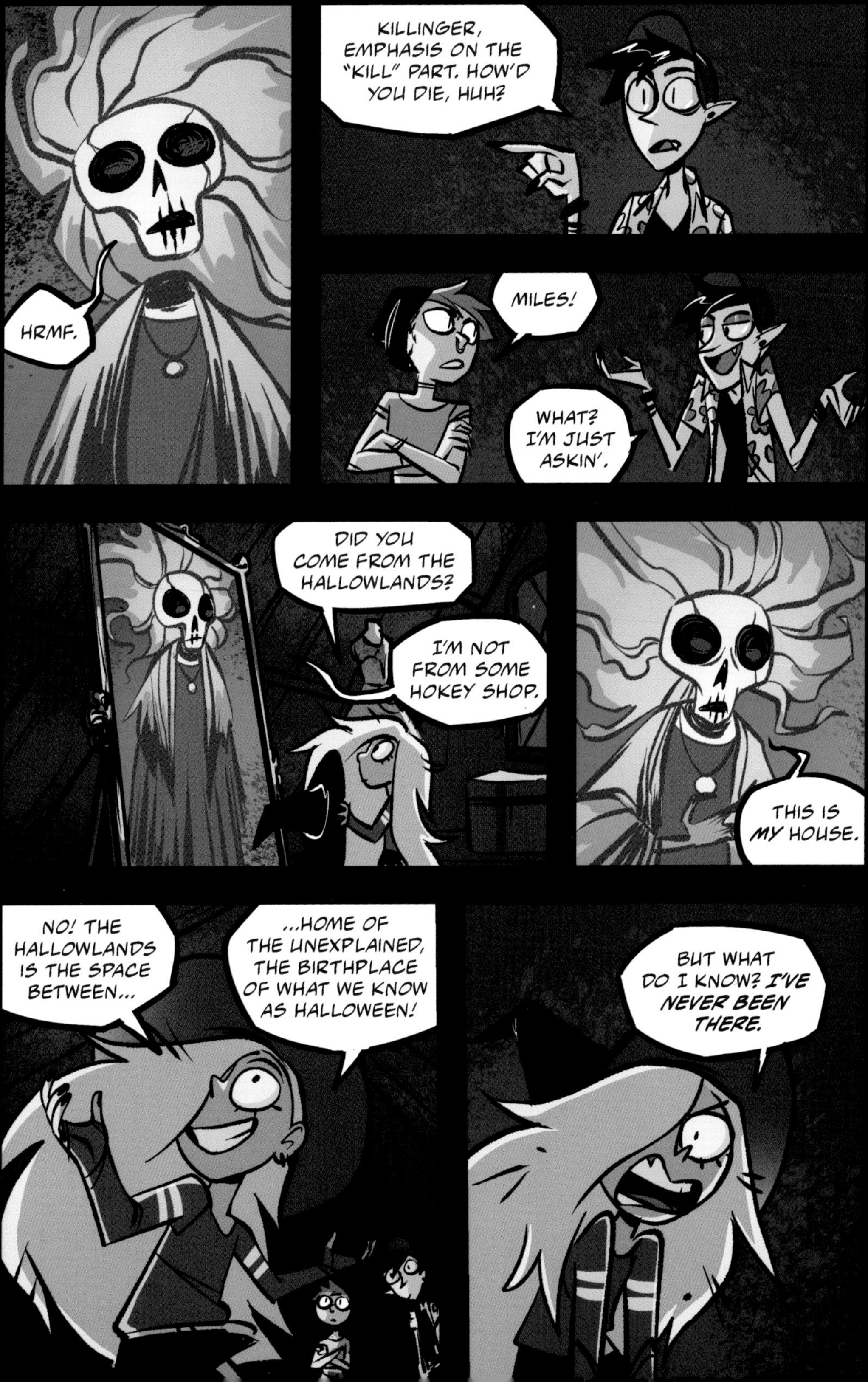
HRMF.
KILLINGER, EMPHASIS ON THE "KILL" PART. HOW'D YOU DIE, HUH?
MILES!
WHAT? I'M JUST ASKIN'.
DID YOU COME FROM THE HALLOWLANDS?
I'M NOT FROM SOME HOKEY SHOP.
THIS IS *MY* HOUSE.
NO! THE HALLOWLANDS IS THE SPACE BETWEEN...
...HOME OF THE UNEXPLAINED, THE BIRTHPLACE OF WHAT WE KNOW AS HALLOWEEN!
BUT WHAT DO I KNOW? *I'VE NEVER BEEN THERE.*

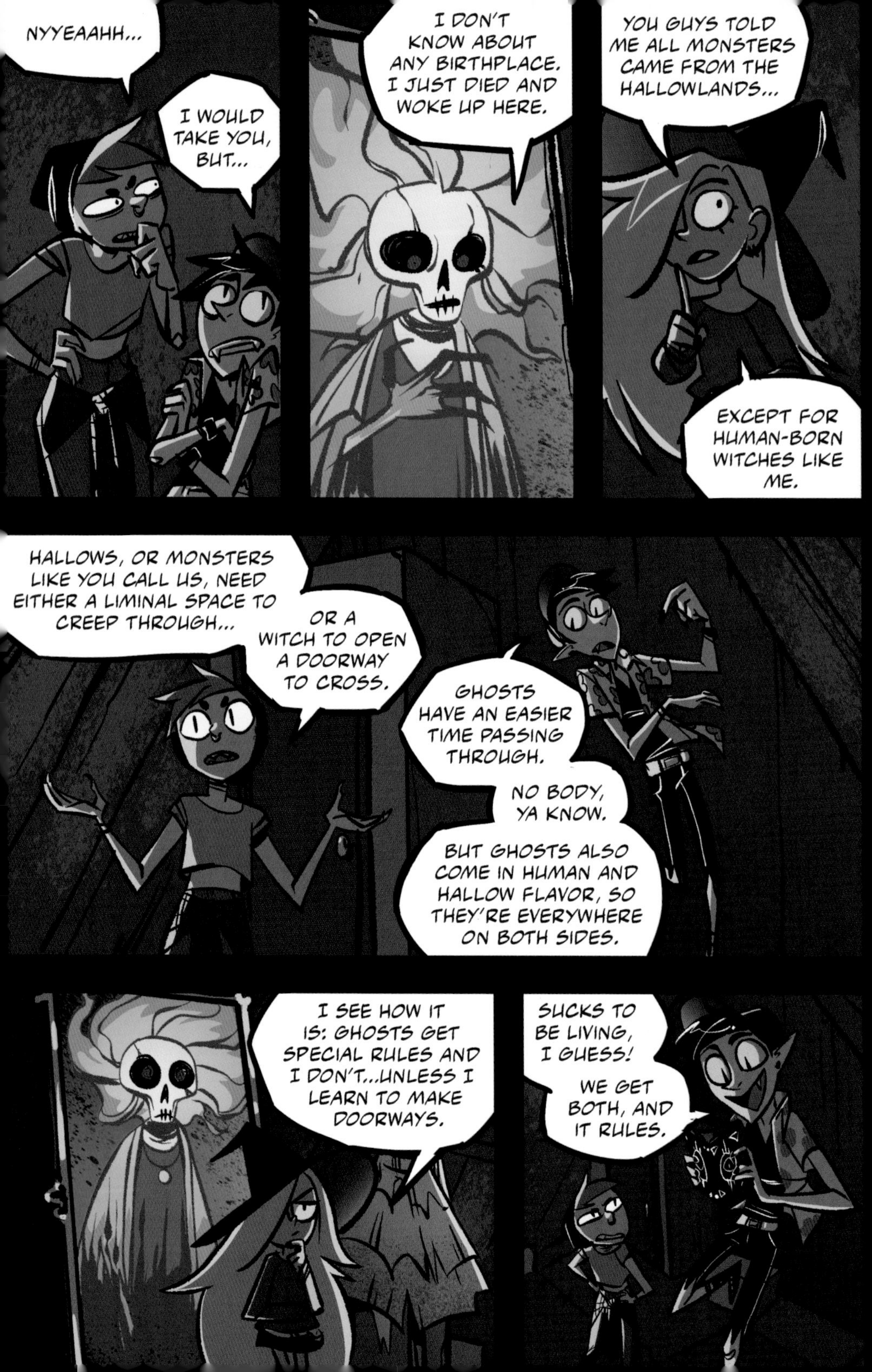
NYYEAAHH...
I WOULD TAKE YOU, BUT...
I DON'T KNOW ABOUT ANY BIRTHPLACE. I JUST DIED AND WOKE UP HERE.
YOU GUYS TOLD ME ALL MONSTERS CAME FROM THE HALLOWLANDS...
EXCEPT FOR HUMAN-BORN WITCHES LIKE ME.
HALLOWS, OR MONSTERS LIKE YOU CALL US, NEED EITHER A LIMINAL SPACE TO CREEP THROUGH...
OR A WITCH TO OPEN A DOORWAY TO CROSS.
GHOSTS HAVE AN EASIER TIME PASSING THROUGH.
NO BODY, YA KNOW.
BUT GHOSTS ALSO COME IN HUMAN AND HALLOW FLAVOR, SO THEY'RE EVERYWHERE ON BOTH SIDES.
I SEE HOW IT IS: GHOSTS GET SPECIAL RULES AND I DON'T...UNLESS I LEARN TO MAKE DOORWAYS.
SUCKS TO BE LIVING, I GUESS!
WE GET BOTH, AND IT RULES.

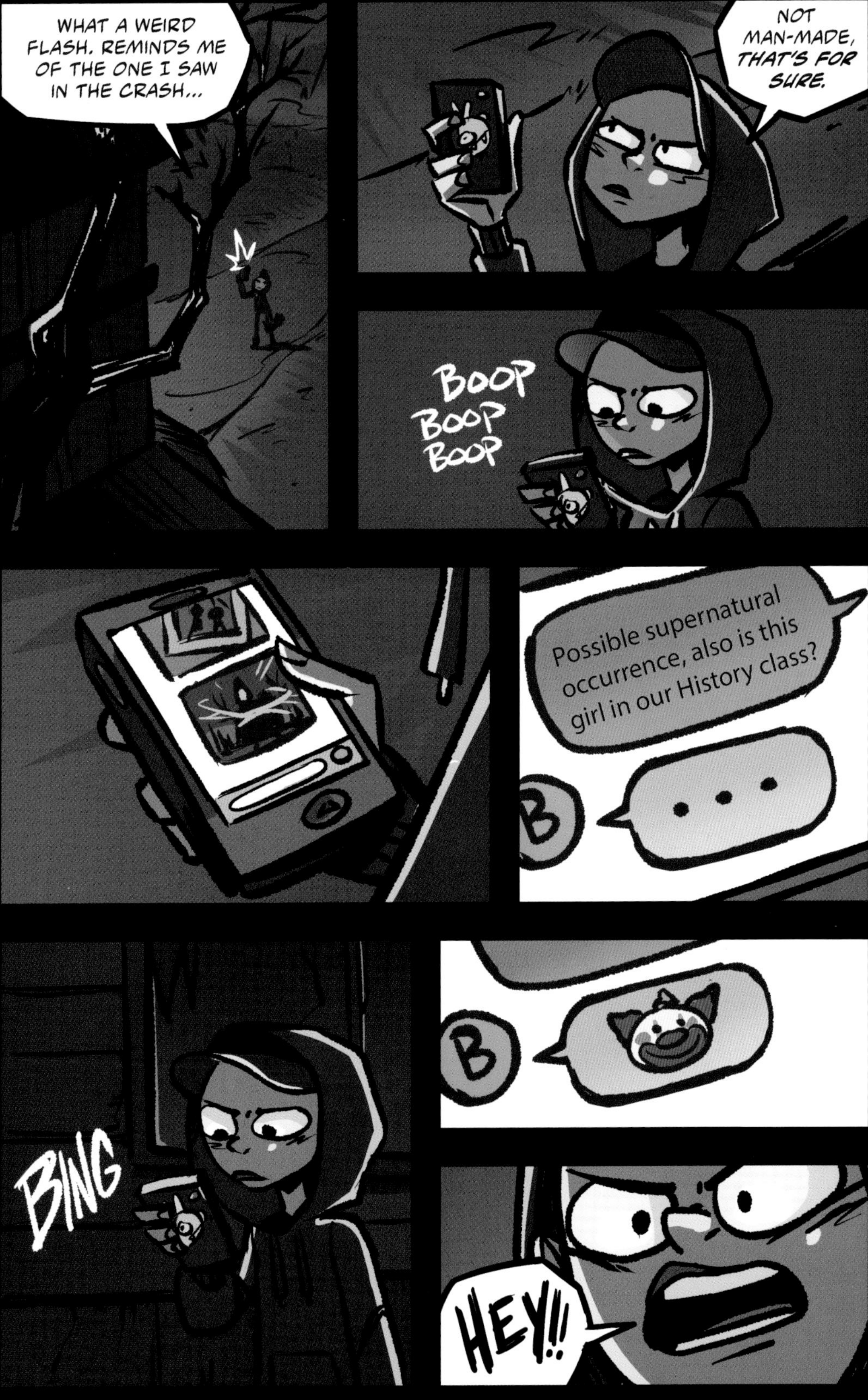
WHAT A WEIRD FLASH. REMINDS ME OF THE ONE I SAW IN THE CRASH...
NOT MAN-MADE, THAT'S FOR SURE.
BOOP BOOP BOOP
Possible supernatural occurrence, also is this girl in our History class?
B
• • •
B
BING
HEY!!!

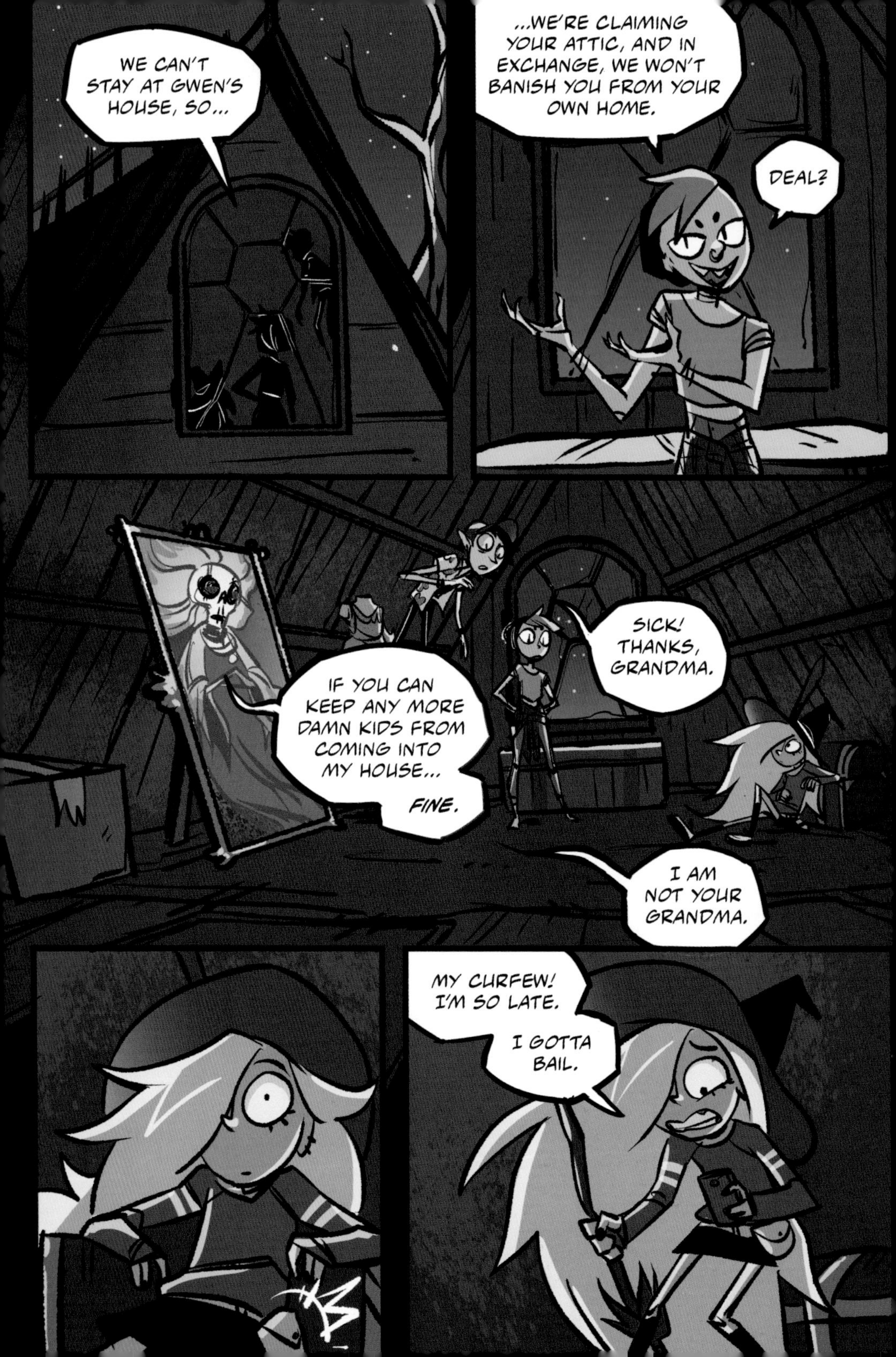

WE CAN'T STAY AT GWEN'S HOUSE, SO...
...WE'RE CLAIMING YOUR ATTIC, AND IN EXCHANGE, WE WON'T BANISH YOU FROM YOUR OWN HOME.
DEAL?
SICK! THANKS, GRANDMA.
IF YOU CAN KEEP ANY MORE DAMN KIDS FROM COMING INTO MY HOUSE...
FINE.
I AM NOT YOUR GRANDMA.
MY CURFEW! I'M SO LATE.
I GOTTA BAIL.

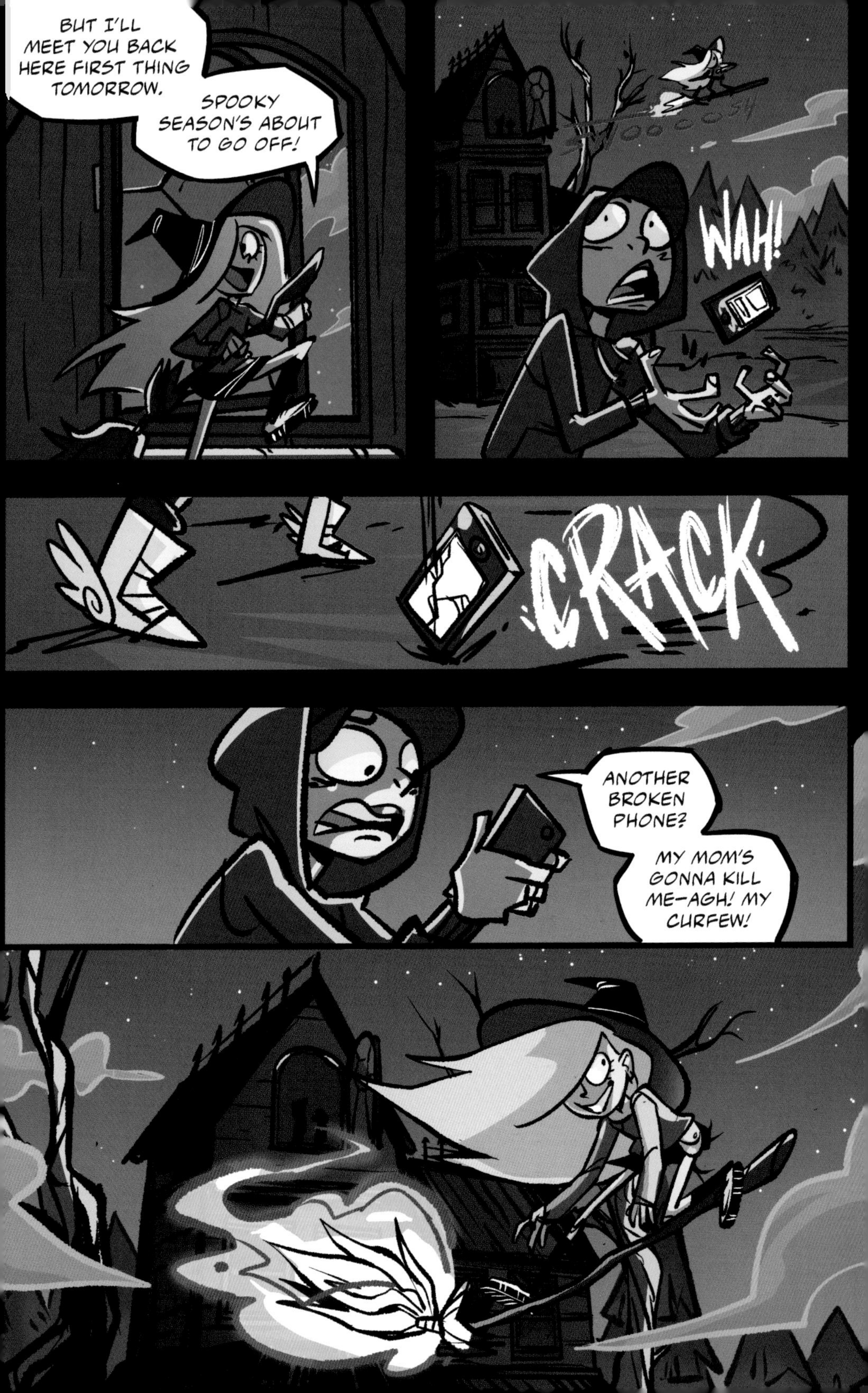
BUT I'LL MEET YOU BACK HERE FIRST THING TOMORROW.
SPOOKY SEASON'S ABOUT TO GO OFF!
SHOOOOOSH
WAH!
CRACK
ANOTHER BROKEN PHONE?
MY MOM'S GONNA KILL ME—AGH! MY CURFEW!

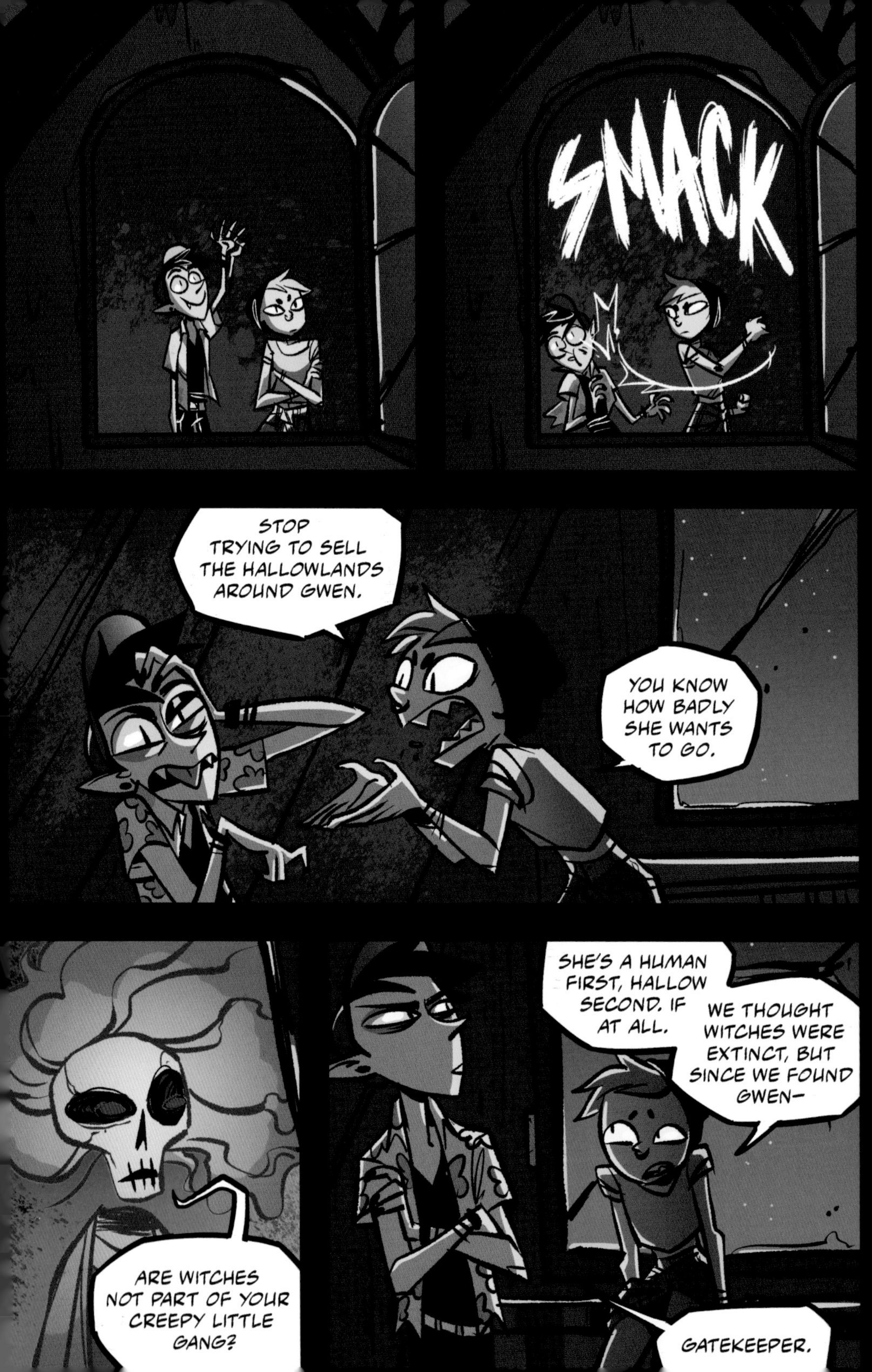
SMACK
STOP TRYING TO SELL THE HALLOWLANDS AROUND GWEN.
YOU KNOW HOW BADLY SHE WANTS TO GO.
ARE WITCHES NOT PART OF YOUR CREEPY LITTLE GANG?
SHE'S A HUMAN FIRST, HALLOW SECOND. IF AT ALL.
WE THOUGHT WITCHES WERE EXTINCT, BUT SINCE WE FOUND GWEN—
GATEKEEPER.

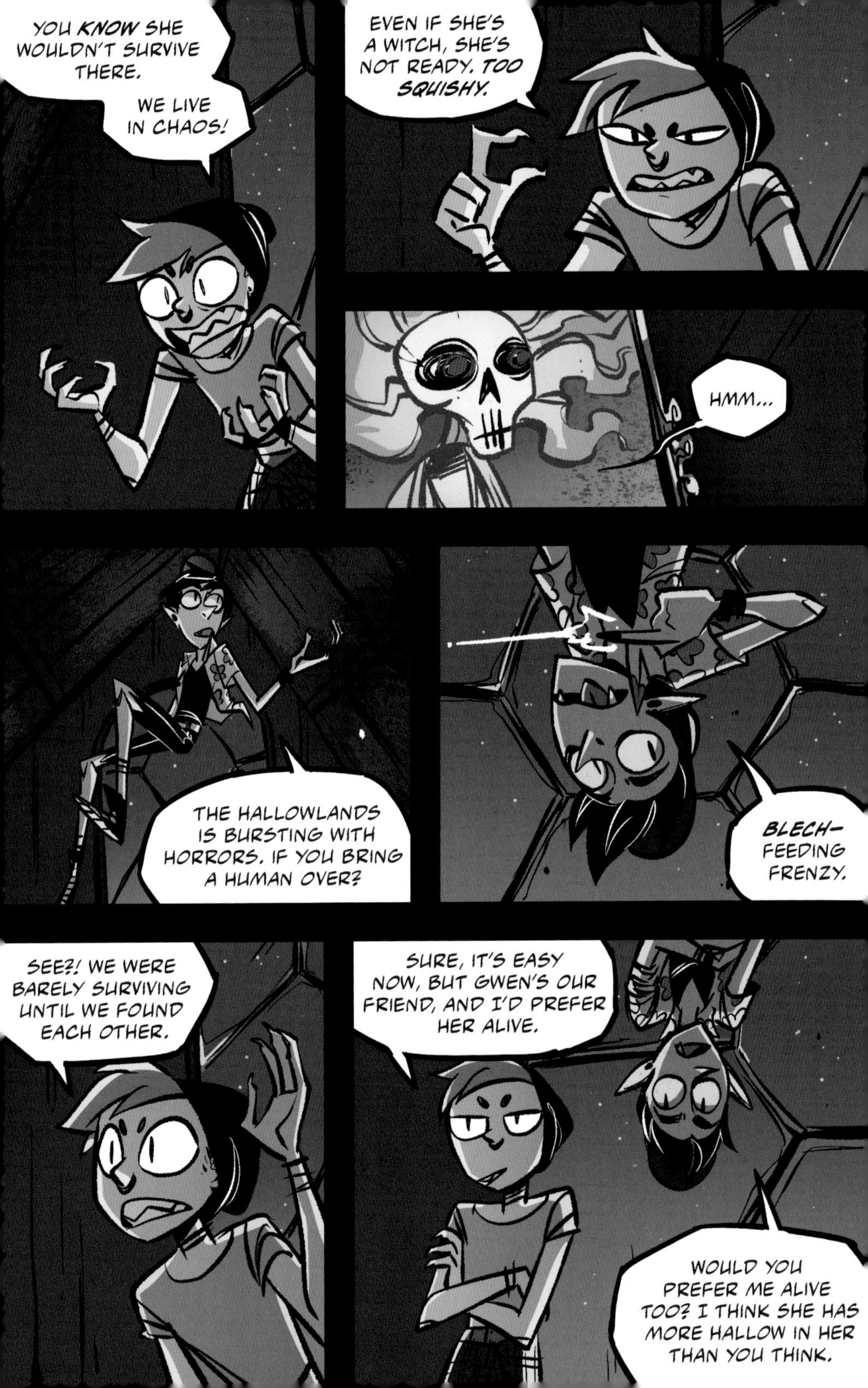
YOU *KNOW* SHE WOULDN'T SURVIVE THERE.
WE LIVE IN CHAOS!
EVEN IF SHE'S A WITCH, SHE'S NOT READY. *TOO SQUISHY.*
HMM...
THE HALLOWLANDS IS BURSTING WITH HORRORS. IF YOU BRING A HUMAN OVER?
*BLECH*— FEEDING FRENZY.
SEE?! WE WERE BARELY SURVIVING UNTIL WE FOUND EACH OTHER.
SURE, IT'S EASY NOW, BUT GWEN'S OUR FRIEND, AND I'D PREFER HER ALIVE.
WOULD YOU PREFER ME ALIVE TOO? I THINK SHE HAS MORE HALLOW IN HER THAN YOU THINK.

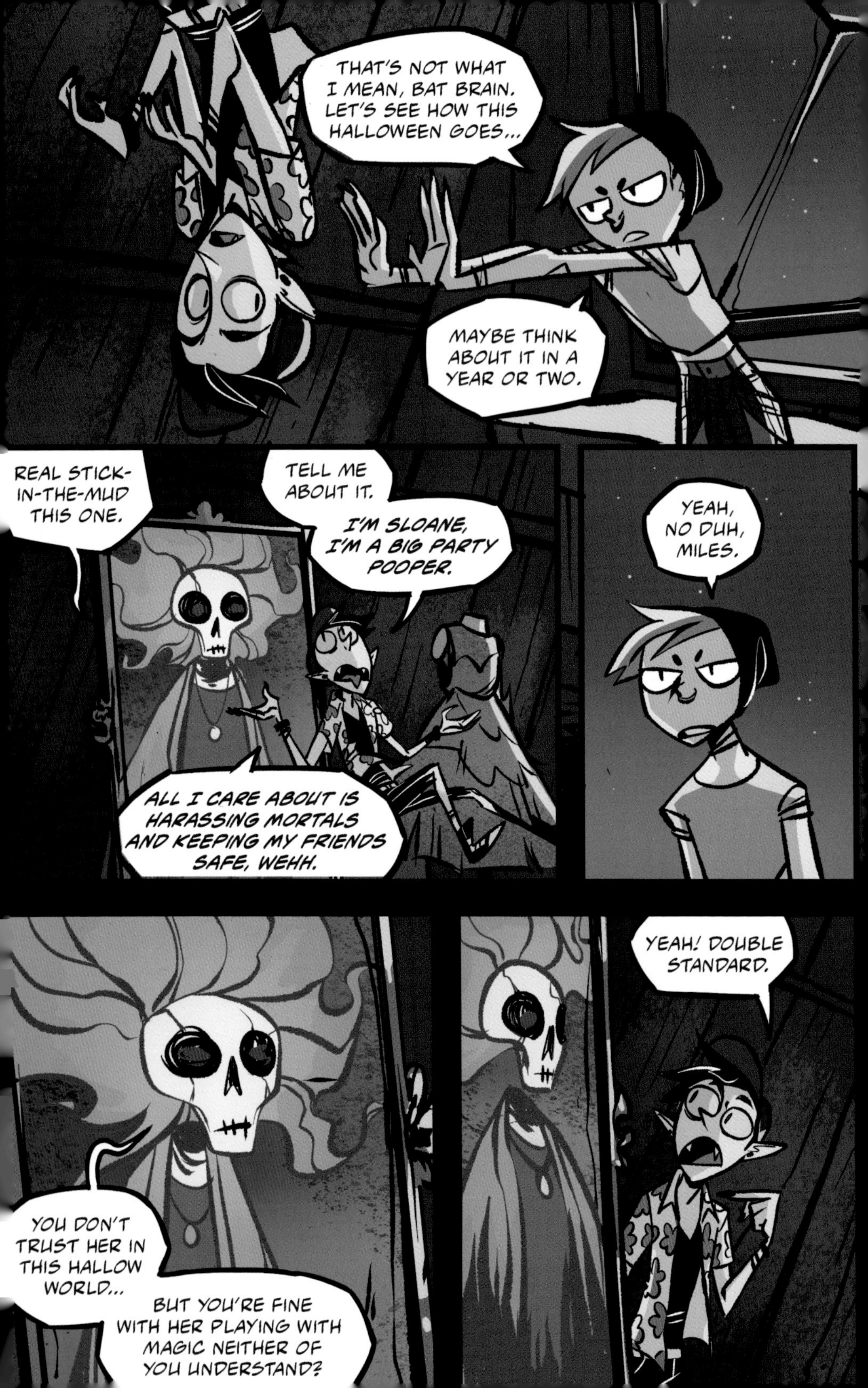
THAT'S NOT WHAT I MEAN, BAT BRAIN. LET'S SEE HOW THIS HALLOWEEN GOES...
MAYBE THINK ABOUT IT IN A YEAR OR TWO.
REAL STICK-IN-THE-MUD THIS ONE.
TELL ME ABOUT IT.
I'M SLOANE, I'M A BIG PARTY POOPER.
ALL I CARE ABOUT IS HARASSING MORTALS AND KEEPING MY FRIENDS SAFE, WEHH.
YEAH, NO DUH, MILES.
YOU DON'T TRUST HER IN THIS HALLOW WORLD...
BUT YOU'RE FINE WITH HER PLAYING WITH MAGIC NEITHER OF YOU UNDERSTAND?
YEAH! DOUBLE STANDARD.

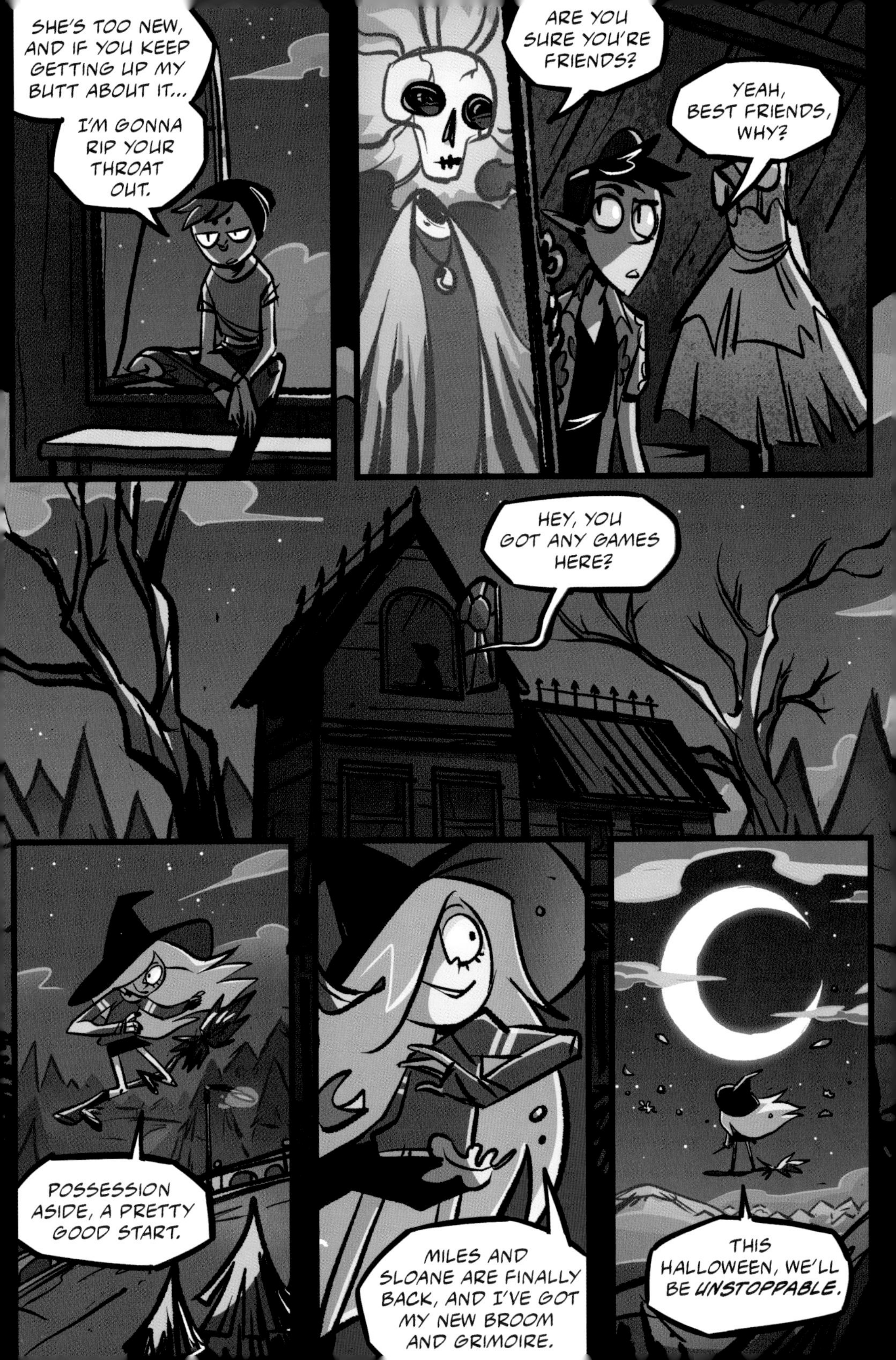
SHE'S TOO NEW, AND IF YOU KEEP GETTING UP MY BUTT ABOUT IT...
I'M GONNA RIP YOUR THROAT OUT.
ARE YOU SURE YOU'RE FRIENDS?
YEAH, BEST FRIENDS, WHY?
HEY, YOU GOT ANY GAMES HERE?
POSSESSION ASIDE, A PRETTY GOOD START.
MILES AND SLOANE ARE FINALLY BACK, AND I'VE GOT MY NEW BROOM AND GRIMOIRE.
THIS HALLOWEEN, WE'LL BE *UNSTOPPABLE.*

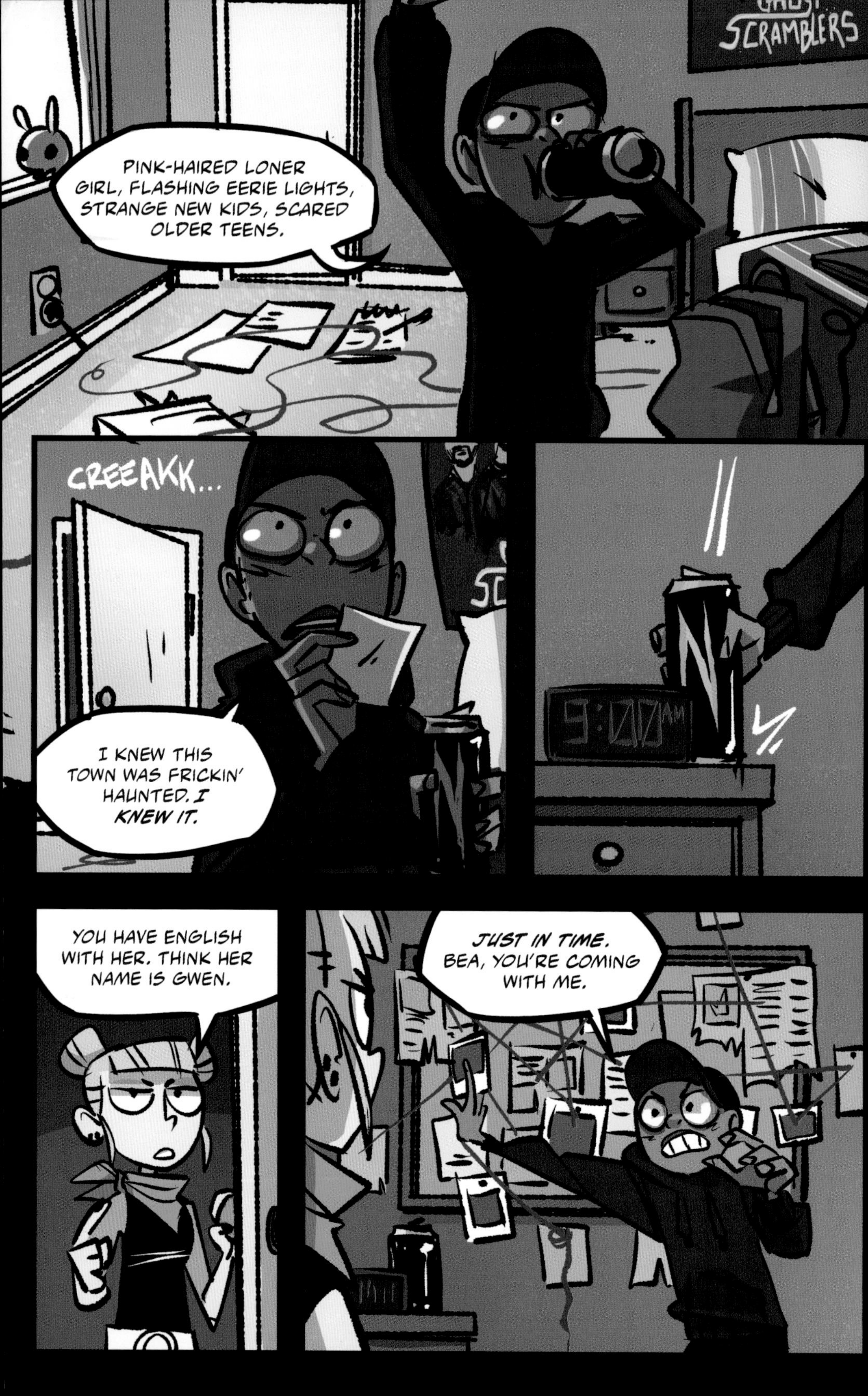
GHOST SCRAMBLERS
PINK-HAIRED LONER GIRL, FLASHING EERIE LIGHTS, STRANGE NEW KIDS, SCARED OLDER TEENS.
CREEAKK...
I KNEW THIS TOWN WAS FRICKIN' HAUNTED. *I KNEW IT.*
9:00 AM
YOU HAVE ENGLISH WITH HER. THINK HER NAME IS GWEN.
*JUST IN TIME.* BEA, YOU'RE COMING WITH ME.

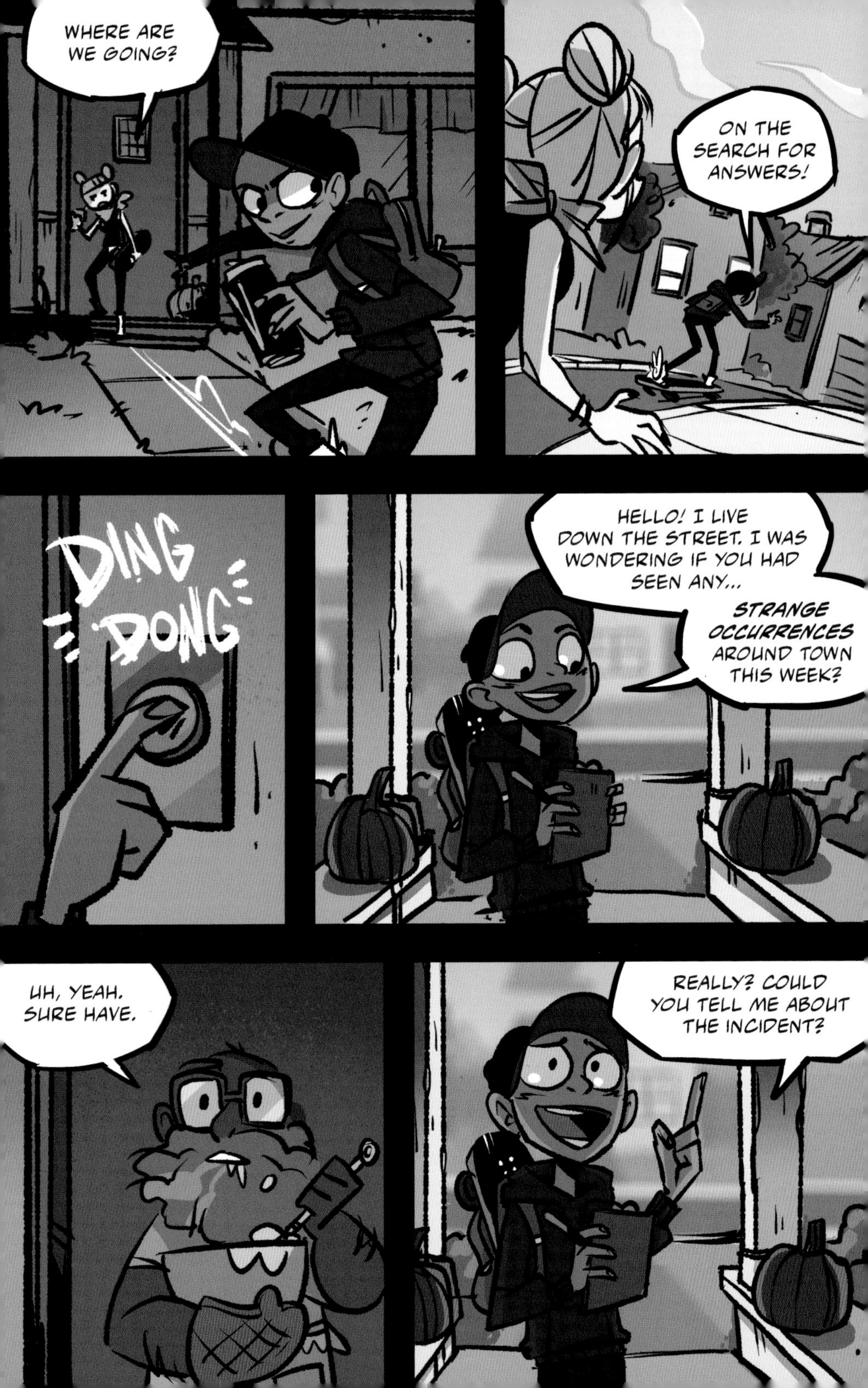
WHERE ARE WE GOING?
ON THE SEARCH FOR ANSWERS!
DING DONG
HELLO! I LIVE DOWN THE STREET. I WAS WONDERING IF YOU HAD SEEN ANY...
STRANGE OCCURRENCES AROUND TOWN THIS WEEK?
UH, YEAH. SURE HAVE.
REALLY? COULD YOU TELL ME ABOUT THE INCIDENT?

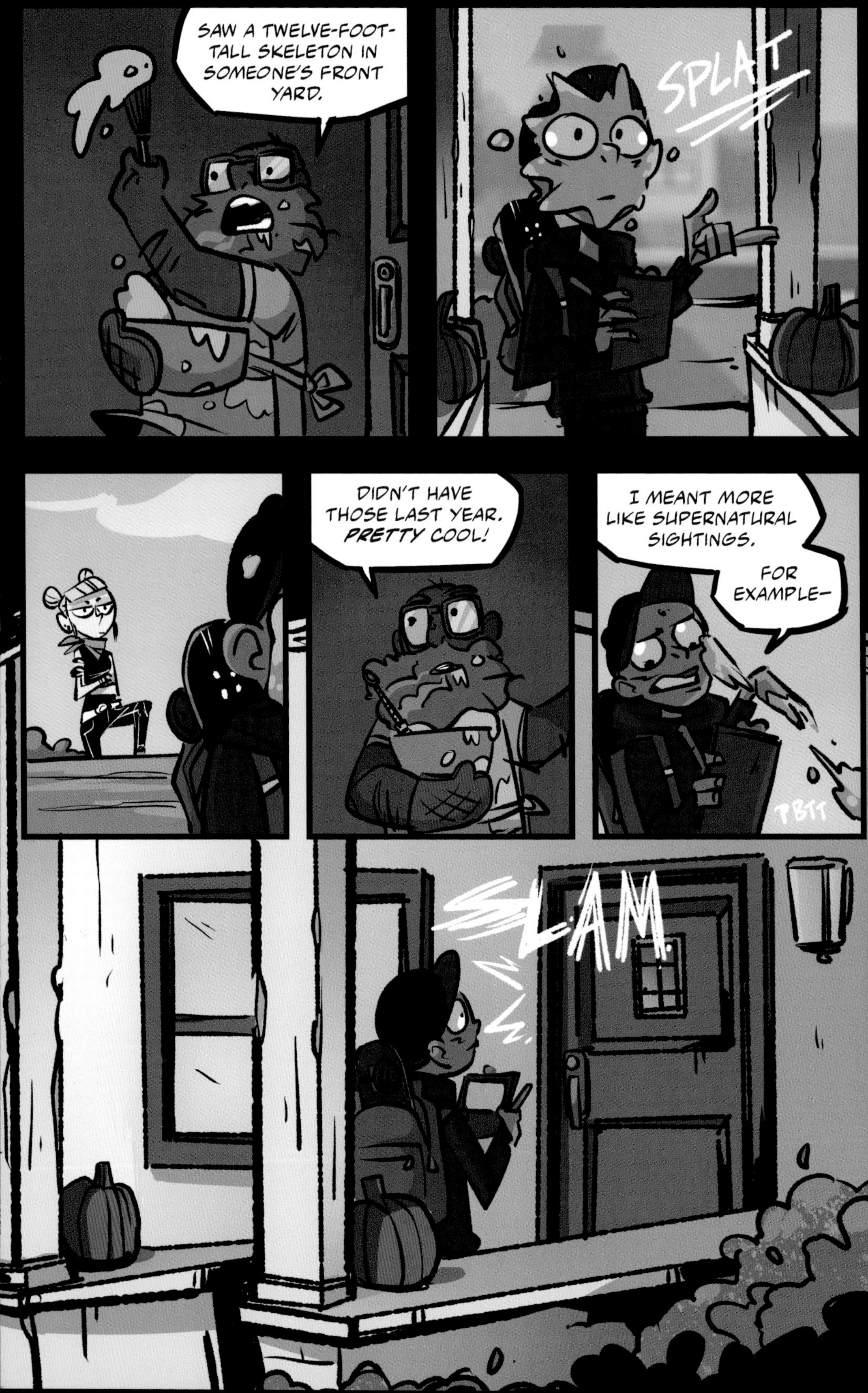
SAW A TWELVE-FOOT-TALL SKELETON IN SOMEONE'S FRONT YARD.
SPLAT
DIDN'T HAVE THOSE LAST YEAR. *PRETTY* COOL!
I MEANT MORE LIKE SUPERNATURAL SIGHTINGS.
FOR EXAMPLE–
PBTT
SLAM.

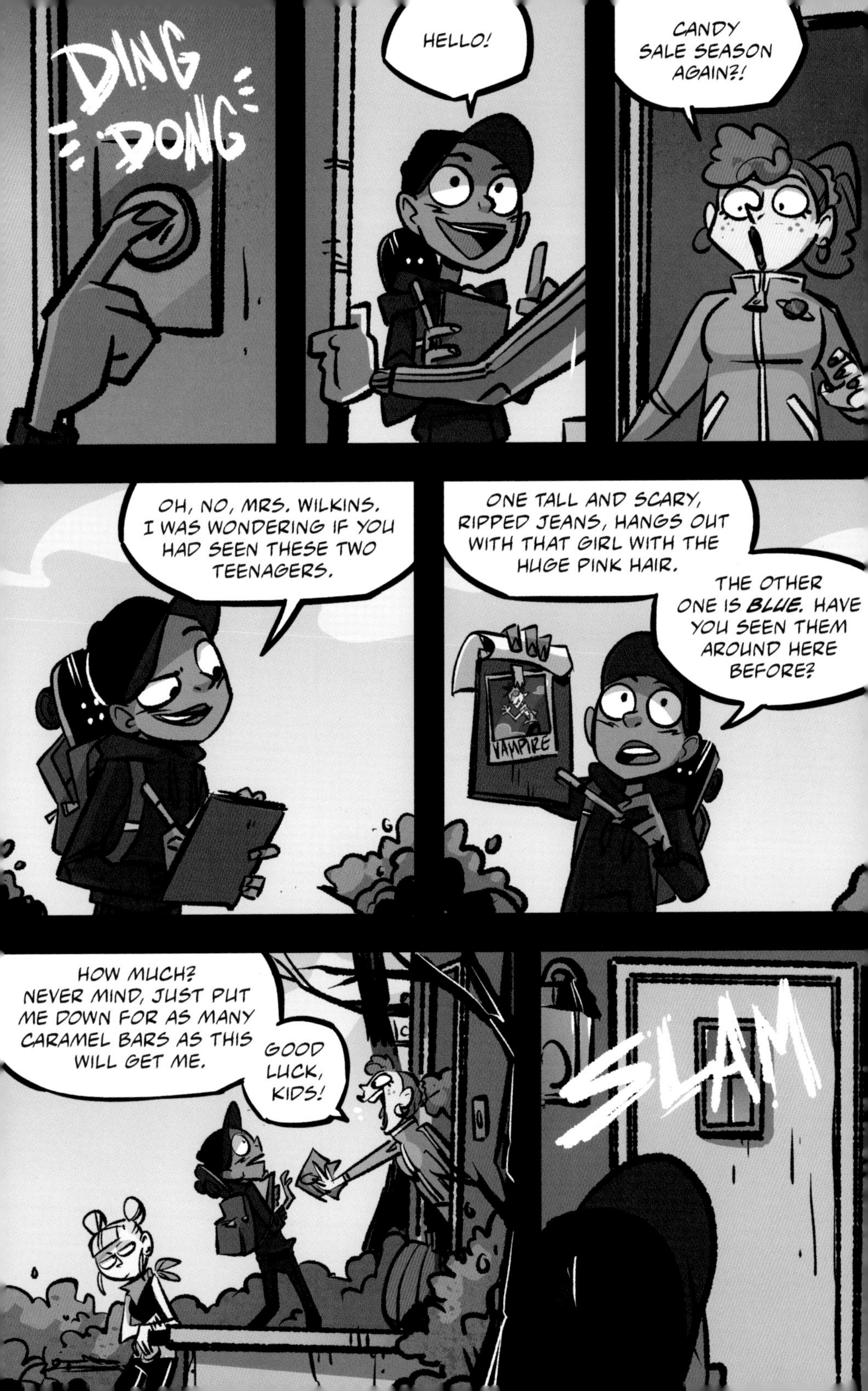
DING DONG
HELLO!
CANDY SALE SEASON AGAIN?!
OH, NO, MRS. WILKINS. I WAS WONDERING IF YOU HAD SEEN THESE TWO TEENAGERS.
ONE TALL AND SCARY, RIPPED JEANS, HANGS OUT WITH THAT GIRL WITH THE HUGE PINK HAIR.
THE OTHER ONE IS BLUE. HAVE YOU SEEN THEM AROUND HERE BEFORE?
VAMPIRE
HOW MUCH? NEVER MIND, JUST PUT ME DOWN FOR AS MANY CARAMEL BARS AS THIS WILL GET ME.
GOOD LUCK, KIDS!
SLAM

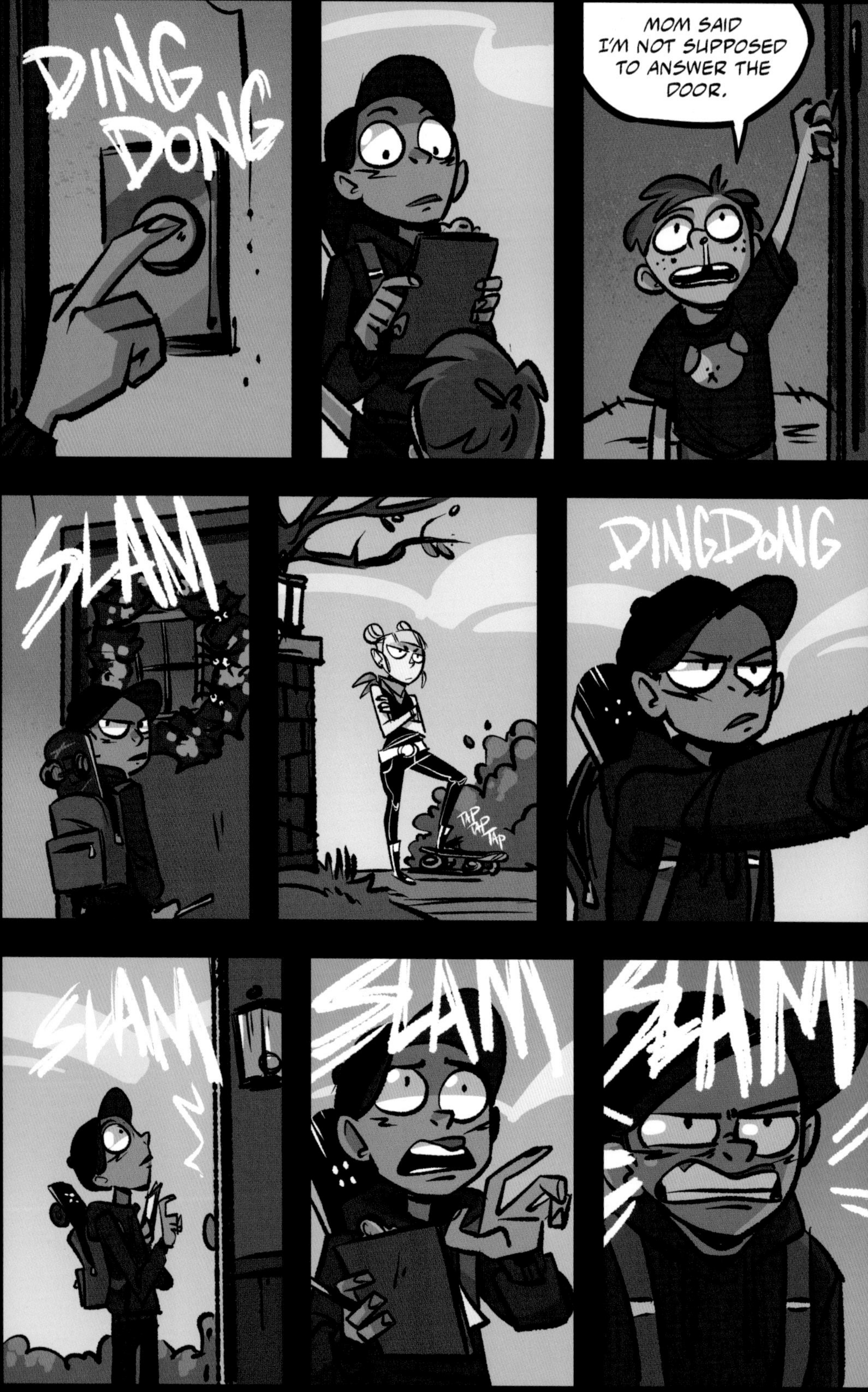
DING DONG
MOM SAID I'M NOT SUPPOSED TO ANSWER THE DOOR.
SLAM
TAP TAP TAP
DINGDONG
SLAM
SLAM
SLAM

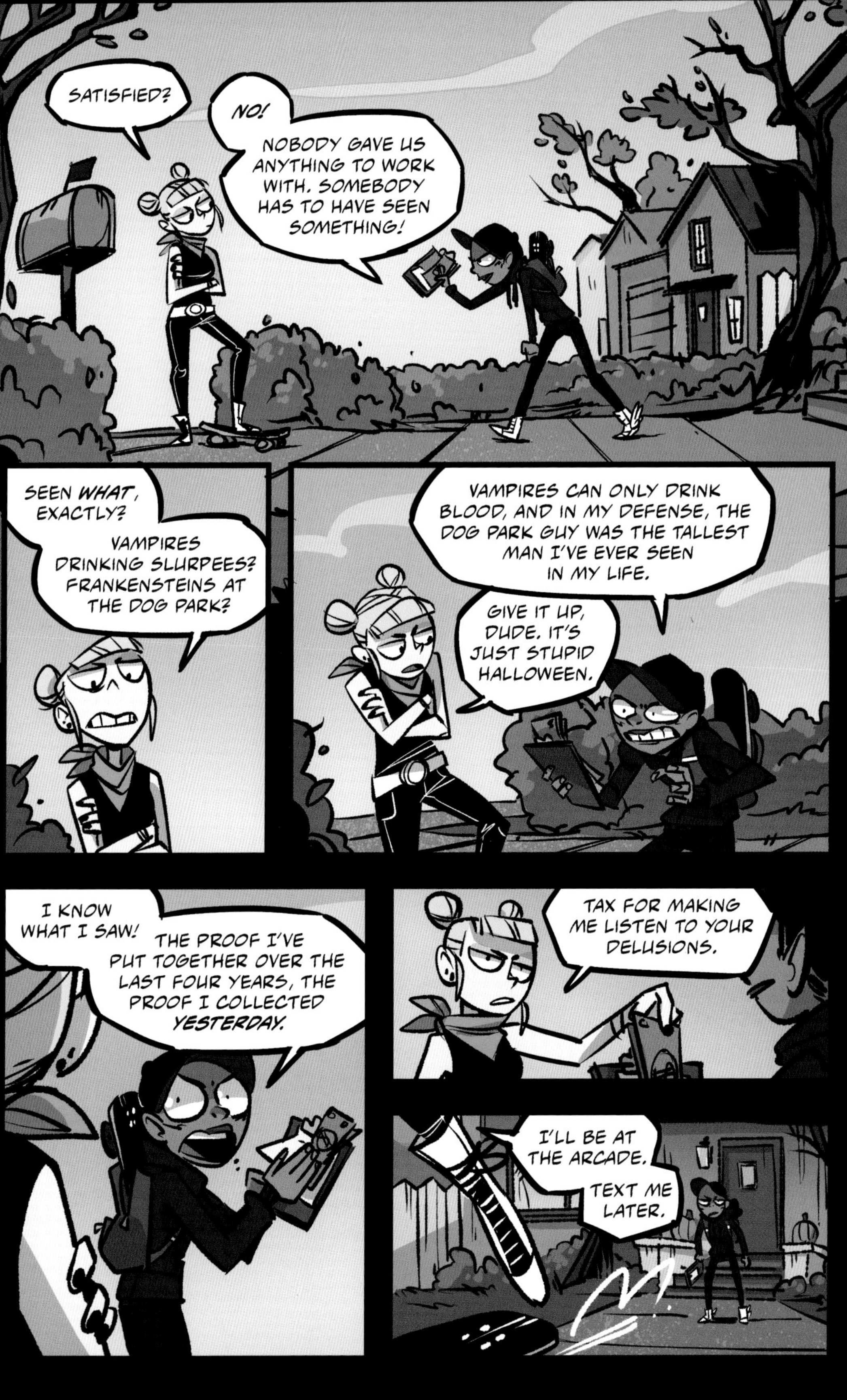
SATISFIED?
NO!
NOBODY GAVE US ANYTHING TO WORK WITH. SOMEBODY HAS TO HAVE SEEN SOMETHING!
SEEN WHAT, EXACTLY?
VAMPIRES DRINKING SLURPEES? FRANKENSTEINS AT THE DOG PARK?
VAMPIRES CAN ONLY DRINK BLOOD, AND IN MY DEFENSE, THE DOG PARK GUY WAS THE TALLEST MAN I'VE EVER SEEN IN MY LIFE.
GIVE IT UP, DUDE. IT'S JUST STUPID HALLOWEEN.
I KNOW WHAT I SAW!
THE PROOF I'VE PUT TOGETHER OVER THE LAST FOUR YEARS, THE PROOF I COLLECTED YESTERDAY.
TAX FOR MAKING ME LISTEN TO YOUR DELUSIONS.
I'LL BE AT THE ARCADE.
TEXT ME LATER.

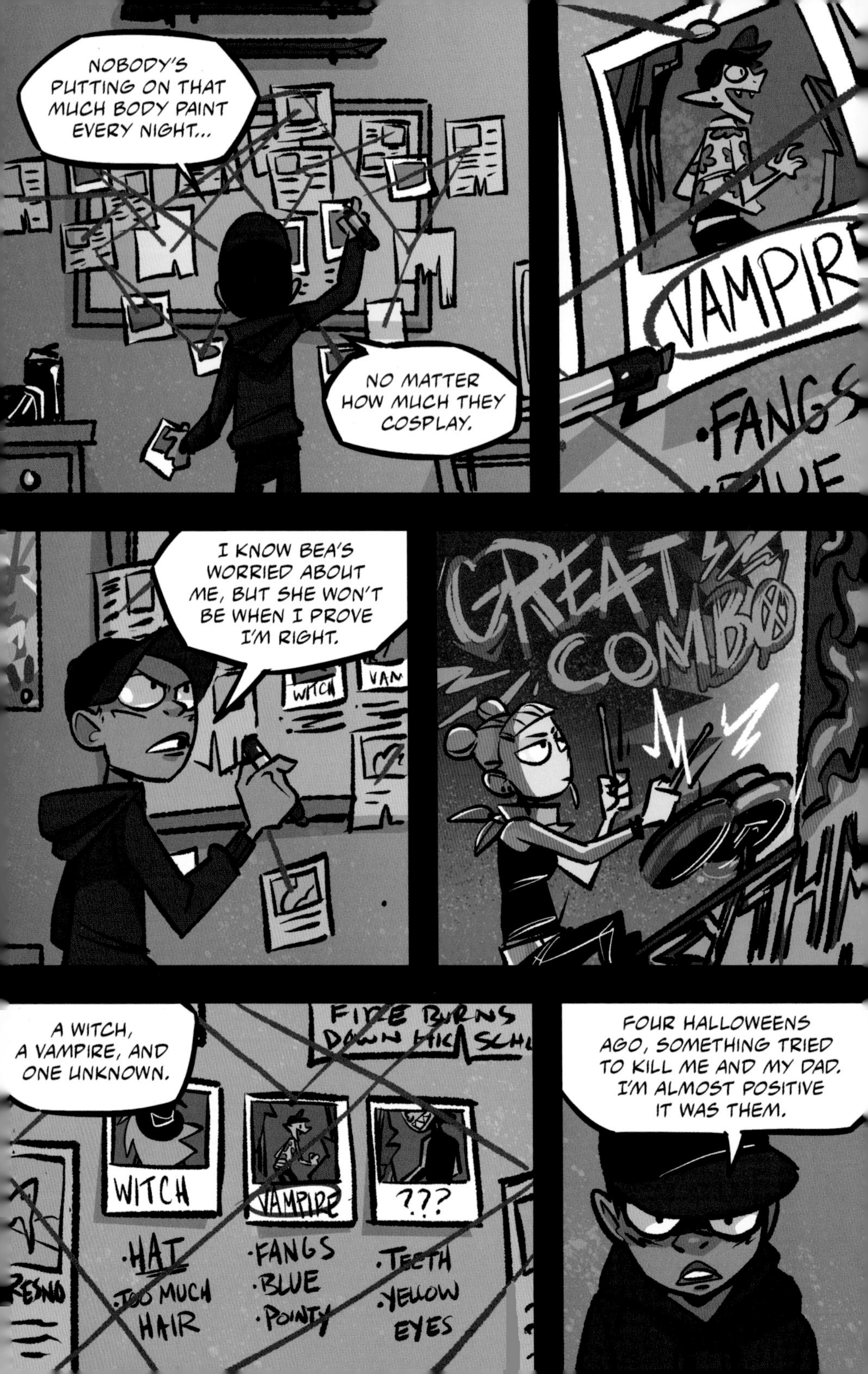
NOBODY'S PUTTING ON THAT MUCH BODY PAINT EVERY NIGHT...
NO MATTER HOW MUCH THEY COSPLAY.
VAMPIRE
•FANGS
I KNOW BEA'S WORRIED ABOUT ME, BUT SHE WON'T BE WHEN I PROVE I'M RIGHT.
WITCH
GREAT COMBO
A WITCH, A VAMPIRE, AND ONE UNKNOWN.
WITCH
VAMPIRE
???
•HAT
•TOO MUCH HAIR
•FANGS
•BLUE
•POINTY
•TEETH
•YELLOW EYES
FOUR HALLOWEENS AGO, SOMETHING TRIED TO KILL ME AND MY DAD. I'M ALMOST POSITIVE IT WAS THEM.

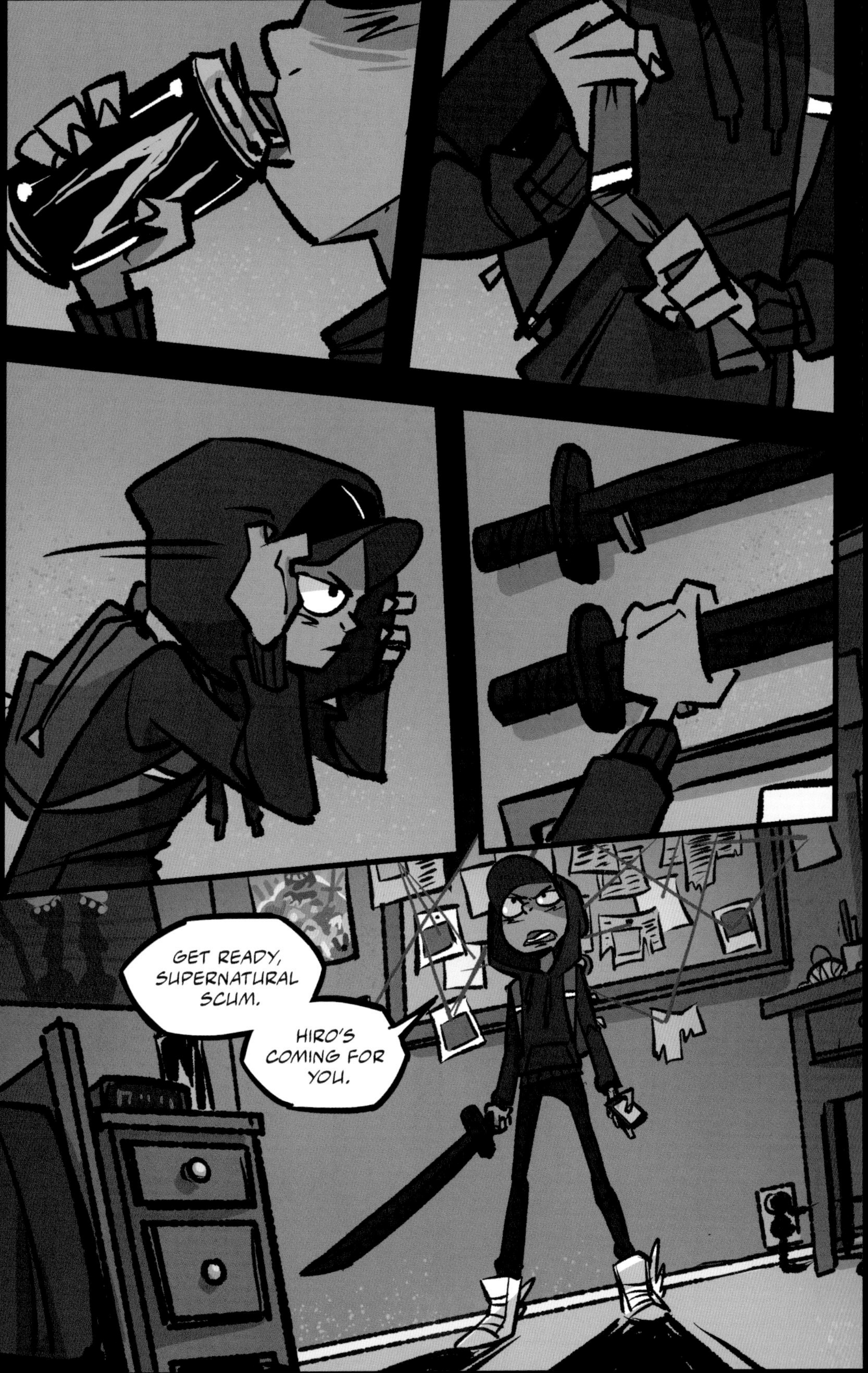
GET READY, SUPERNATURAL SCUM.
HIRO'S COMING FOR YOU.

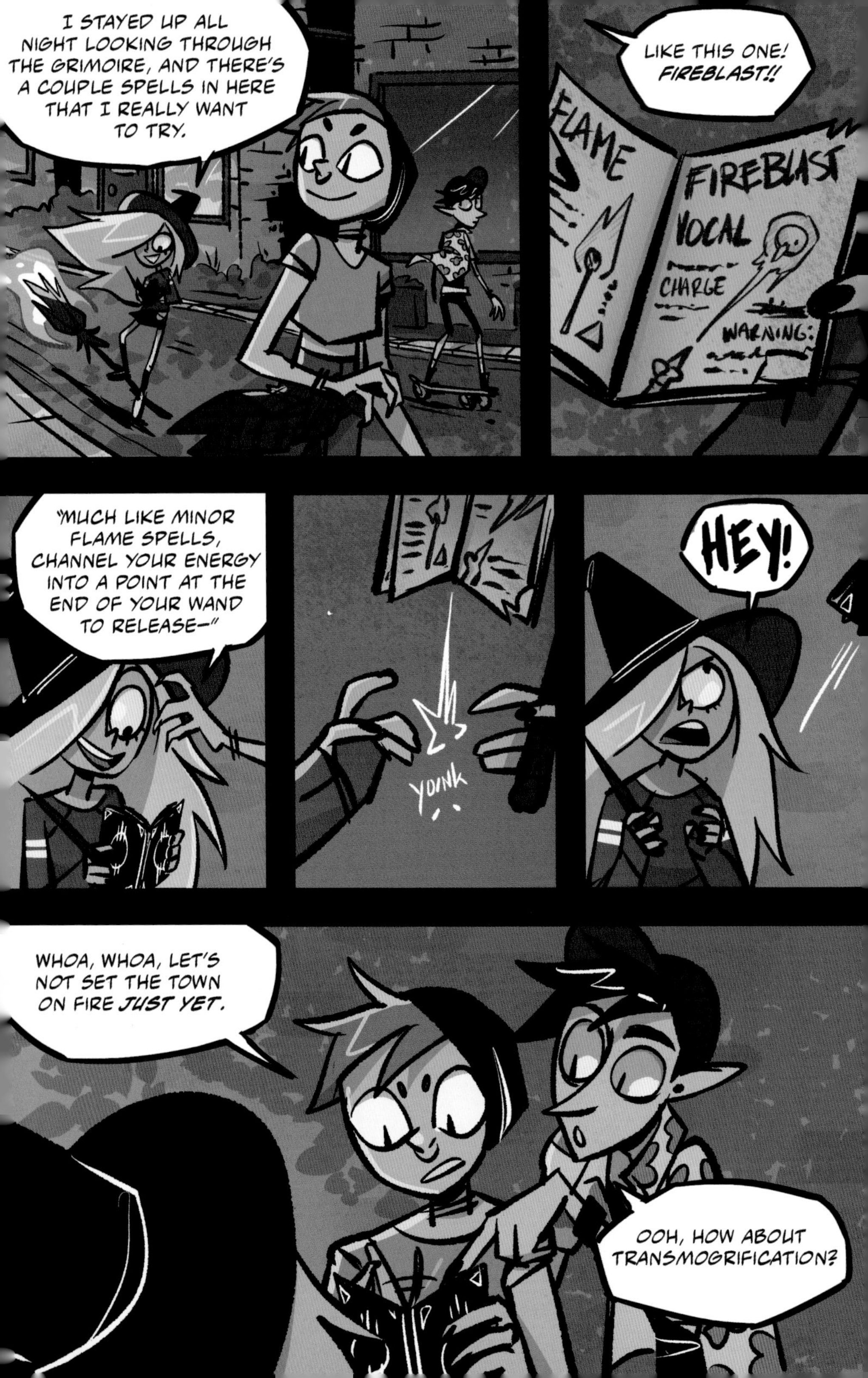
I STAYED UP ALL NIGHT LOOKING THROUGH THE GRIMOIRE, AND THERE'S A COUPLE SPELLS IN HERE THAT I REALLY WANT TO TRY.
LIKE THIS ONE! FIREBLAST!!
FLAME
FIREBLAST
VOCAL
CHARGE
WARNING:
"MUCH LIKE MINOR FLAME SPELLS, CHANNEL YOUR ENERGY INTO A POINT AT THE END OF YOUR WAND TO RELEASE—"
YOINK
HEY!
WHOA, WHOA, LET'S NOT SET THE TOWN ON FIRE JUST YET.
OOH, HOW ABOUT TRANSMOGRIFICATION?

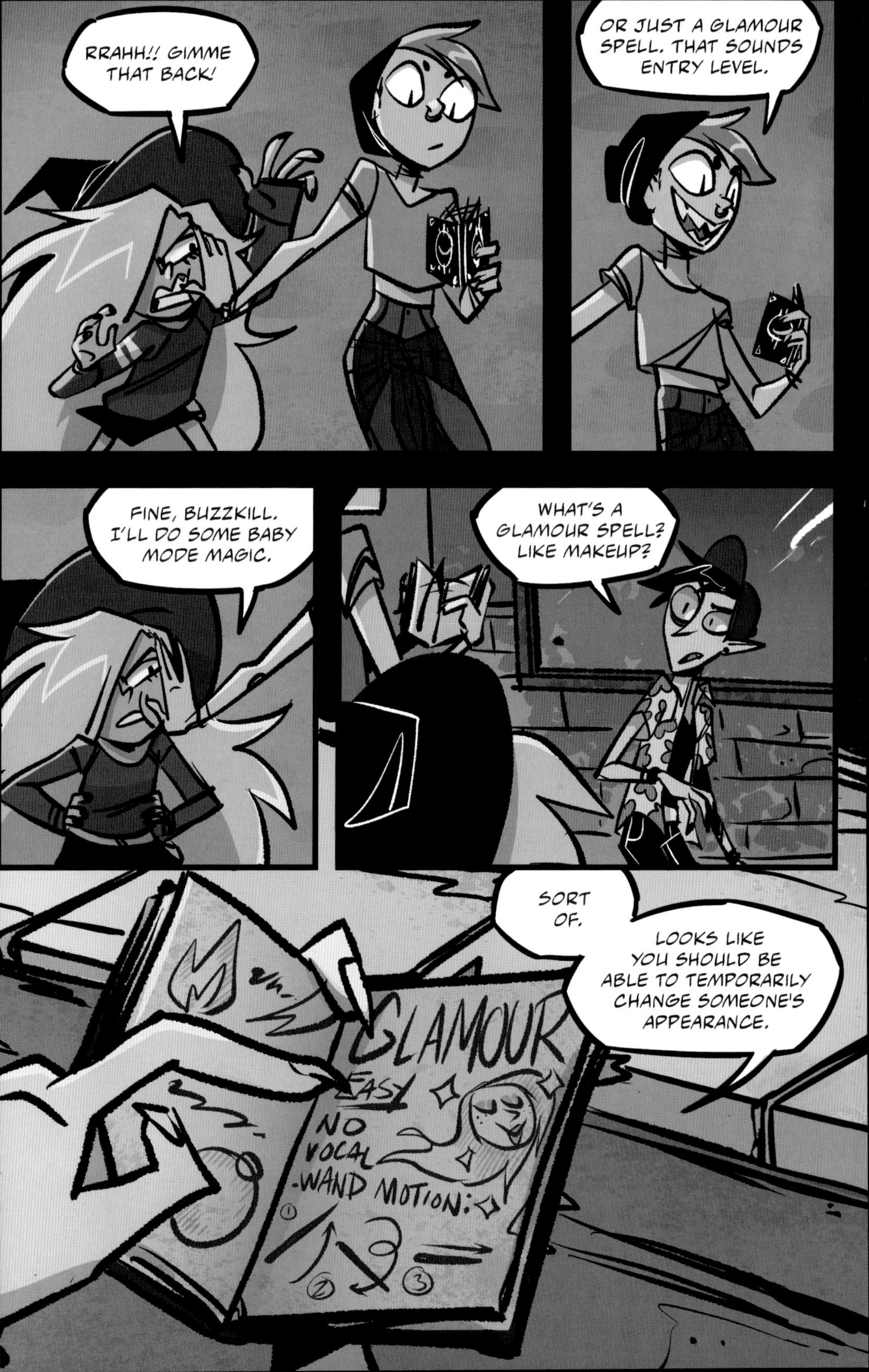
RRAHH!! GIMME THAT BACK!
OR JUST A GLAMOUR SPELL. THAT SOUNDS ENTRY LEVEL.
FINE, BUZZKILL. I'LL DO SOME BABY MODE MAGIC.
WHAT'S A GLAMOUR SPELL? LIKE MAKEUP?
SORT OF.
LOOKS LIKE YOU SHOULD BE ABLE TO TEMPORARILY CHANGE SOMEONE'S APPEARANCE.
GLAMOUR
EASY
NO VOCAL
-WAND MOTION:
1
2
3

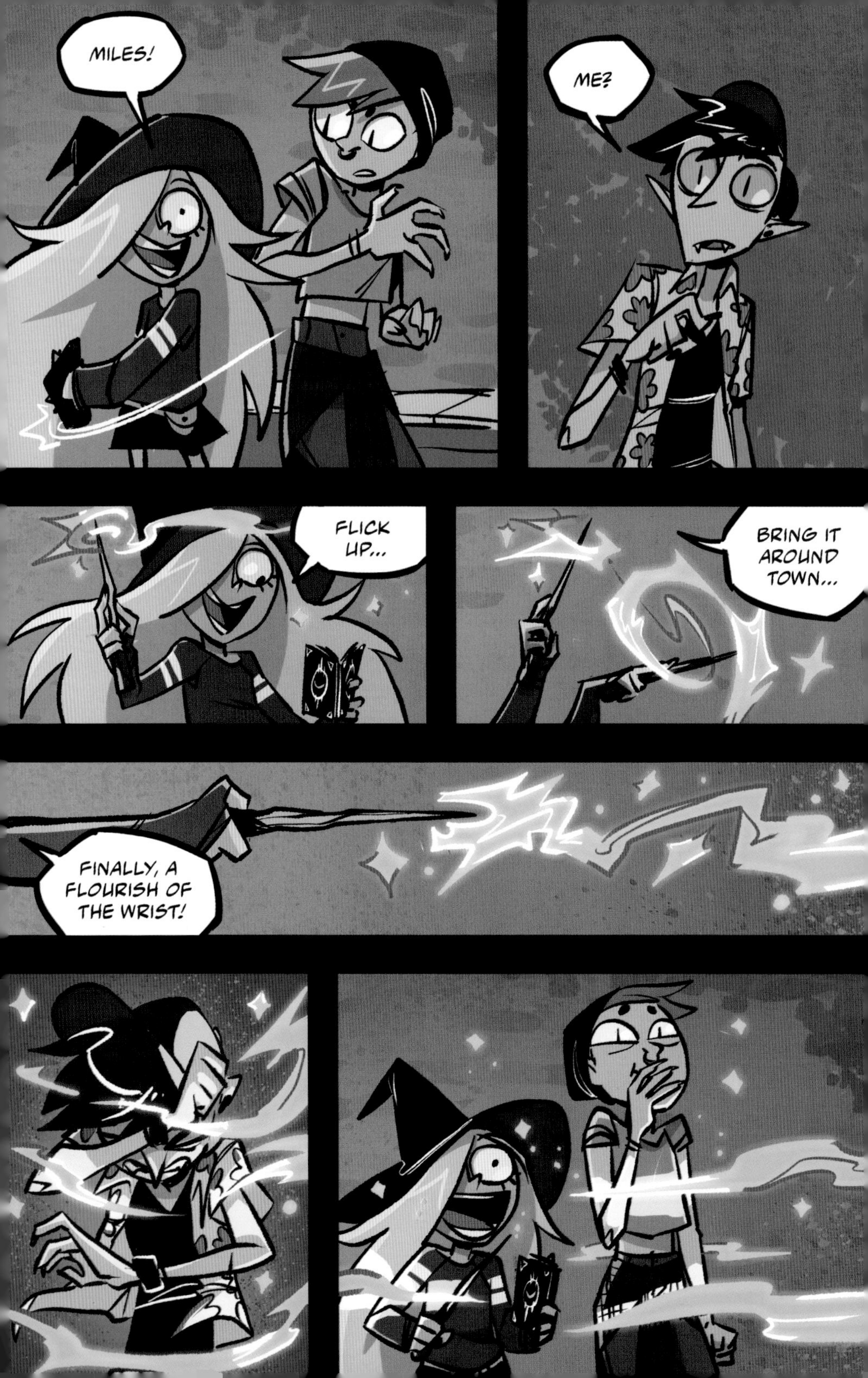
MILES!
ME?
FLICK UP...
BRING IT AROUND TOWN...
FINALLY, A FLOURISH OF THE WRIST!

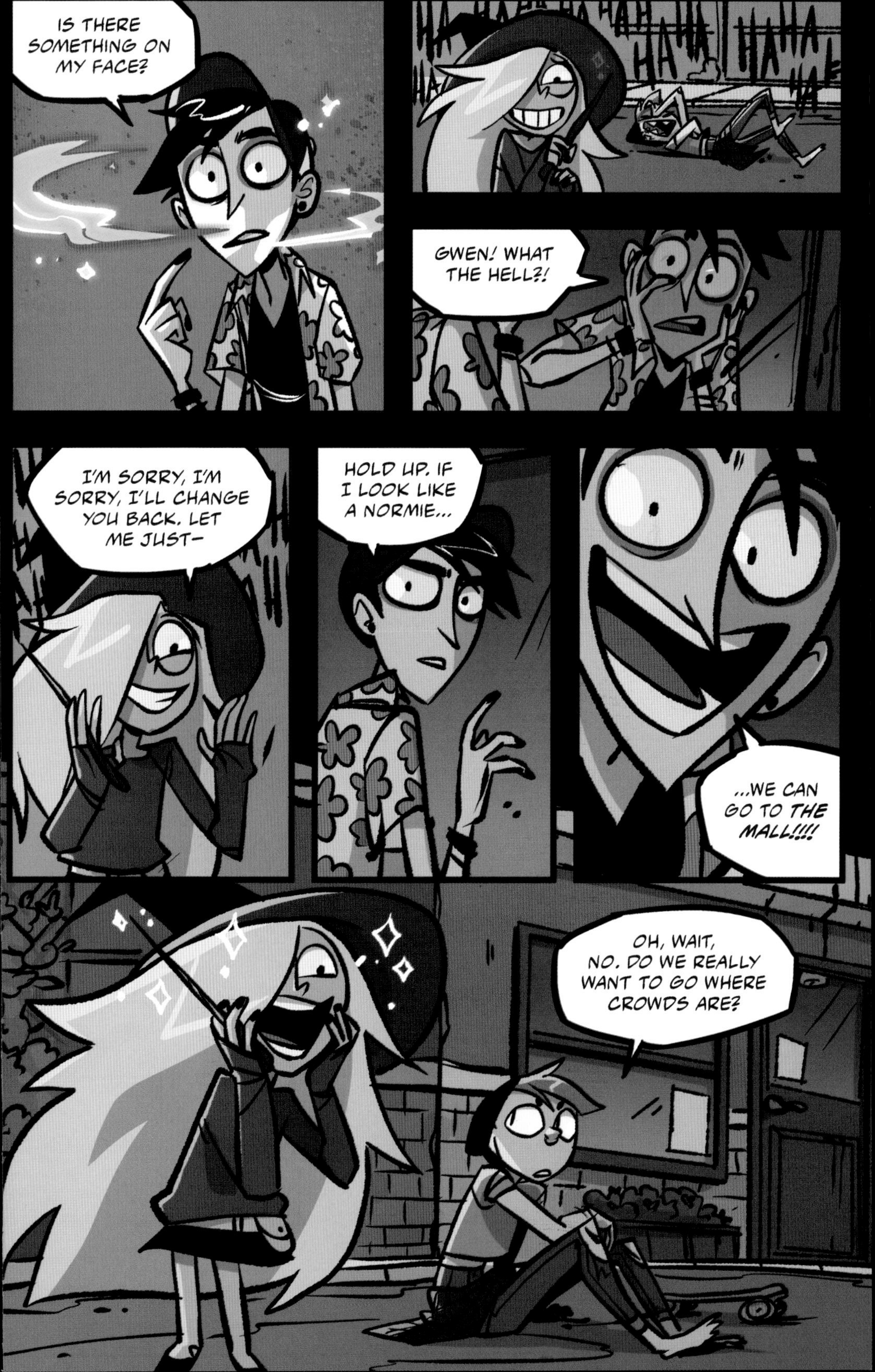
IS THERE SOMETHING ON MY FACE?
HA HA HA HA HA HA HA HA HA HA HA HA HA
GWEN! WHAT THE HELL?!
I'M SORRY, I'M SORRY, I'LL CHANGE YOU BACK. LET ME JUST–
HOLD UP. IF I LOOK LIKE A NORMIE...
...WE CAN GO TO THE MALL!!!!
OH, WAIT, NO. DO WE REALLY WANT TO GO WHERE CROWDS ARE?

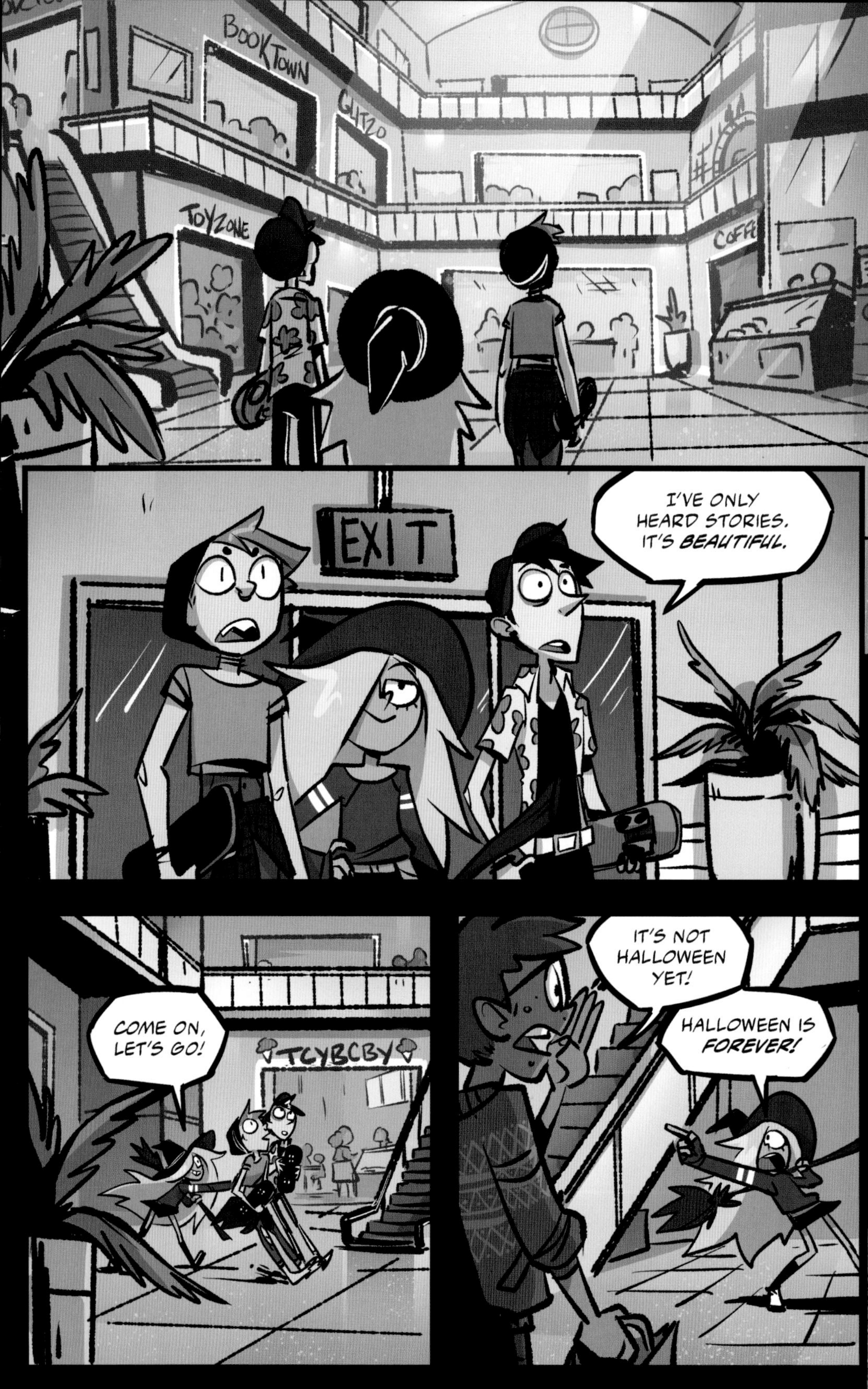
BOOKTOWN
TOYZONE
EXIT
I'VE ONLY HEARD STORIES. IT'S *BEAUTIFUL.*
COME ON, LET'S GO!
TCYBCBY
IT'S NOT HALLOWEEN YET!
HALLOWEEN IS *FOREVER!*

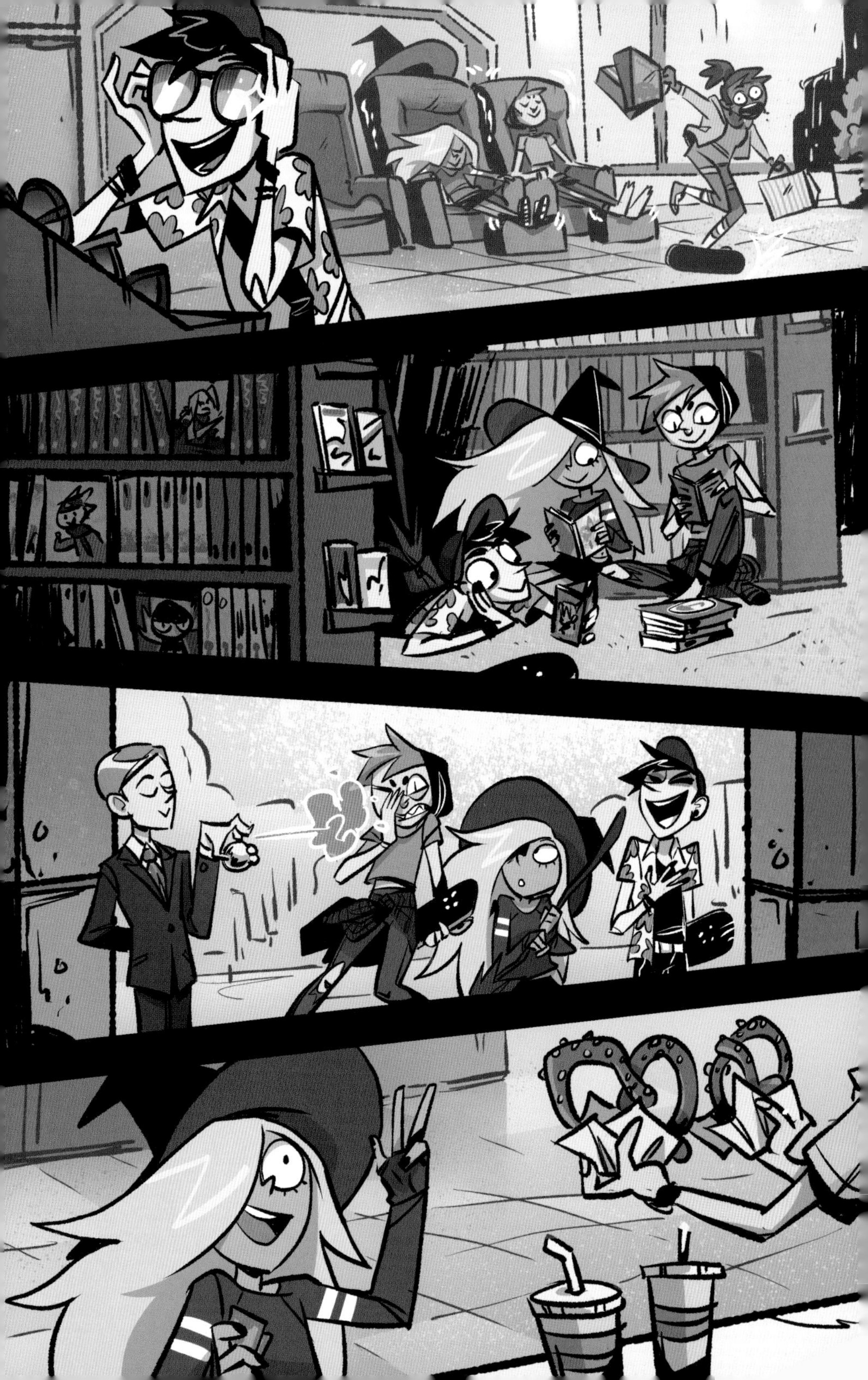

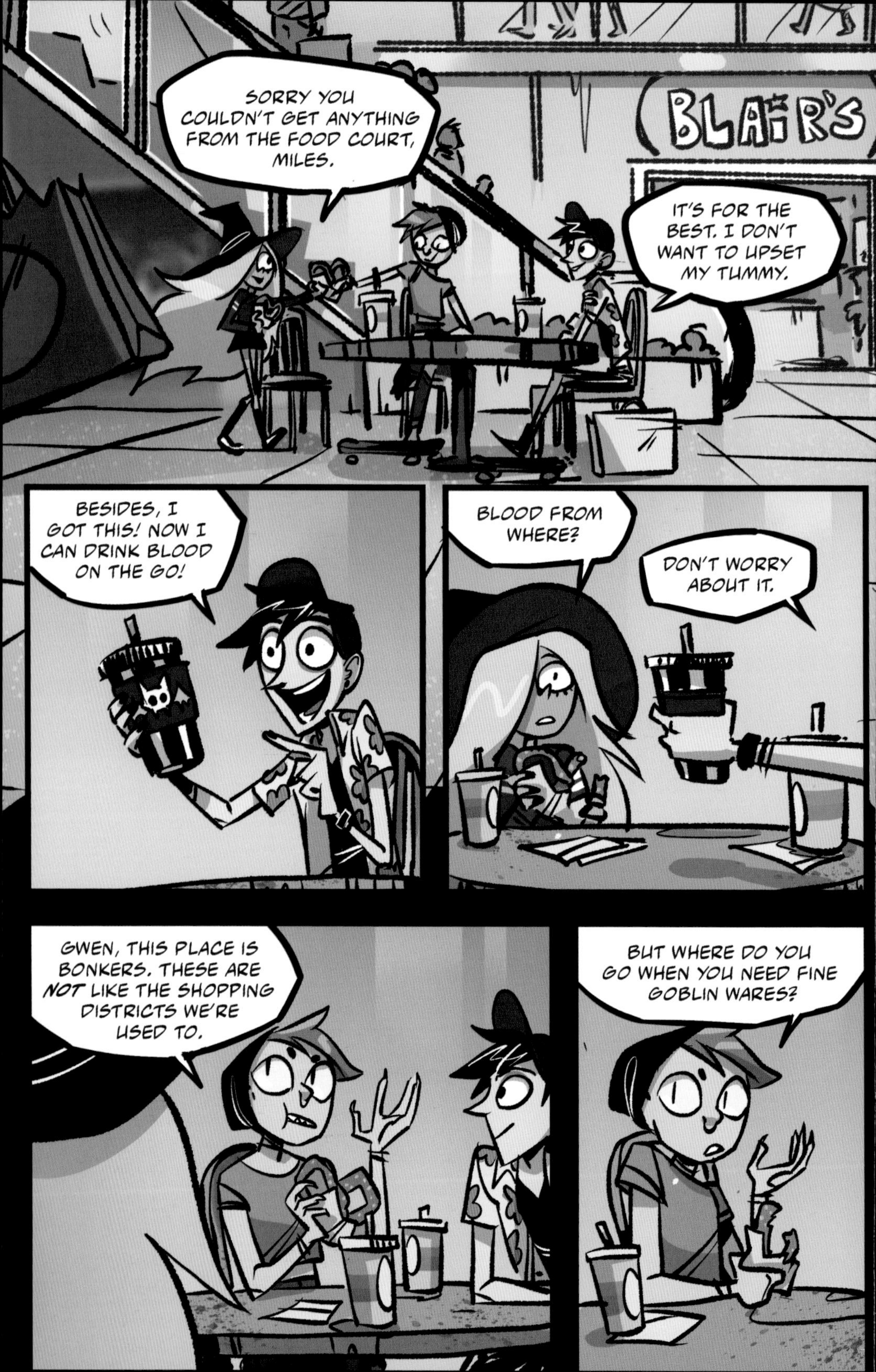
SORRY YOU COULDN'T GET ANYTHING FROM THE FOOD COURT, MILES.
BLAIR'S
IT'S FOR THE BEST. I DON'T WANT TO UPSET MY TUMMY.
BESIDES, I GOT THIS! NOW I CAN DRINK BLOOD ON THE GO!
BLOOD FROM WHERE?
DON'T WORRY ABOUT IT.
GWEN, THIS PLACE IS BONKERS. THESE ARE *NOT* LIKE THE SHOPPING DISTRICTS WE'RE USED TO.
BUT WHERE DO YOU GO WHEN YOU NEED FINE GOBLIN WARES?

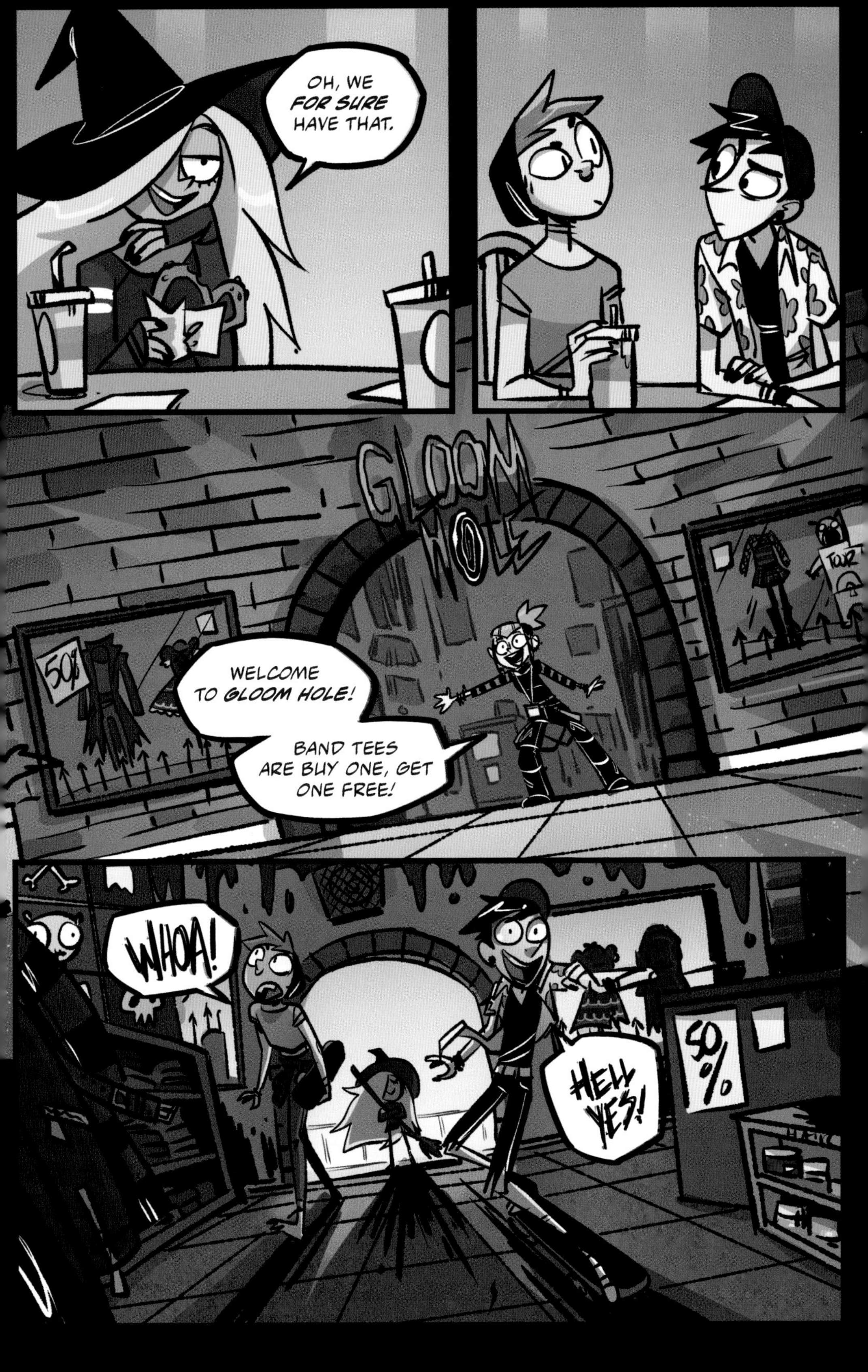
OH, WE *FOR SURE* HAVE THAT.
GLOOM HOLE
50%
TOUR
WELCOME TO *GLOOM HOLE!*
BAND TEES ARE BUY ONE, GET ONE FREE!
WHOA!
HELL YES!
50%

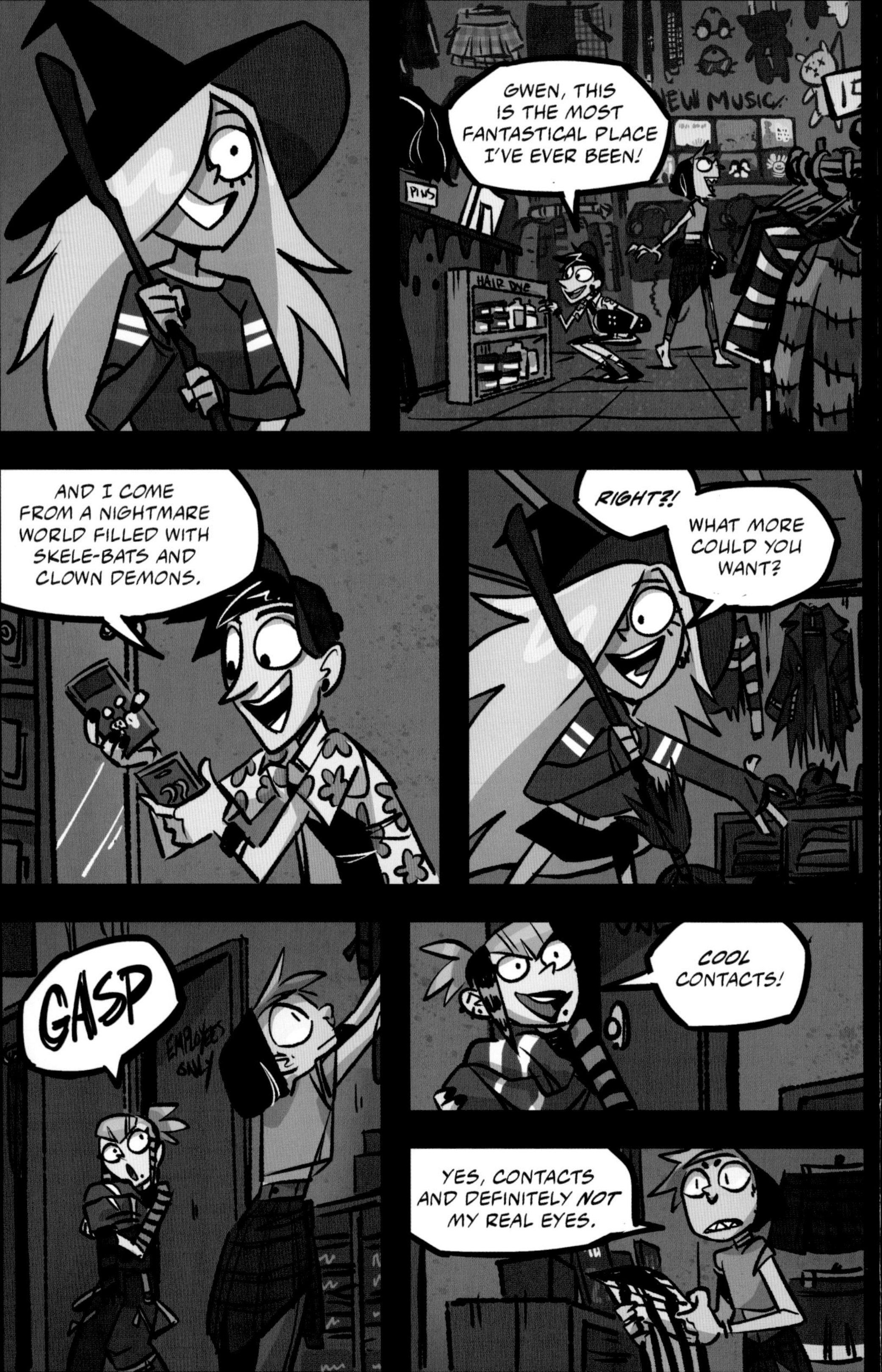
GWEN, THIS IS THE MOST FANTASTICAL PLACE I'VE EVER BEEN!
NEW MUSIC
PINS
HAIR DYE
AND I COME FROM A NIGHTMARE WORLD FILLED WITH SKELE-BATS AND CLOWN DEMONS.
RIGHT?!
WHAT MORE COULD YOU WANT?
GASP
EMPLOYEES ONLY
COOL CONTACTS!
YES, CONTACTS AND DEFINITELY *NOT* MY REAL EYES.

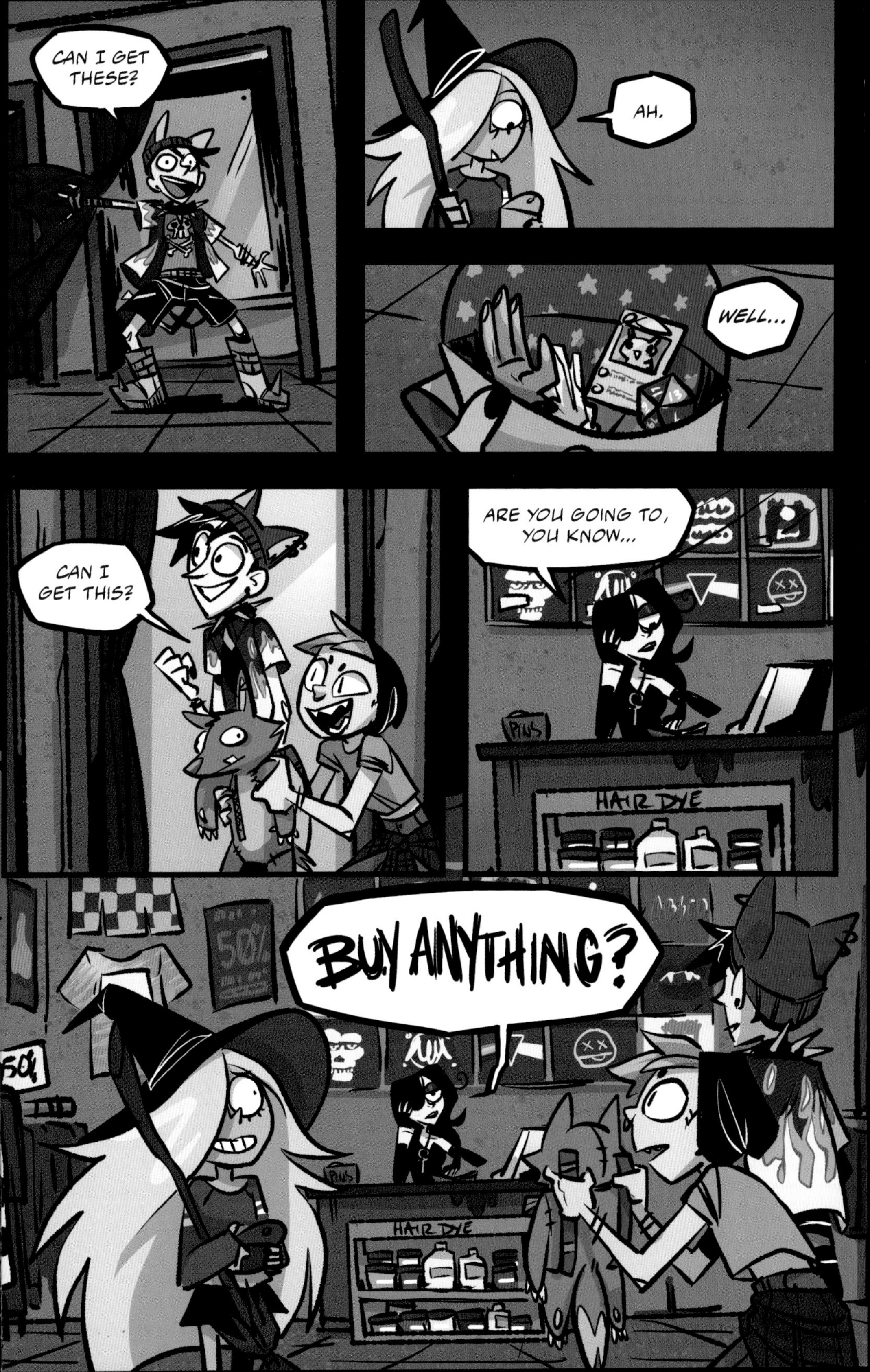
CAN I GET THESE?
AH.
WELL...
CAN I GET THIS?
ARE YOU GOING TO, YOU KNOW...
PINS
HAIR DYE
50%
BUY ANYTHING?
50%
PINS
HAIR DYE

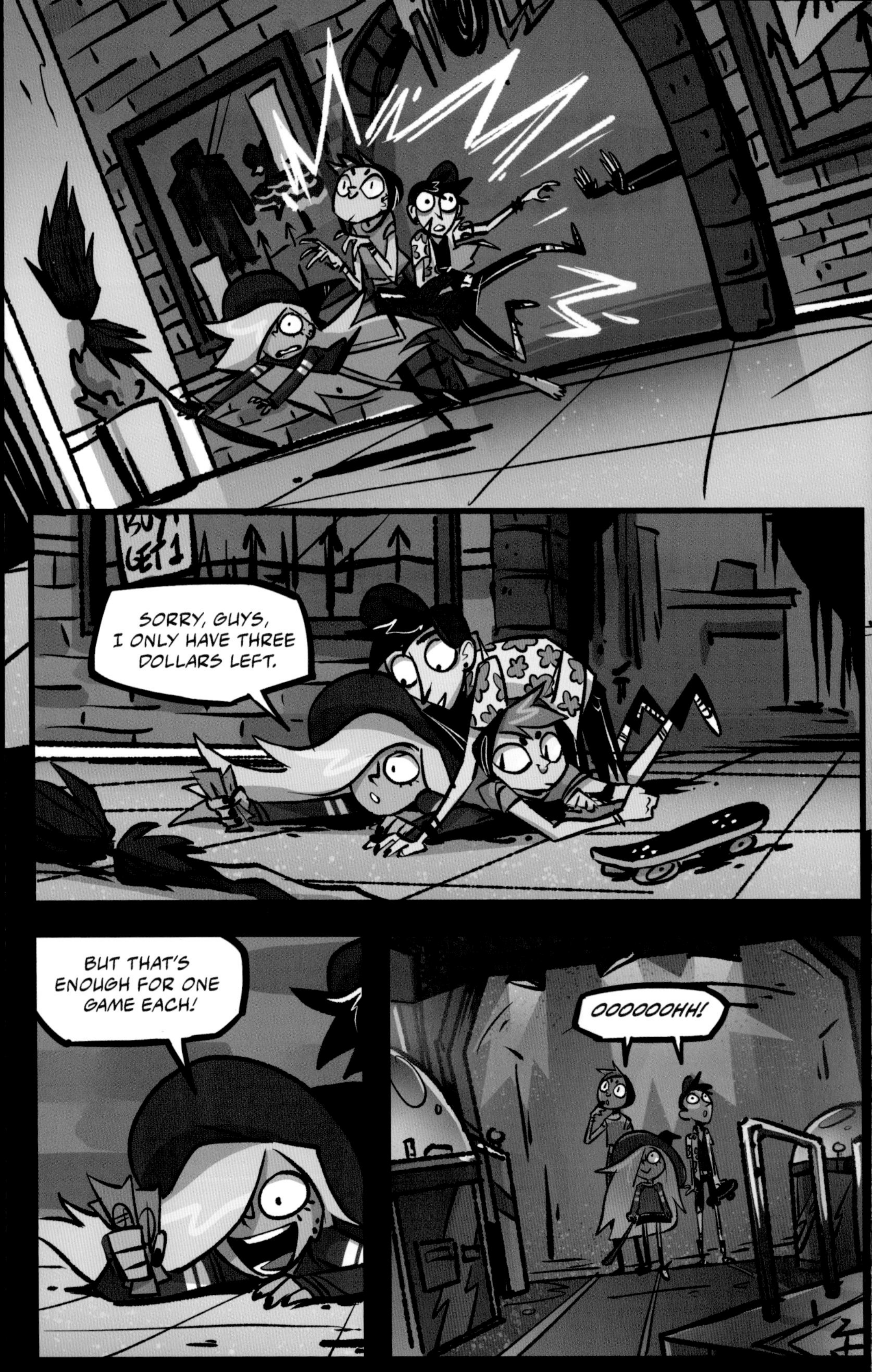
BUY GET 1
SORRY, GUYS, I ONLY HAVE THREE DOLLARS LEFT.
BUT THAT'S ENOUGH FOR ONE GAME EACH!
OOOOOOHH!

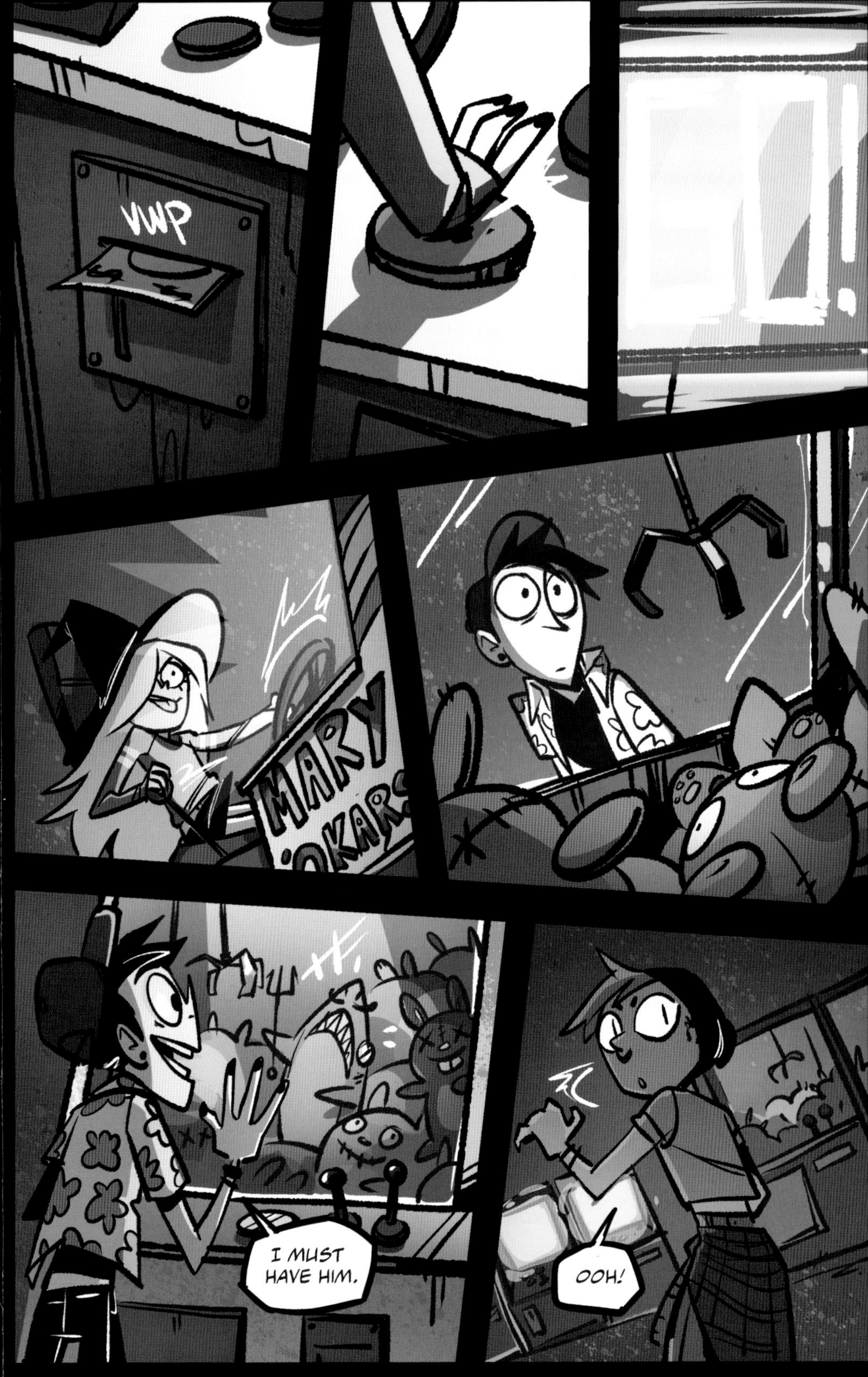
VWP
MARY
OKAR
I MUST HAVE HIM.
OOH!

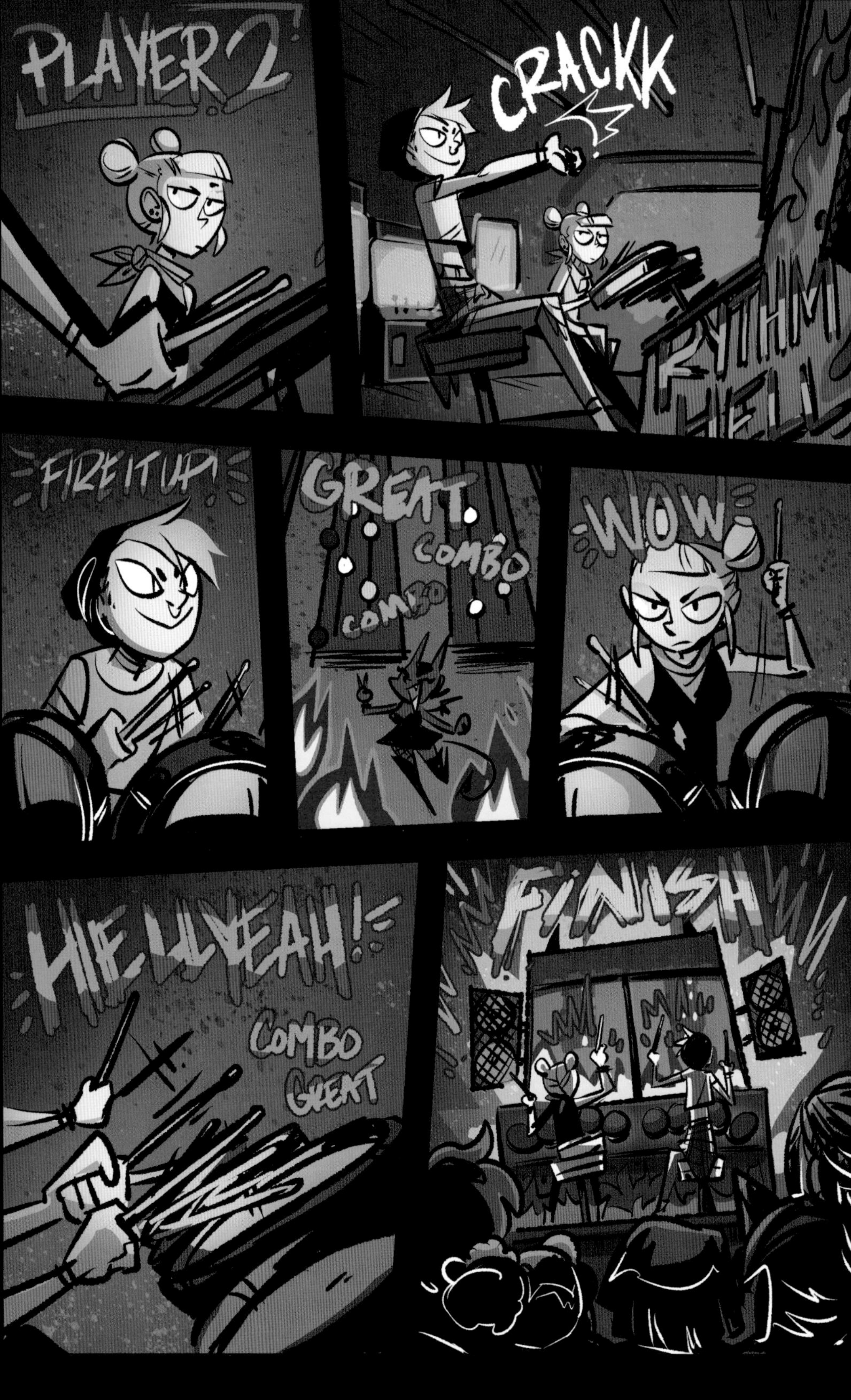
PLAYER 2
CRACKK
RYTHM
FIRE IT UP!
GREAT
COMBO
WOW
HELLYEAH!
COMBO
GREAT
FINISH

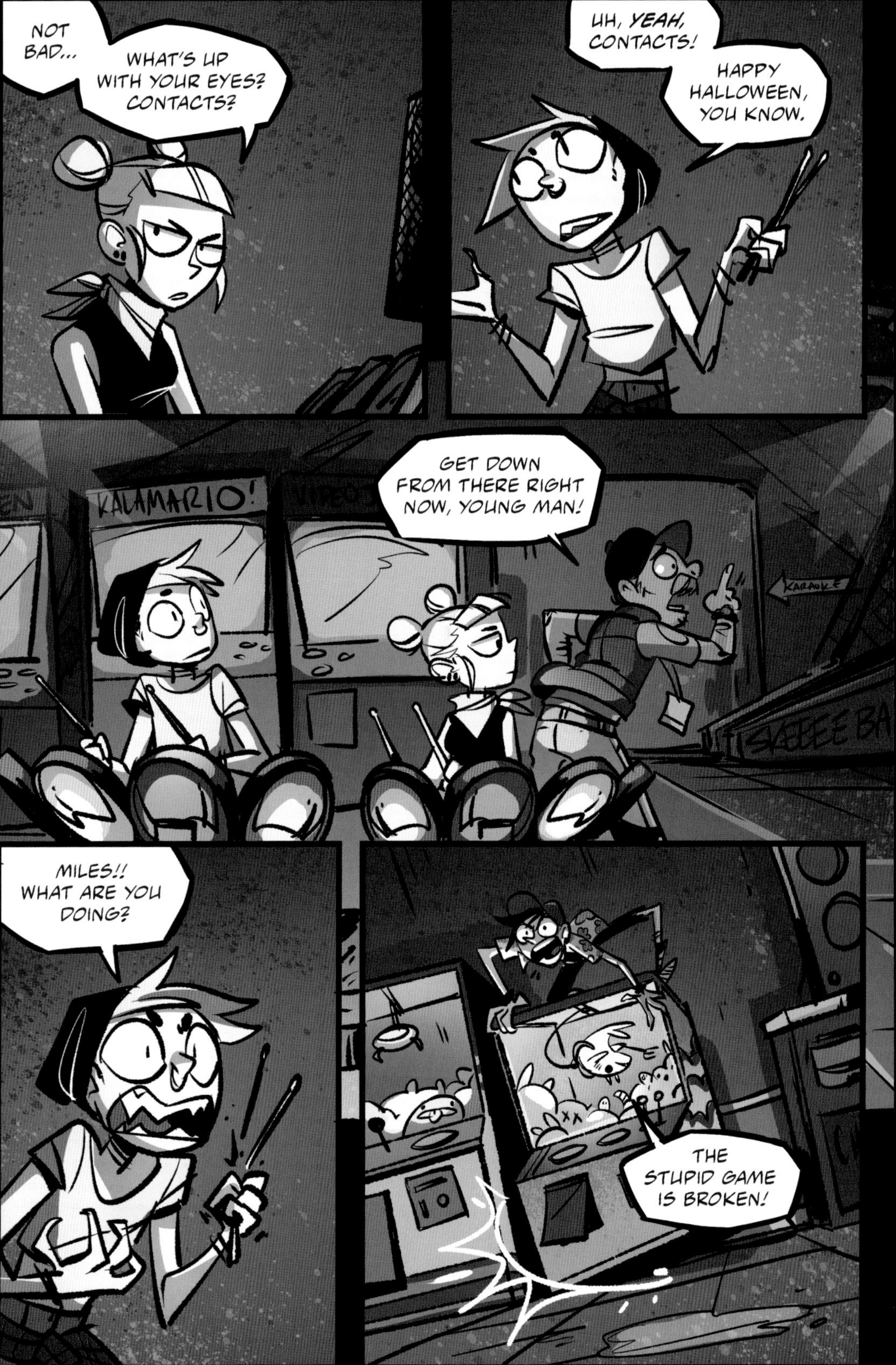
NOT BAD...
WHAT'S UP WITH YOUR EYES? CONTACTS?
UH, YEAH, CONTACTS!
HAPPY HALLOWEEN, YOU KNOW.
KALAMARIO!
GET DOWN FROM THERE RIGHT NOW, YOUNG MAN!
MILES!! WHAT ARE YOU DOING?
THE STUPID GAME IS BROKEN!

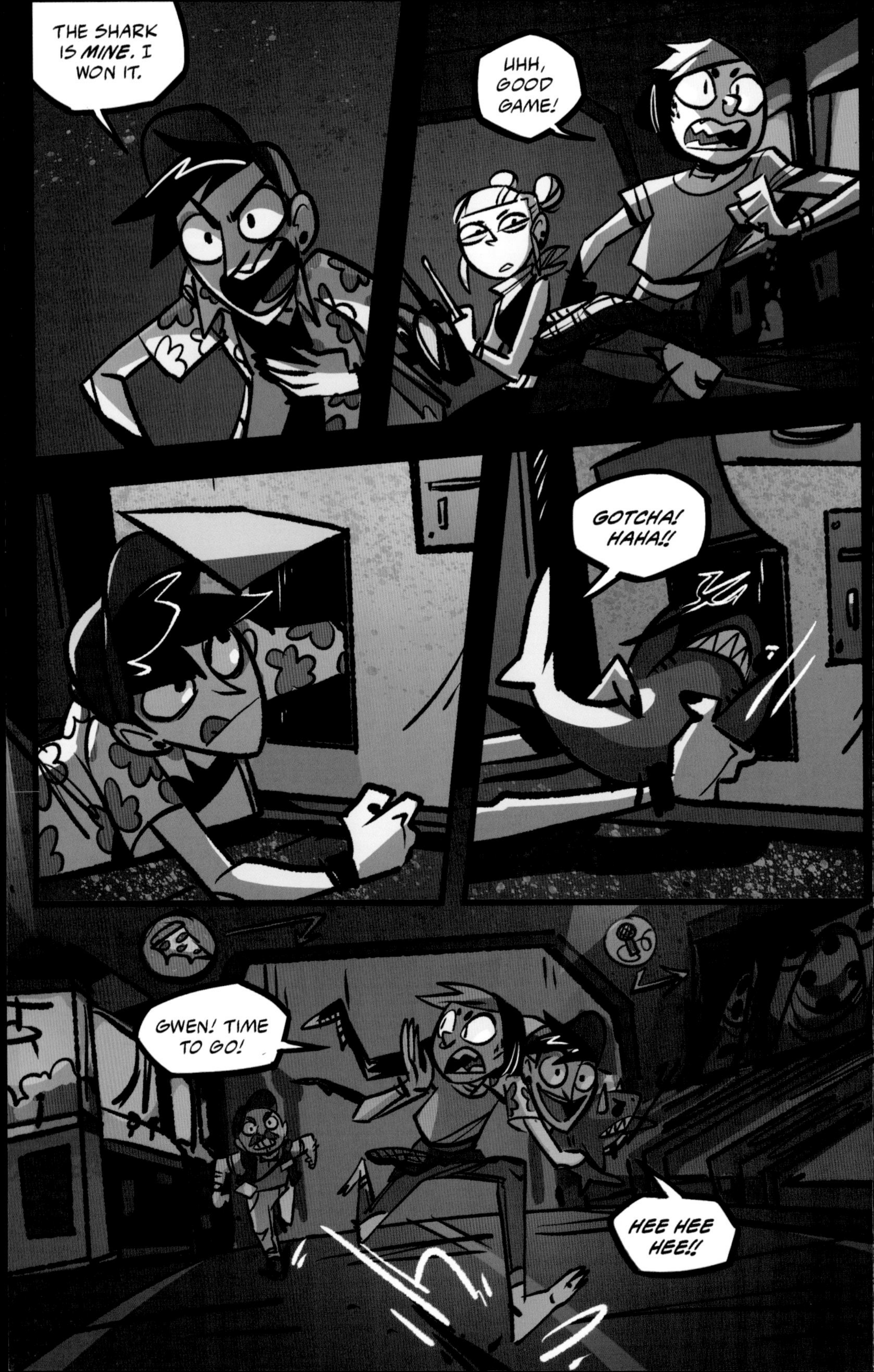
THE SHARK IS *MINE*. I WON IT.
UHH, GOOD GAME!
GOTCHA! HAHA!!
GWEN! TIME TO GO!
HEE HEE HEE!!

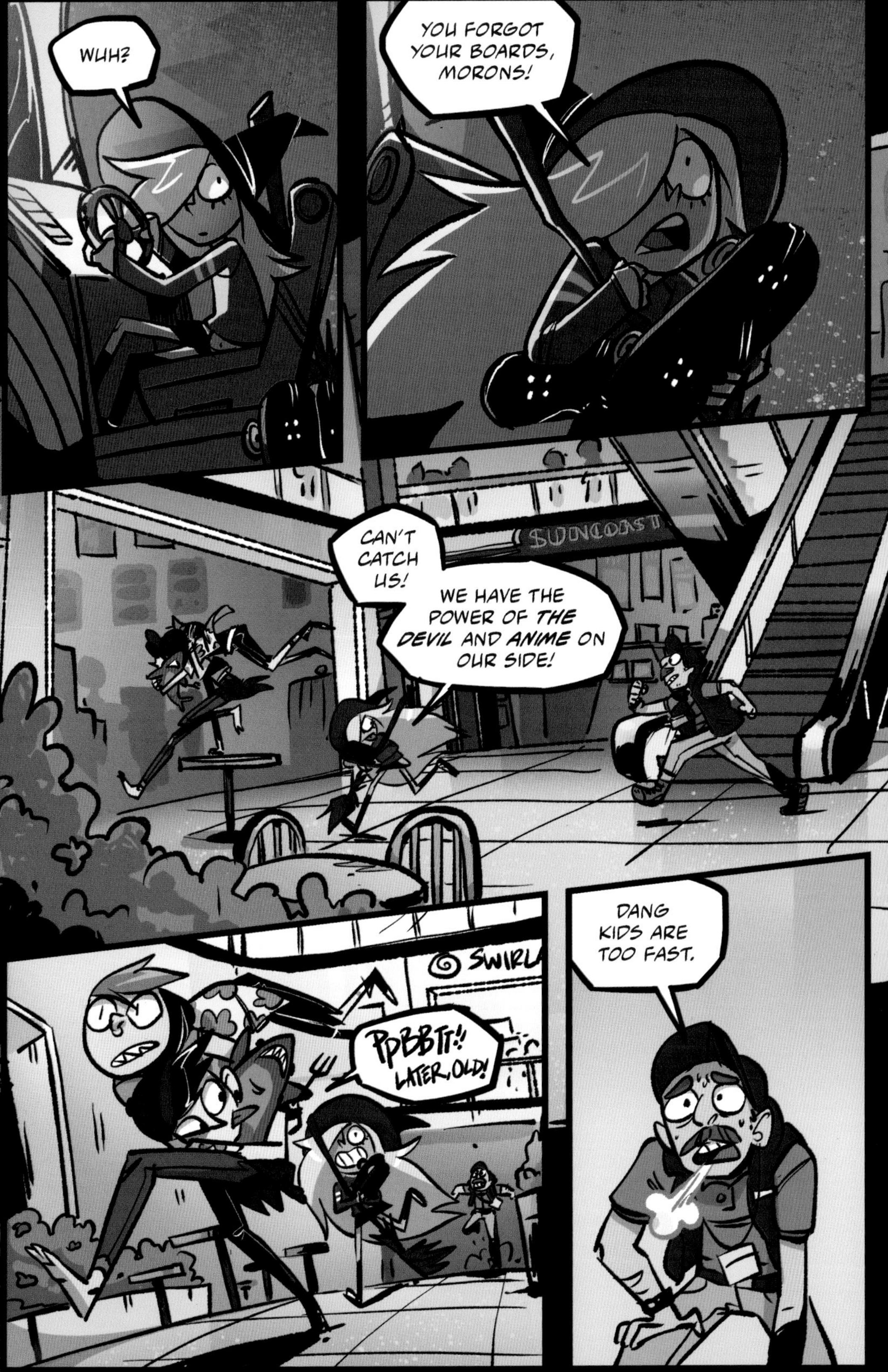
WUH?
YOU FORGOT YOUR BOARDS, MORONS!
SUNCOAST
CAN'T CATCH US!
WE HAVE THE POWER OF *THE DEVIL* AND *ANIME* ON OUR SIDE!
SWIRL
PPBBTT!! LATER, OLD!
DANG KIDS ARE TOO FAST.

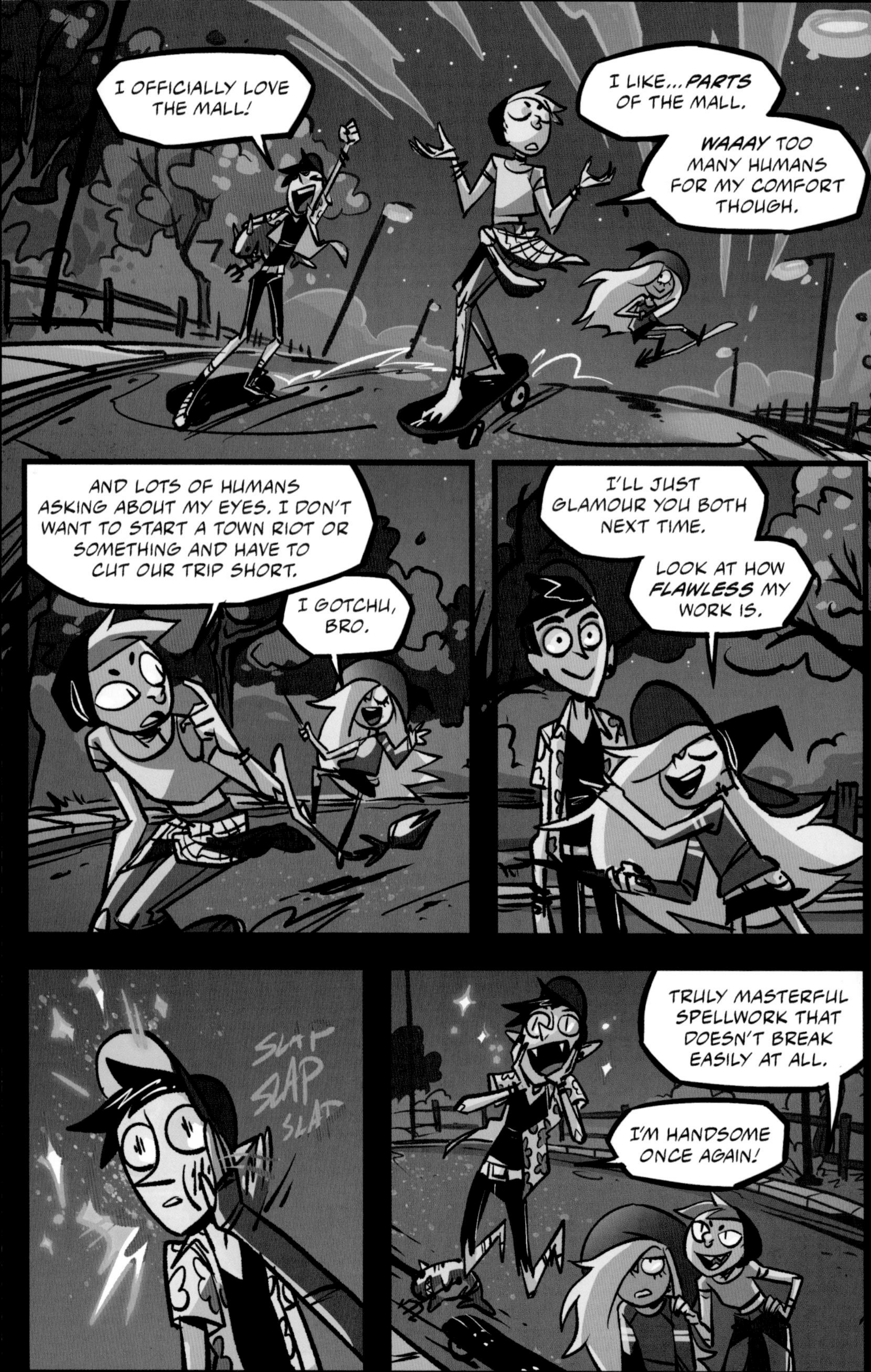
I OFFICIALLY LOVE THE MALL!
I LIKE... PARTS OF THE MALL.
WAAAY TOO MANY HUMANS FOR MY COMFORT THOUGH.
AND LOTS OF HUMANS ASKING ABOUT MY EYES. I DON'T WANT TO START A TOWN RIOT OR SOMETHING AND HAVE TO CUT OUR TRIP SHORT.
I GOTCHU, BRO.
I'LL JUST GLAMOUR YOU BOTH NEXT TIME.
LOOK AT HOW FLAWLESS MY WORK IS.
SLAP
SLAP
SLAP
TRULY MASTERFUL SPELLWORK THAT DOESN'T BREAK EASILY AT ALL.
I'M HANDSOME ONCE AGAIN!

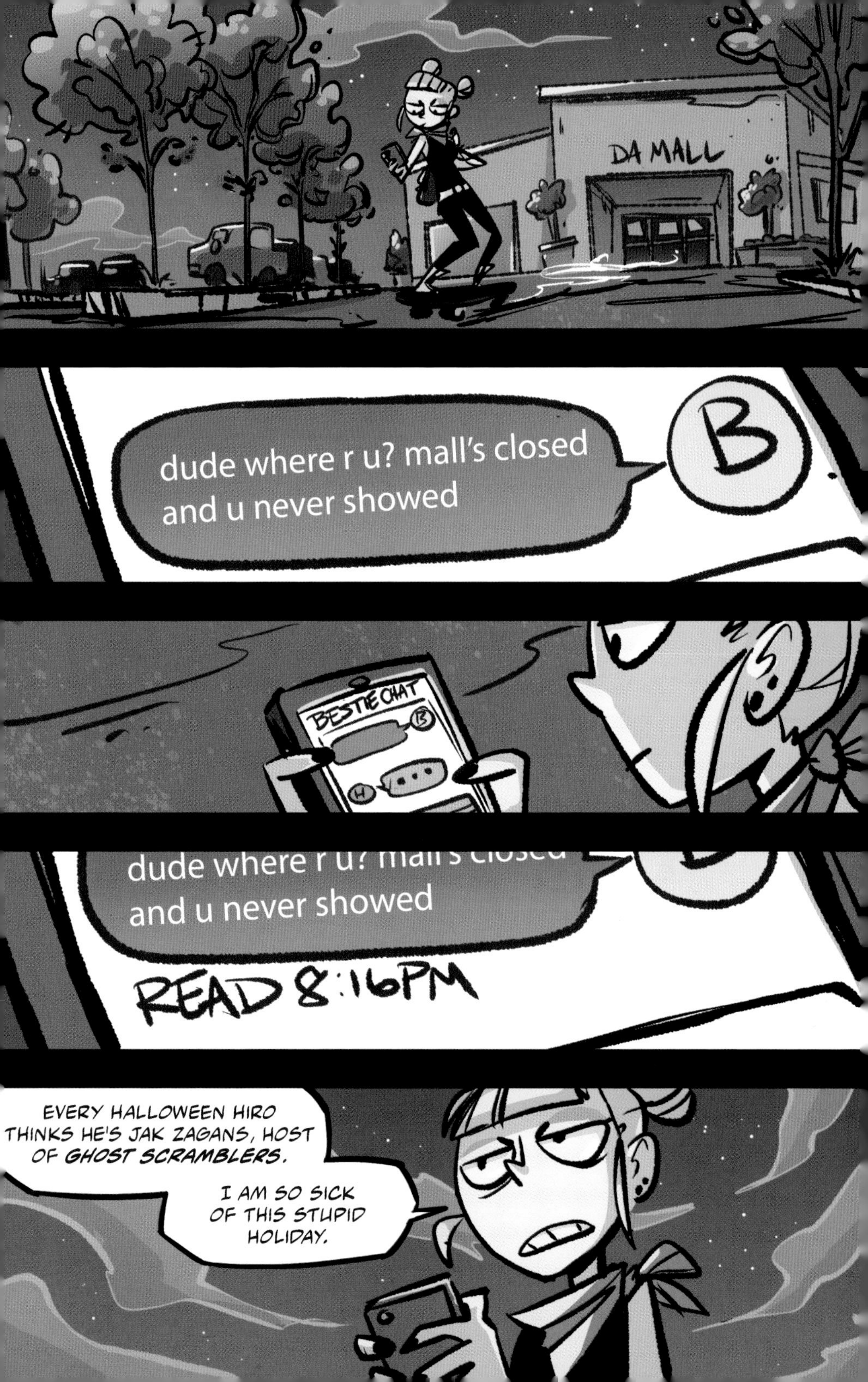
DA MALL
dude where r u? mall's closed and u never showed
B
BESTIE CHAT
B
H
dude where r u? mall's closed and u never showed
READ 8:16PM
EVERY HALLOWEEN HIRO THINKS HE'S JAK ZAGANS, HOST OF *GHOST SCRAMBLERS*.
I AM SO SICK OF THIS STUPID HOLIDAY.

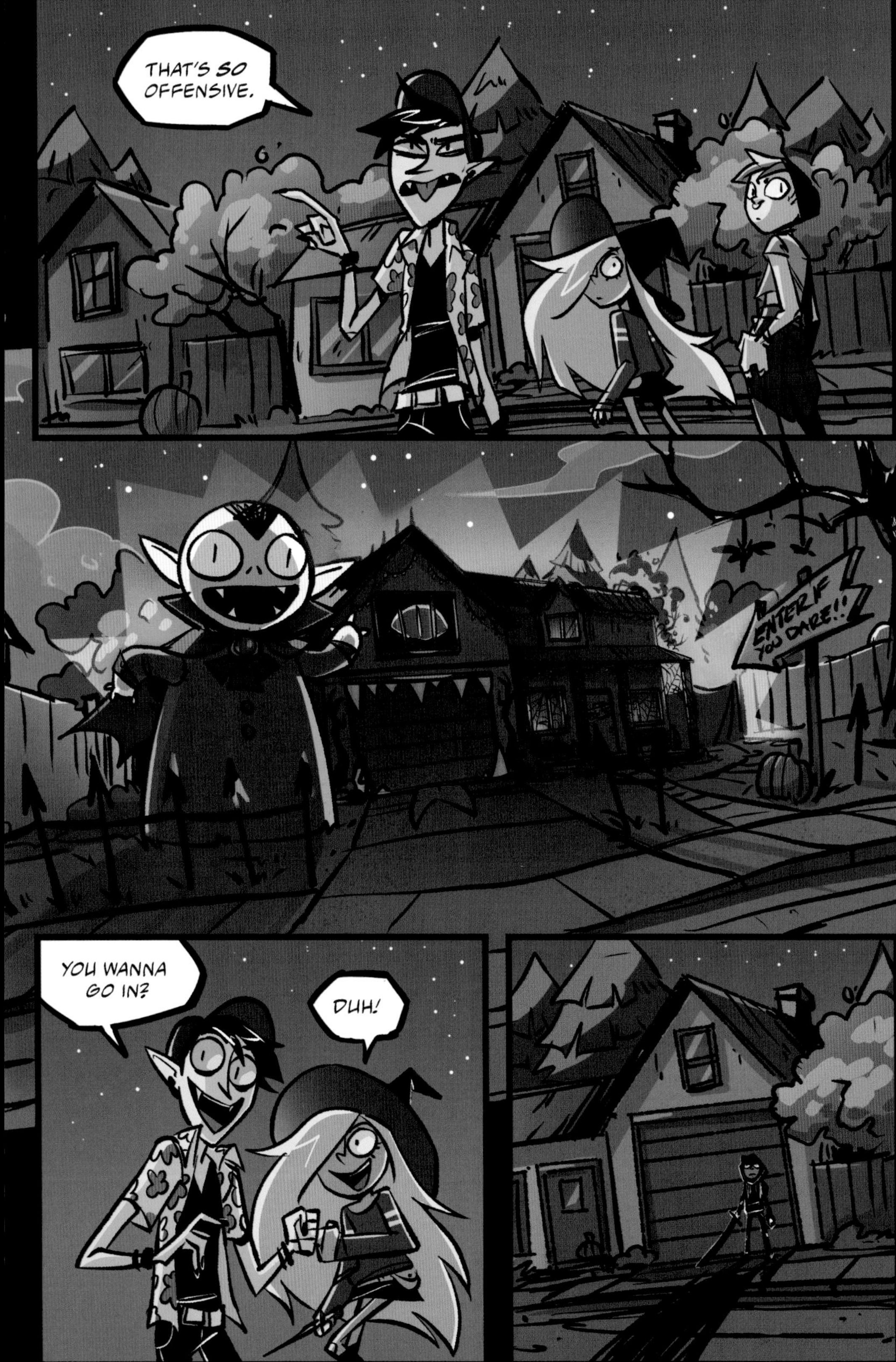
THAT'S SO OFFENSIVE.
ENTER IF YOU DARE!!
YOU WANNA GO IN?
DUH!

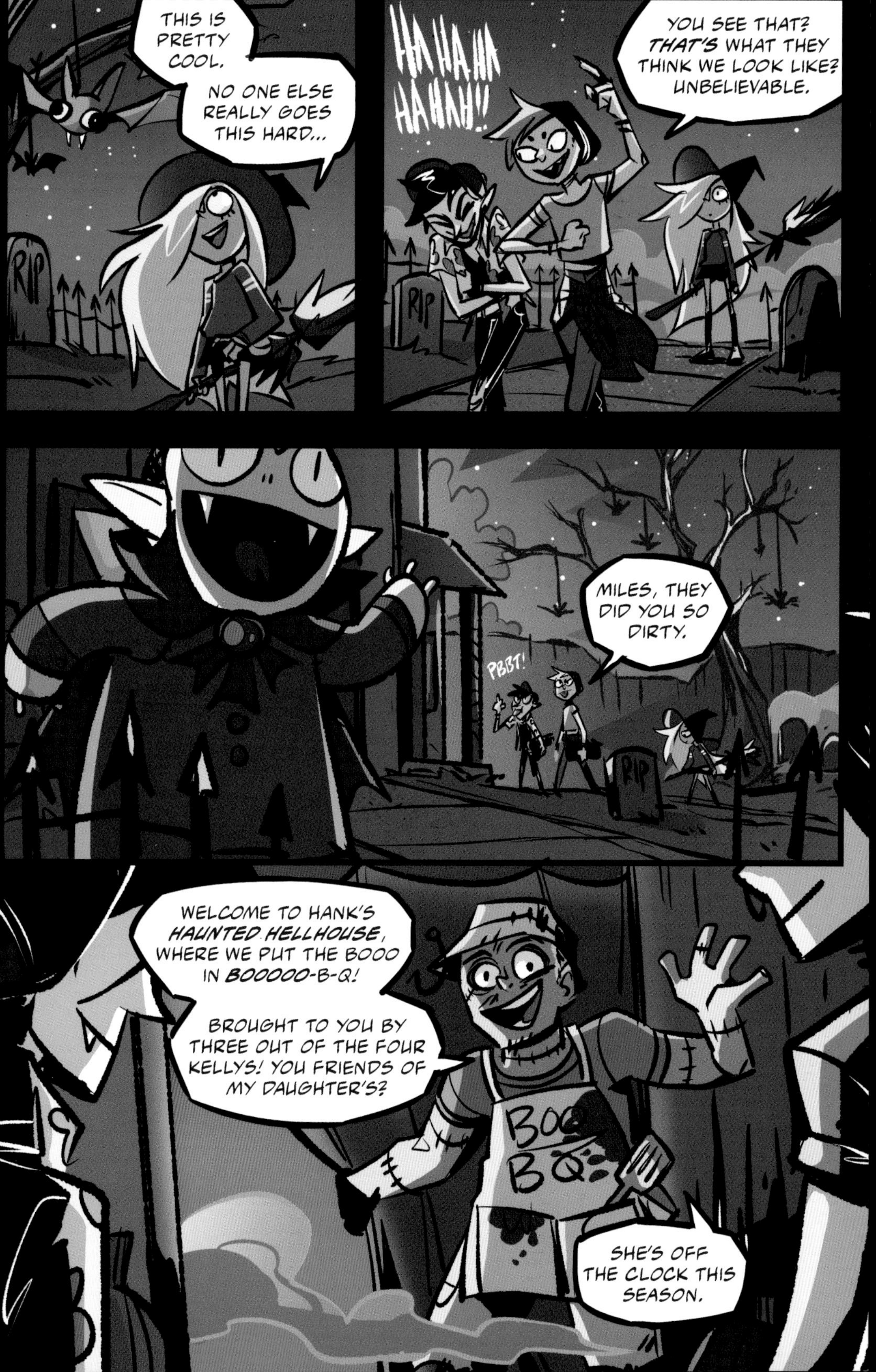
THIS IS PRETTY COOL.
NO ONE ELSE REALLY GOES THIS HARD...
HAHAHA HAHAH!!
YOU SEE THAT? THAT'S WHAT THEY THINK WE LOOK LIKE? UNBELIEVABLE.
MILES, THEY DID YOU SO DIRTY.
PBBT!
RIP
WELCOME TO HANK'S HAUNTED HELLHOUSE, WHERE WE PUT THE BOOO IN BOOOOO-B-Q!
BROUGHT TO YOU BY THREE OUT OF THE FOUR KELLYS! YOU FRIENDS OF MY DAUGHTER'S?
SHE'S OFF THE CLOCK THIS SEASON.

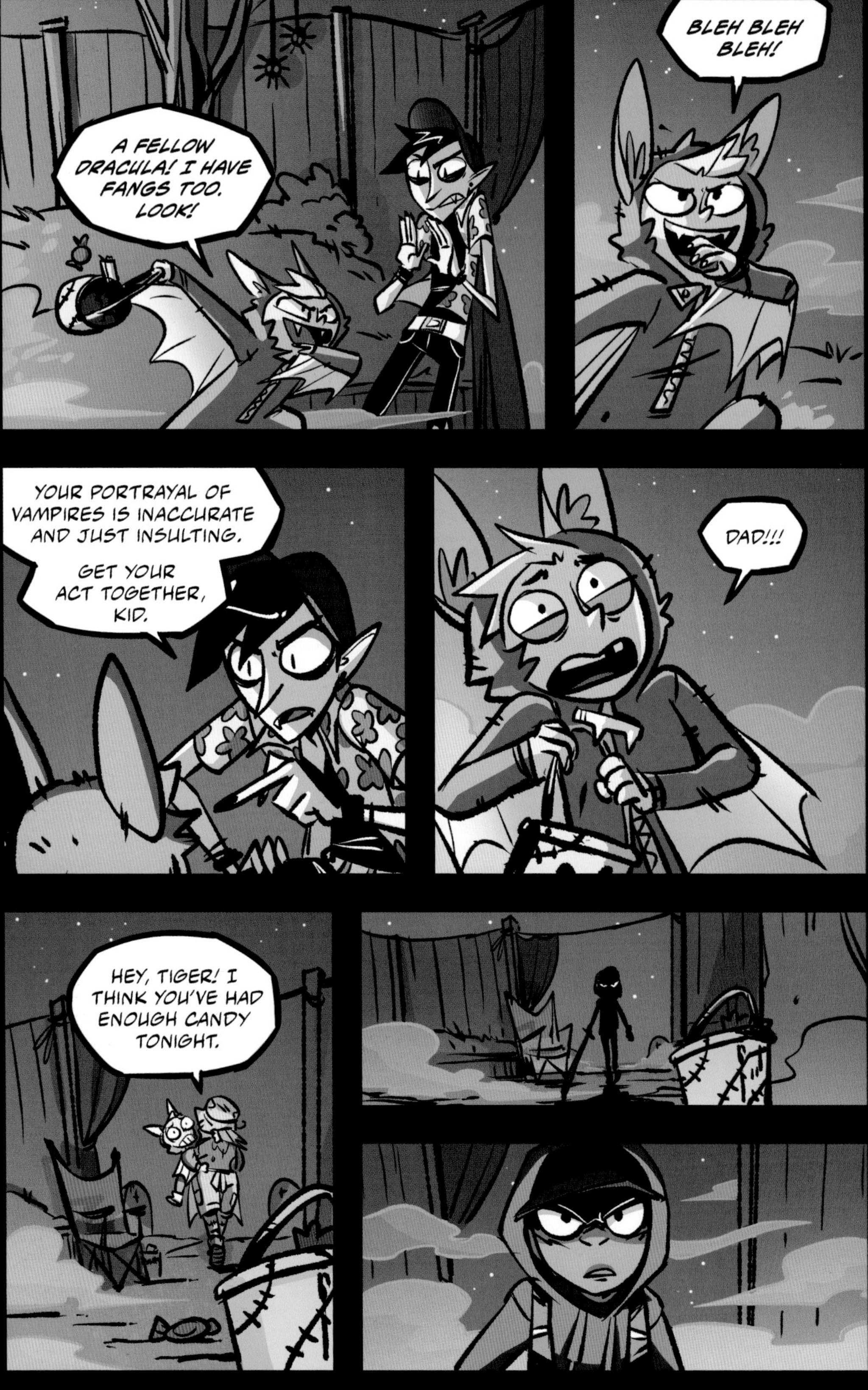
A FELLOW DRACULA! I HAVE FANGS TOO. LOOK!
BLEH BLEH BLEH!
YOUR PORTRAYAL OF VAMPIRES IS INACCURATE AND JUST INSULTING.
GET YOUR ACT TOGETHER, KID.
DAD!!!
HEY, TIGER! I THINK YOU'VE HAD ENOUGH CANDY TONIGHT.

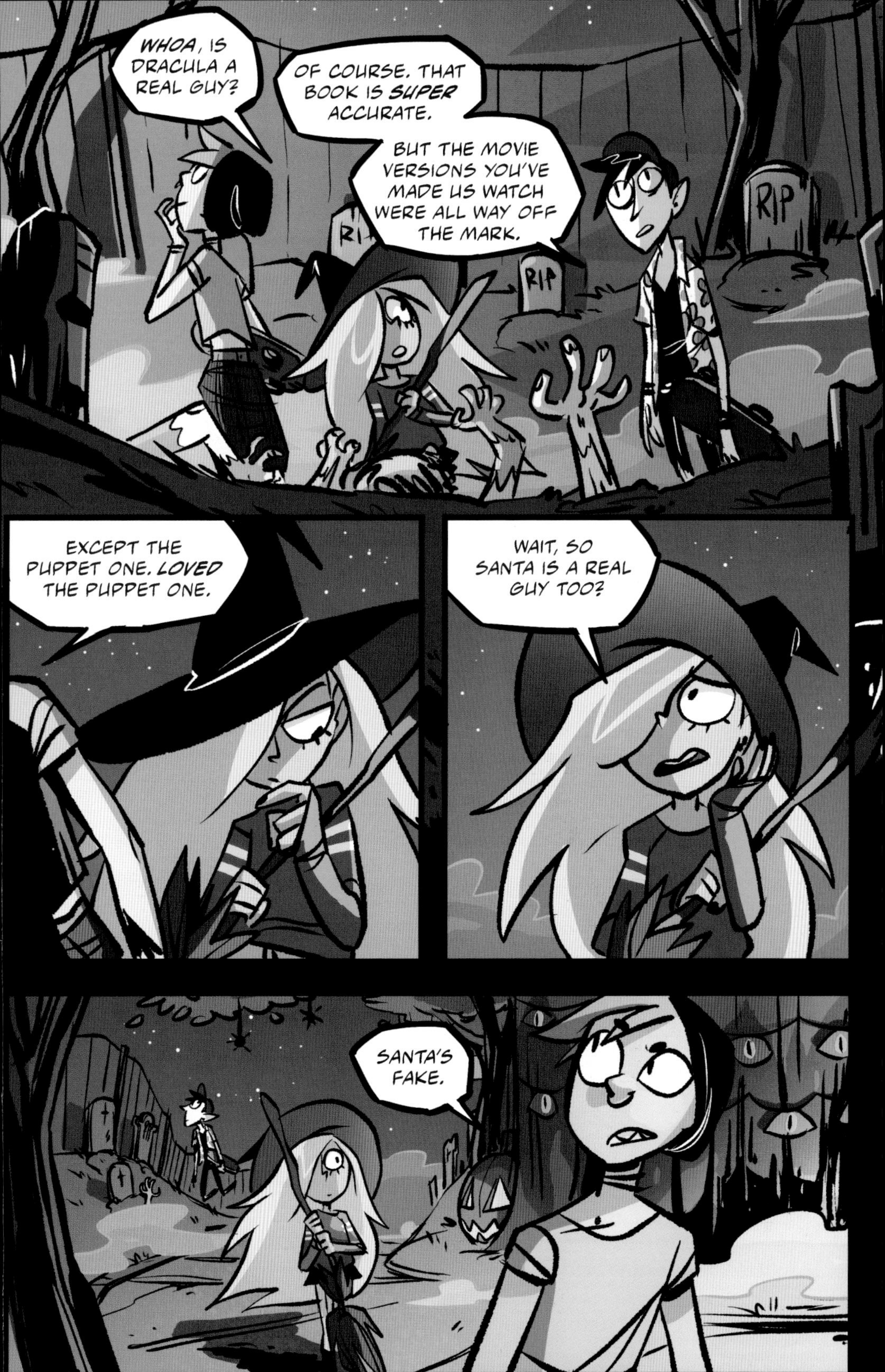
WHOA, IS DRACULA A REAL GUY?
OF COURSE. THAT BOOK IS SUPER ACCURATE.
BUT THE MOVIE VERSIONS YOU'VE MADE US WATCH WERE ALL WAY OFF THE MARK.
RIP
RIP
EXCEPT THE PUPPET ONE. LOVED THE PUPPET ONE.
WAIT, SO SANTA IS A REAL GUY TOO?
SANTA'S FAKE.

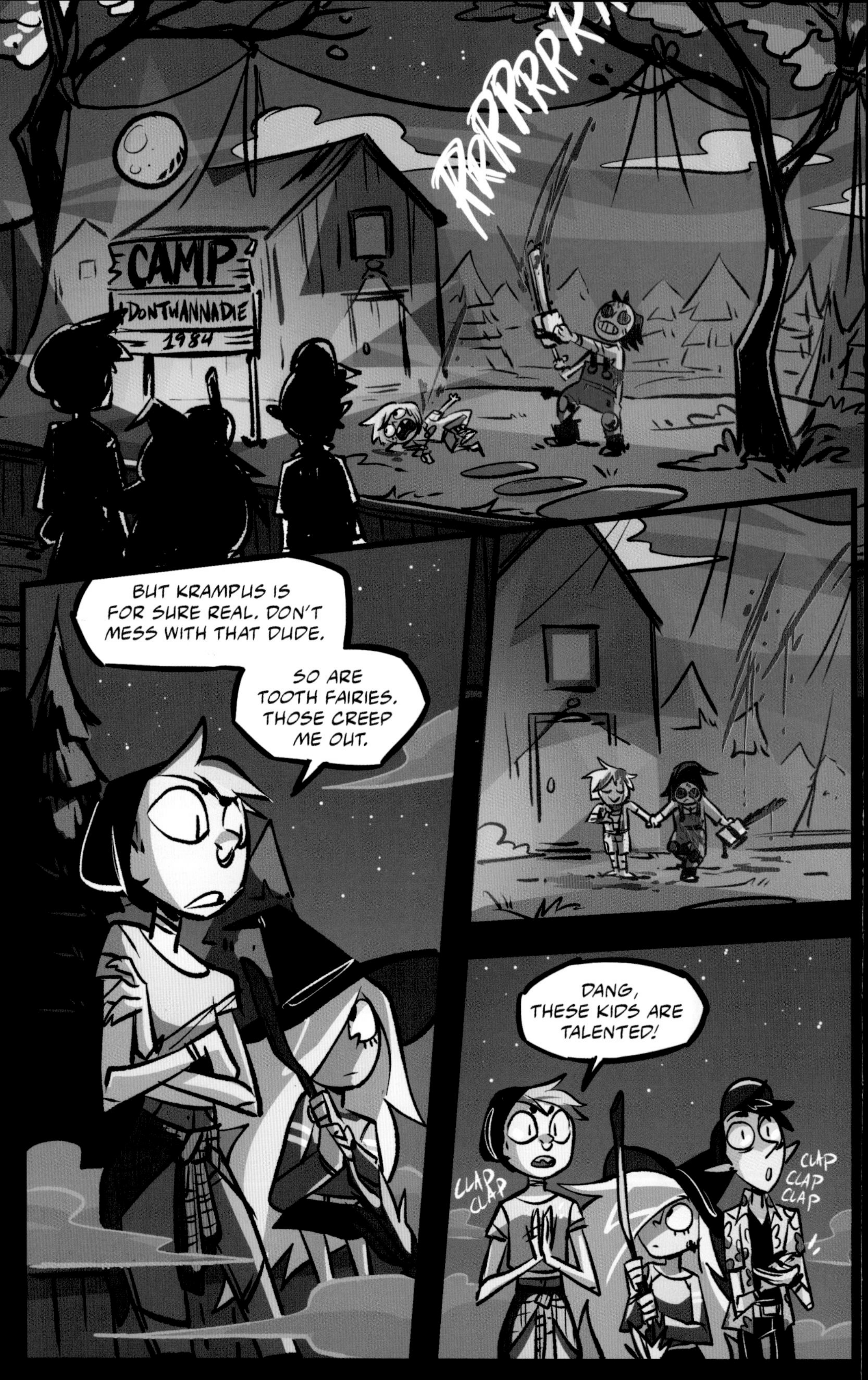
CAMP
DONTWANNADIE
1984
RRRRRRR
BUT KRAMPUS IS FOR SURE REAL. DON'T MESS WITH THAT DUDE.
SO ARE TOOTH FAIRIES. THOSE CREEP ME OUT.
DANG, THESE KIDS ARE TALENTED!
CLAP CLAP
CLAP CLAP CLAP

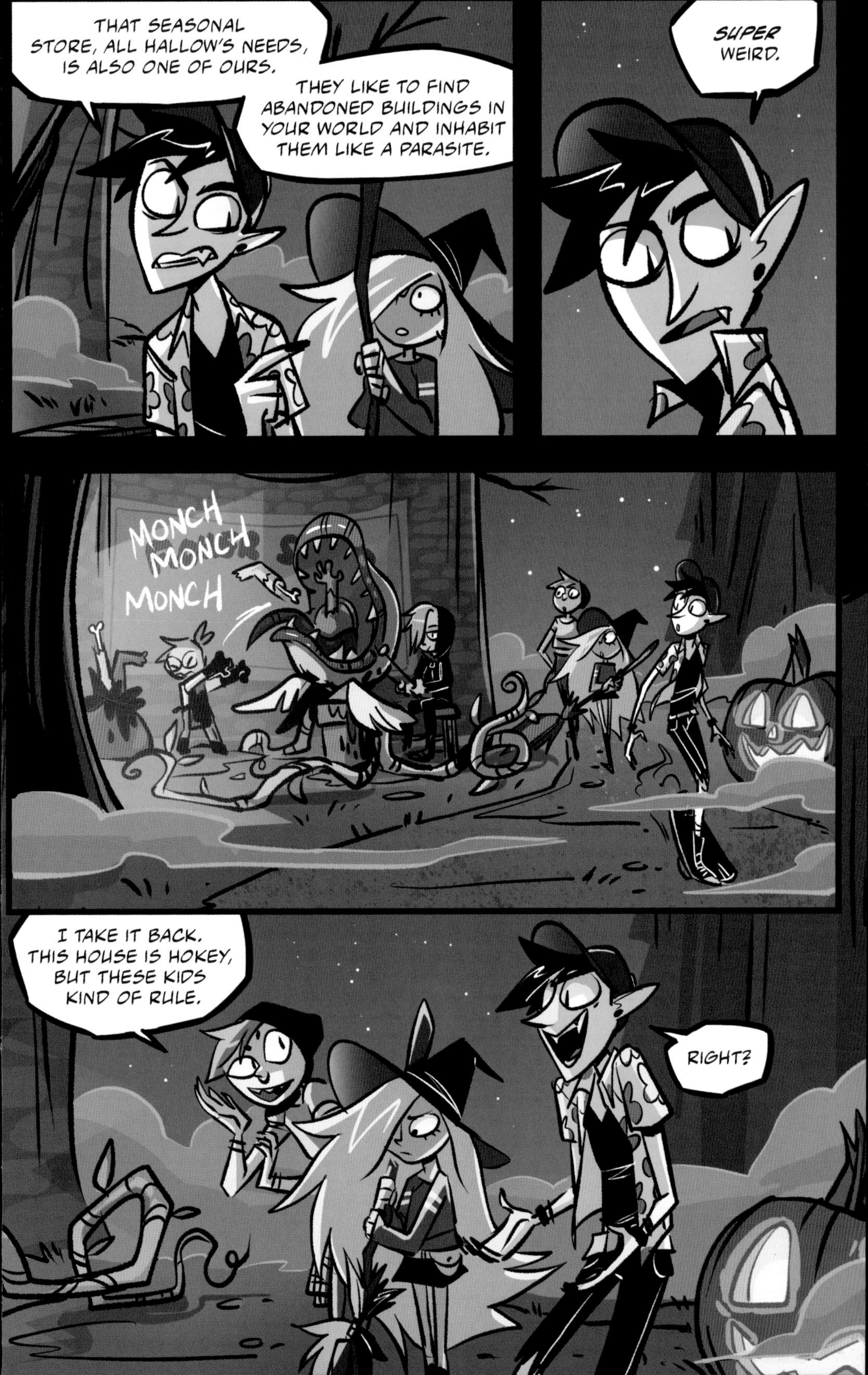

THAT SEASONAL STORE, ALL HALLOW'S NEEDS, IS ALSO ONE OF OURS.
THEY LIKE TO FIND ABANDONED BUILDINGS IN YOUR WORLD AND INHABIT THEM LIKE A PARASITE.
SUPER WEIRD.
MONCH MONCH MONCH
I TAKE IT BACK. THIS HOUSE IS HOKEY, BUT THESE KIDS KIND OF RULE.
RIGHT?

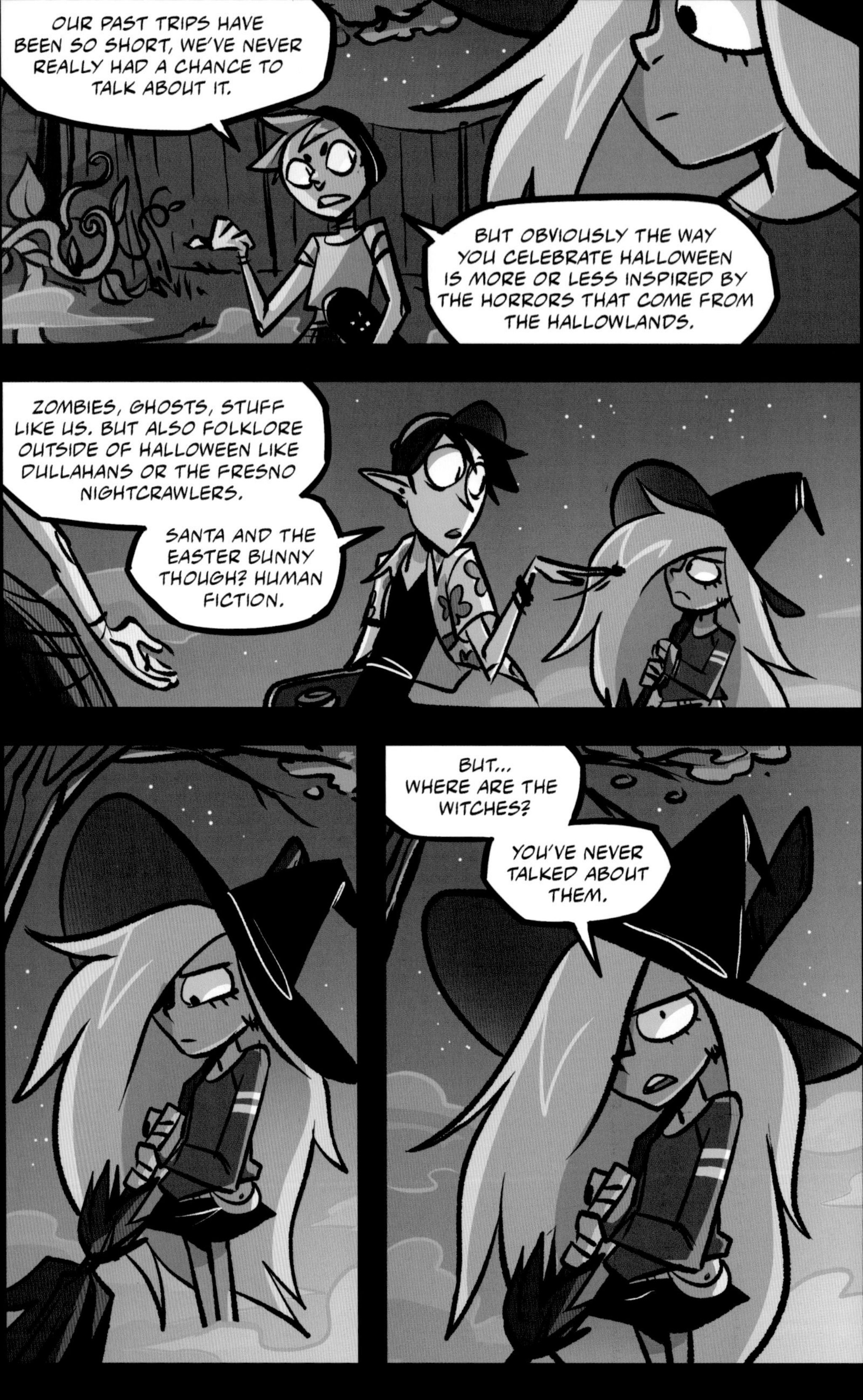
OUR PAST TRIPS HAVE BEEN SO SHORT, WE'VE NEVER REALLY HAD A CHANCE TO TALK ABOUT IT.
BUT OBVIOUSLY THE WAY YOU CELEBRATE HALLOWEEN IS MORE OR LESS INSPIRED BY THE HORRORS THAT COME FROM THE HALLOWLANDS.
ZOMBIES, GHOSTS, STUFF LIKE US. BUT ALSO FOLKLORE OUTSIDE OF HALLOWEEN LIKE DULLAHANS OR THE FRESNO NIGHTCRAWLERS.
SANTA AND THE EASTER BUNNY THOUGH? HUMAN FICTION.
BUT... WHERE ARE THE WITCHES?
YOU'VE NEVER TALKED ABOUT THEM.

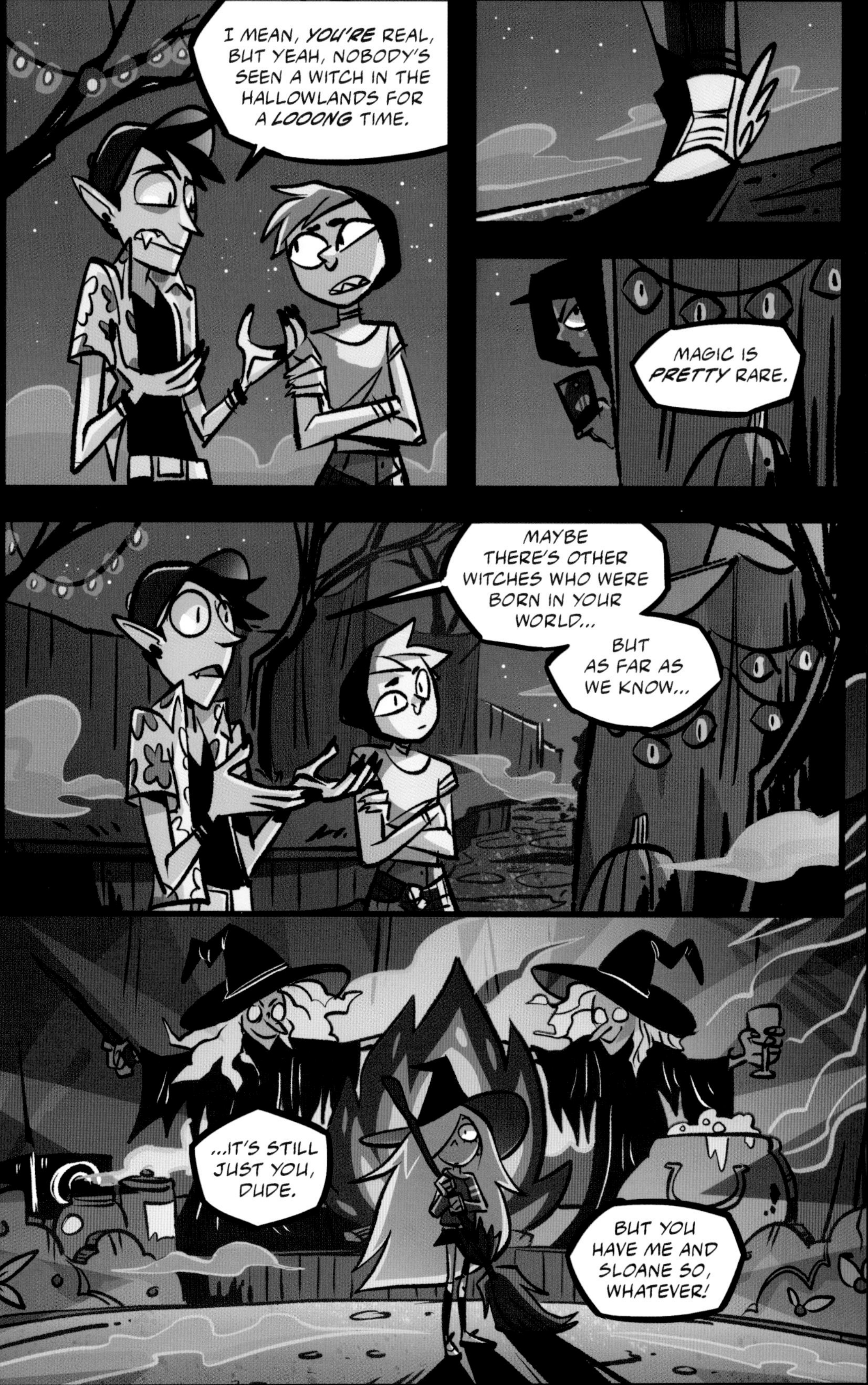
I MEAN, YOU'RE REAL, BUT YEAH, NOBODY'S SEEN A WITCH IN THE HALLOWLANDS FOR A LOOONG TIME.
MAGIC IS PRETTY RARE.
MAYBE THERE'S OTHER WITCHES WHO WERE BORN IN YOUR WORLD...
BUT AS FAR AS WE KNOW...
...IT'S STILL JUST YOU, DUDE.
BUT YOU HAVE ME AND SLOANE SO, WHATEVER!

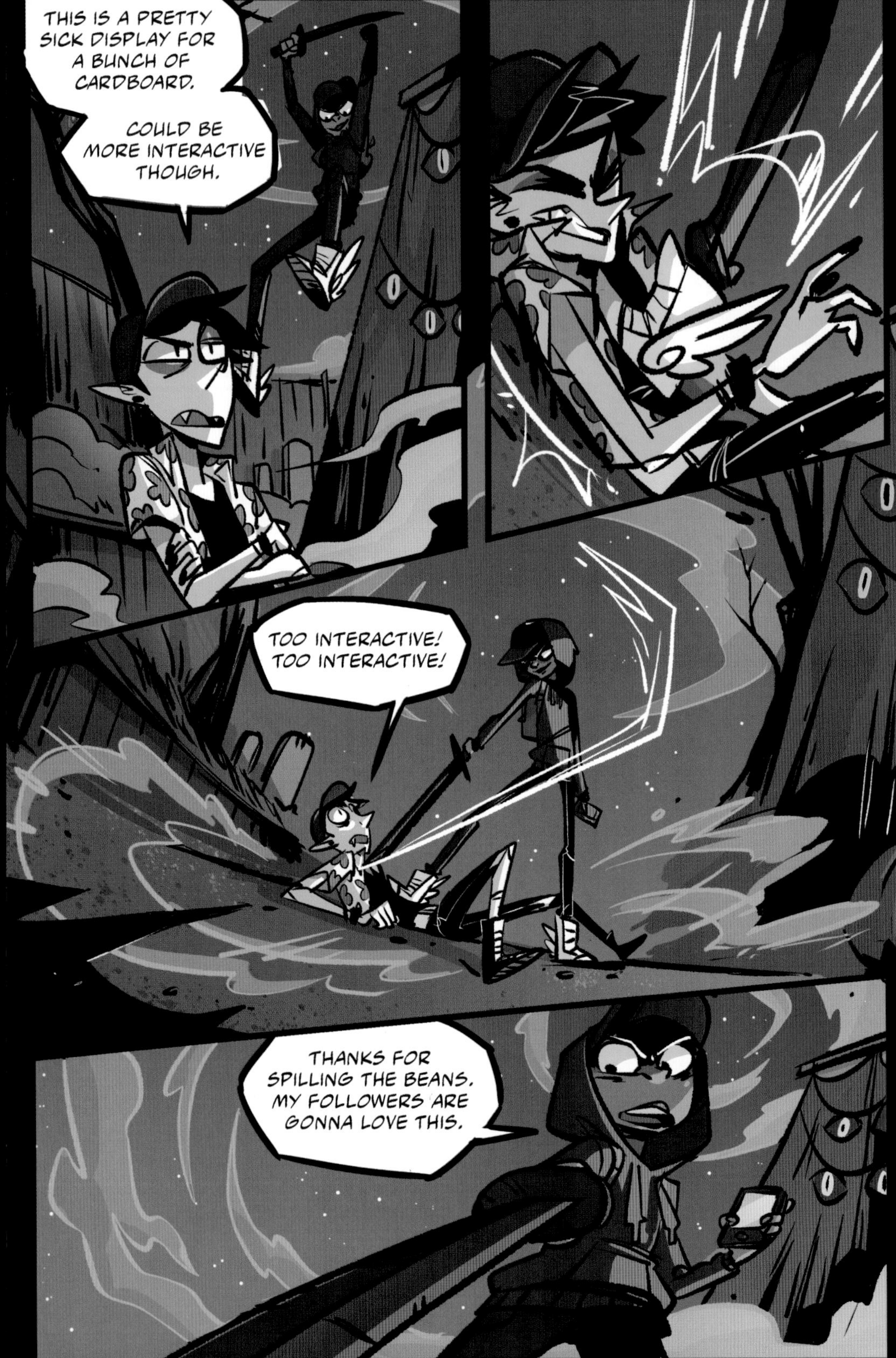
THIS IS A PRETTY SICK DISPLAY FOR A BUNCH OF CARDBOARD.
COULD BE MORE INTERACTIVE THOUGH.
TOO INTERACTIVE! TOO INTERACTIVE!
THANKS FOR SPILLING THE BEANS. MY FOLLOWERS ARE GONNA LOVE THIS.

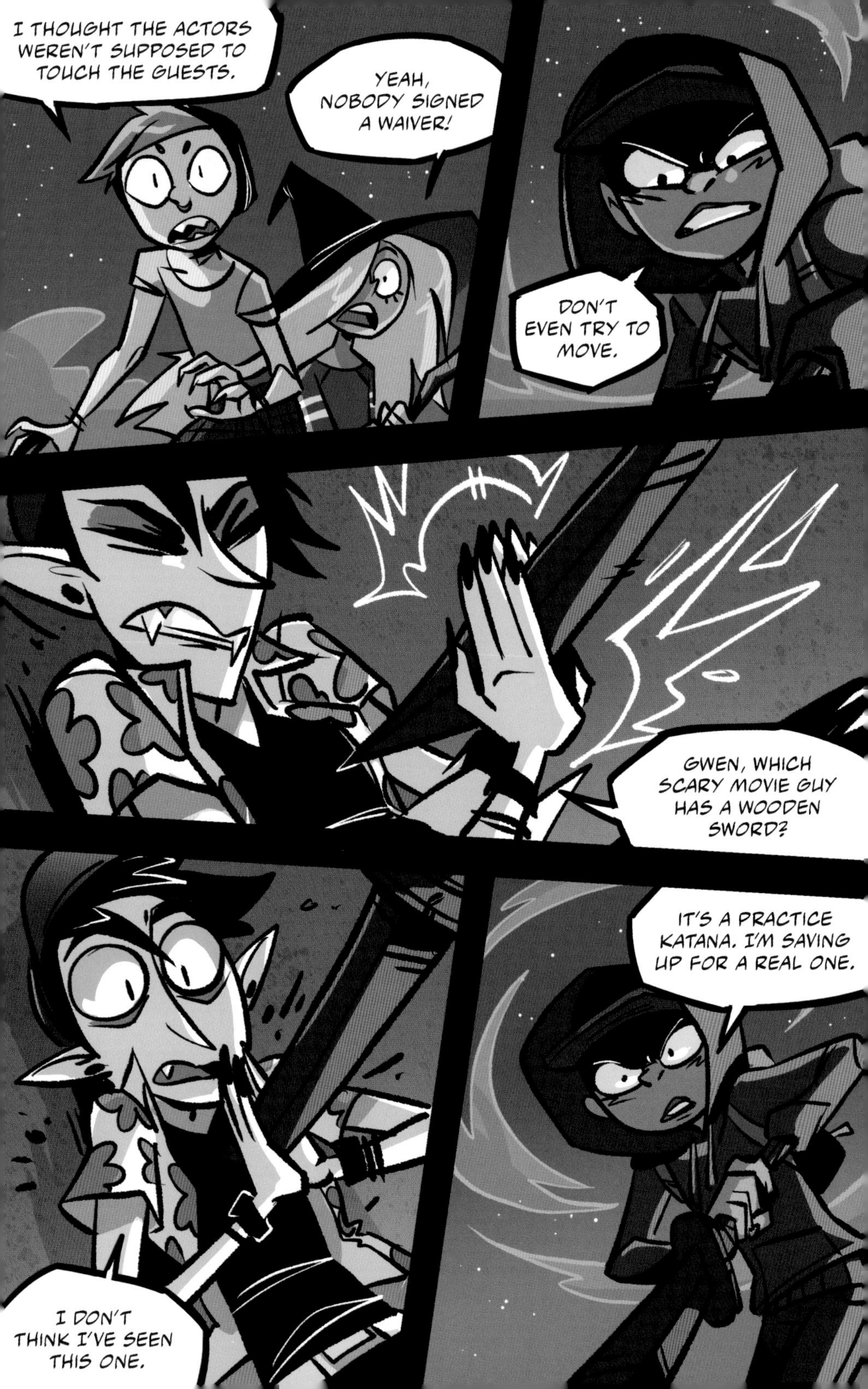
I THOUGHT THE ACTORS WEREN'T SUPPOSED TO TOUCH THE GUESTS.
YEAH, NOBODY SIGNED A WAIVER!
DON'T EVEN TRY TO MOVE.
GWEN, WHICH SCARY MOVIE GUY HAS A WOODEN SWORD?
IT'S A PRACTICE KATANA. I'M SAVING UP FOR A REAL ONE.
I DON'T THINK I'VE SEEN THIS ONE.

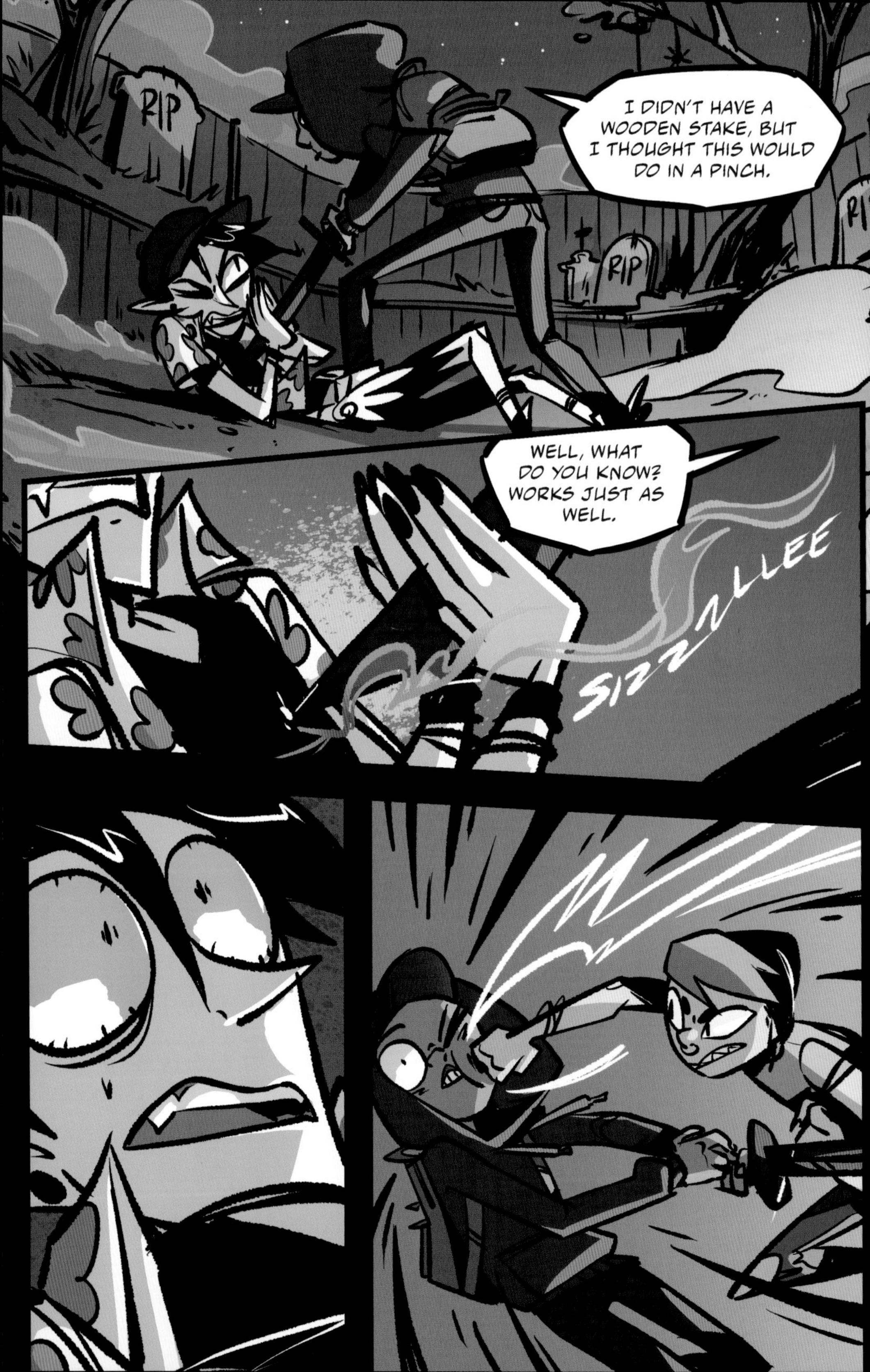
I DIDN'T HAVE A WOODEN STAKE, BUT I THOUGHT THIS WOULD DO IN A PINCH.
WELL, WHAT DO YOU KNOW? WORKS JUST AS WELL.
SIZZZLLEE

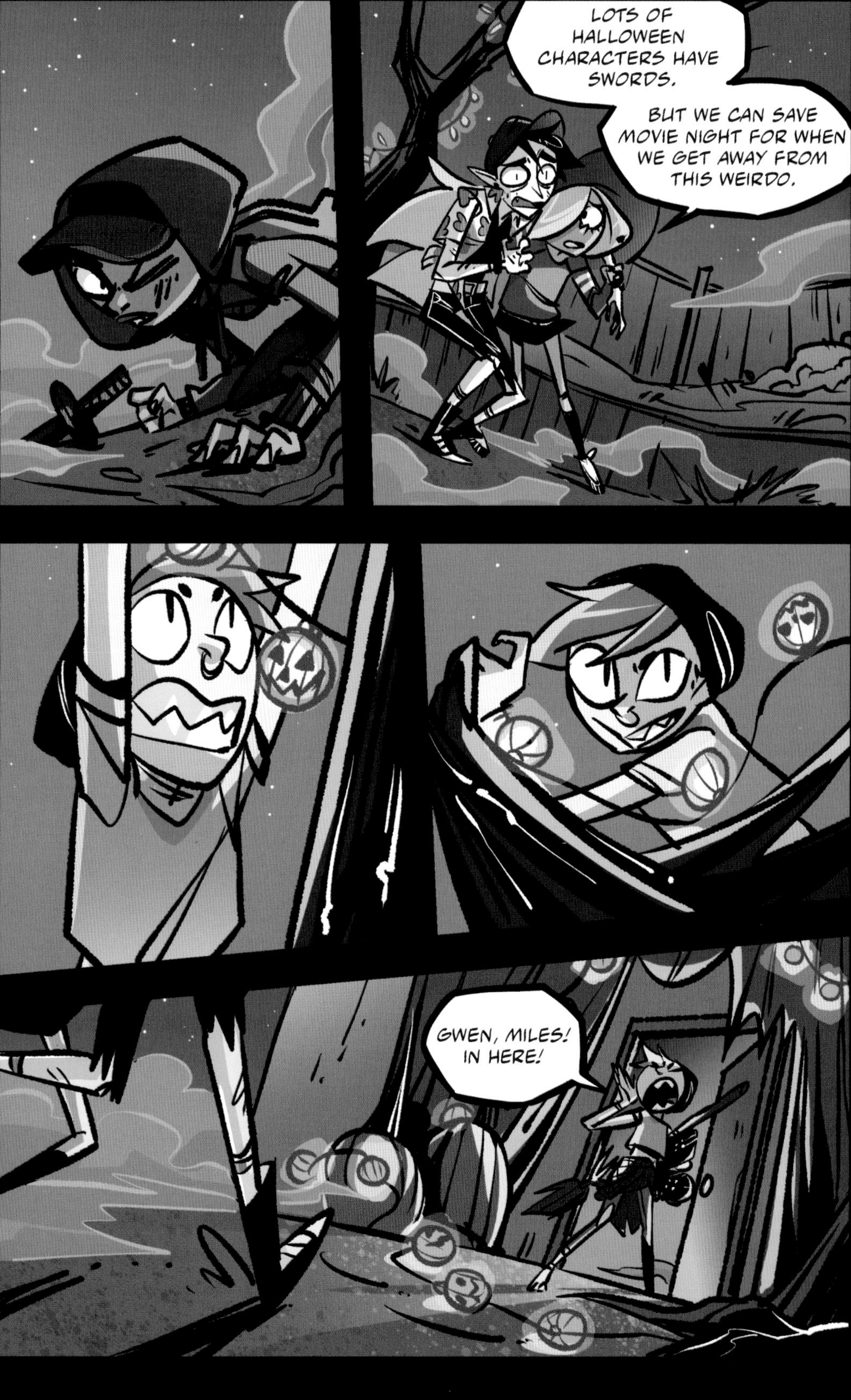
LOTS OF HALLOWEEN CHARACTERS HAVE SWORDS.
BUT WE CAN SAVE MOVIE NIGHT FOR WHEN WE GET AWAY FROM THIS WEIRDO.
GWEN, MILES! IN HERE!

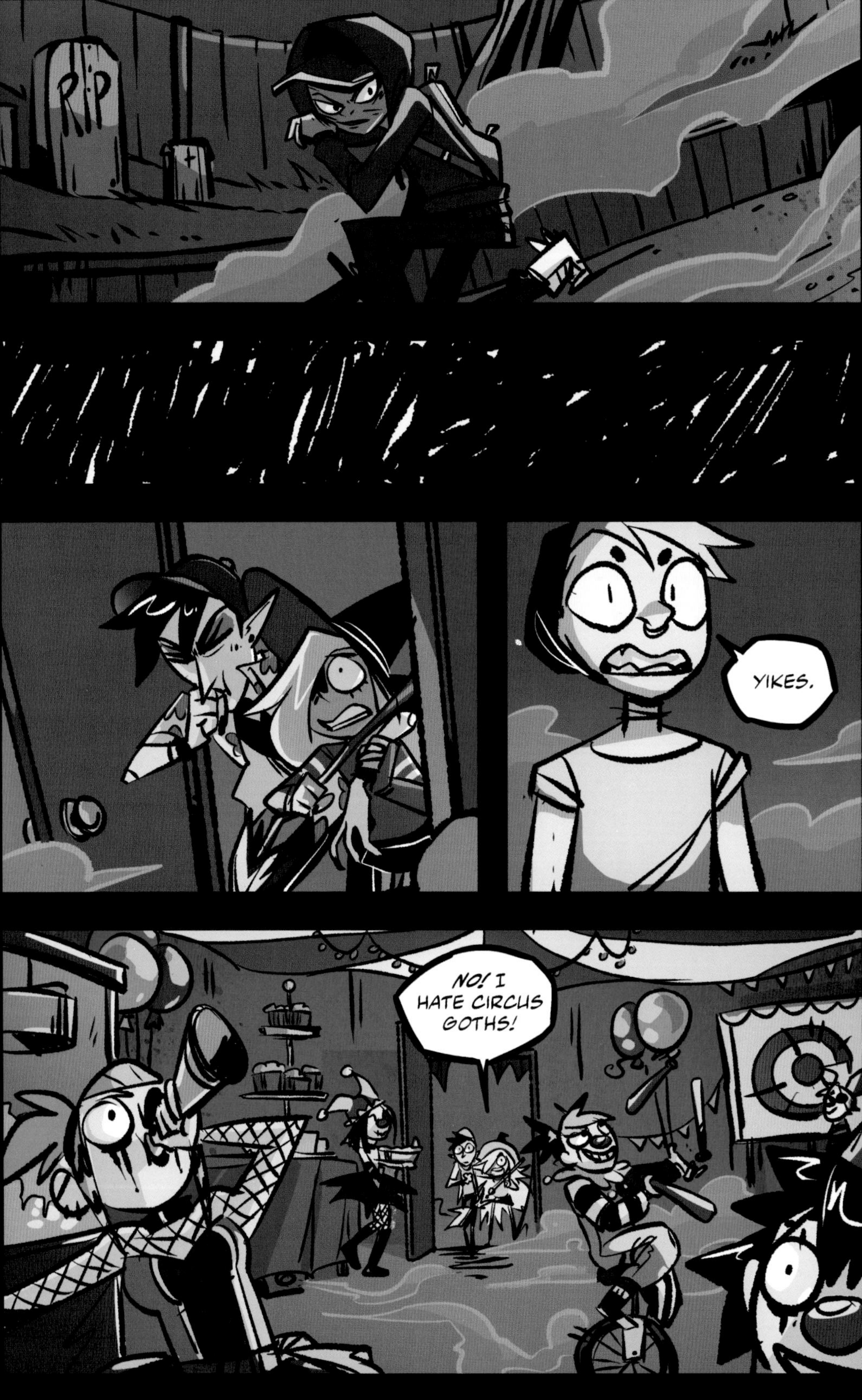

YIKES.
NO! I HATE CIRCUS GOTHS!

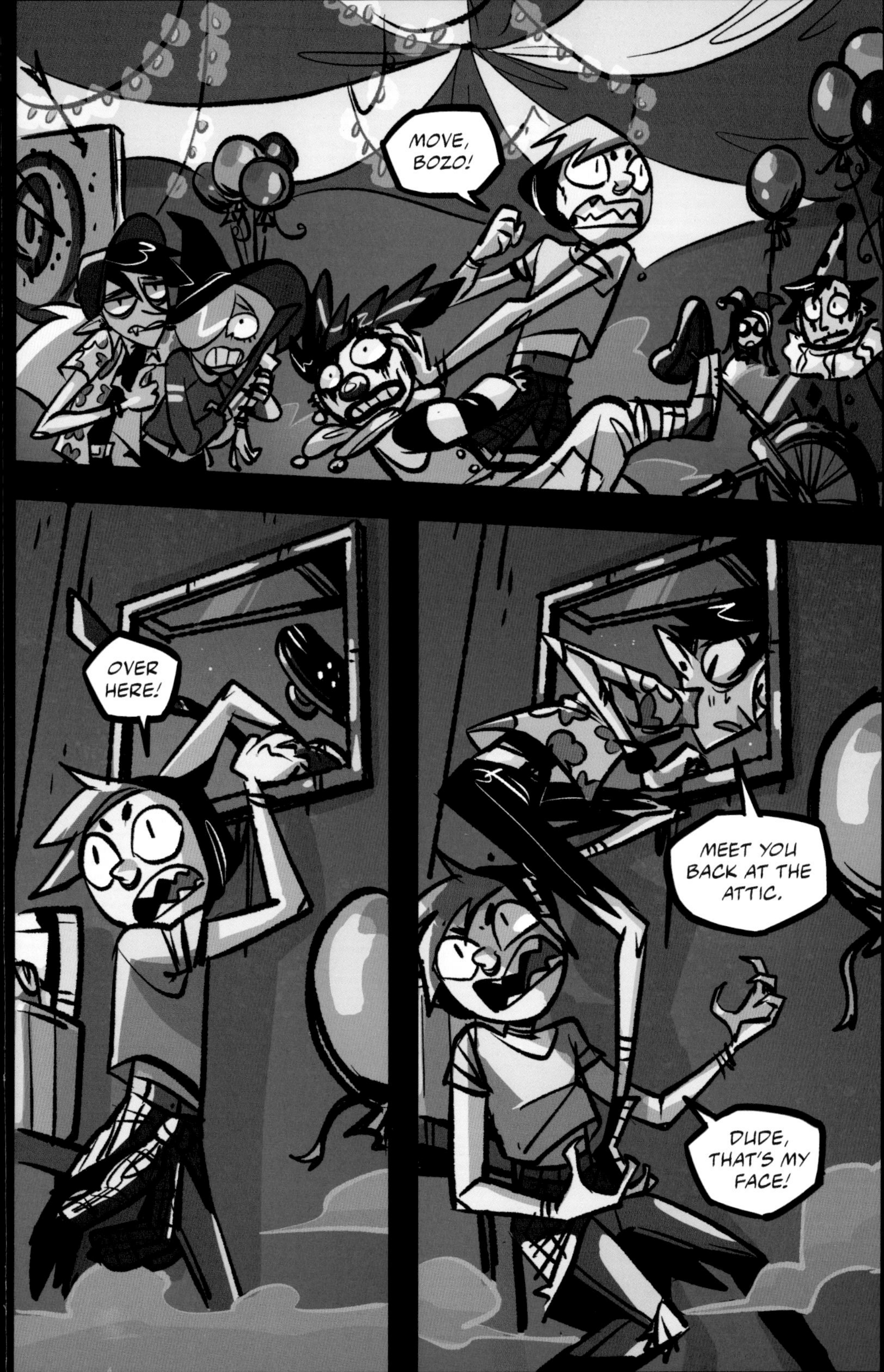
MOVE, BOZO!
OVER HERE!
MEET YOU BACK AT THE ATTIC.
DUDE, THAT'S MY FACE!

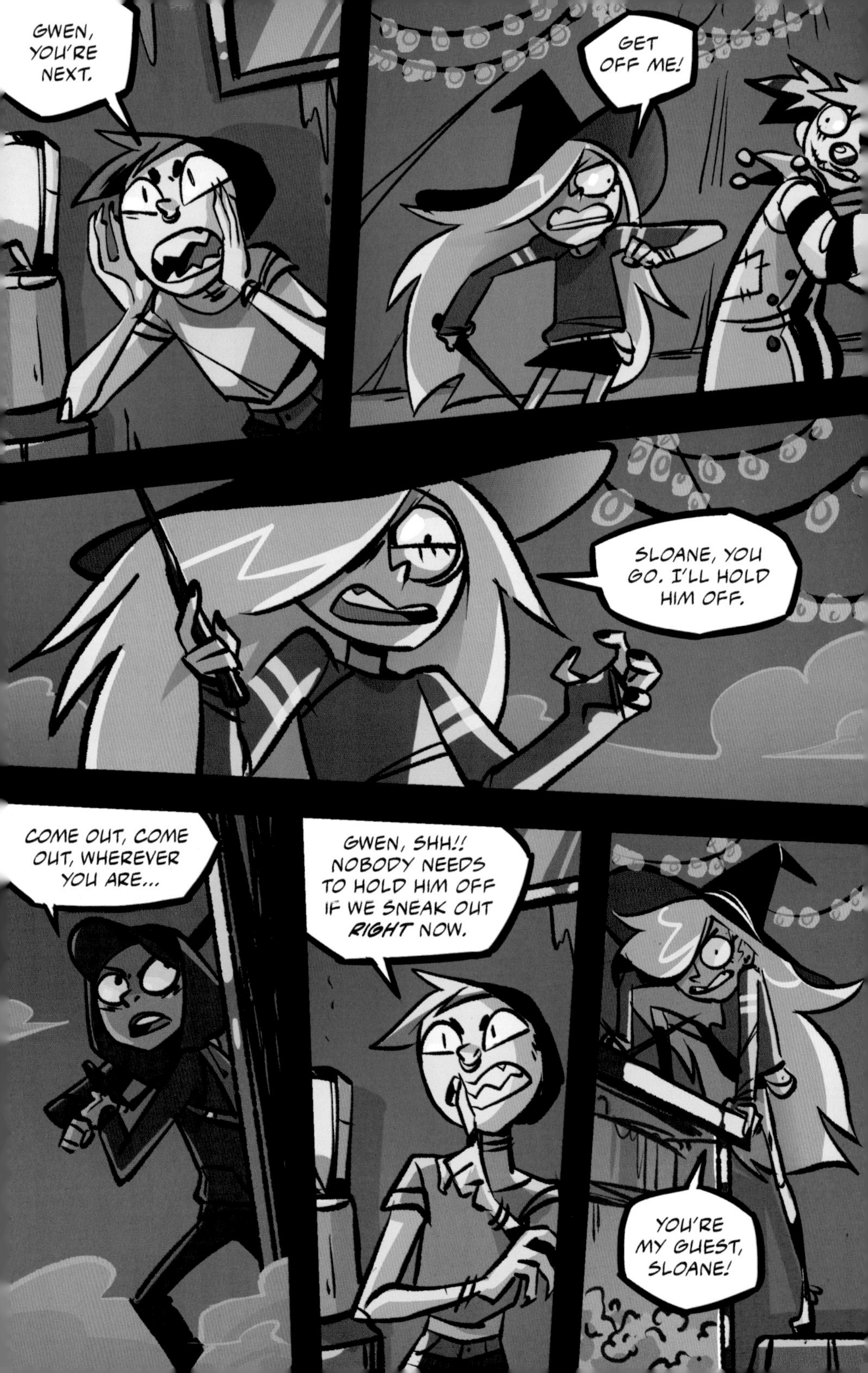
GWEN, YOU'RE NEXT.
GET OFF ME!
SLOANE, YOU GO. I'LL HOLD HIM OFF.
COME OUT, COME OUT, WHEREVER YOU ARE...
GWEN, SHH!! NOBODY NEEDS TO HOLD HIM OFF IF WE SNEAK OUT *RIGHT* NOW.
YOU'RE MY GUEST, SLOANE!

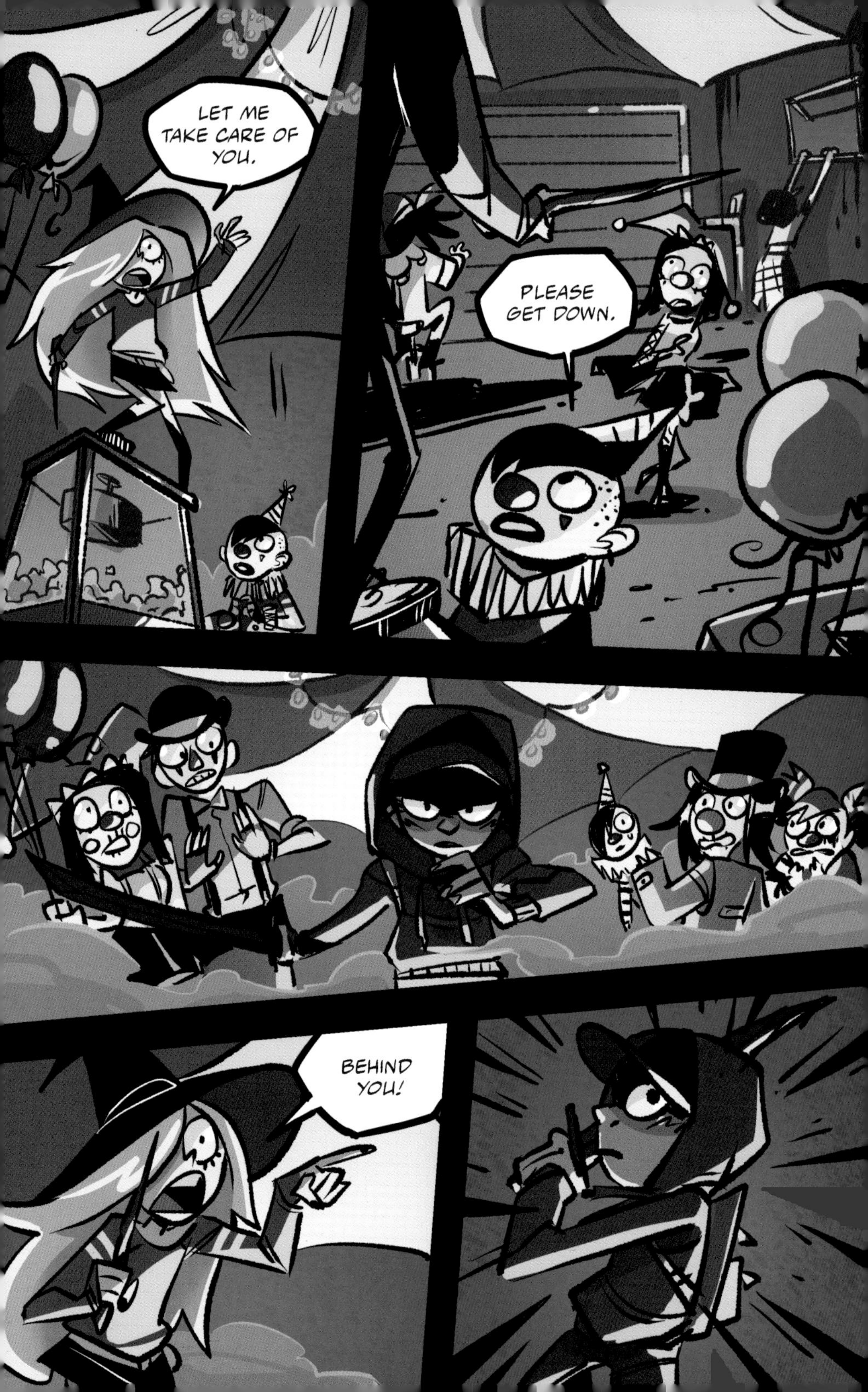
LET ME TAKE CARE OF YOU.
PLEASE GET DOWN.
BEHIND YOU!

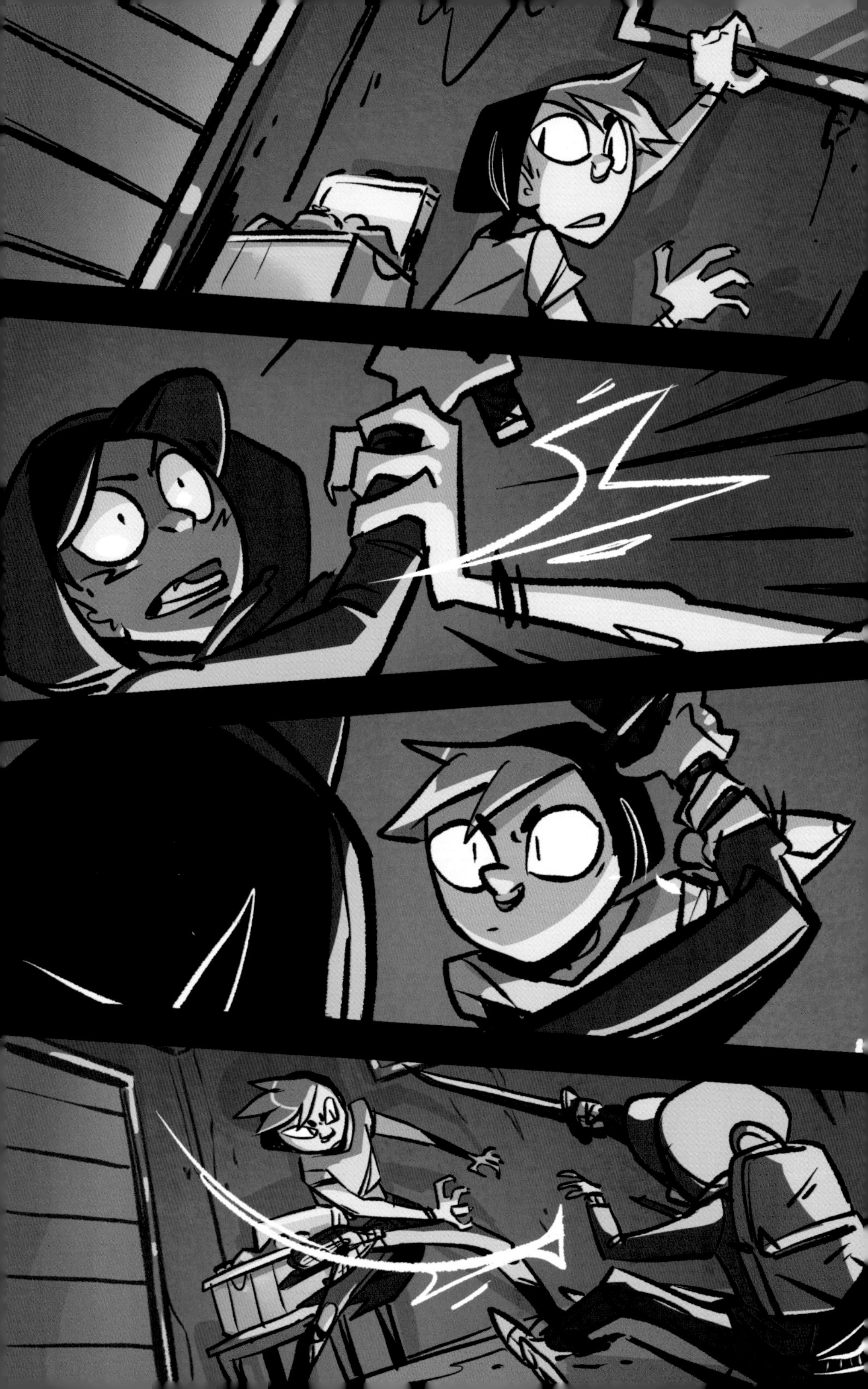

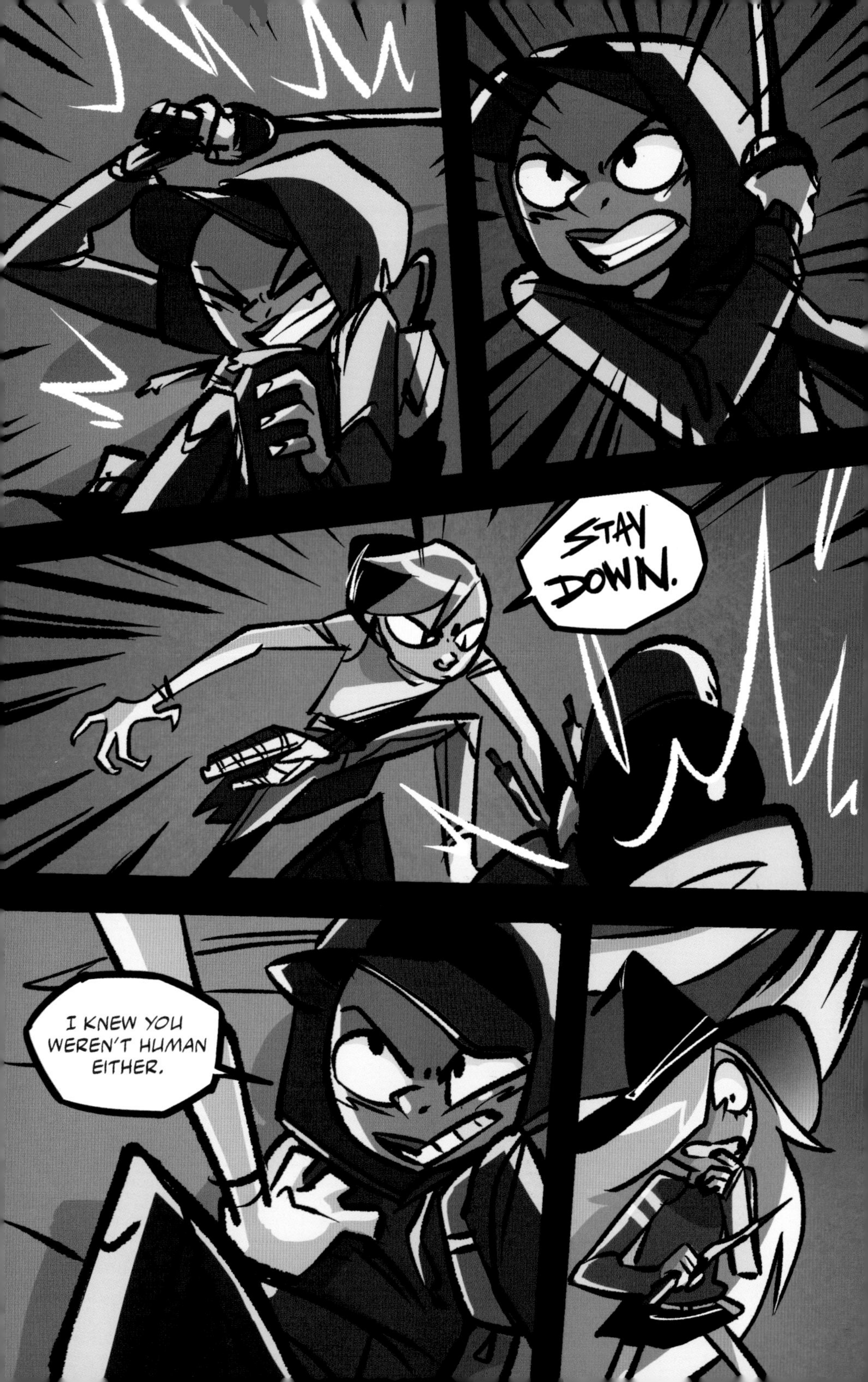
STAY DOWN.
I KNEW YOU WEREN'T HUMAN EITHER.

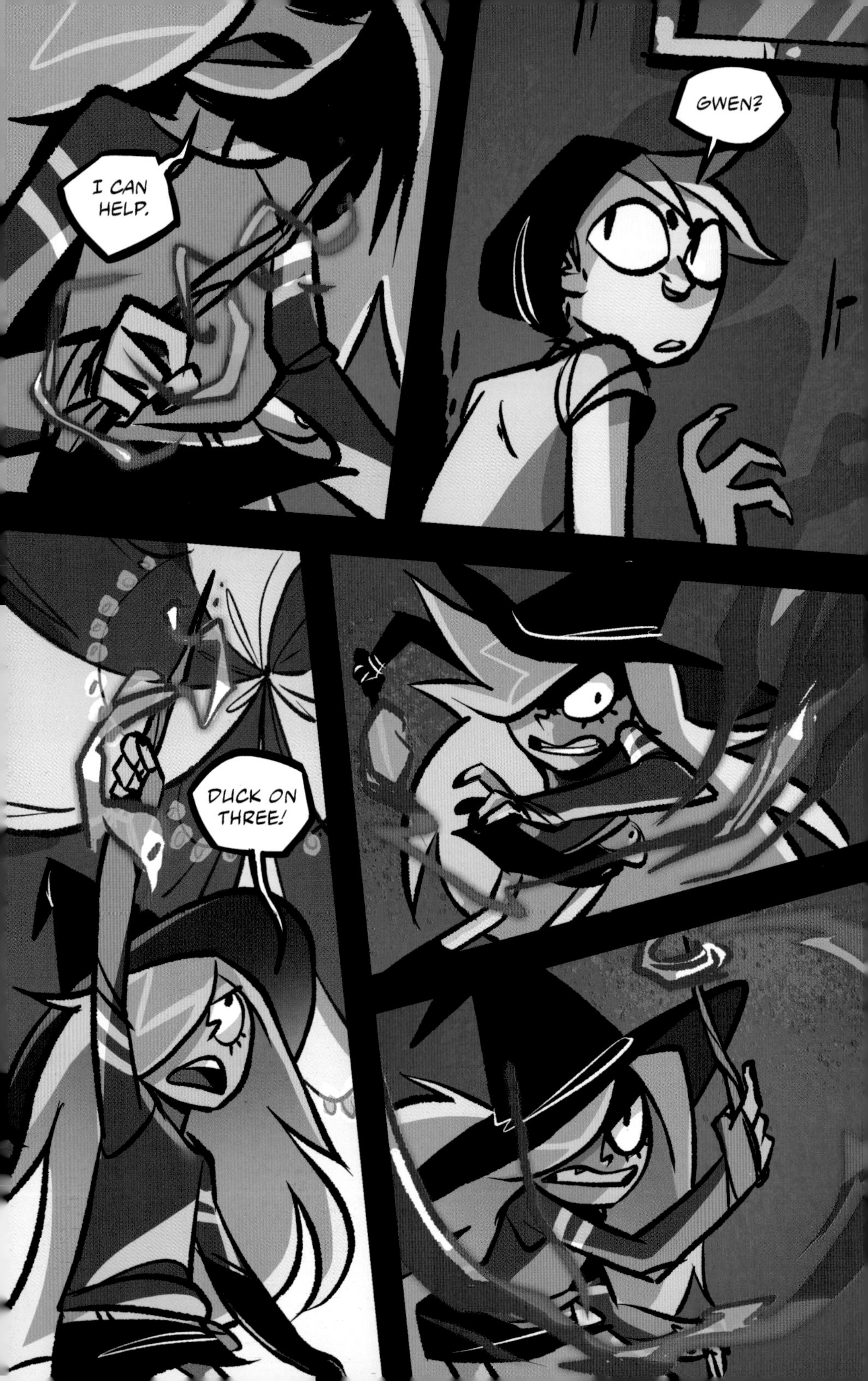
I CAN HELP.
GWEN?
DUCK ON THREE!

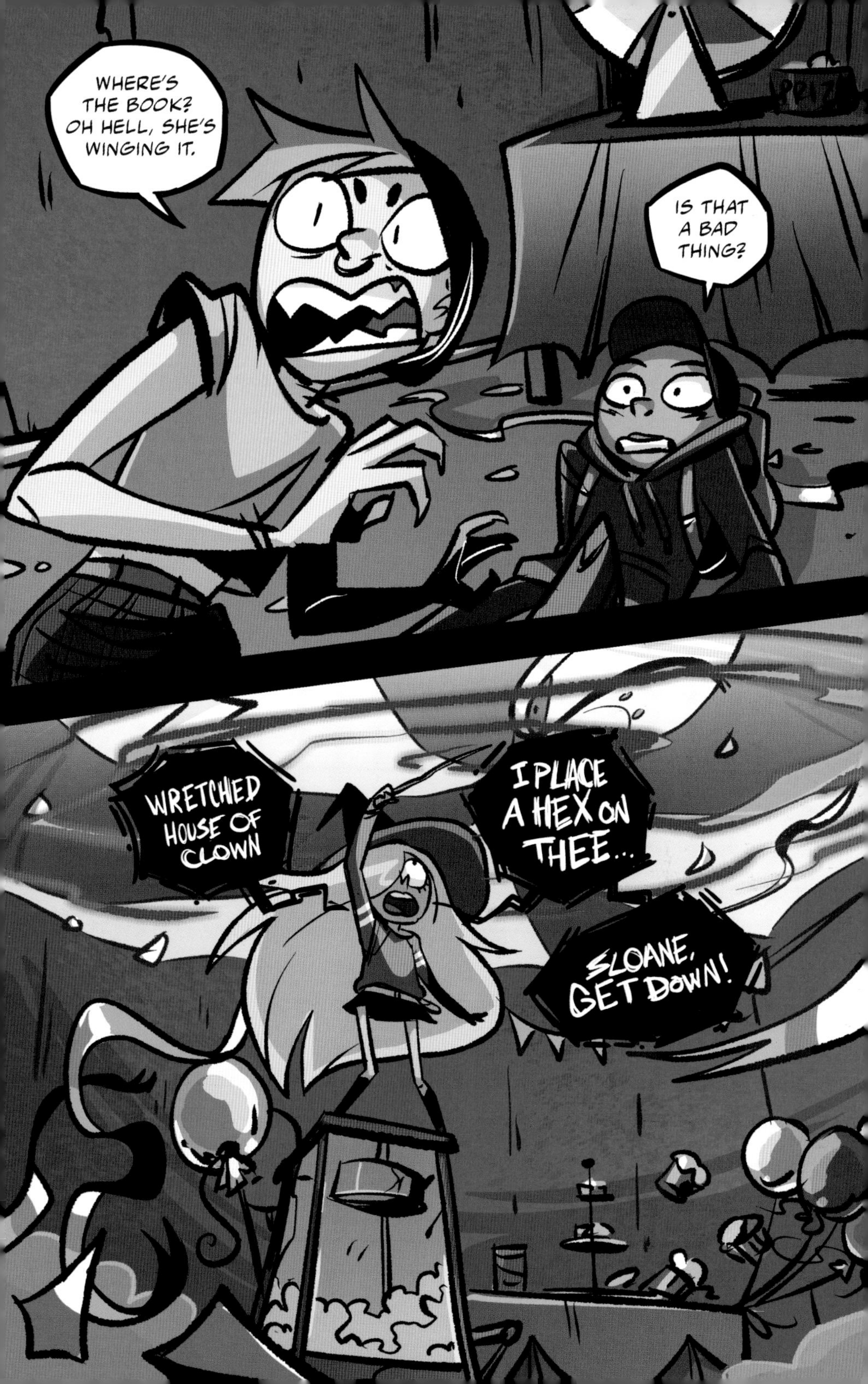
WHERE'S THE BOOK? OH HELL, SHE'S WINGING IT.
IS THAT A BAD THING?
WRETCHED HOUSE OF CLOWN
I PLACE A HEX ON THEE...
SLOANE, GET DOWN!

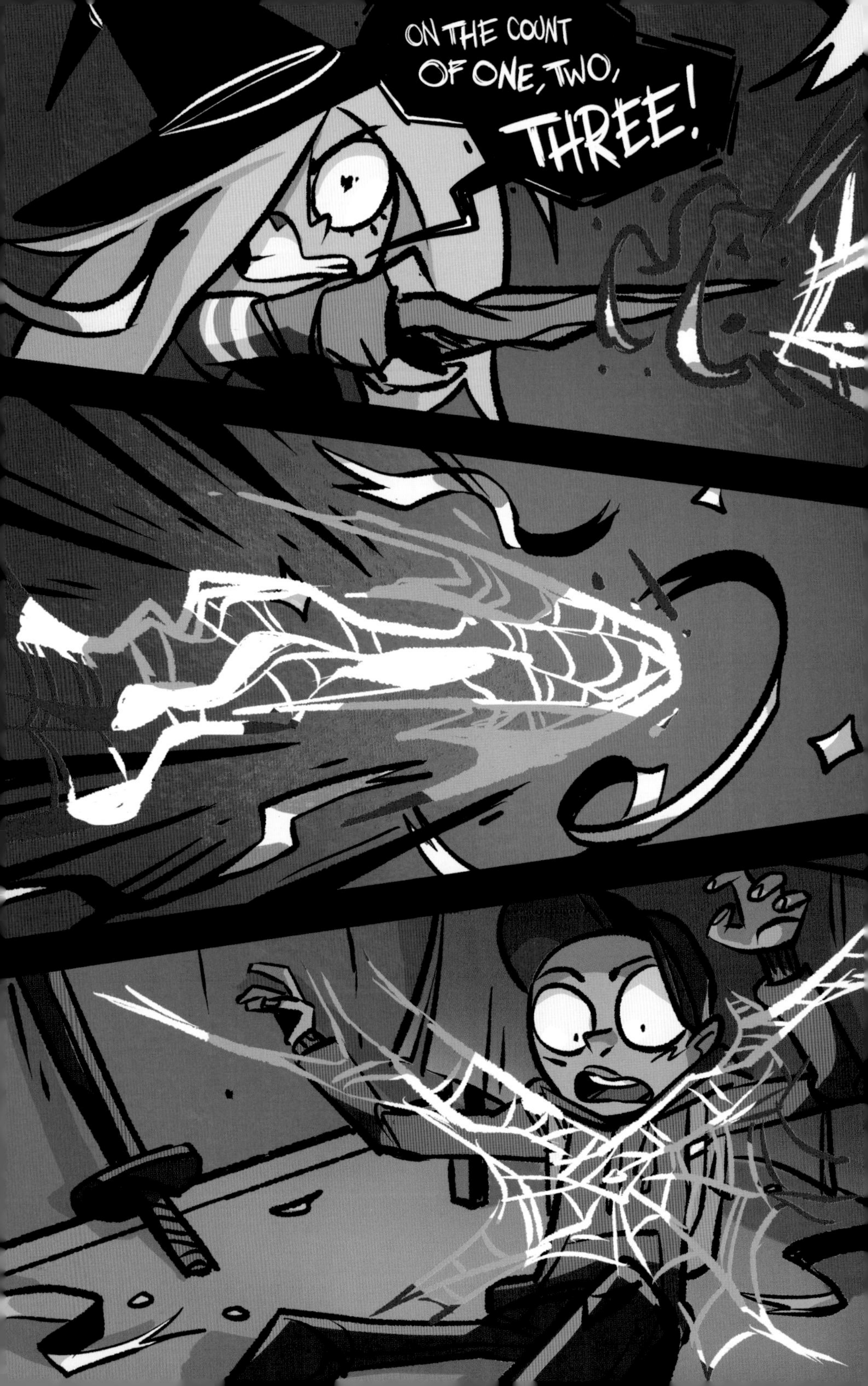
ON THE COUNT OF ONE, TWO, THREE!

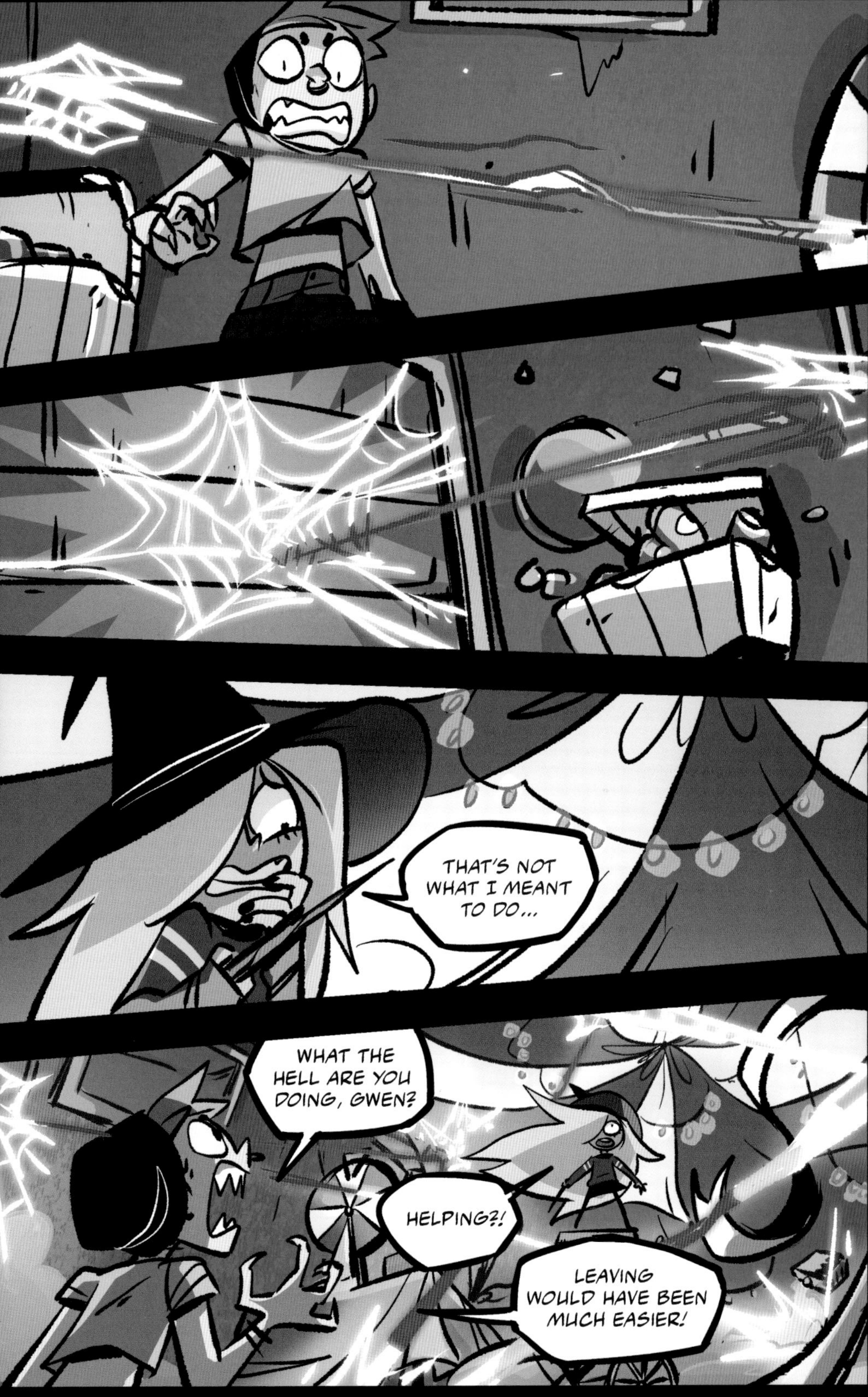

THAT'S NOT WHAT I MEANT TO DO...
WHAT THE HELL ARE YOU DOING, GWEN?
HELPING?!
LEAVING WOULD HAVE BEEN MUCH EASIER!

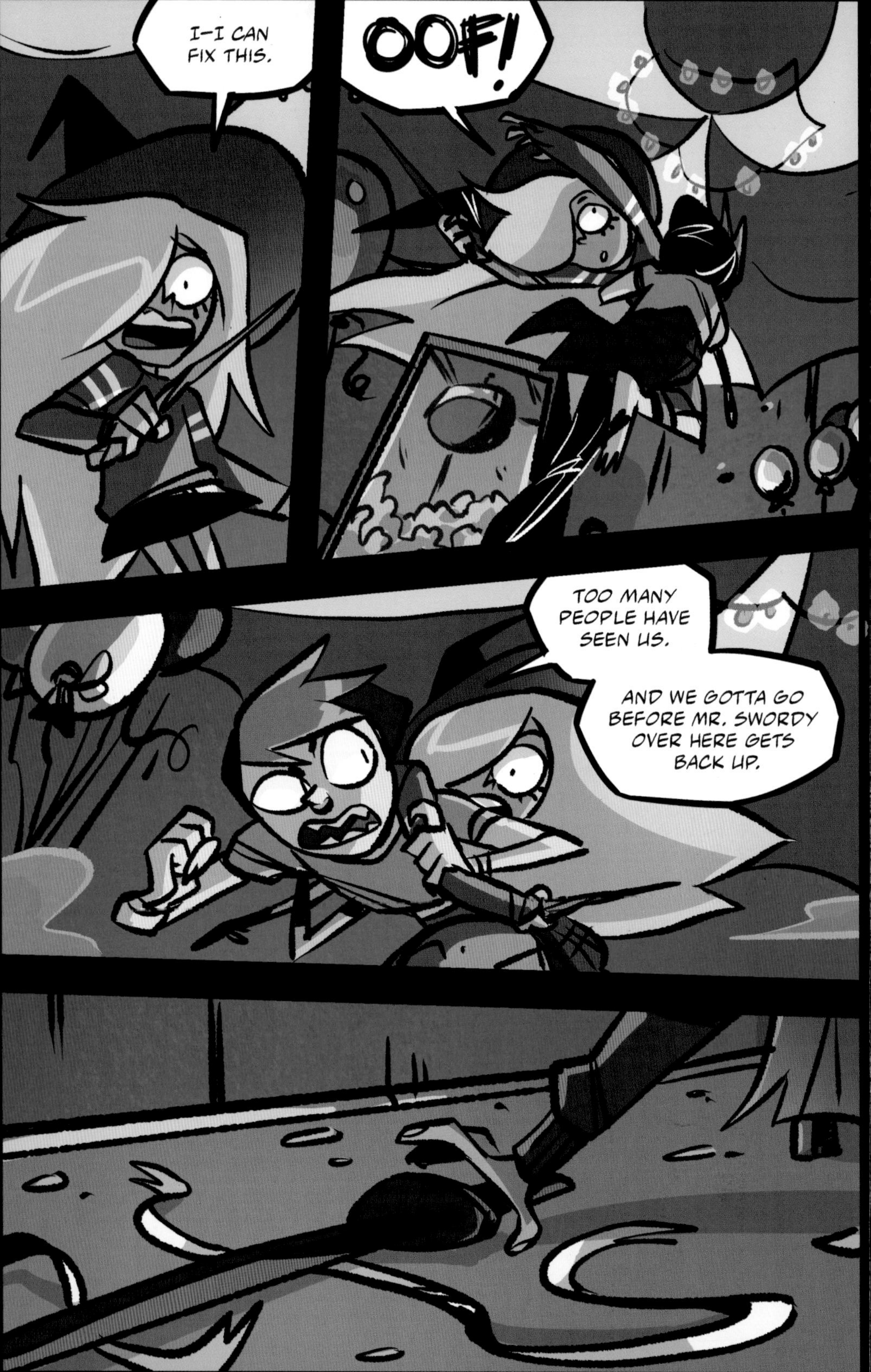
I-I CAN FIX THIS.
OOF!
TOO MANY PEOPLE HAVE SEEN US.
AND WE GOTTA GO BEFORE MR. SWORDY OVER HERE GETS BACK UP.

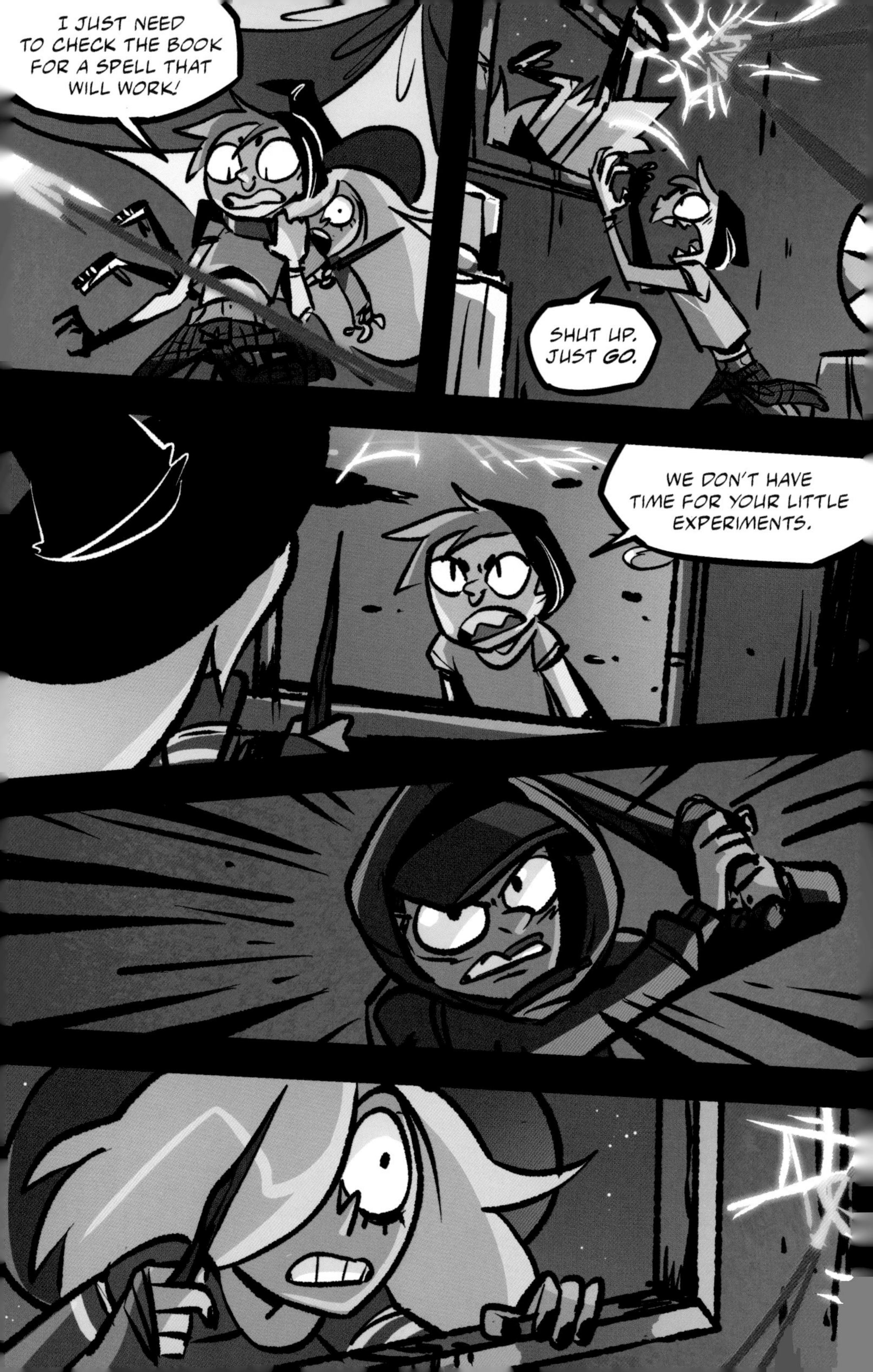
I JUST NEED TO CHECK THE BOOK FOR A SPELL THAT WILL WORK!
SHUT UP. JUST GO.
WE DON'T HAVE TIME FOR YOUR LITTLE EXPERIMENTS.

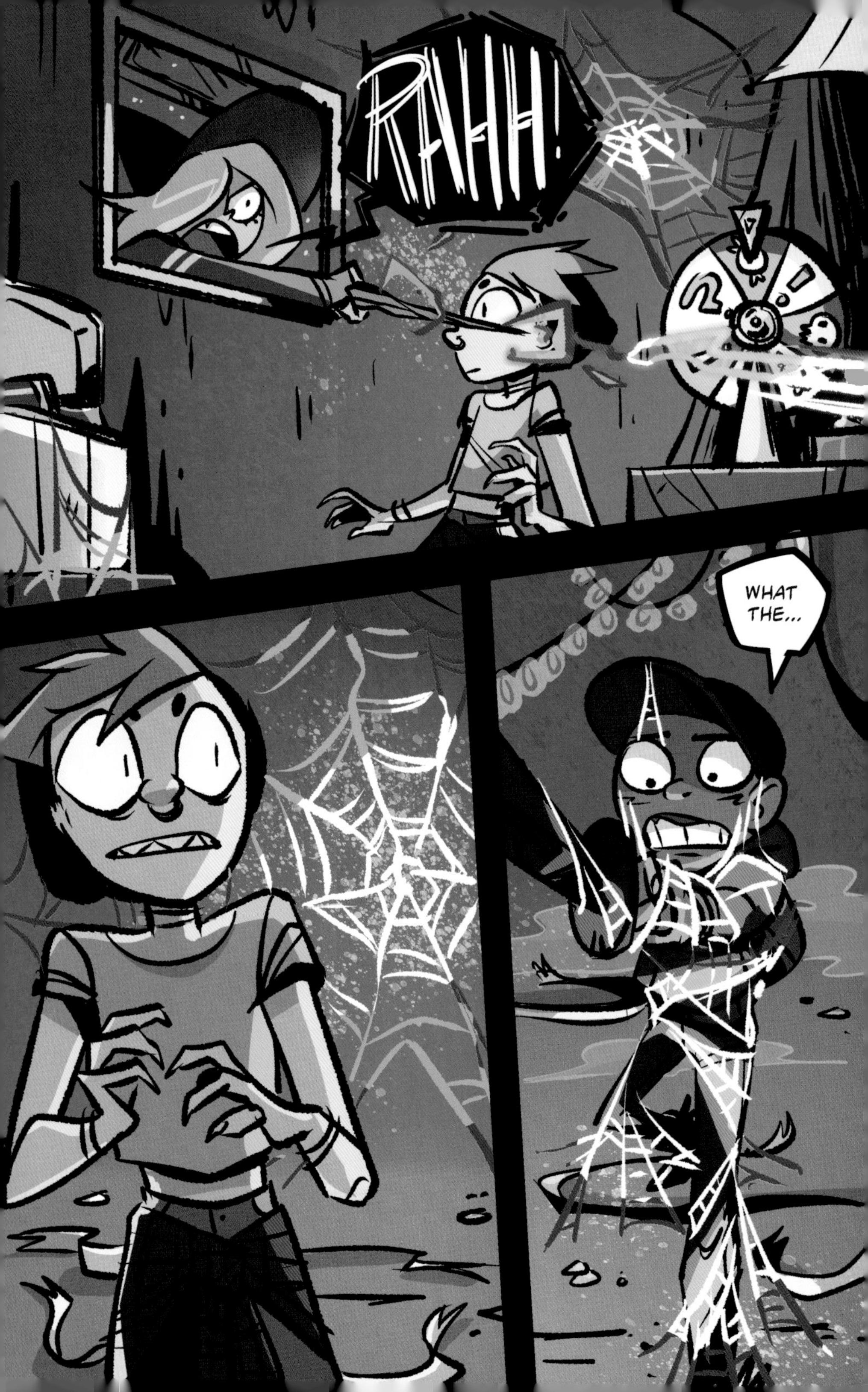
RAHH!
WHAT THE...

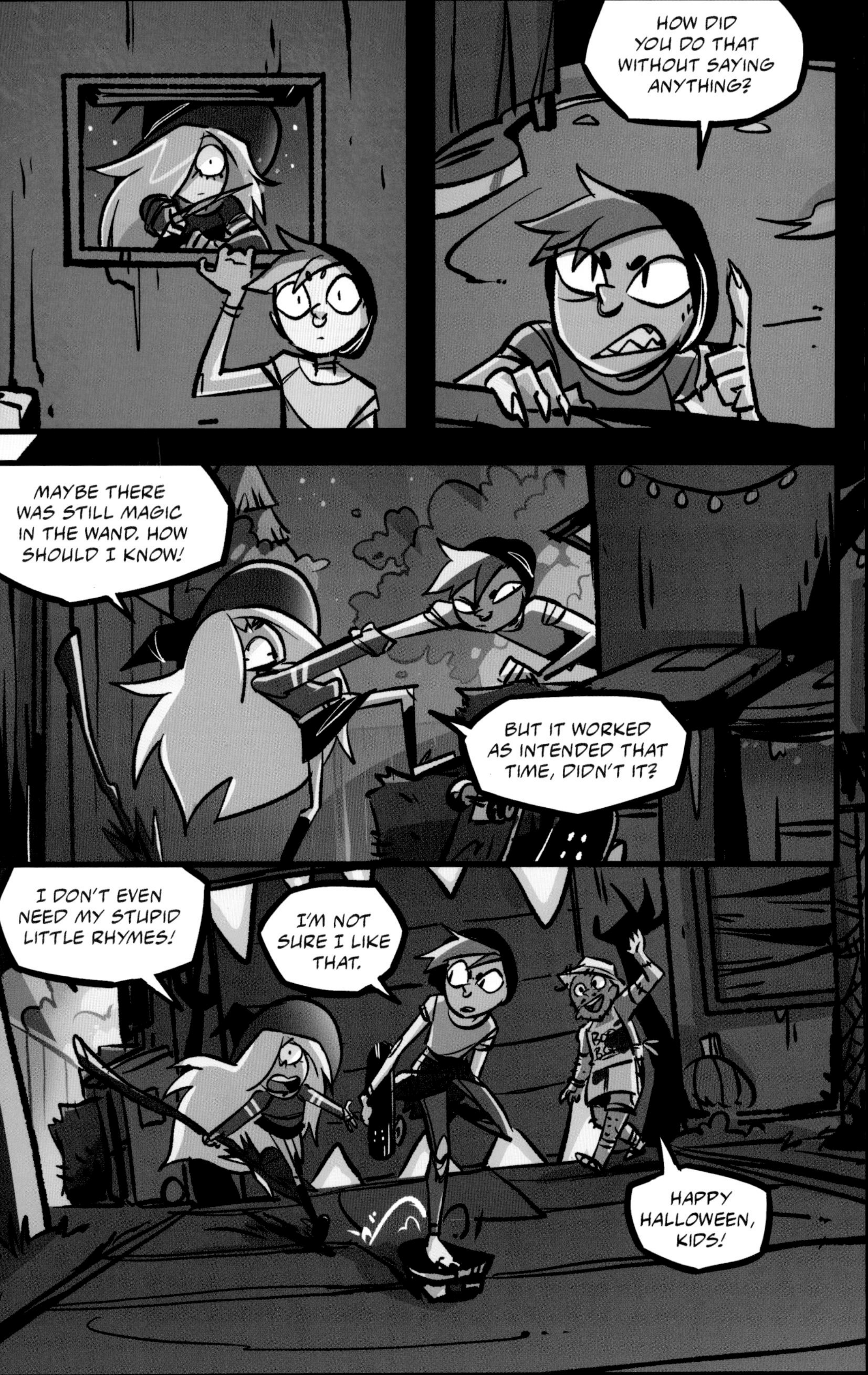
HOW DID YOU DO THAT WITHOUT SAYING ANYTHING?
MAYBE THERE WAS STILL MAGIC IN THE WAND. HOW SHOULD I KNOW!
BUT IT WORKED AS INTENDED THAT TIME, DIDN'T IT?
I DON'T EVEN NEED MY STUPID LITTLE RHYMES!
I'M NOT SURE I LIKE THAT.
HAPPY HALLOWEEN, KIDS!

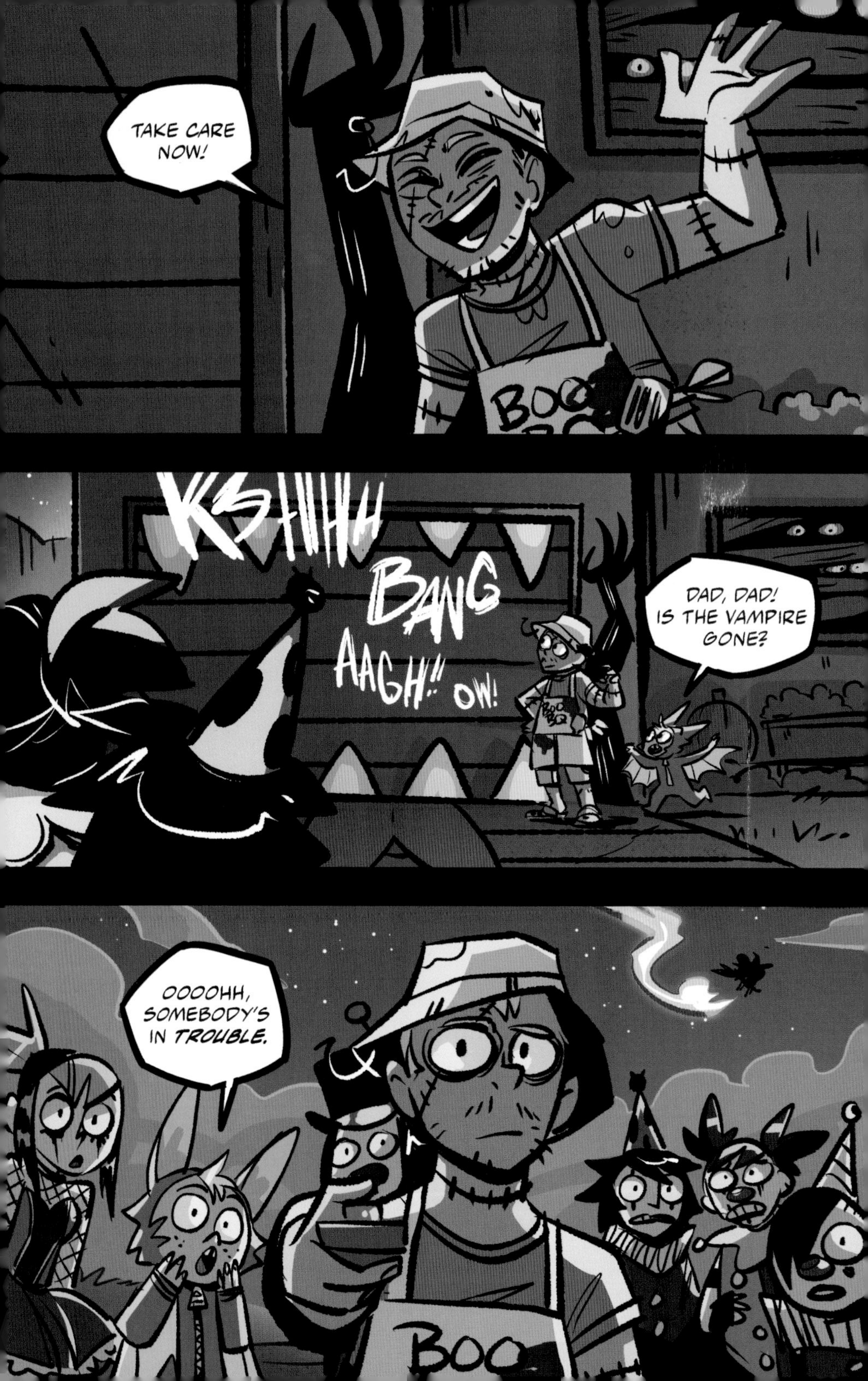
TAKE CARE NOW!
BOO
KSHHHH
BANG
AAGH!! OW!
DAD, DAD! IS THE VAMPIRE GONE?
OOOOHH, SOMEBODY'S IN *TROUBLE.*
BOO

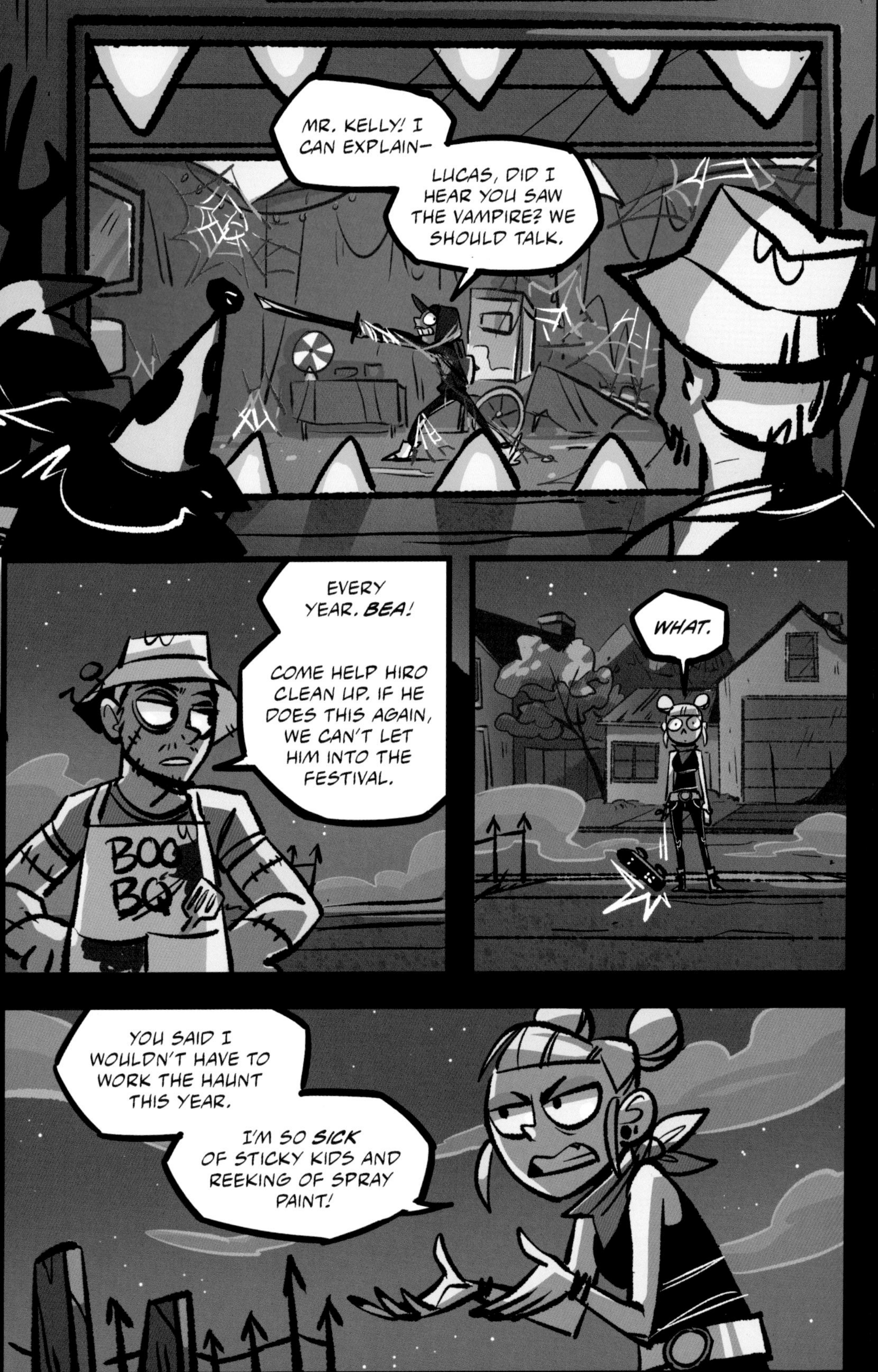
MR. KELLY! I CAN EXPLAIN—
LUCAS, DID I HEAR YOU SAW THE VAMPIRE? WE SHOULD TALK.
EVERY YEAR. BEA!
COME HELP HIRO CLEAN UP. IF HE DOES THIS AGAIN, WE CAN'T LET HIM INTO THE FESTIVAL.
BOO BOO
WHAT.
YOU SAID I WOULDN'T HAVE TO WORK THE HAUNT THIS YEAR.
I'M SO SICK OF STICKY KIDS AND REEKING OF SPRAY PAINT!

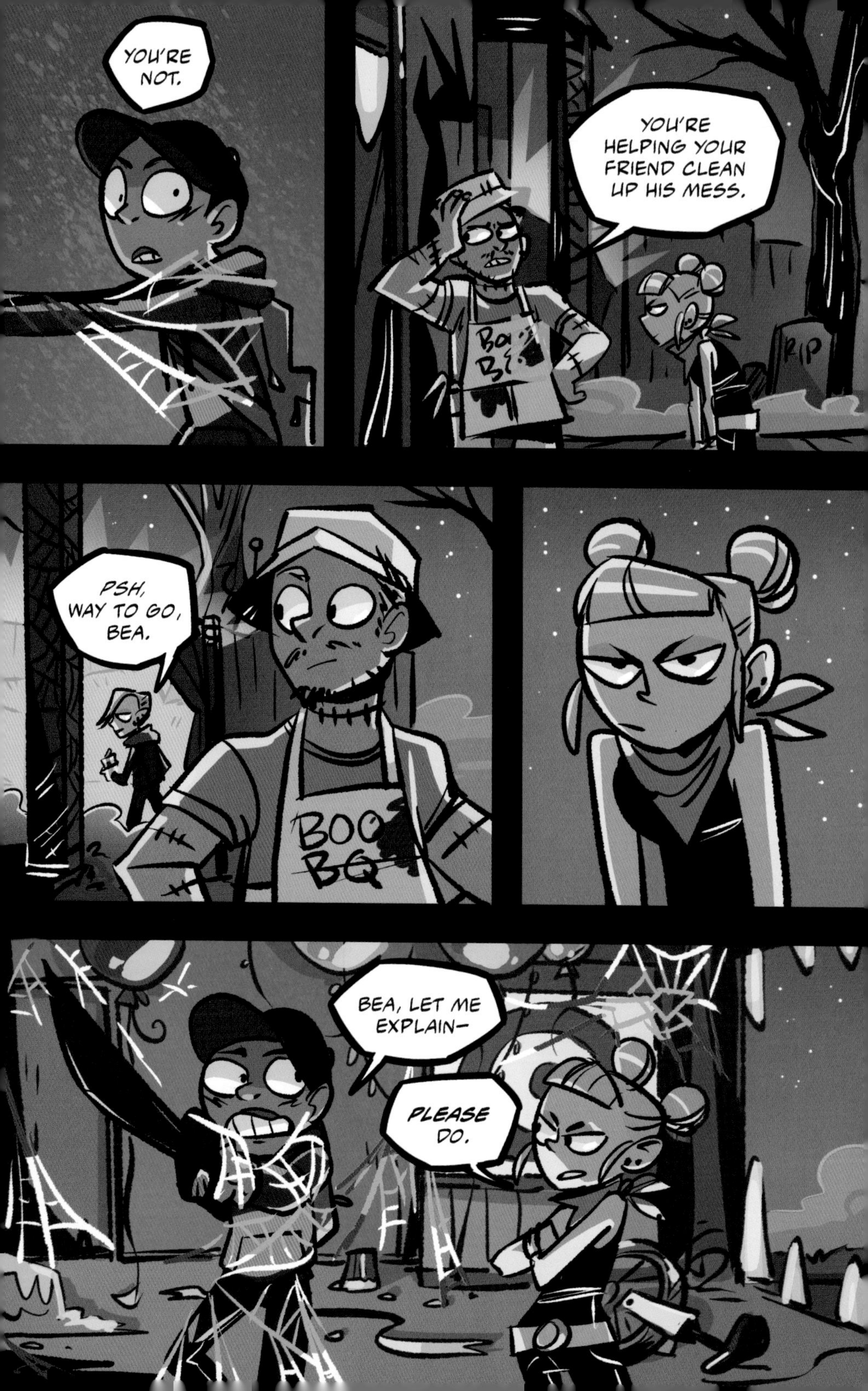
YOU'RE NOT.
YOU'RE HELPING YOUR FRIEND CLEAN UP HIS MESS.
RIP
BOO BQ
PSH, WAY TO GO, BEA.
BOO BQ
BEA, LET ME EXPLAIN—
PLEASE DO.

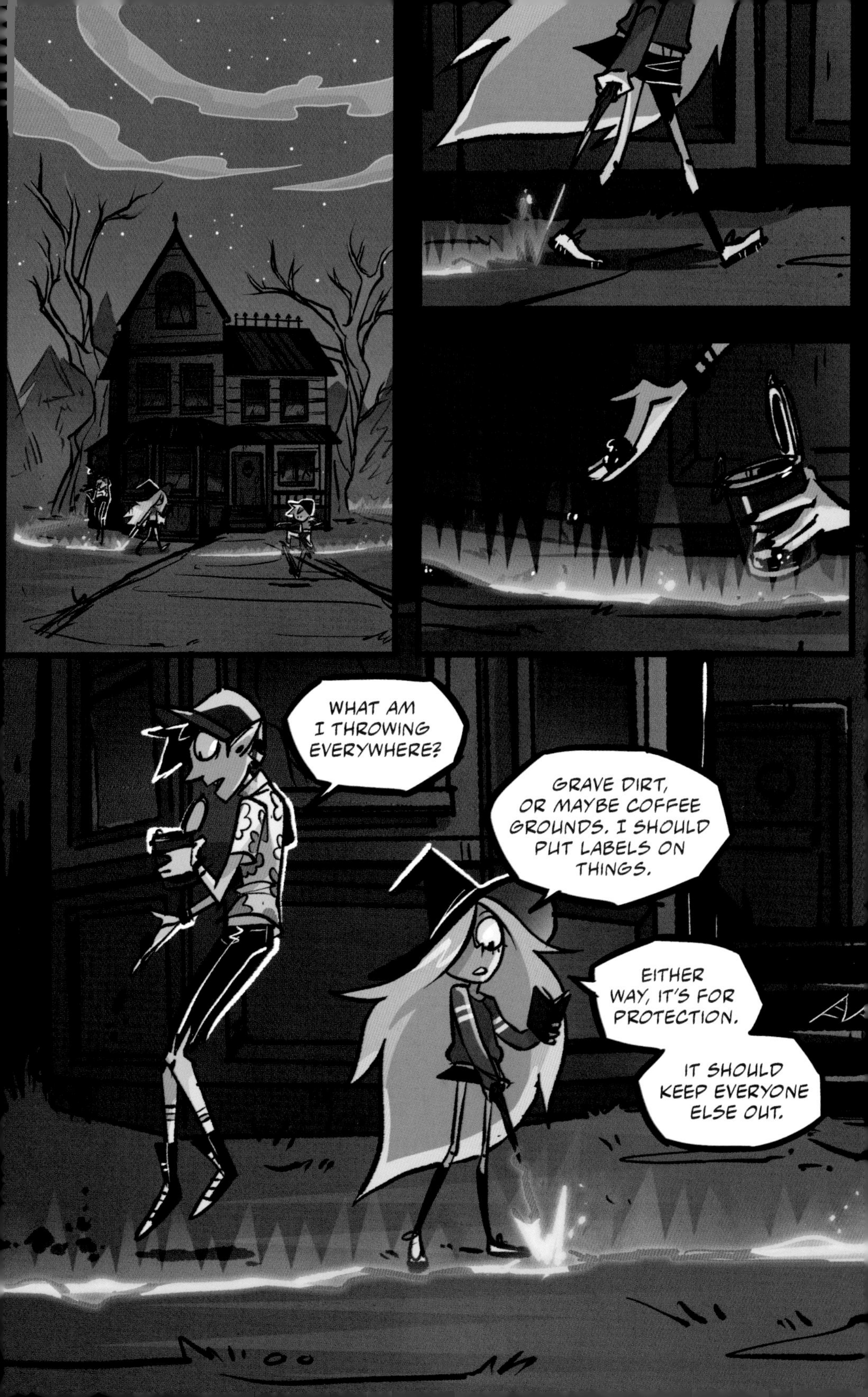
WHAT AM I THROWING EVERYWHERE?
GRAVE DIRT, OR MAYBE COFFEE GROUNDS. I SHOULD PUT LABELS ON THINGS.
EITHER WAY, IT'S FOR PROTECTION.
IT SHOULD KEEP EVERYONE ELSE OUT.

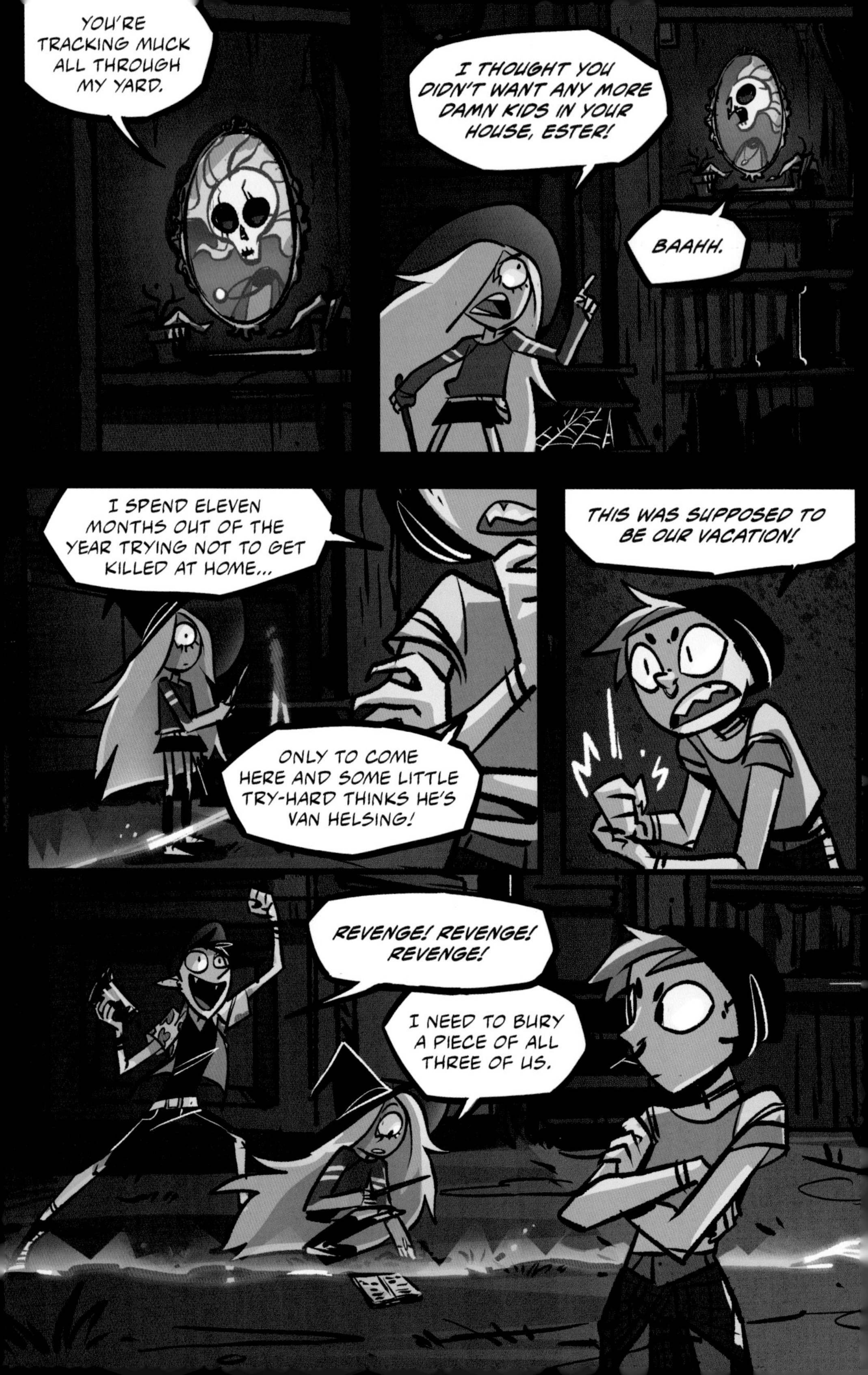
YOU'RE TRACKING MUCK ALL THROUGH MY YARD.
I THOUGHT YOU DIDN'T WANT ANY MORE DAMN KIDS IN YOUR HOUSE, ESTER!
BAAHH.
I SPEND ELEVEN MONTHS OUT OF THE YEAR TRYING NOT TO GET KILLED AT HOME...
ONLY TO COME HERE AND SOME LITTLE TRY-HARD THINKS HE'S VAN HELSING!
THIS WAS SUPPOSED TO BE OUR VACATION!
REVENGE! REVENGE! REVENGE!
I NEED TO BURY A PIECE OF ALL THREE OF US.

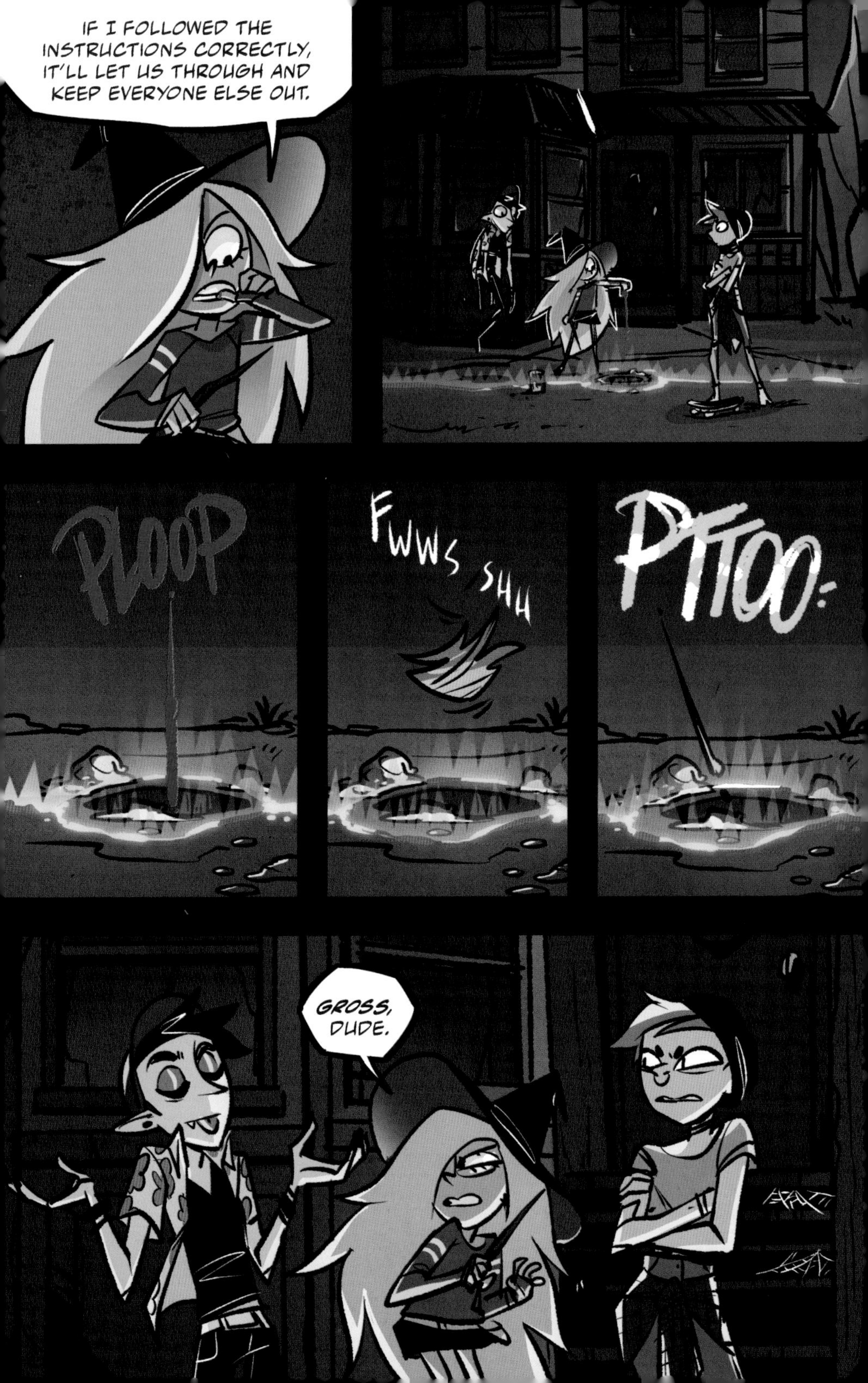
IF I FOLLOWED THE INSTRUCTIONS CORRECTLY, IT'LL LET US THROUGH AND KEEP EVERYONE ELSE OUT.
PLOOP
FWWS SHH
PTOO
GROSS, DUDE.

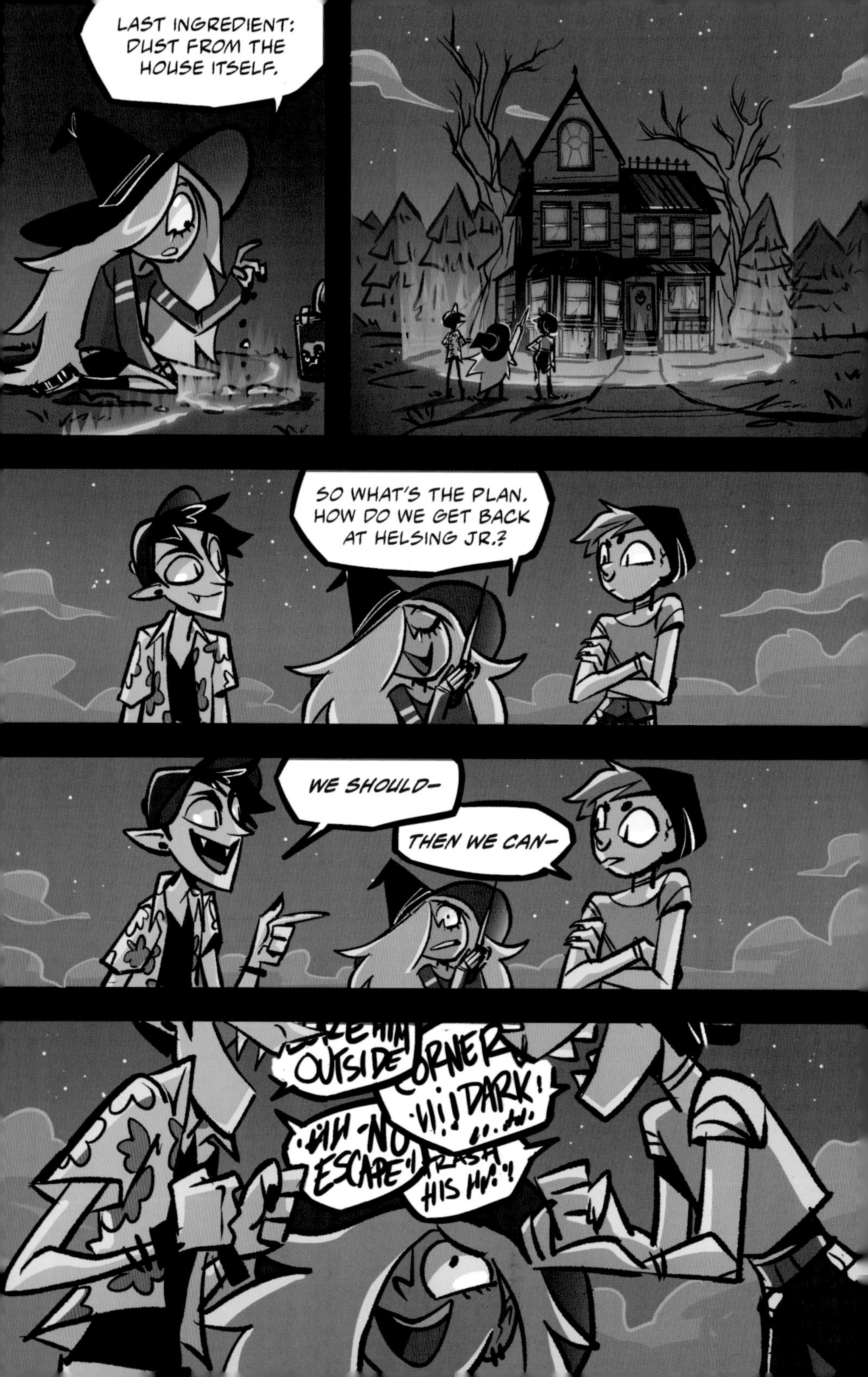
LAST INGREDIENT: DUST FROM THE HOUSE ITSELF.
SO WHAT'S THE PLAN. HOW DO WE GET BACK AT HELSING JR.?
WE SHOULD—
THEN WE CAN—
OUTSIDE
CORNER
DARK!
NO ESCAPE
HIS

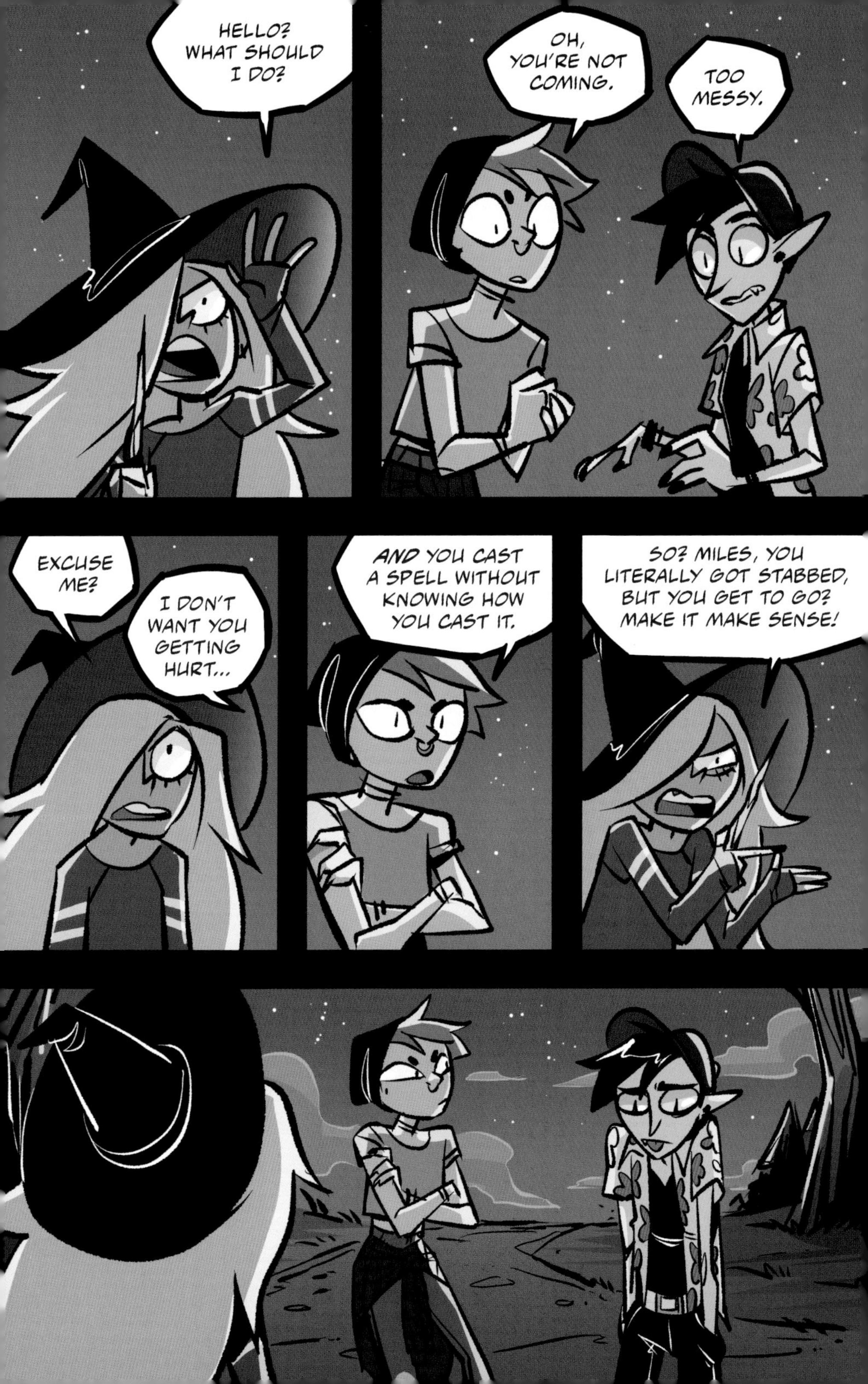
HELLO? WHAT SHOULD I DO?
OH, YOU'RE NOT COMING.
TOO MESSY.
EXCUSE ME?
I DON'T WANT YOU GETTING HURT...
AND YOU CAST A SPELL WITHOUT KNOWING HOW YOU CAST IT.
SO? MILES, YOU LITERALLY GOT STABBED, BUT YOU GET TO GO? MAKE IT MAKE SENSE!

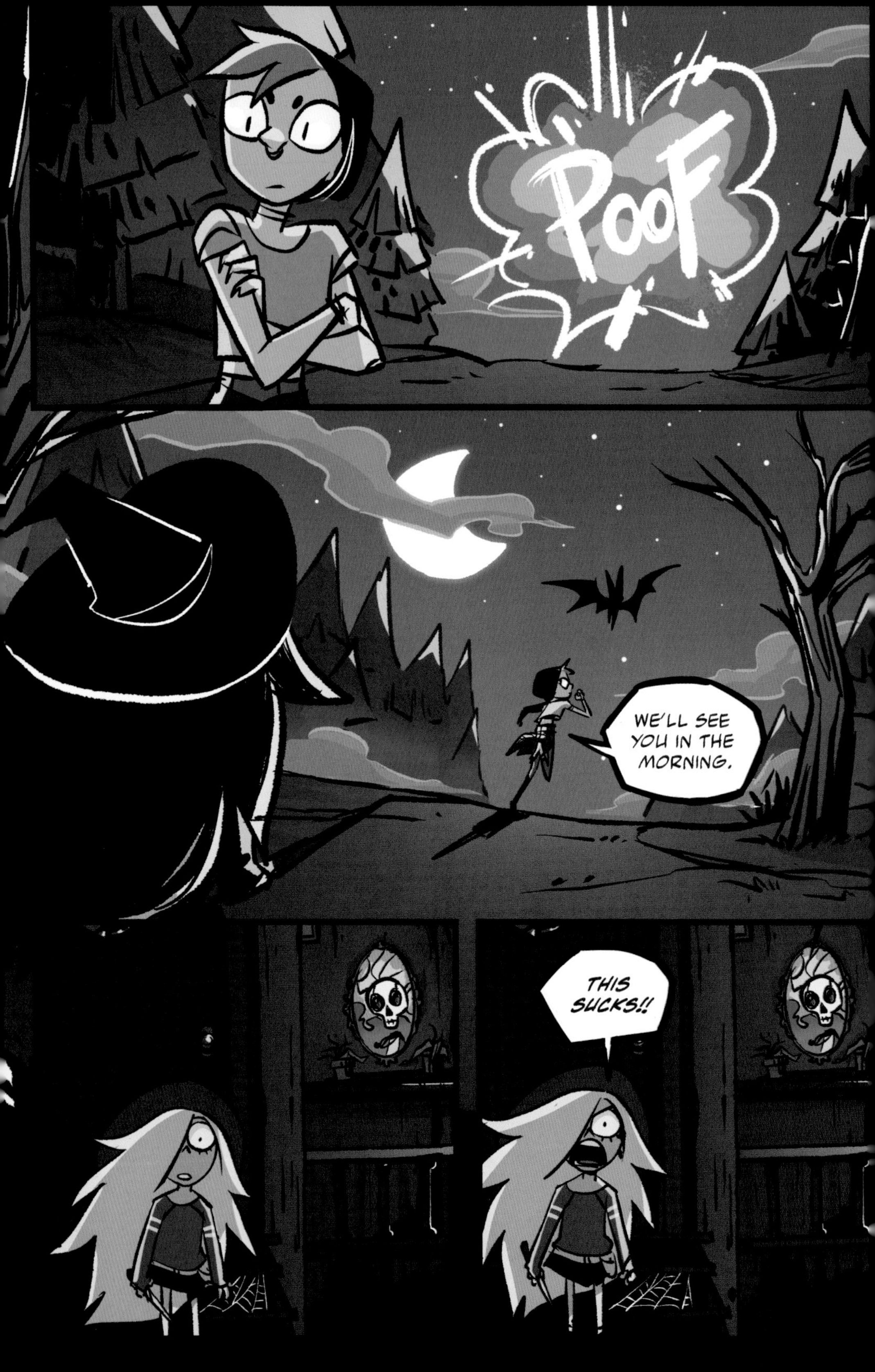
POOF
WE'LL SEE YOU IN THE MORNING.
THIS SUCKS!!

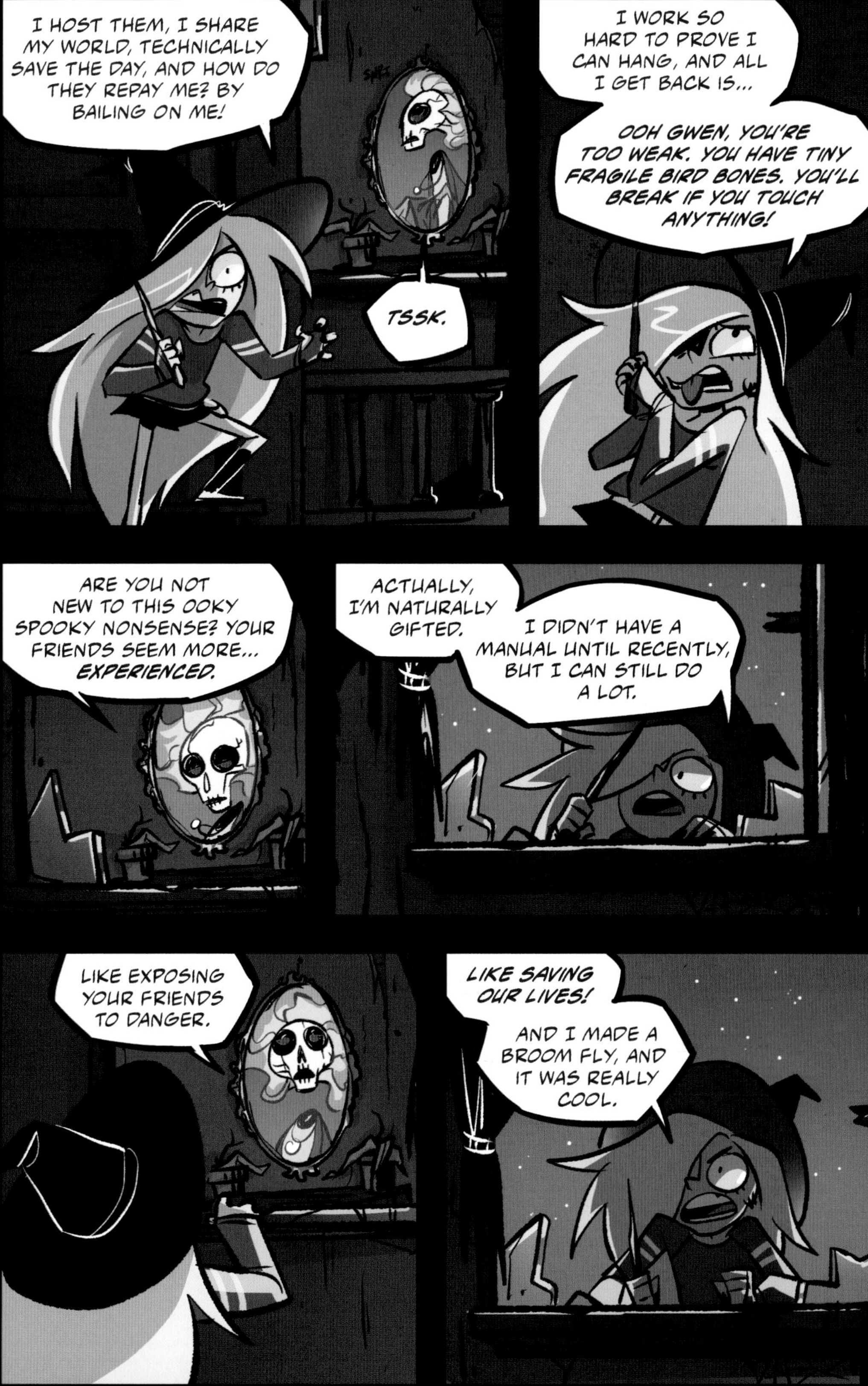
I HOST THEM, I SHARE MY WORLD, TECHNICALLY SAVE THE DAY, AND HOW DO THEY REPAY ME? BY BAILING ON ME!
TSSK.
I WORK SO HARD TO PROVE I CAN HANG, AND ALL I GET BACK IS...
OOH GWEN, YOU'RE TOO WEAK. YOU HAVE TINY FRAGILE BIRD BONES. YOU'LL BREAK IF YOU TOUCH ANYTHING!
ARE YOU NOT NEW TO THIS OOKY SPOOKY NONSENSE? YOUR FRIENDS SEEM MORE... EXPERIENCED.
ACTUALLY, I'M NATURALLY GIFTED.
I DIDN'T HAVE A MANUAL UNTIL RECENTLY, BUT I CAN STILL DO A LOT.
LIKE EXPOSING YOUR FRIENDS TO DANGER.
LIKE SAVING OUR LIVES!
AND I MADE A BROOM FLY, AND IT WAS REALLY COOL.

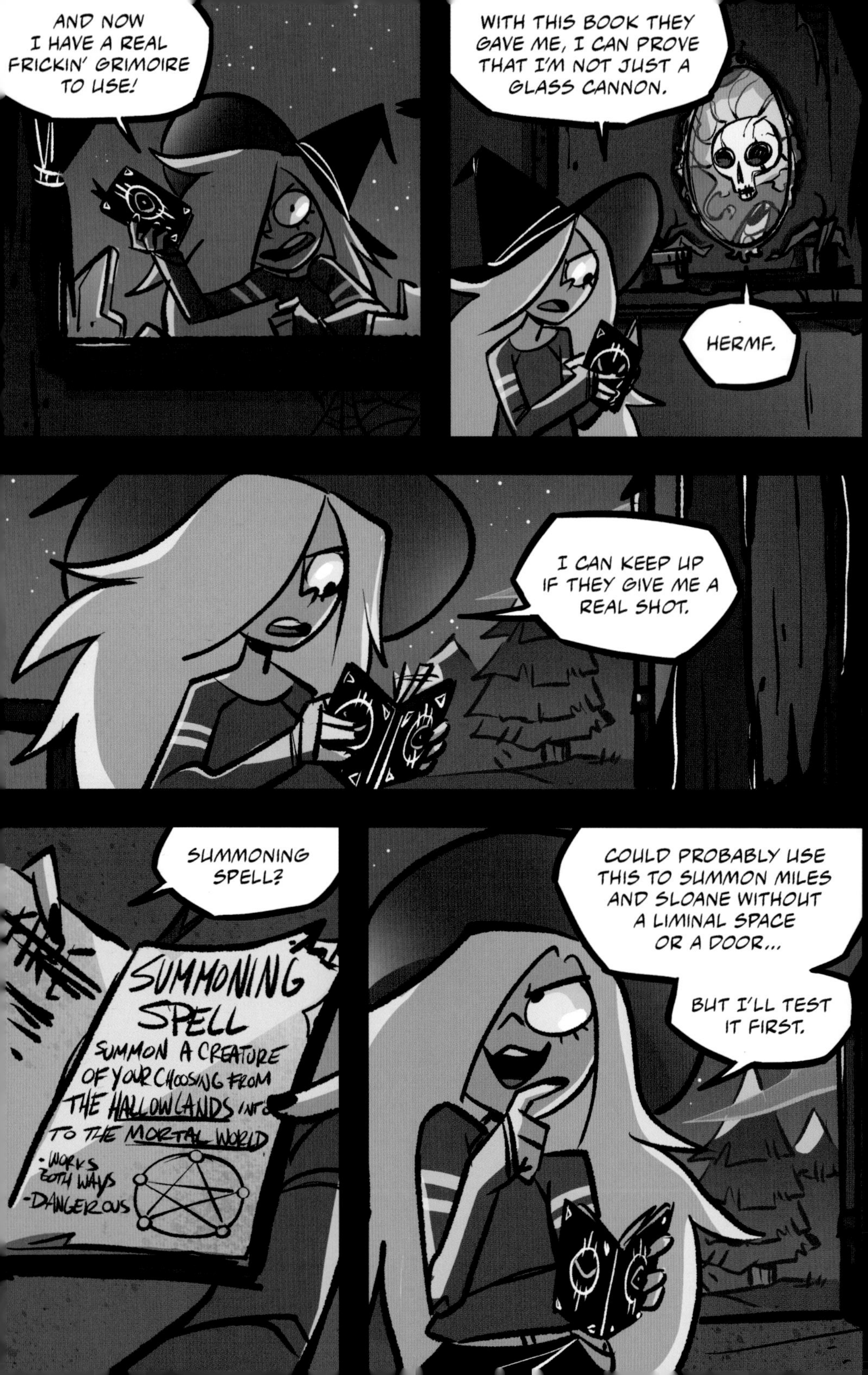
AND NOW I HAVE A REAL FRICKIN' GRIMOIRE TO USE!
WITH THIS BOOK THEY GAVE ME, I CAN PROVE THAT I'M NOT JUST A GLASS CANNON.
HERMF.
I CAN KEEP UP IF THEY GIVE ME A REAL SHOT.
SUMMONING SPELL?
SUMMONING SPELL
SUMMON A CREATURE OF YOUR CHOOSING FROM THE HALLOWLANDS INTO TO THE MORTAL WORLD
-WORKS BOTH WAYS
-DANGEROUS
COULD PROBABLY USE THIS TO SUMMON MILES AND SLOANE WITHOUT A LIMINAL SPACE OR A DOOR...
BUT I'LL TEST IT FIRST.

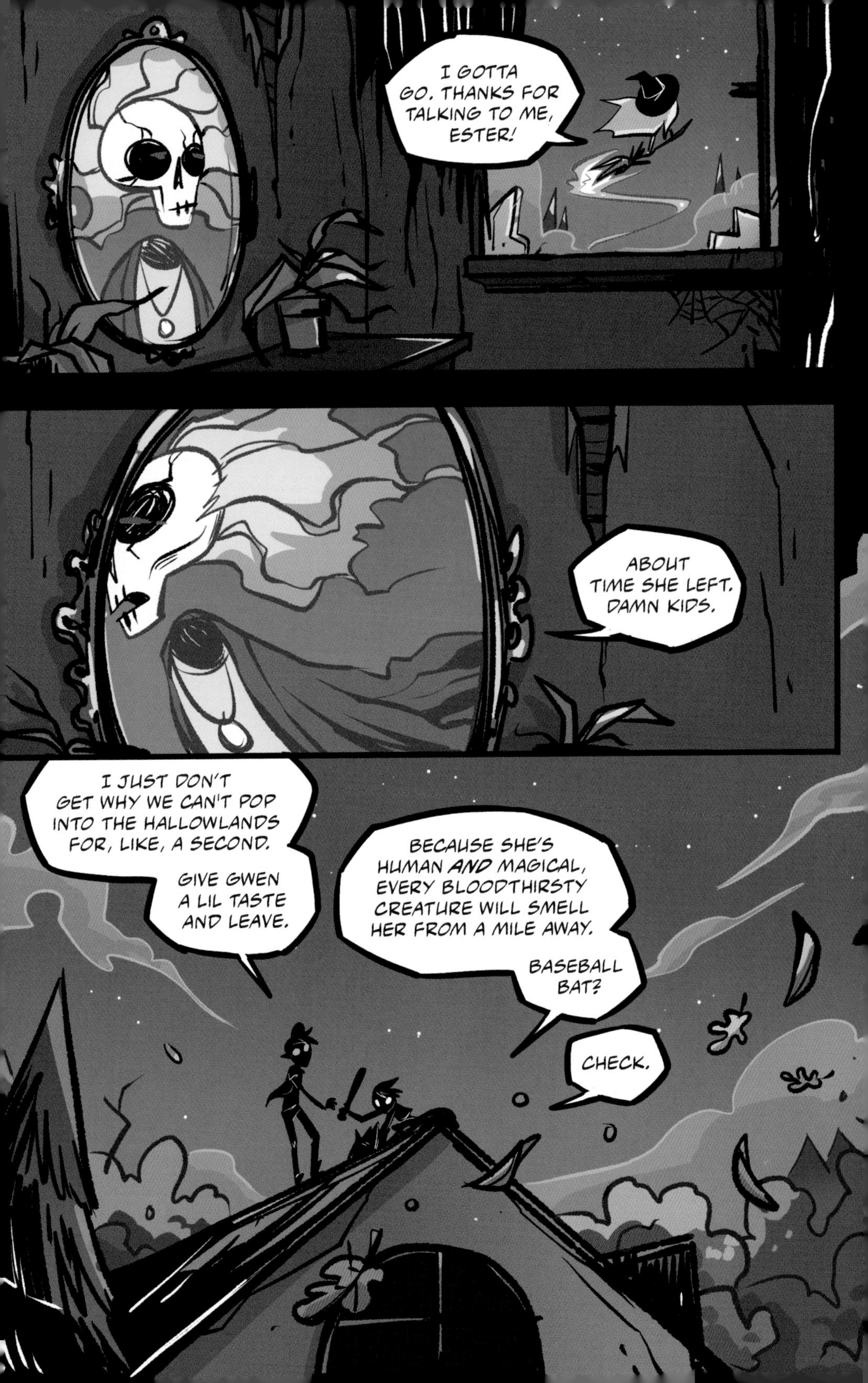
I GOTTA GO. THANKS FOR TALKING TO ME, ESTER!
ABOUT TIME SHE LEFT. DAMN KIDS.
I JUST DON'T GET WHY WE CAN'T POP INTO THE HALLOWLANDS FOR, LIKE, A SECOND.
GIVE GWEN A LIL TASTE AND LEAVE.
BECAUSE SHE'S HUMAN AND MAGICAL, EVERY BLOODTHIRSTY CREATURE WILL SMELL HER FROM A MILE AWAY.
BASEBALL BAT?
CHECK.

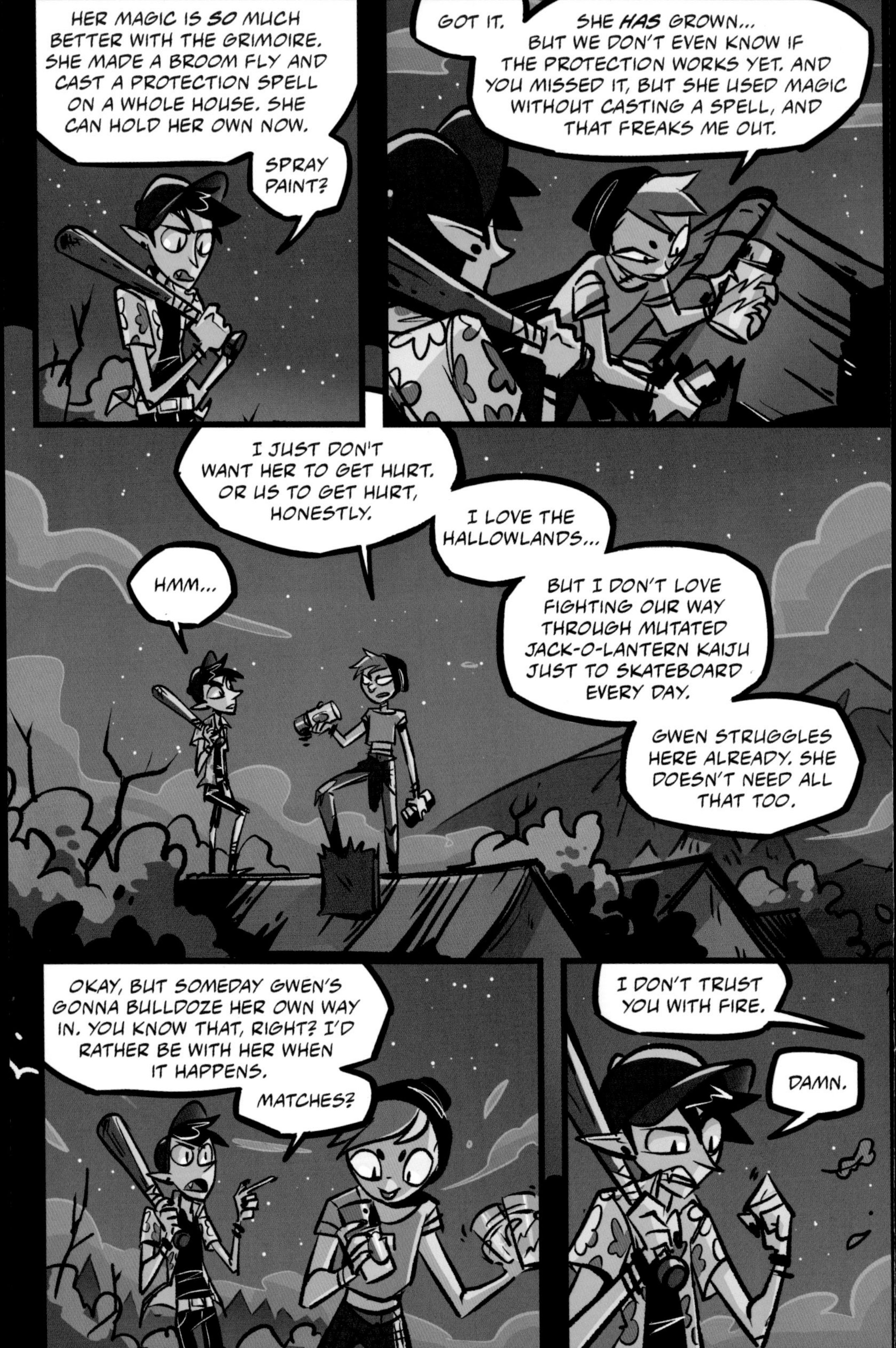
HER MAGIC IS SO MUCH BETTER WITH THE GRIMOIRE. SHE MADE A BROOM FLY AND CAST A PROTECTION SPELL ON A WHOLE HOUSE. SHE CAN HOLD HER OWN NOW.
SPRAY PAINT?
GOT IT.
SHE HAS GROWN... BUT WE DON'T EVEN KNOW IF THE PROTECTION WORKS YET. AND YOU MISSED IT, BUT SHE USED MAGIC WITHOUT CASTING A SPELL, AND THAT FREAKS ME OUT.
I JUST DON'T WANT HER TO GET HURT. OR US TO GET HURT, HONESTLY.
HMM...
I LOVE THE HALLOWLANDS...
BUT I DON'T LOVE FIGHTING OUR WAY THROUGH MUTATED JACK-O-LANTERN KAIJU JUST TO SKATEBOARD EVERY DAY.
GWEN STRUGGLES HERE ALREADY. SHE DOESN'T NEED ALL THAT TOO.
OKAY, BUT SOMEDAY GWEN'S GONNA BULLDOZE HER OWN WAY IN. YOU KNOW THAT, RIGHT? I'D RATHER BE WITH HER WHEN IT HAPPENS.
MATCHES?
I DON'T TRUST YOU WITH FIRE.
DAMN.

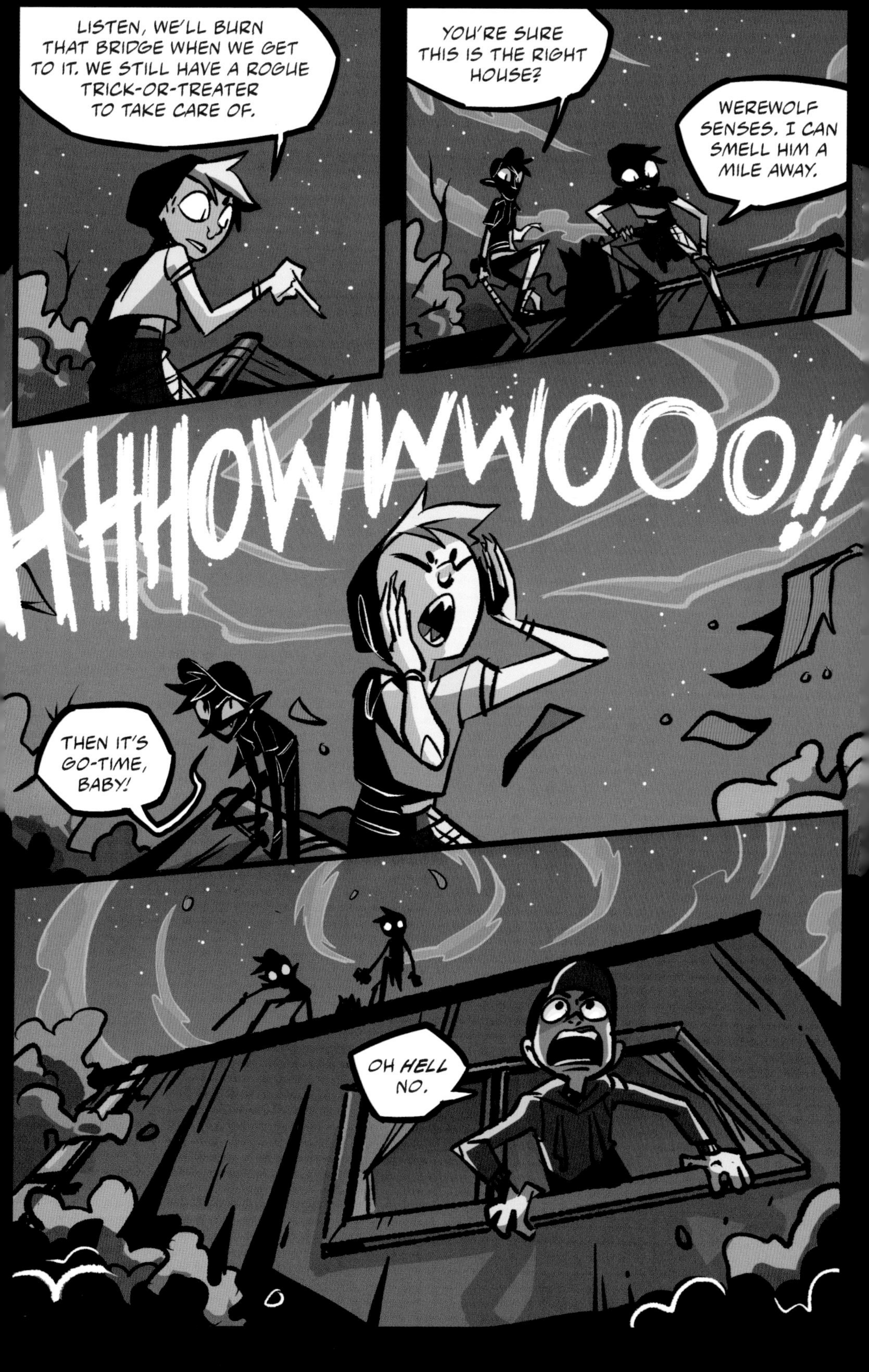
LISTEN, WE'LL BURN THAT BRIDGE WHEN WE GET TO IT. WE STILL HAVE A ROGUE TRICK-OR-TREATER TO TAKE CARE OF.
YOU'RE SURE THIS IS THE RIGHT HOUSE?
WEREWOLF SENSES. I CAN SMELL HIM A MILE AWAY.
HHHOWWWOOO!!
THEN IT'S GO-TIME, BABY!
OH HELL NO.

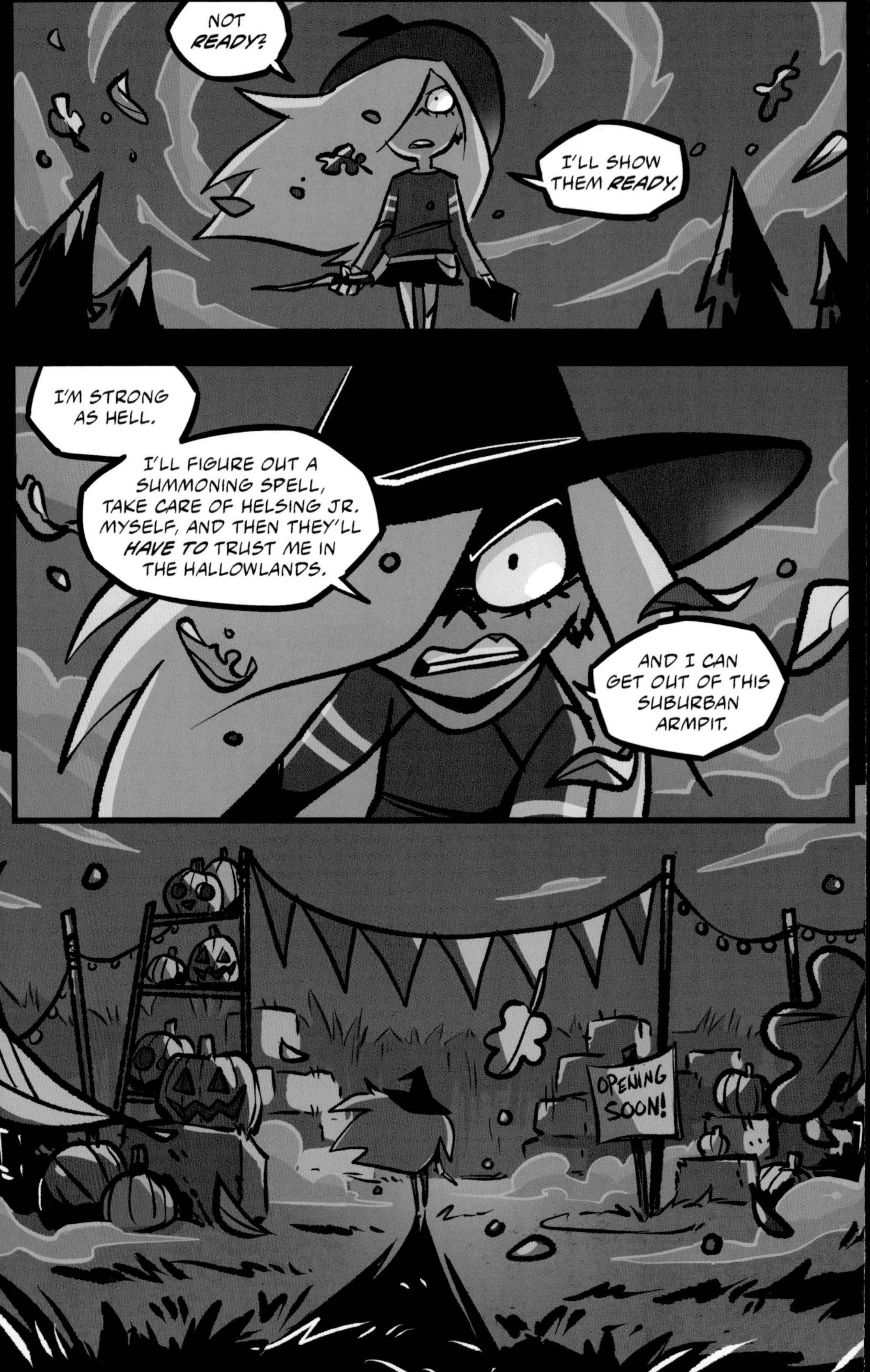
NOT READY?
I'LL SHOW THEM READY.
I'M STRONG AS HELL.
I'LL FIGURE OUT A SUMMONING SPELL, TAKE CARE OF HELSING JR. MYSELF, AND THEN THEY'LL HAVE TO TRUST ME IN THE HALLOWLANDS.
AND I CAN GET OUT OF THIS SUBURBAN ARMPIT.
OPENING SOON!

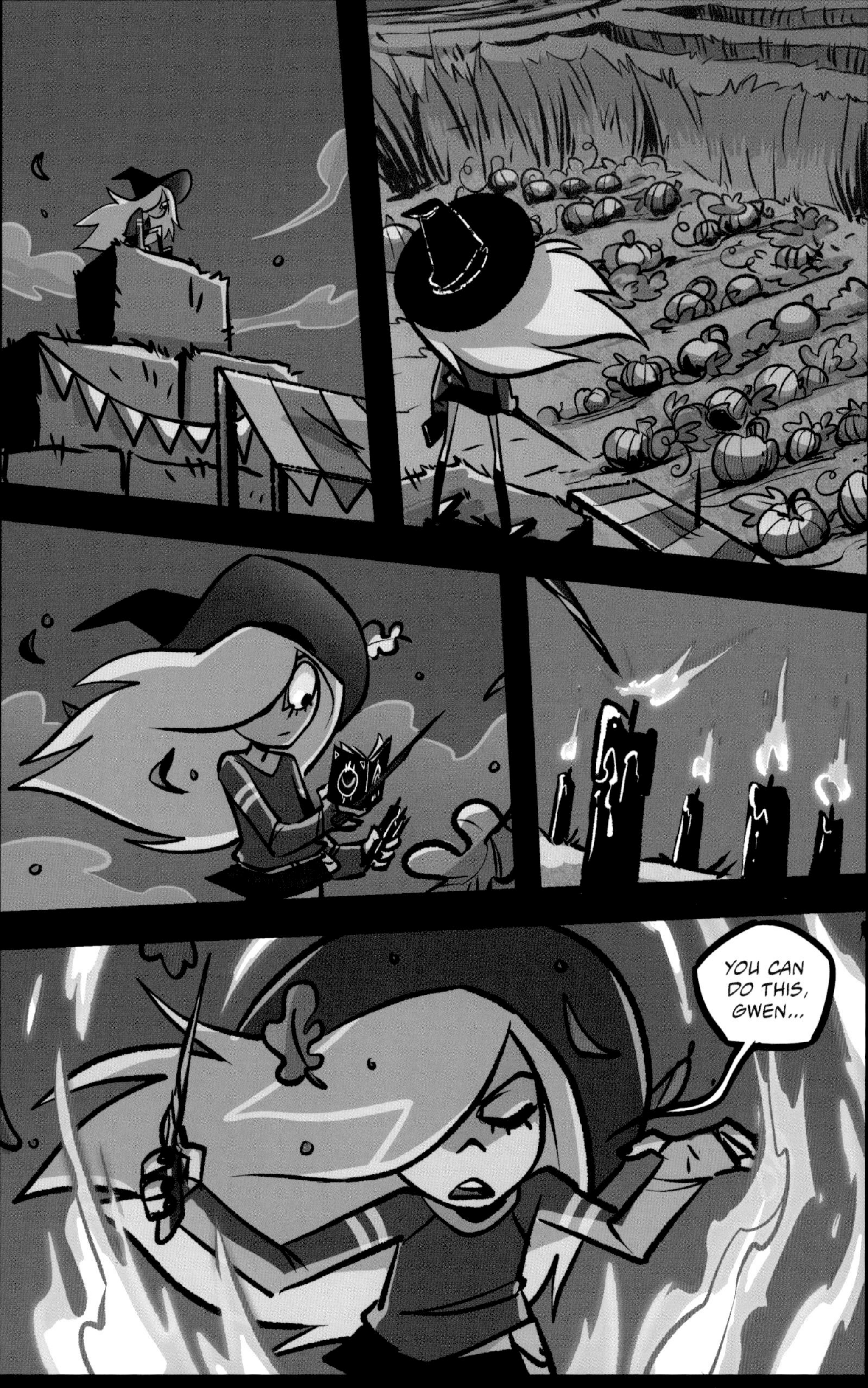
YOU CAN DO THIS, GWEN...

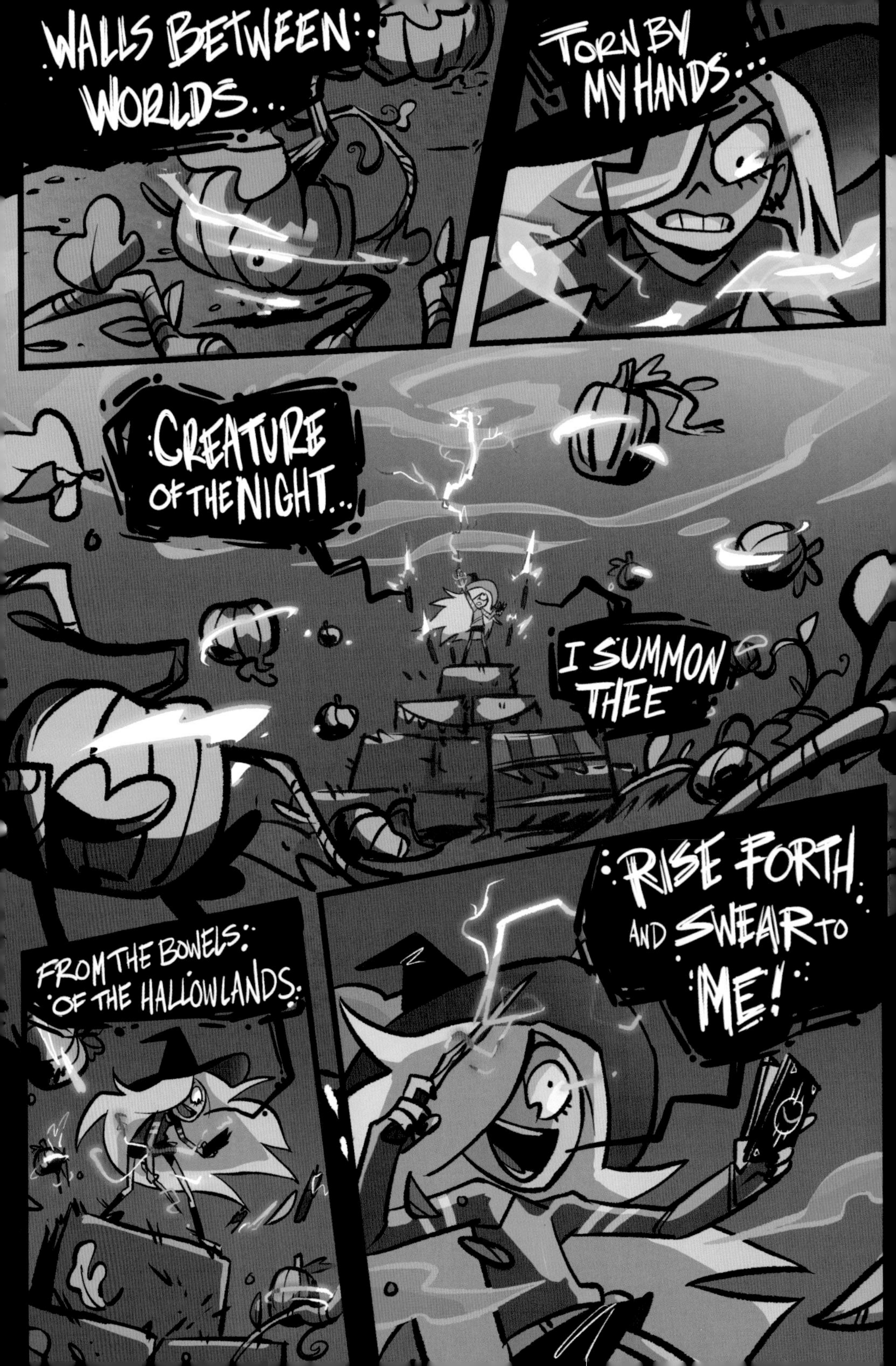
WALLS BETWEEN WORLDS...
TORN BY MY HANDS...
CREATURE OF THE NIGHT...
I SUMMON THEE
FROM THE BOWELS OF THE HALLOWLANDS
RISE FORTH AND SWEAR TO ME!

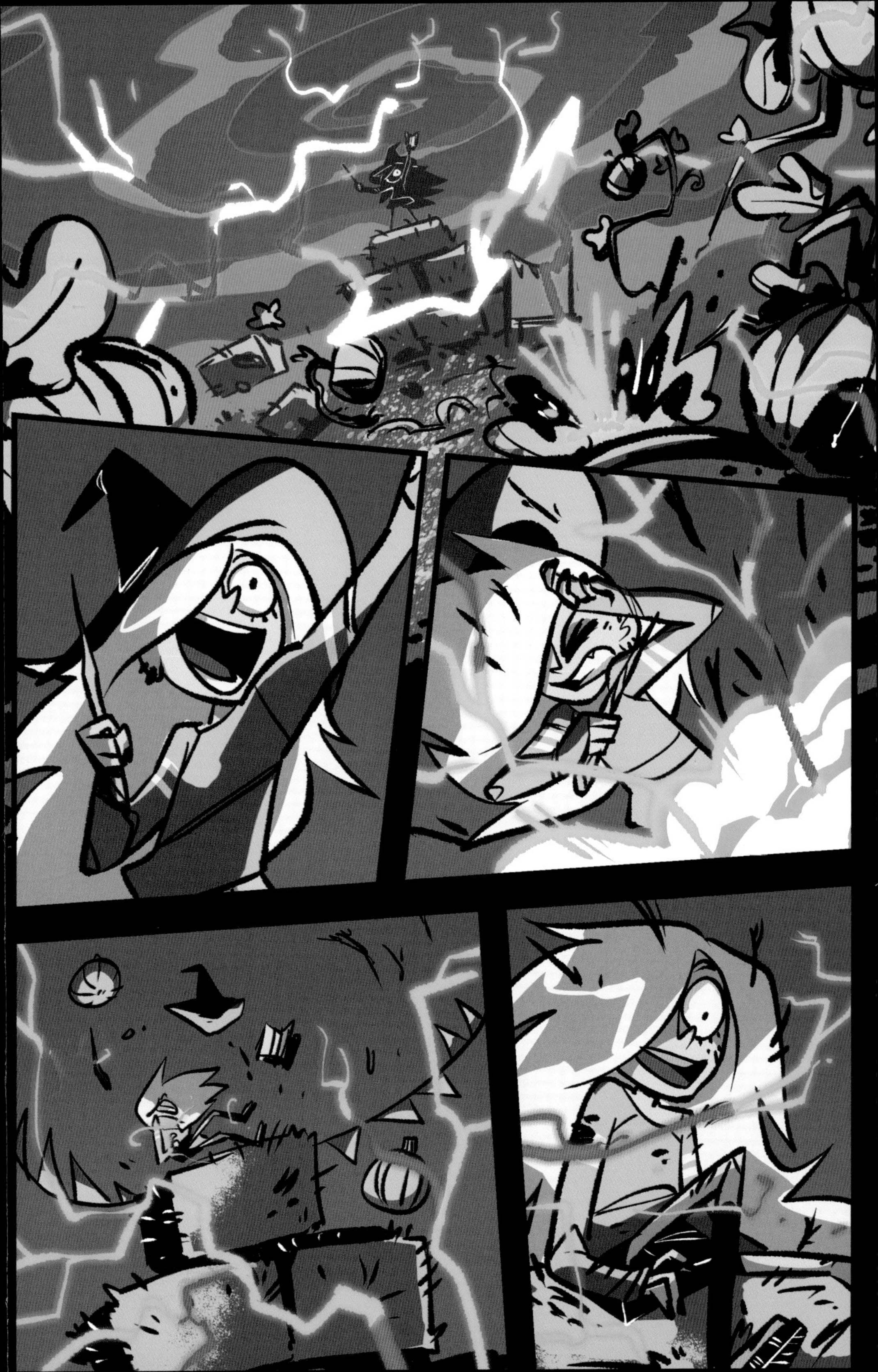

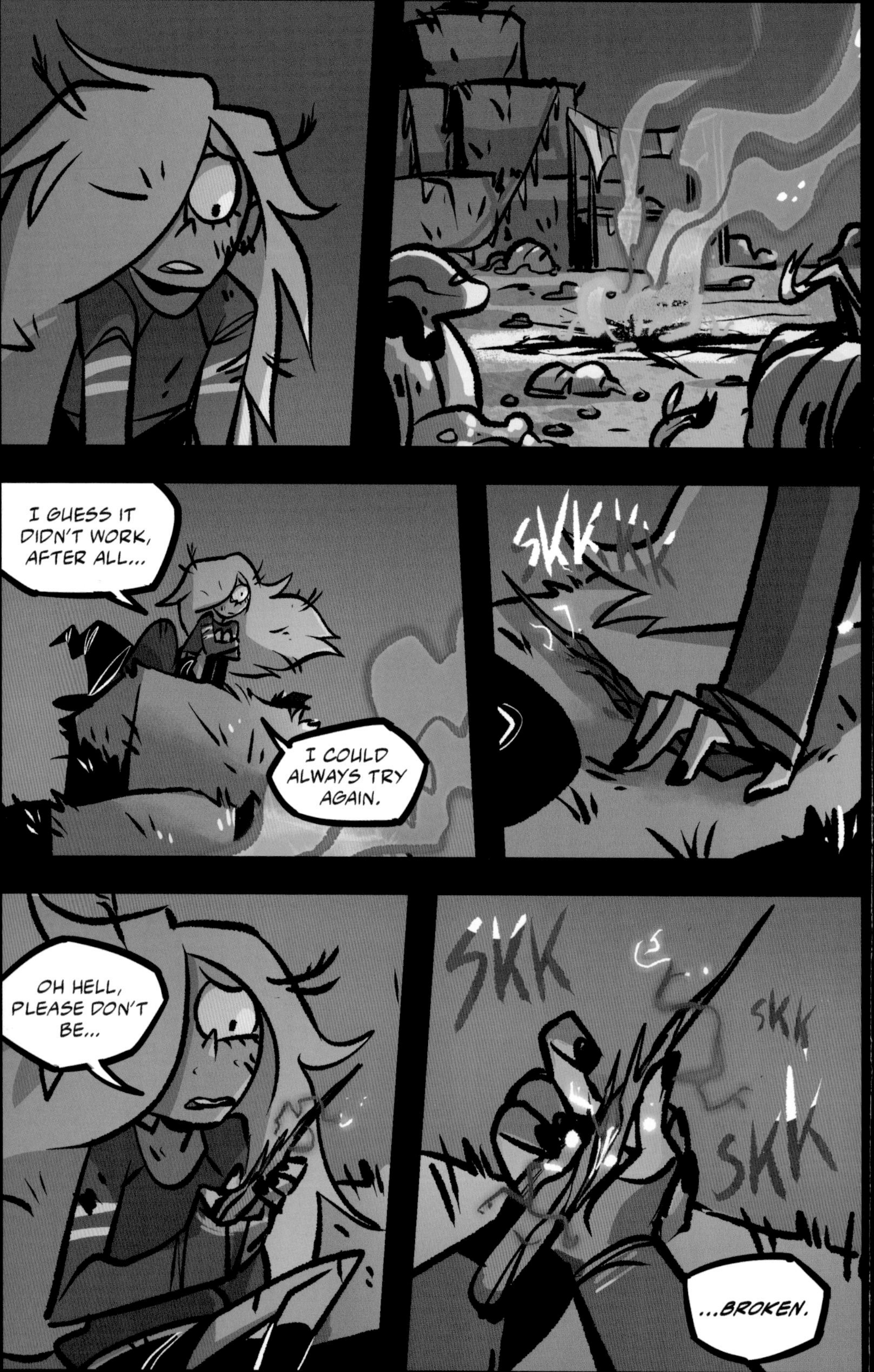
I GUESS IT DIDN'T WORK, AFTER ALL...
I COULD ALWAYS TRY AGAIN.
SKK
OH HELL, PLEASE DON'T BE...
SKK
SKK
SKK
...BROKEN.

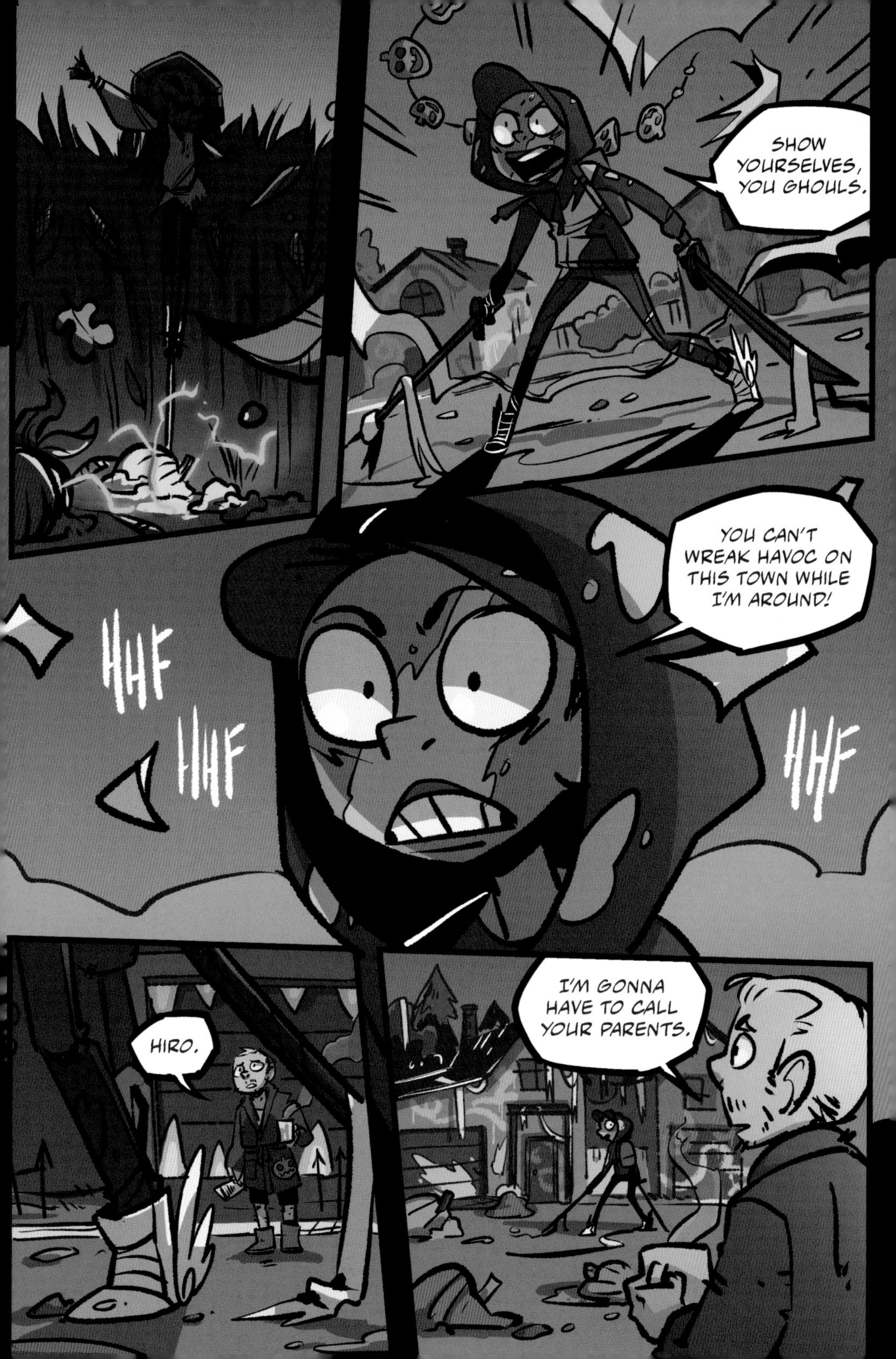
SHOW YOURSELVES, YOU GHOULS.
YOU CAN'T WREAK HAVOC ON THIS TOWN WHILE I'M AROUND!
HHF
HHF
HHF
HIRO.
I'M GONNA HAVE TO CALL YOUR PARENTS.

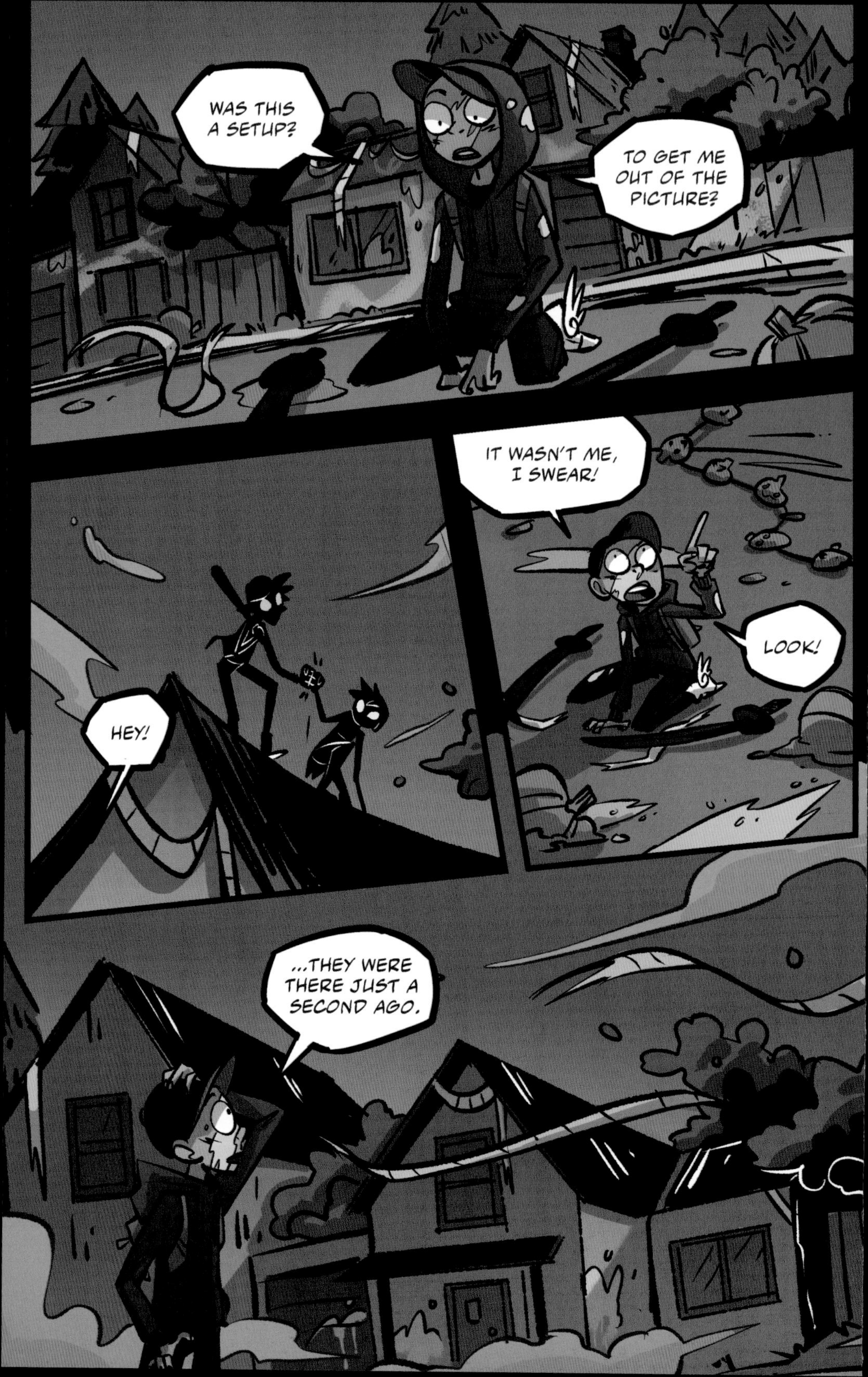
WAS THIS A SETUP?
TO GET ME OUT OF THE PICTURE?
HEY!
IT WASN'T ME, I SWEAR!
LOOK!
...THEY WERE THERE JUST A SECOND AGO.

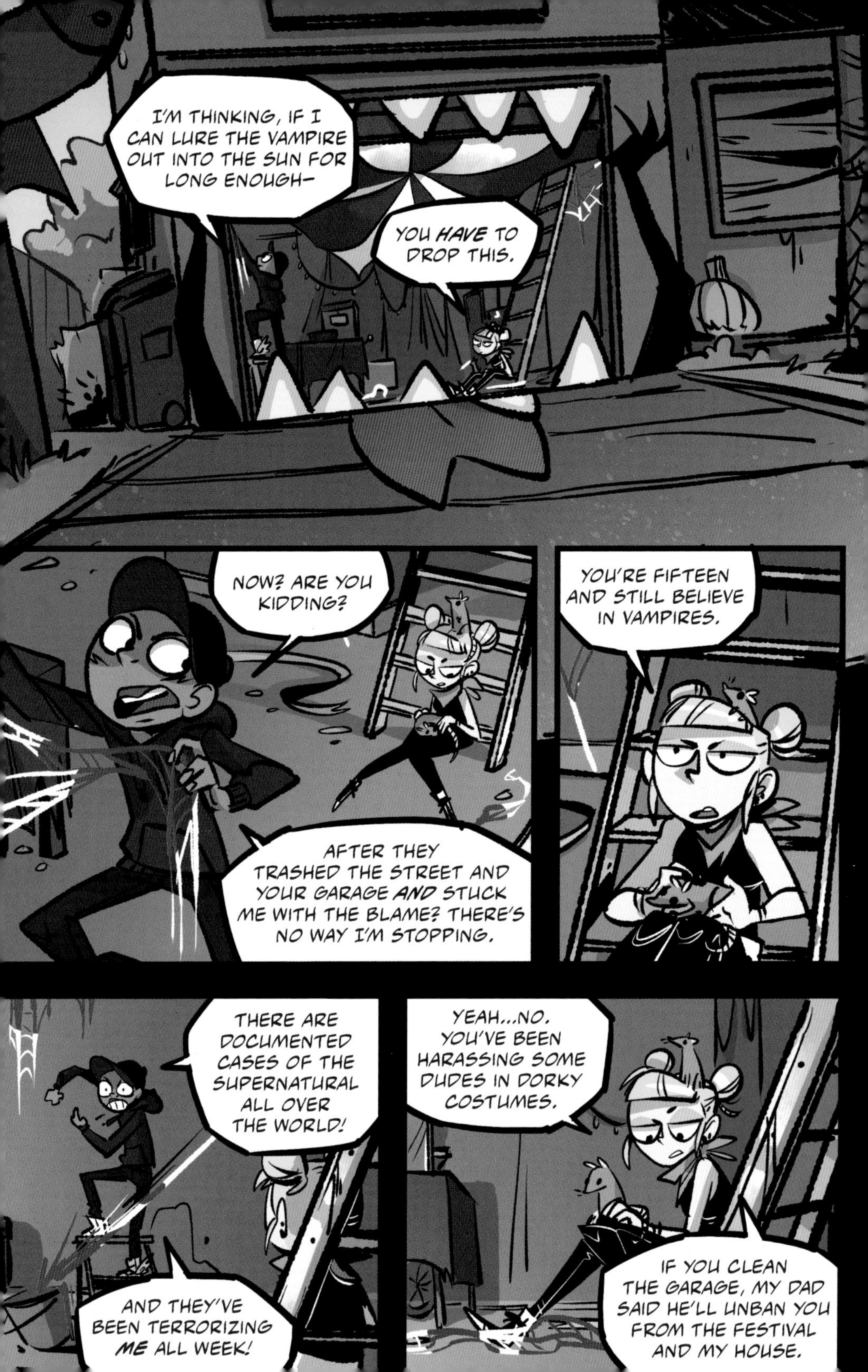
I'M THINKING, IF I CAN LURE THE VAMPIRE OUT INTO THE SUN FOR LONG ENOUGH–
YOU *HAVE* TO DROP THIS.
NOW? ARE YOU KIDDING?
AFTER THEY TRASHED THE STREET AND YOUR GARAGE *AND* STUCK ME WITH THE BLAME? THERE'S NO WAY I'M STOPPING.
YOU'RE FIFTEEN AND STILL BELIEVE IN VAMPIRES.
THERE ARE DOCUMENTED CASES OF THE SUPERNATURAL ALL OVER THE WORLD!
AND THEY'VE BEEN TERRORIZING *ME* ALL WEEK!
YEAH...NO. YOU'VE BEEN HARASSING SOME DUDES IN DORKY COSTUMES.
IF YOU CLEAN THE GARAGE, MY DAD SAID HE'LL UNBAN YOU FROM THE FESTIVAL AND MY HOUSE.

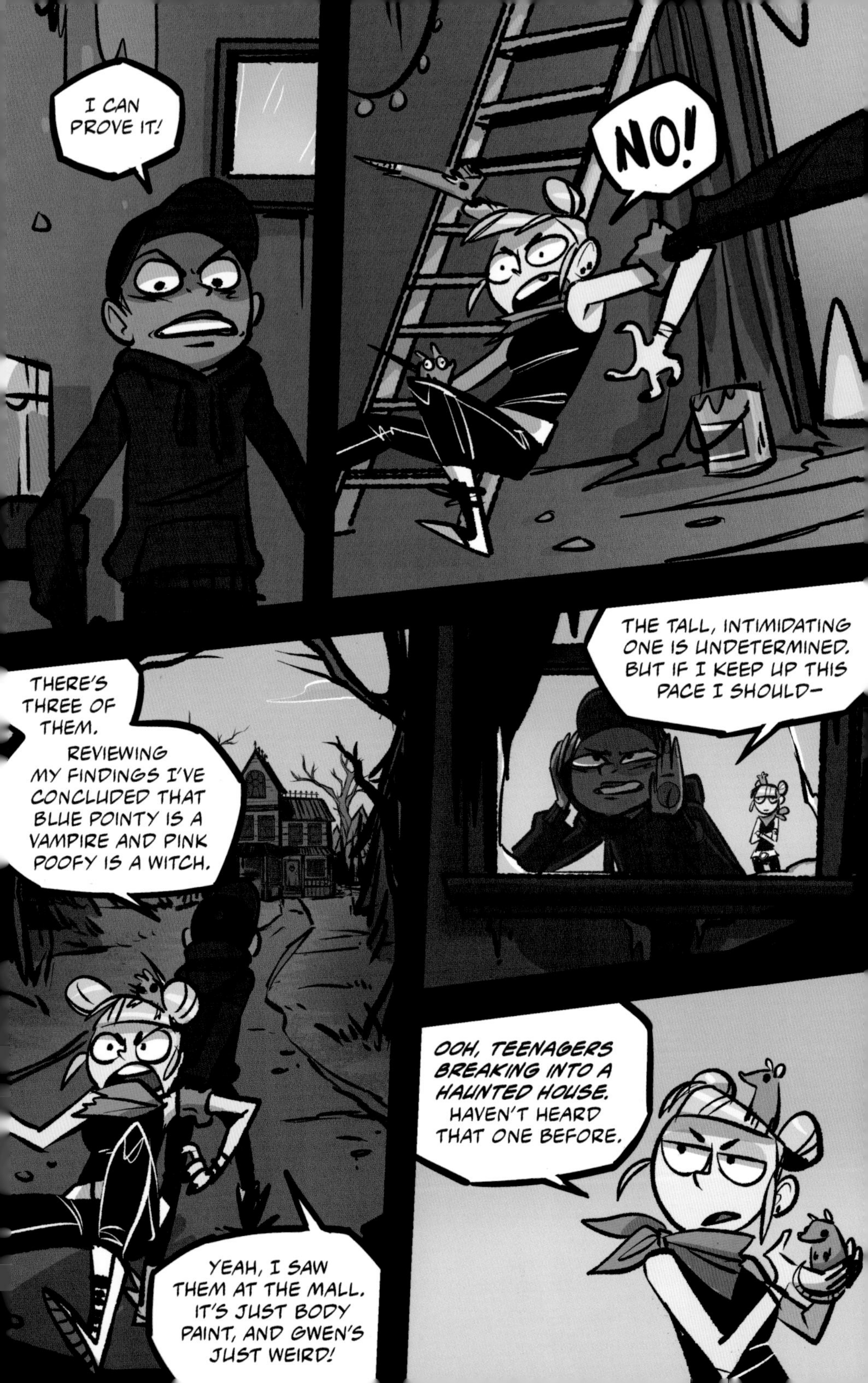
I CAN PROVE IT!
NO!
THERE'S THREE OF THEM. REVIEWING MY FINDINGS I'VE CONCLUDED THAT BLUE POINTY IS A VAMPIRE AND PINK POOFY IS A WITCH.
THE TALL, INTIMIDATING ONE IS UNDETERMINED. BUT IF I KEEP UP THIS PACE I SHOULD—
YEAH, I SAW THEM AT THE MALL. IT'S JUST BODY PAINT, AND GWEN'S JUST WEIRD!
*OOH, TEENAGERS BREAKING INTO A HAUNTED HOUSE.* HAVEN'T HEARD THAT ONE BEFORE.

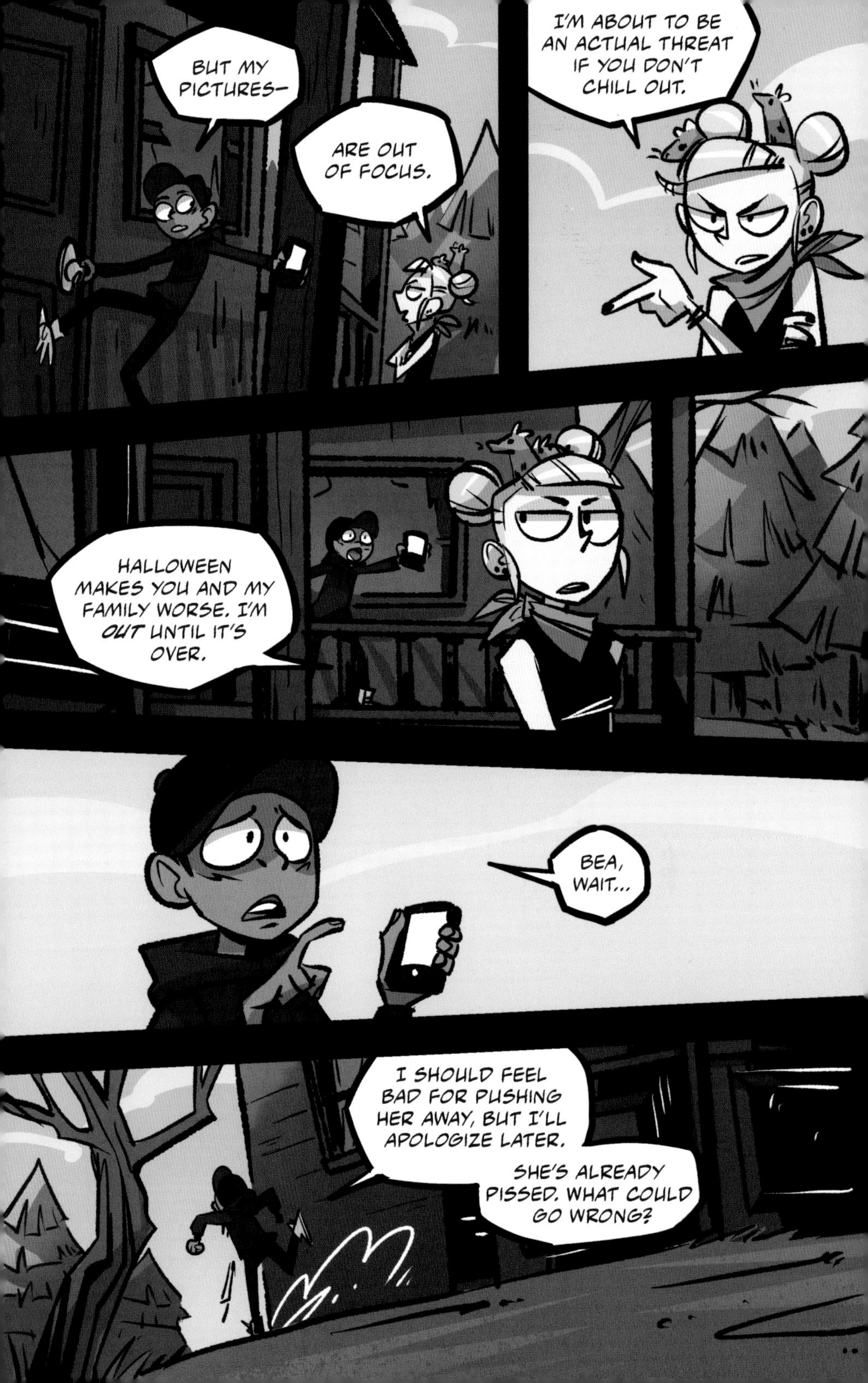
BUT MY PICTURES—
ARE OUT OF FOCUS.
I'M ABOUT TO BE AN ACTUAL THREAT IF YOU DON'T CHILL OUT.
HALLOWEEN MAKES YOU AND MY FAMILY WORSE. I'M *OUT* UNTIL IT'S OVER.
BEA, WAIT...
I SHOULD FEEL BAD FOR PUSHING HER AWAY, BUT I'LL APOLOGIZE LATER.
SHE'S ALREADY PISSED. WHAT COULD GO WRONG?

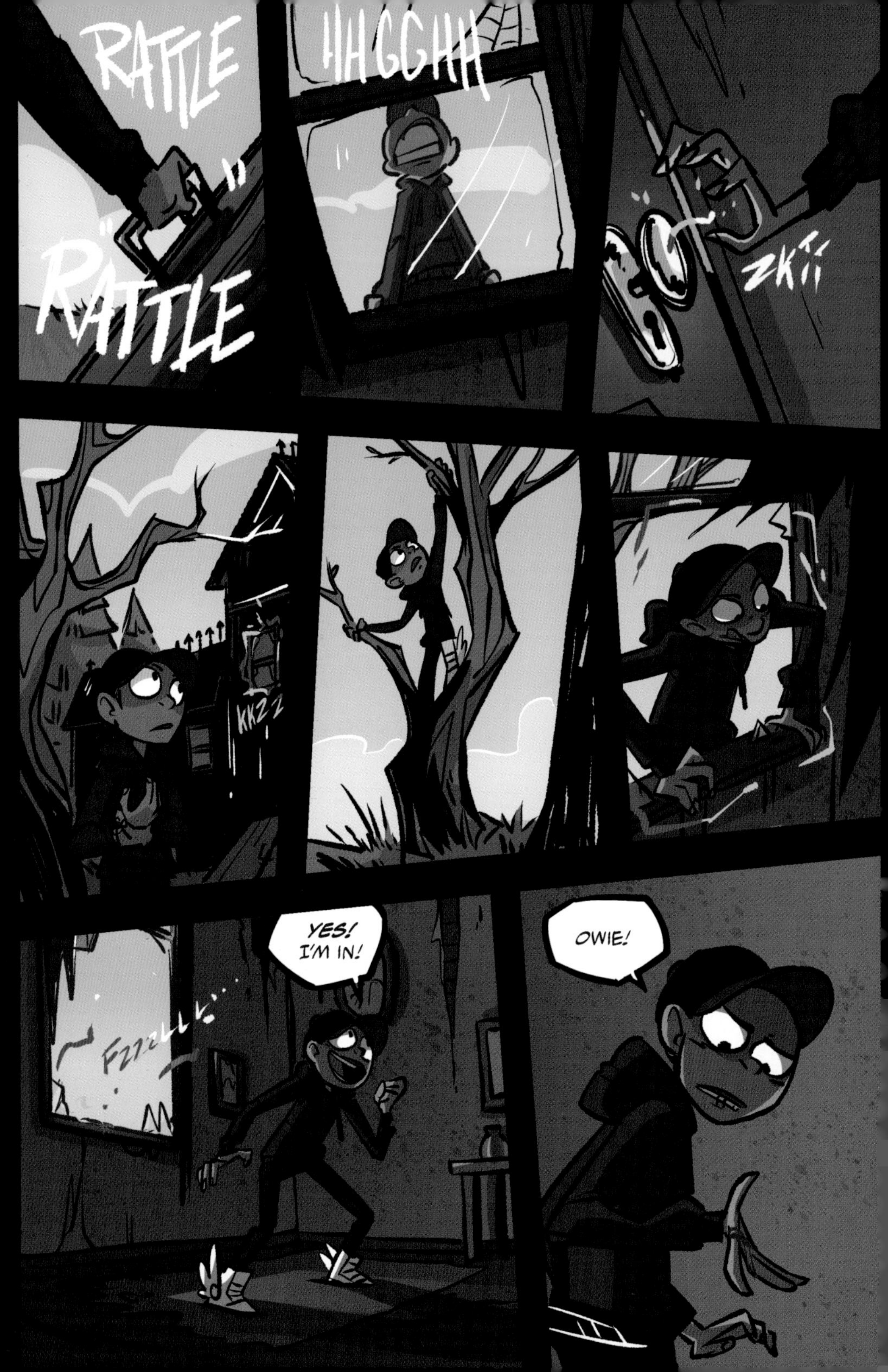
RATTLE
RATTLE
HHGGHH
ZKT
KKZZ
YES! I'M IN!
OWIE!
FZZZLLL...

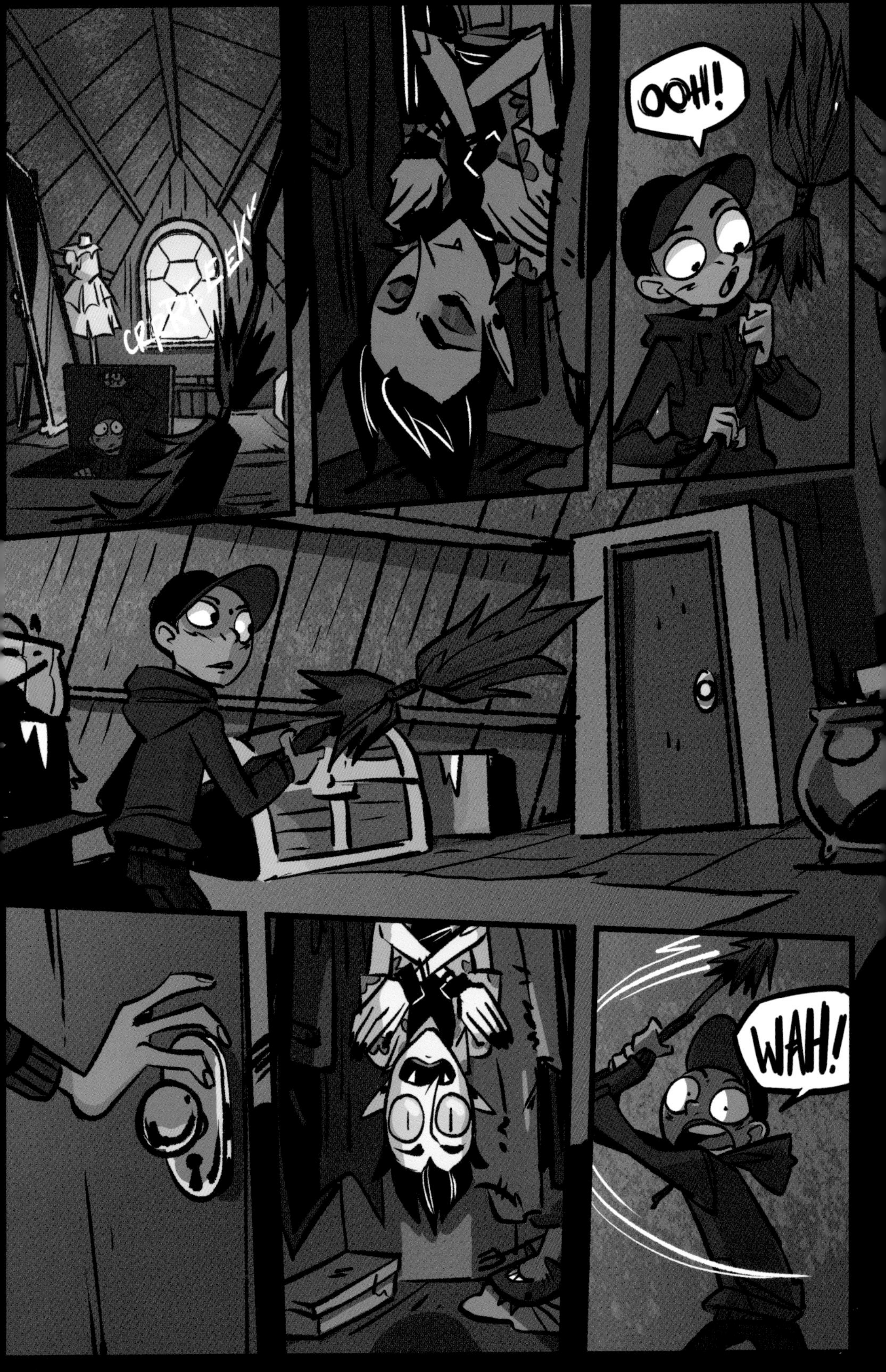
CRRREEEKK
OOH!
WAH!

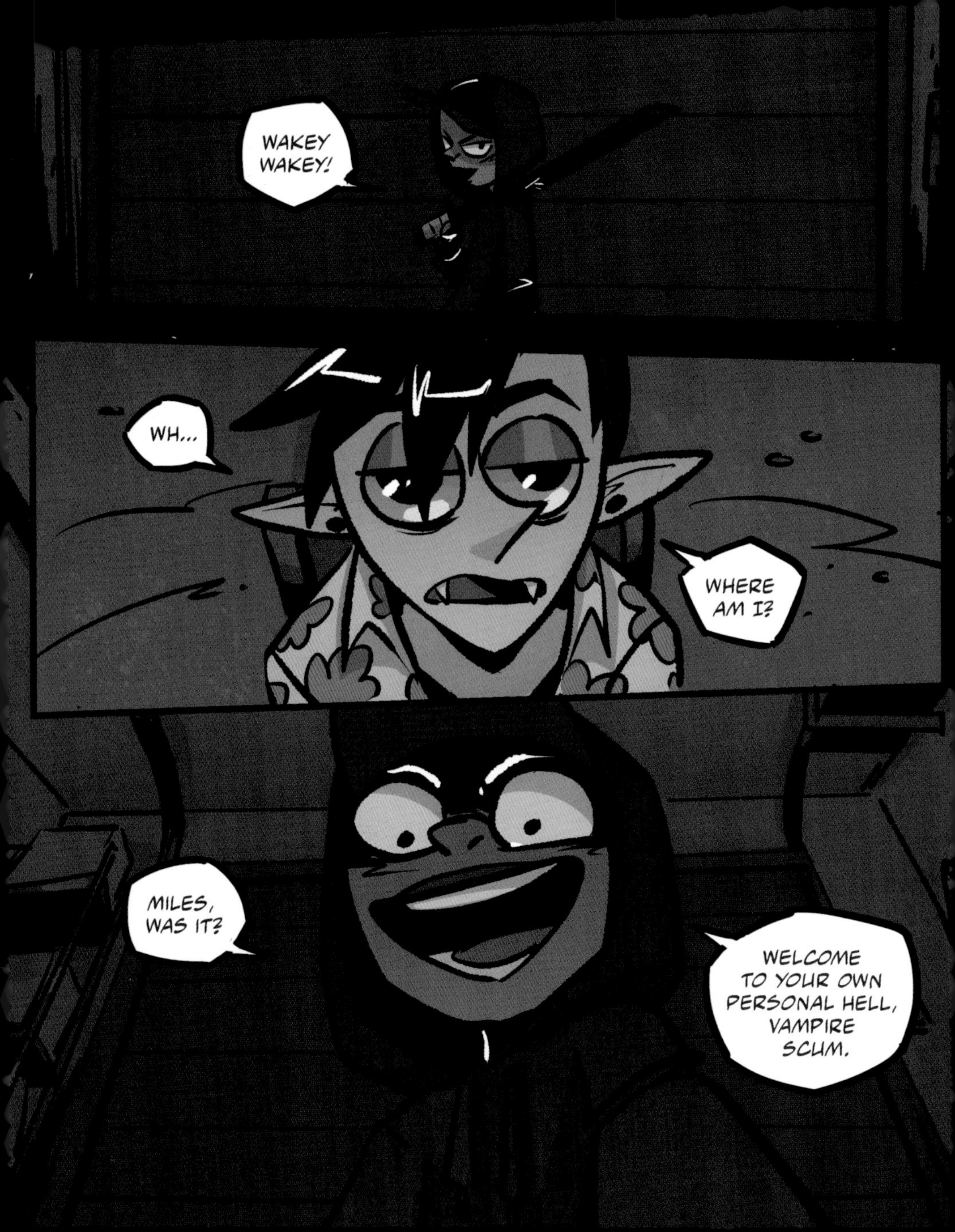
WAKEY WAKEY!
WH...
WHERE AM I?
MILES, WAS IT?
WELCOME TO YOUR OWN PERSONAL HELL, VAMPIRE SCUM.

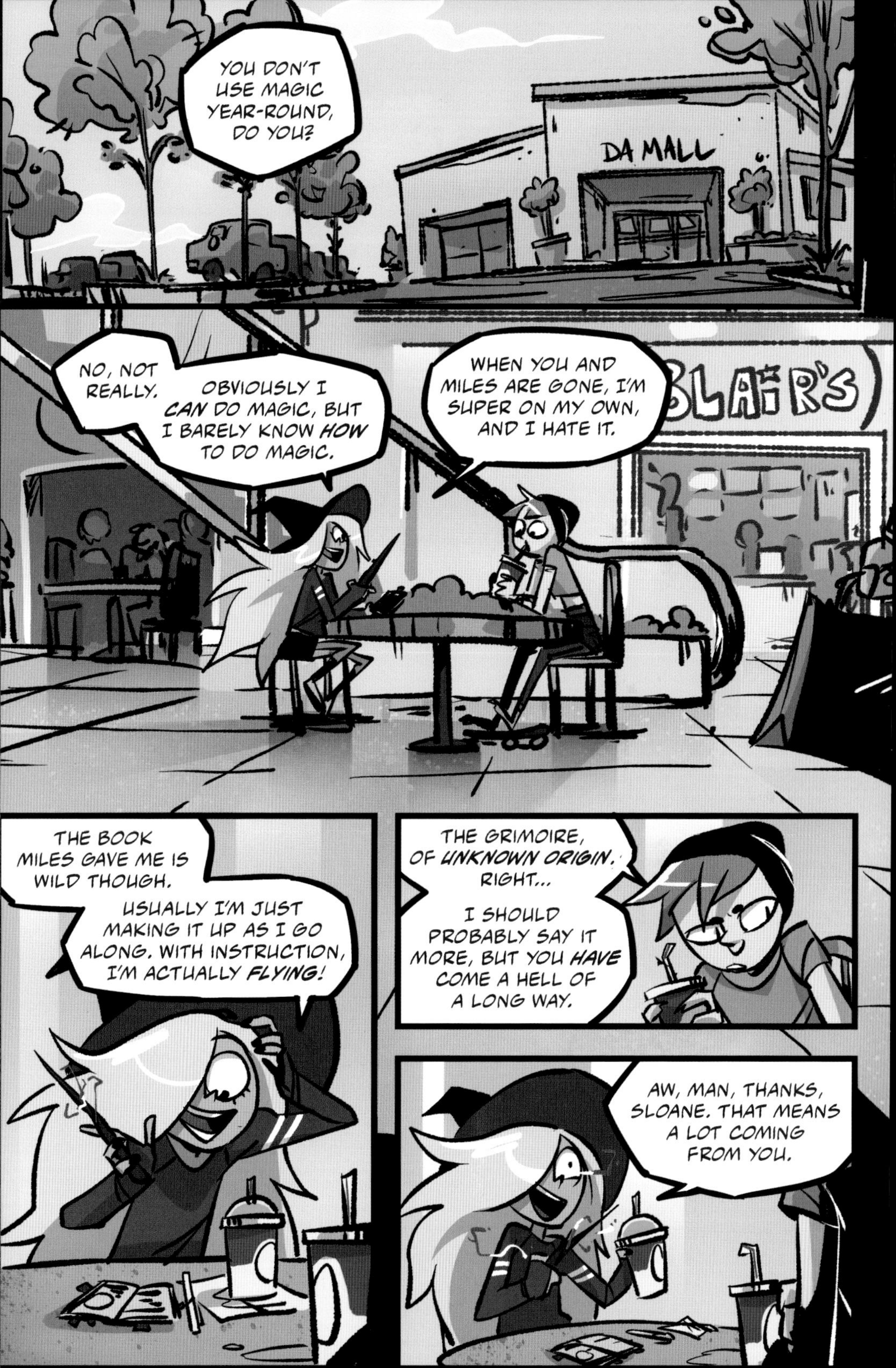

YOU DON'T USE MAGIC YEAR-ROUND, DO YOU?
DA MALL
NO, NOT REALLY.
OBVIOUSLY I *CAN* DO MAGIC, BUT I BARELY KNOW *HOW* TO DO MAGIC.
WHEN YOU AND MILES ARE GONE, I'M SUPER ON MY OWN, AND I HATE IT.
BLAIR'S
THE BOOK MILES GAVE ME IS WILD THOUGH.
USUALLY I'M JUST MAKING IT UP AS I GO ALONG. WITH INSTRUCTION, I'M ACTUALLY *FLYING!*
THE GRIMOIRE, OF *UNKNOWN ORIGIN*. RIGHT...
I SHOULD PROBABLY SAY IT MORE, BUT YOU *HAVE* COME A HELL OF A LONG WAY.
AW, MAN, THANKS, SLOANE. THAT MEANS A LOT COMING FROM YOU.

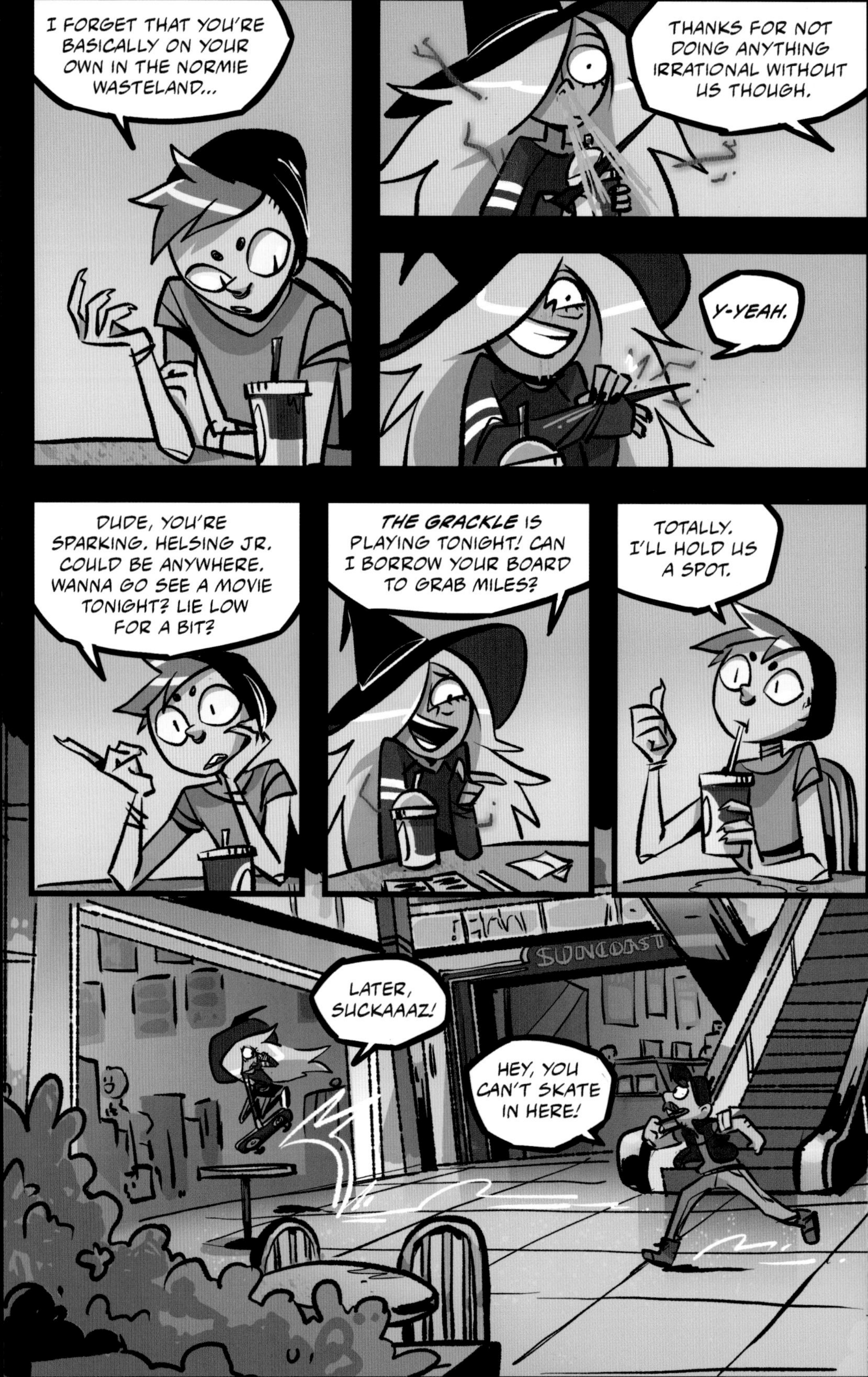
I FORGET THAT YOU'RE BASICALLY ON YOUR OWN IN THE NORMIE WASTELAND...
THANKS FOR NOT DOING ANYTHING IRRATIONAL WITHOUT US THOUGH.
Y-YEAH.
DUDE, YOU'RE SPARKING. HELSING JR. COULD BE ANYWHERE. WANNA GO SEE A MOVIE TONIGHT? LIE LOW FOR A BIT?
*THE GRACKLE* IS PLAYING TONIGHT! CAN I BORROW YOUR BOARD TO GRAB MILES?
TOTALLY. I'LL HOLD US A SPOT.
SUNCOAST
LATER, SUCKAAAZ!
HEY, YOU CAN'T SKATE IN HERE!

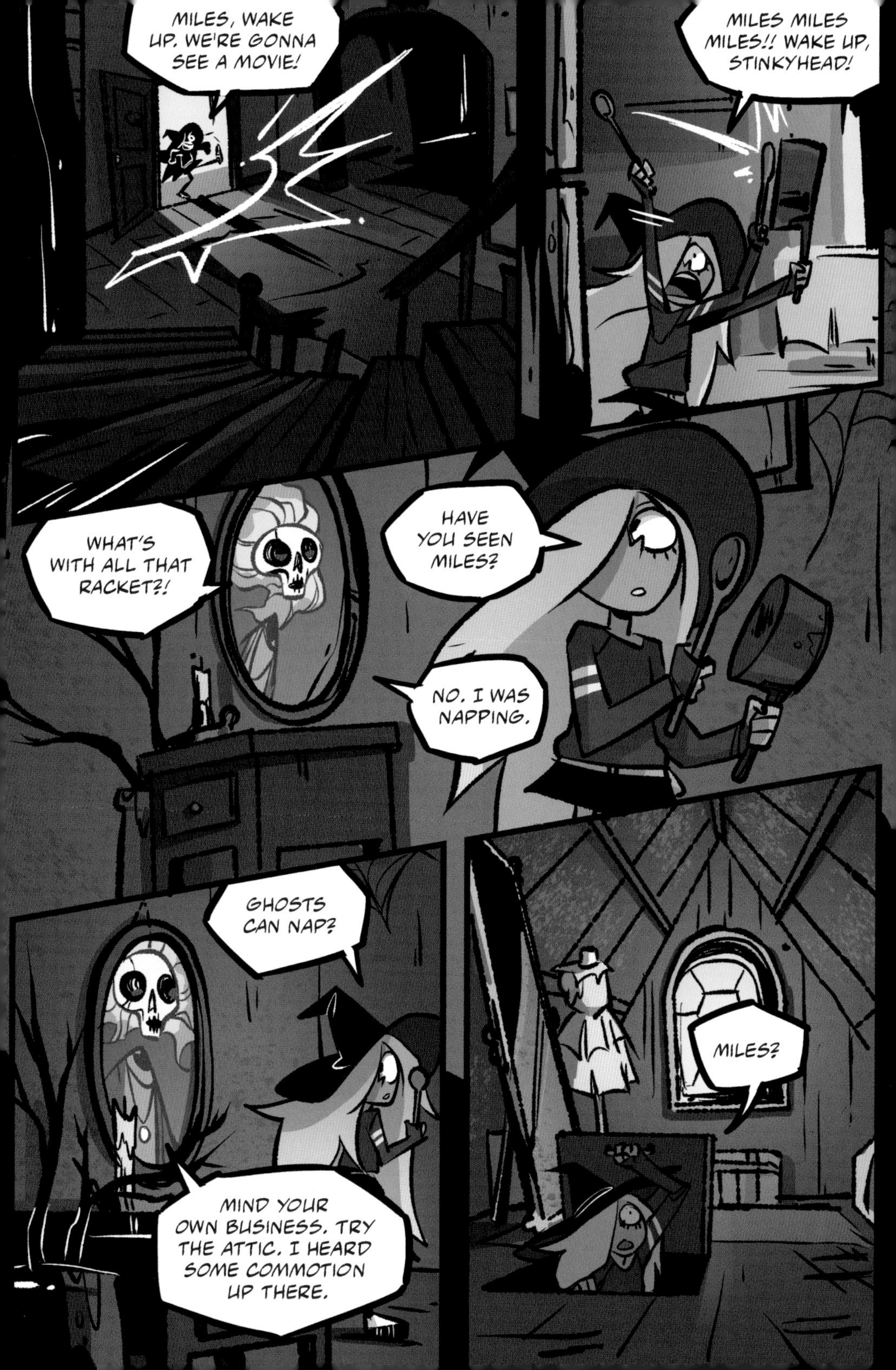
MILES, WAKE UP. WE'RE GONNA SEE A MOVIE!
MILES MILES MILES!! WAKE UP, STINKYHEAD!
WHAT'S WITH ALL THAT RACKET?!
HAVE YOU SEEN MILES?
NO. I WAS NAPPING.
GHOSTS CAN NAP?
MIND YOUR OWN BUSINESS. TRY THE ATTIC. I HEARD SOME COMMOTION UP THERE.
MILES?

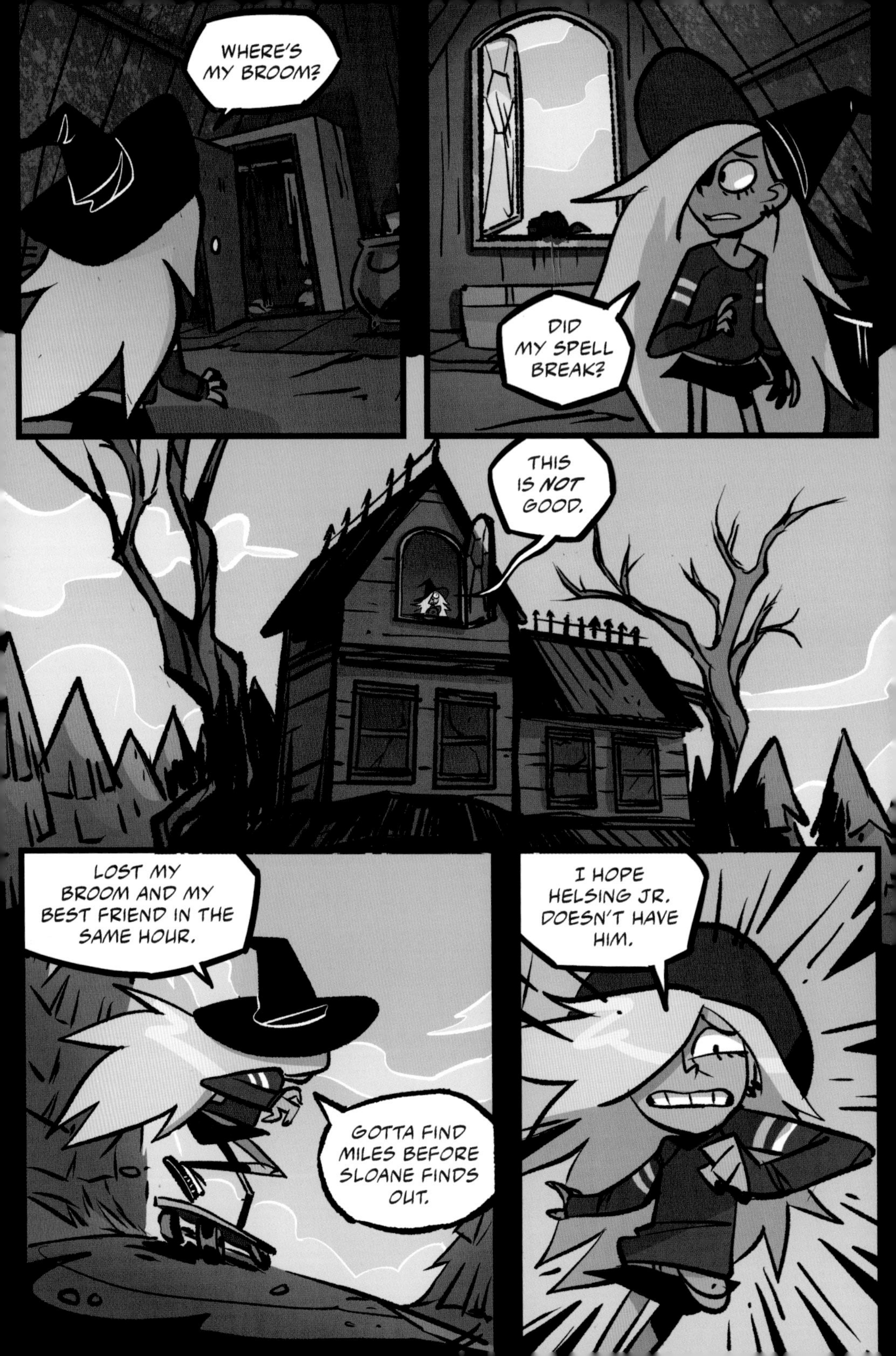
WHERE'S MY BROOM?
DID MY SPELL BREAK?
THIS IS *NOT* GOOD.
LOST MY BROOM AND MY BEST FRIEND IN THE SAME HOUR.
GOTTA FIND MILES BEFORE SLOANE FINDS OUT.
I HOPE HELSING JR. DOESN'T HAVE HIM.

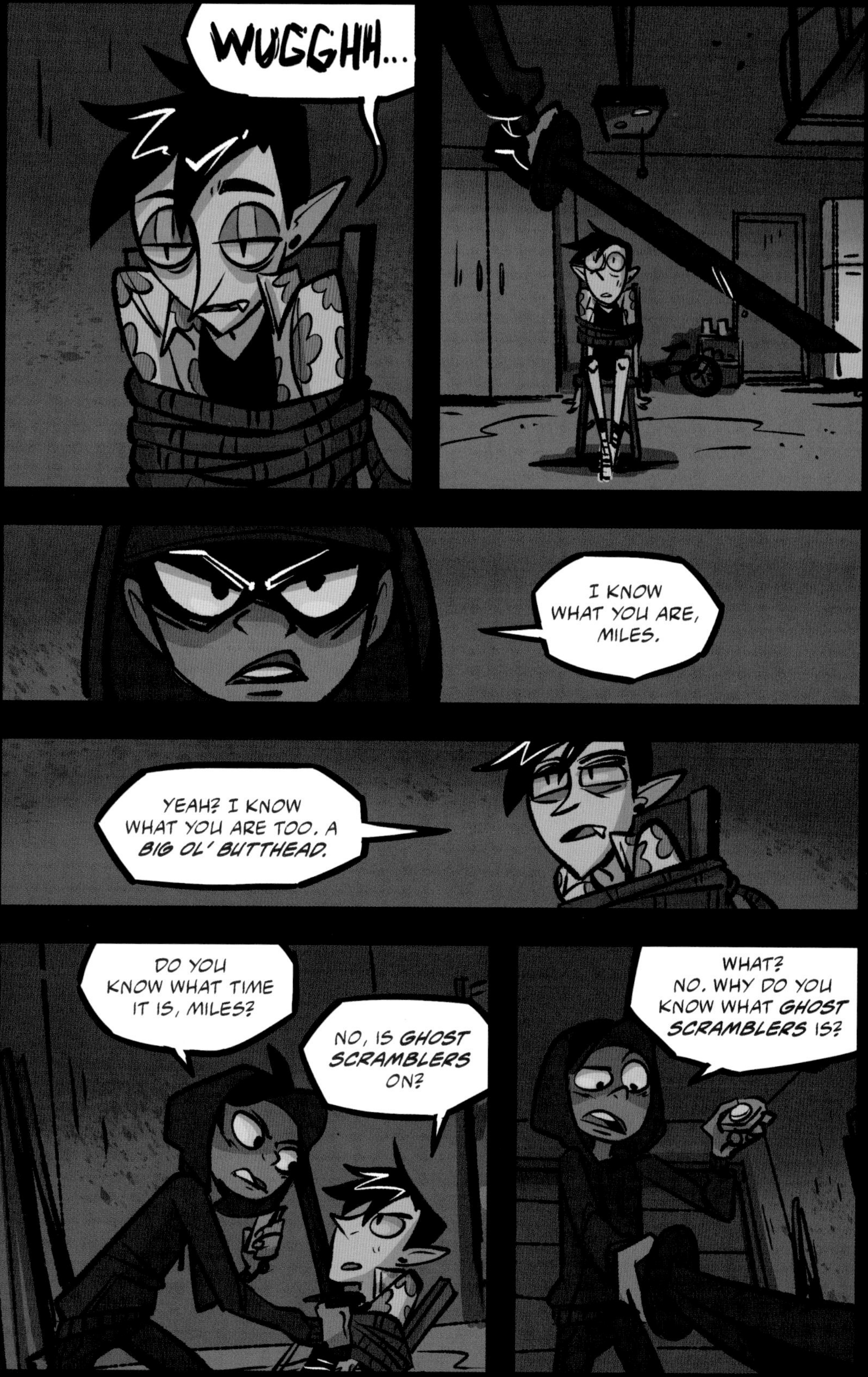
WUGGHH...
I KNOW WHAT YOU ARE, MILES.
YEAH? I KNOW WHAT YOU ARE TOO. A *BIG OL' BUTTHEAD.*
DO YOU KNOW WHAT TIME IT IS, MILES?
NO, IS *GHOST SCRAMBLERS* ON?
WHAT? NO. WHY DO YOU KNOW WHAT *GHOST SCRAMBLERS* IS?

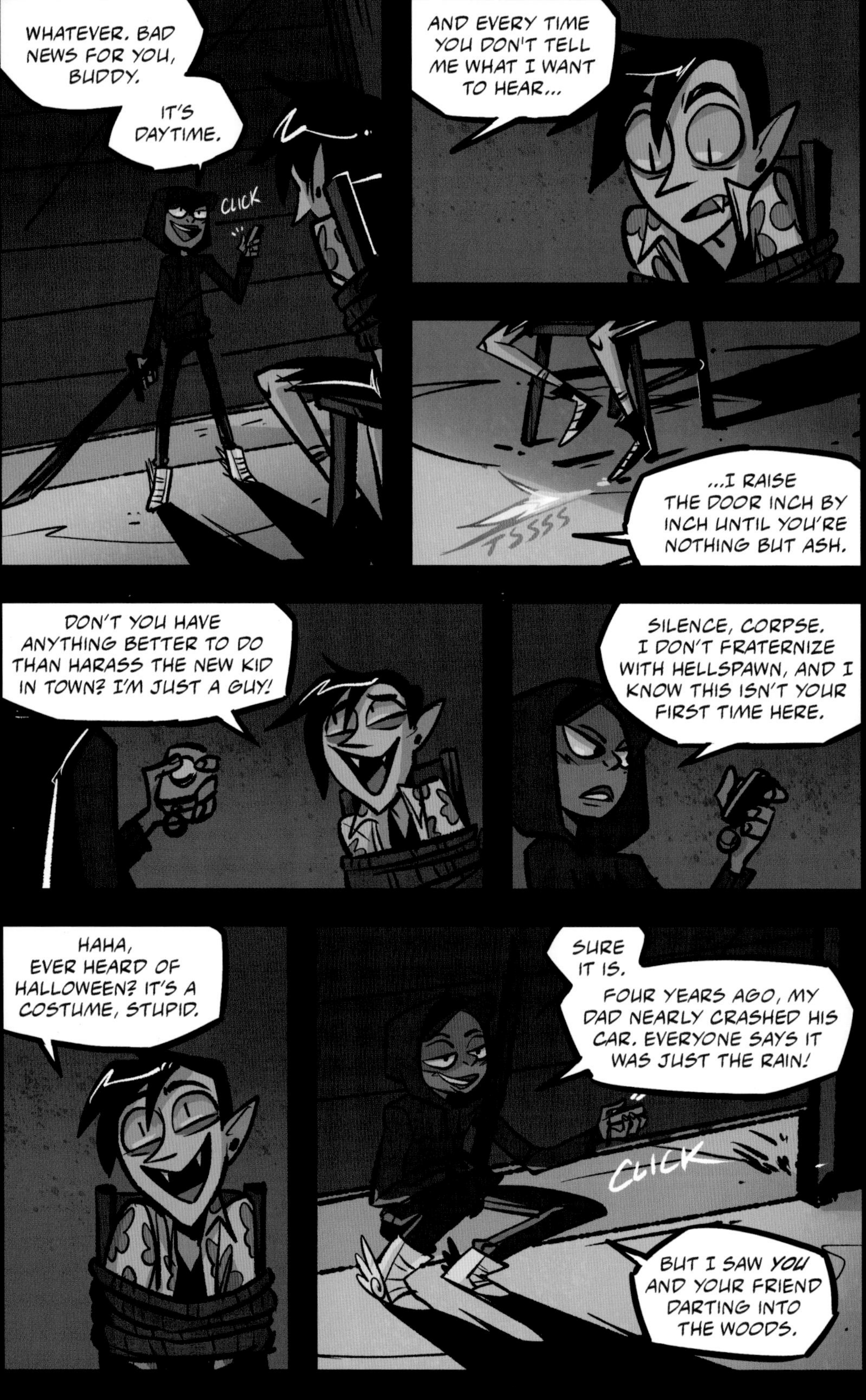
WHATEVER. BAD NEWS FOR YOU, BUDDY.
IT'S DAYTIME.
CLICK
AND EVERY TIME YOU DON'T TELL ME WHAT I WANT TO HEAR...
...I RAISE THE DOOR INCH BY INCH UNTIL YOU'RE NOTHING BUT ASH.
TSSSS
DON'T YOU HAVE ANYTHING BETTER TO DO THAN HARASS THE NEW KID IN TOWN? I'M JUST A GUY!
SILENCE, CORPSE. I DON'T FRATERNIZE WITH HELLSPAWN, AND I KNOW THIS ISN'T YOUR FIRST TIME HERE.
HAHA, EVER HEARD OF HALLOWEEN? IT'S A COSTUME, STUPID.
SURE IT IS.
FOUR YEARS AGO, MY DAD NEARLY CRASHED HIS CAR. EVERYONE SAYS IT WAS JUST THE RAIN!
CLICK
BUT I SAW *YOU* AND YOUR FRIEND DARTING INTO THE WOODS.

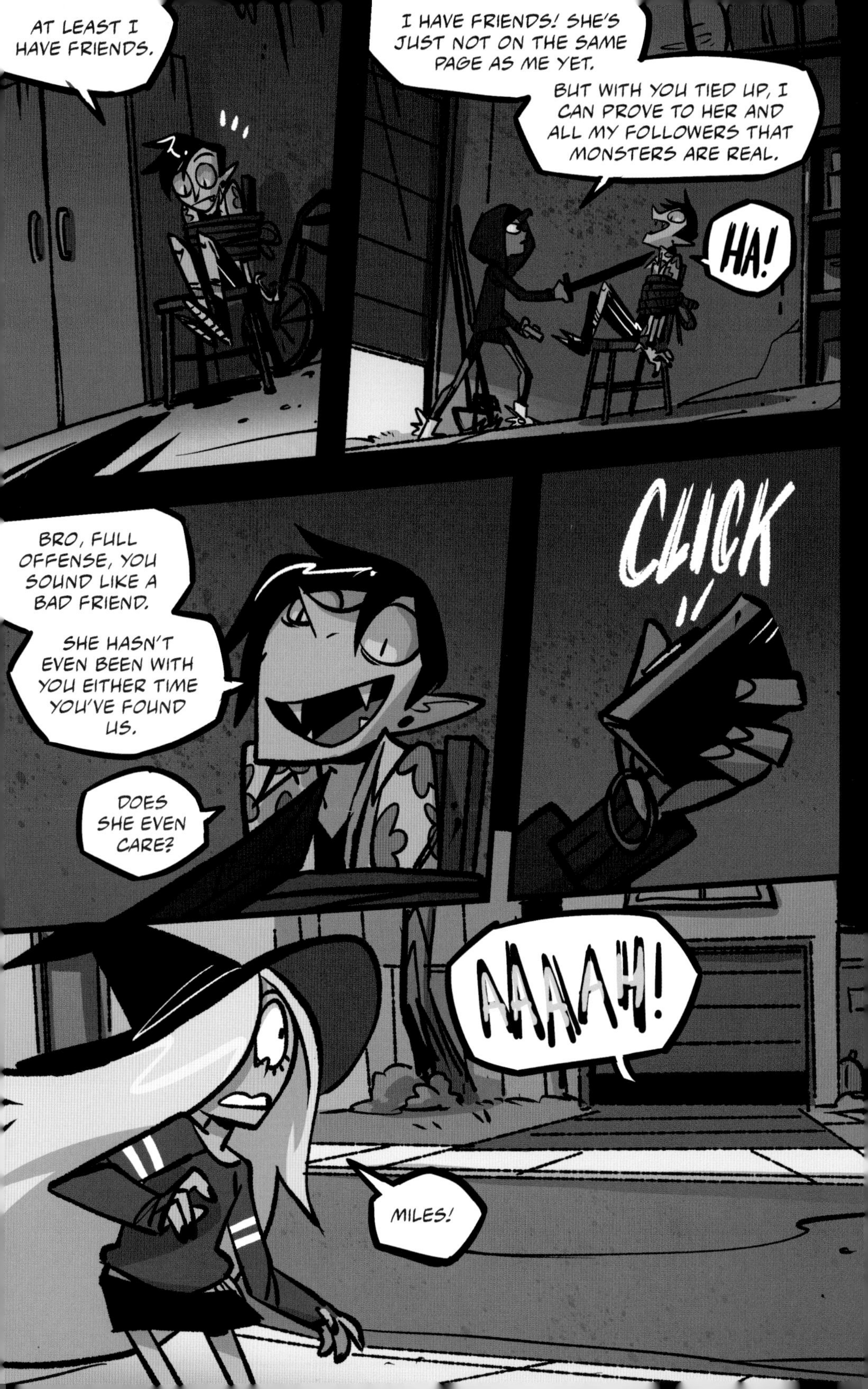
AT LEAST I HAVE FRIENDS.
I HAVE FRIENDS! SHE'S JUST NOT ON THE SAME PAGE AS ME YET.
BUT WITH YOU TIED UP, I CAN PROVE TO HER AND ALL MY FOLLOWERS THAT MONSTERS ARE REAL.
HA!
BRO, FULL OFFENSE, YOU SOUND LIKE A BAD FRIEND.
SHE HASN'T EVEN BEEN WITH YOU EITHER TIME YOU'VE FOUND US.
DOES SHE EVEN CARE?
CLICK
AAAAH!
MILES!

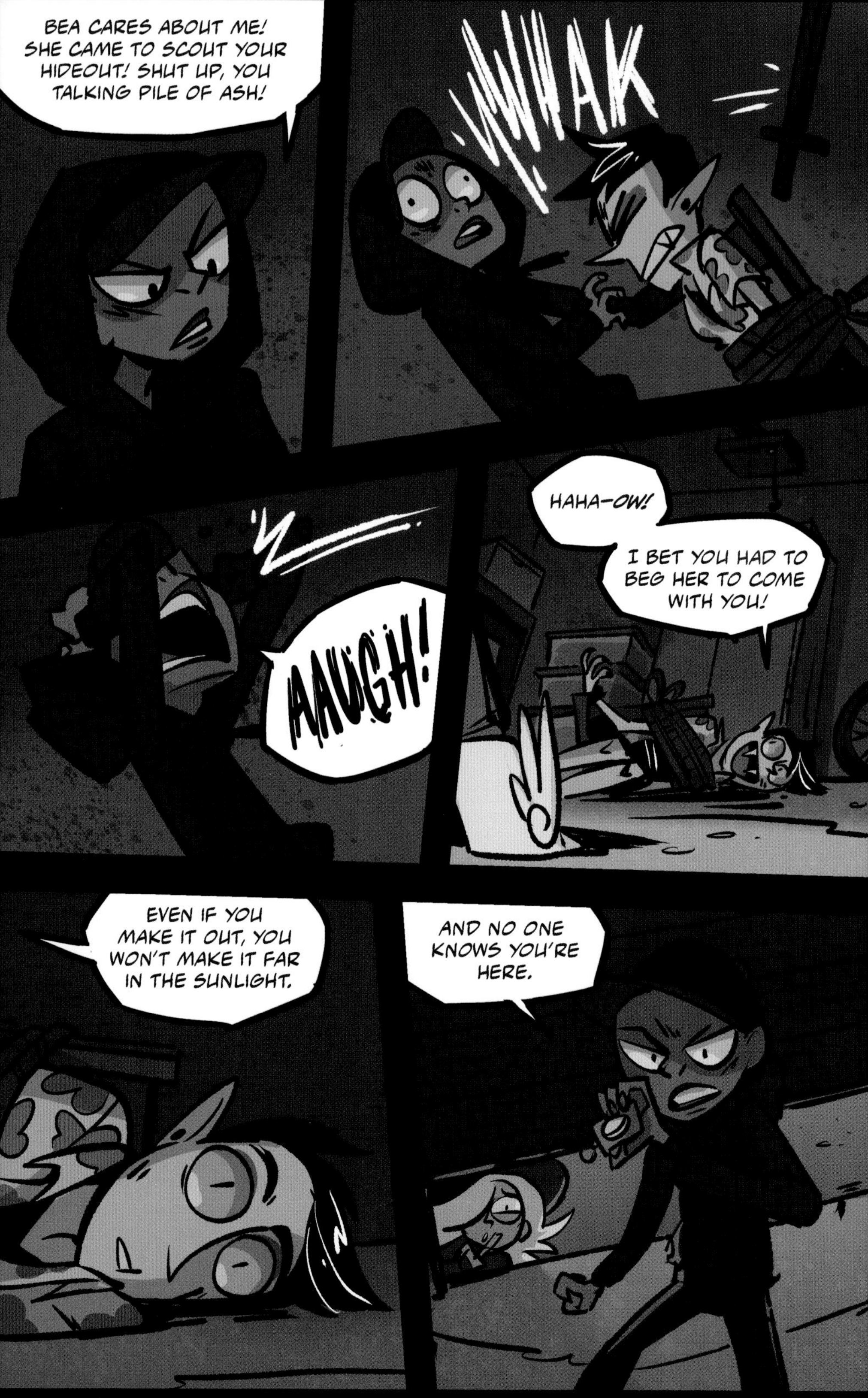
BEA CARES ABOUT ME! SHE CAME TO SCOUT YOUR HIDEOUT! SHUT UP, YOU TALKING PILE OF ASH!
WHAK
AAUGH!
HAHA-OW!
I BET YOU HAD TO BEG HER TO COME WITH YOU!
EVEN IF YOU MAKE IT OUT, YOU WON'T MAKE IT FAR IN THE SUNLIGHT.
AND NO ONE KNOWS YOU'RE HERE.

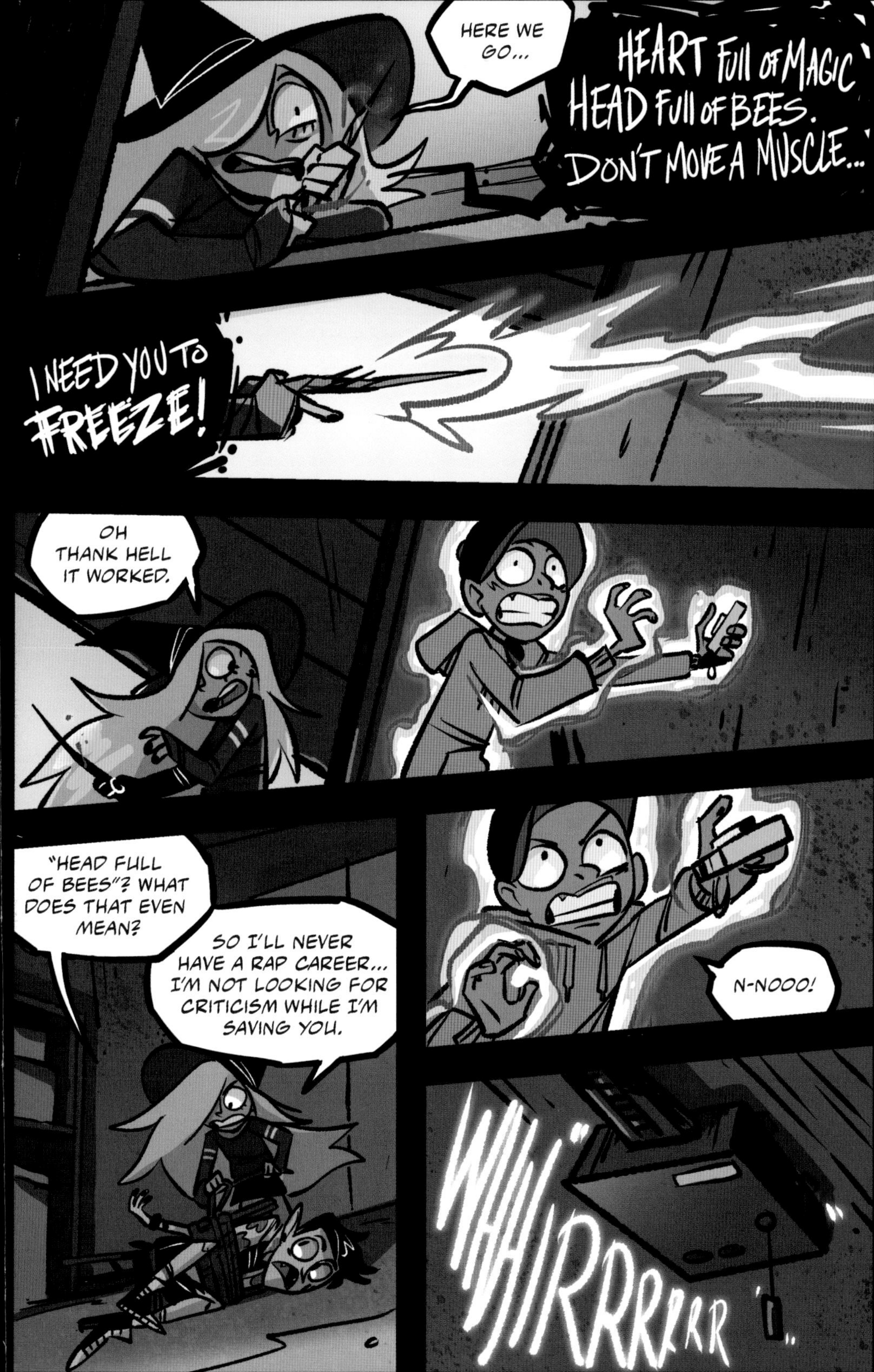
HERE WE GO...
HEART FULL OF MAGIC HEAD FULL OF BEES. DON'T MOVE A MUSCLE...
I NEED YOU TO FREEZE!
OH THANK HELL IT WORKED.
"HEAD FULL OF BEES"? WHAT DOES THAT EVEN MEAN?
SO I'LL NEVER HAVE A RAP CAREER... I'M NOT LOOKING FOR CRITICISM WHILE I'M SAVING YOU.
N-NOOO!
WHHIRRRRRRR

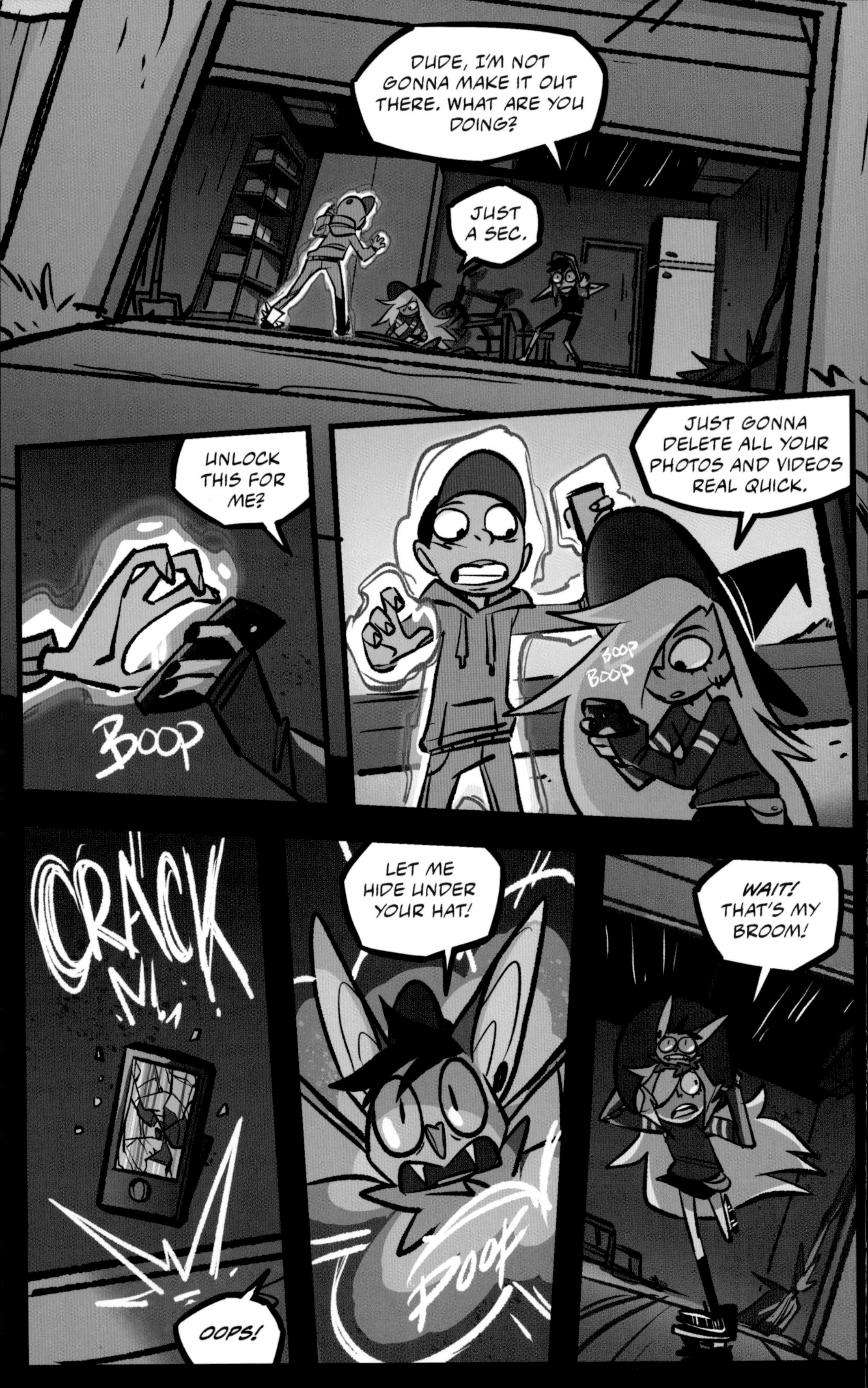
DUDE, I'M NOT GONNA MAKE IT OUT THERE. WHAT ARE YOU DOING?
JUST A SEC.
UNLOCK THIS FOR ME?
BOOP
JUST GONNA DELETE ALL YOUR PHOTOS AND VIDEOS REAL QUICK.
BOOP BOOP
CRACK
OOPS!
LET ME HIDE UNDER YOUR HAT!
POOF
WAIT! THAT'S MY BROOM!

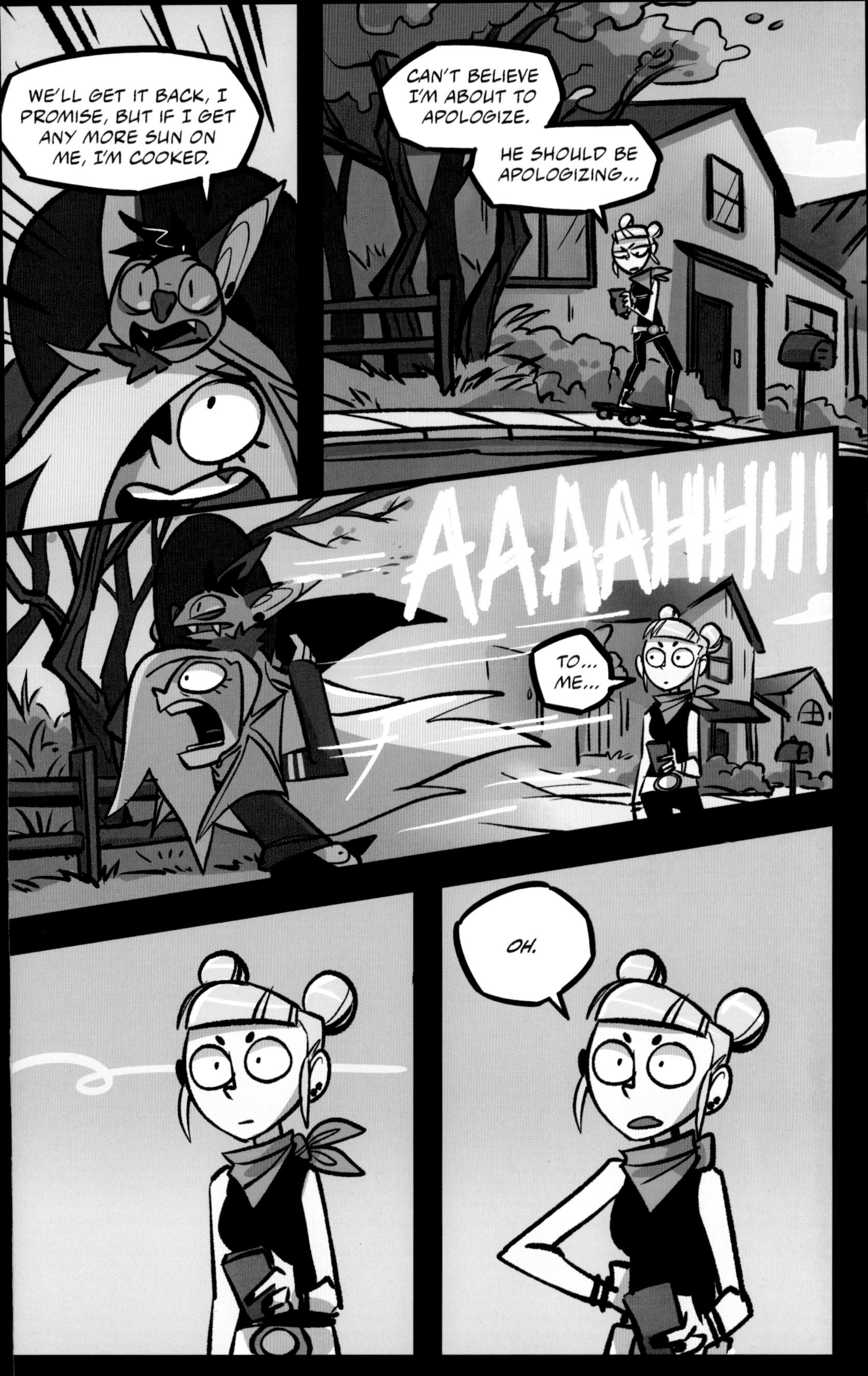
WE'LL GET IT BACK, I PROMISE, BUT IF I GET ANY MORE SUN ON ME, I'M COOKED.
CAN'T BELIEVE I'M ABOUT TO APOLOGIZE.
HE SHOULD BE APOLOGIZING...
AAAAHHHH
TO... ME...
OH.

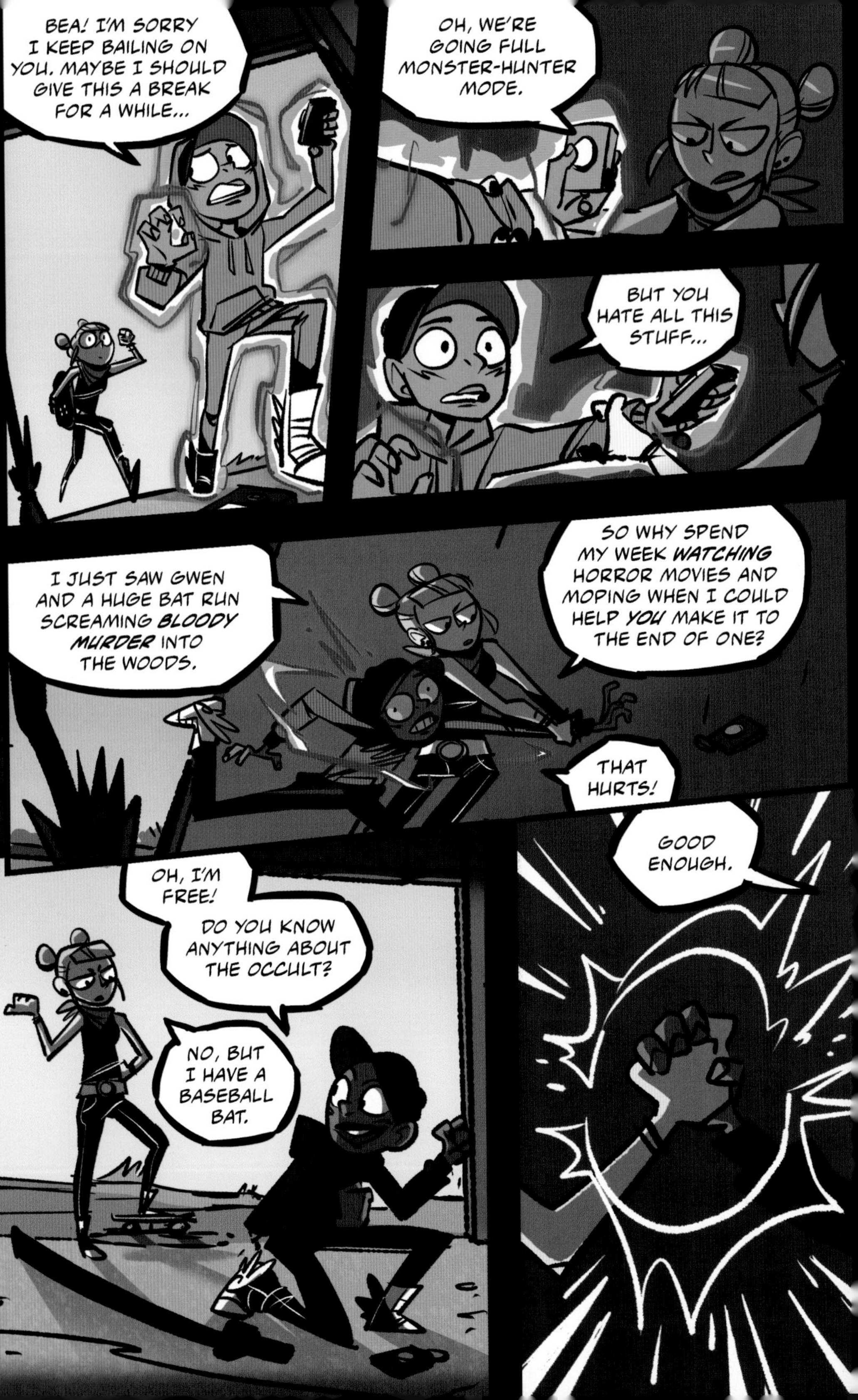
BEA! I'M SORRY I KEEP BAILING ON YOU. MAYBE I SHOULD GIVE THIS A BREAK FOR A WHILE...
OH, WE'RE GOING FULL MONSTER-HUNTER MODE.
BUT YOU HATE ALL THIS STUFF...
I JUST SAW GWEN AND A HUGE BAT RUN SCREAMING *BLOODY MURDER* INTO THE WOODS.
SO WHY SPEND MY WEEK *WATCHING* HORROR MOVIES AND MOPING WHEN I COULD HELP *YOU* MAKE IT TO THE END OF ONE?
THAT HURTS!
OH, I'M FREE!
DO YOU KNOW ANYTHING ABOUT THE OCCULT?
NO, BUT I HAVE A BASEBALL BAT.
GOOD ENOUGH.

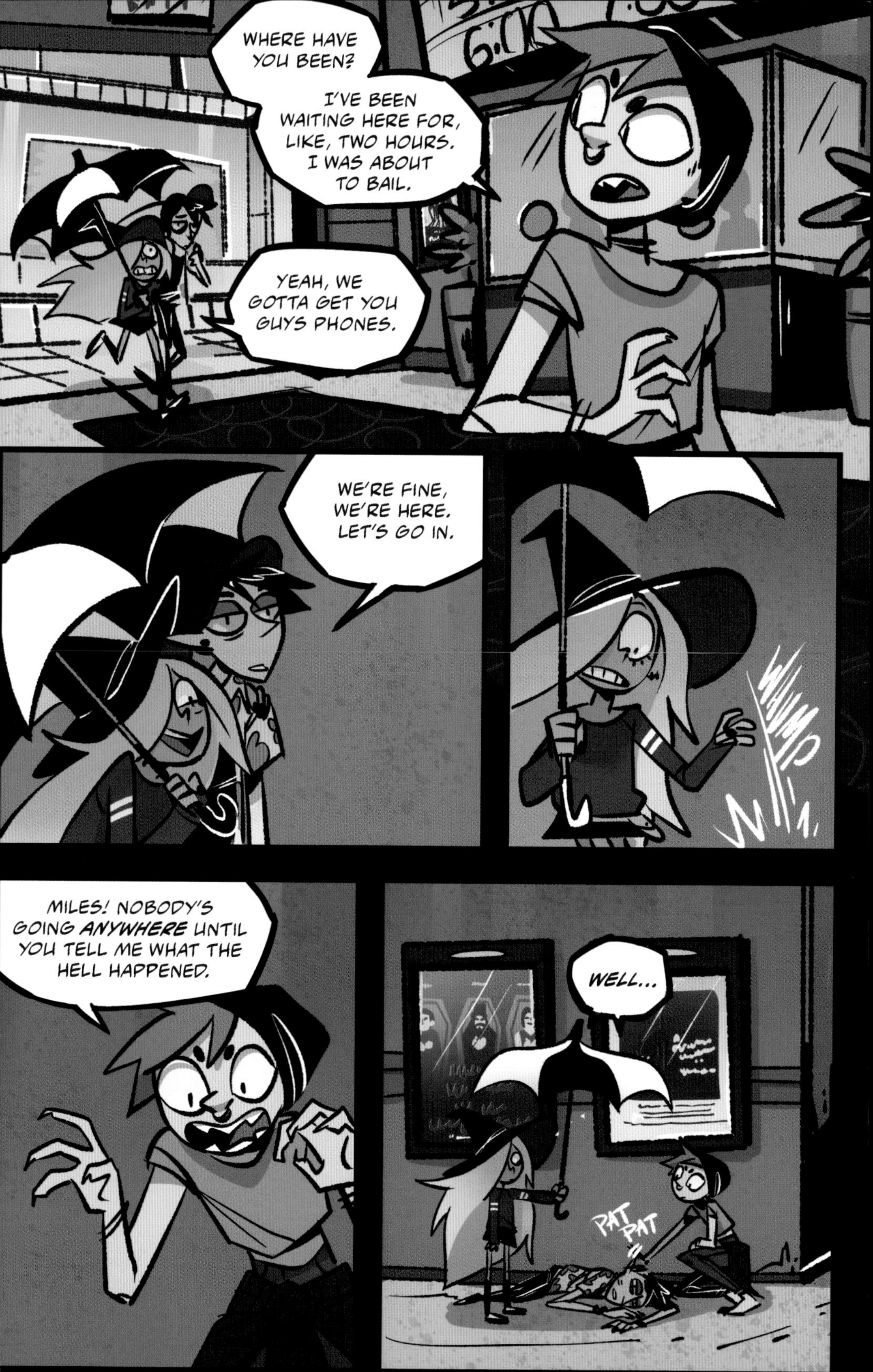
WHERE HAVE YOU BEEN?
I'VE BEEN WAITING HERE FOR, LIKE, TWO HOURS. I WAS ABOUT TO BAIL.
YEAH, WE GOTTA GET YOU GUYS PHONES.
WE'RE FINE, WE'RE HERE. LET'S GO IN.
WHUMP
MILES! NOBODY'S GOING ANYWHERE UNTIL YOU TELL ME WHAT THE HELL HAPPENED.
WELL...
PAT PAT

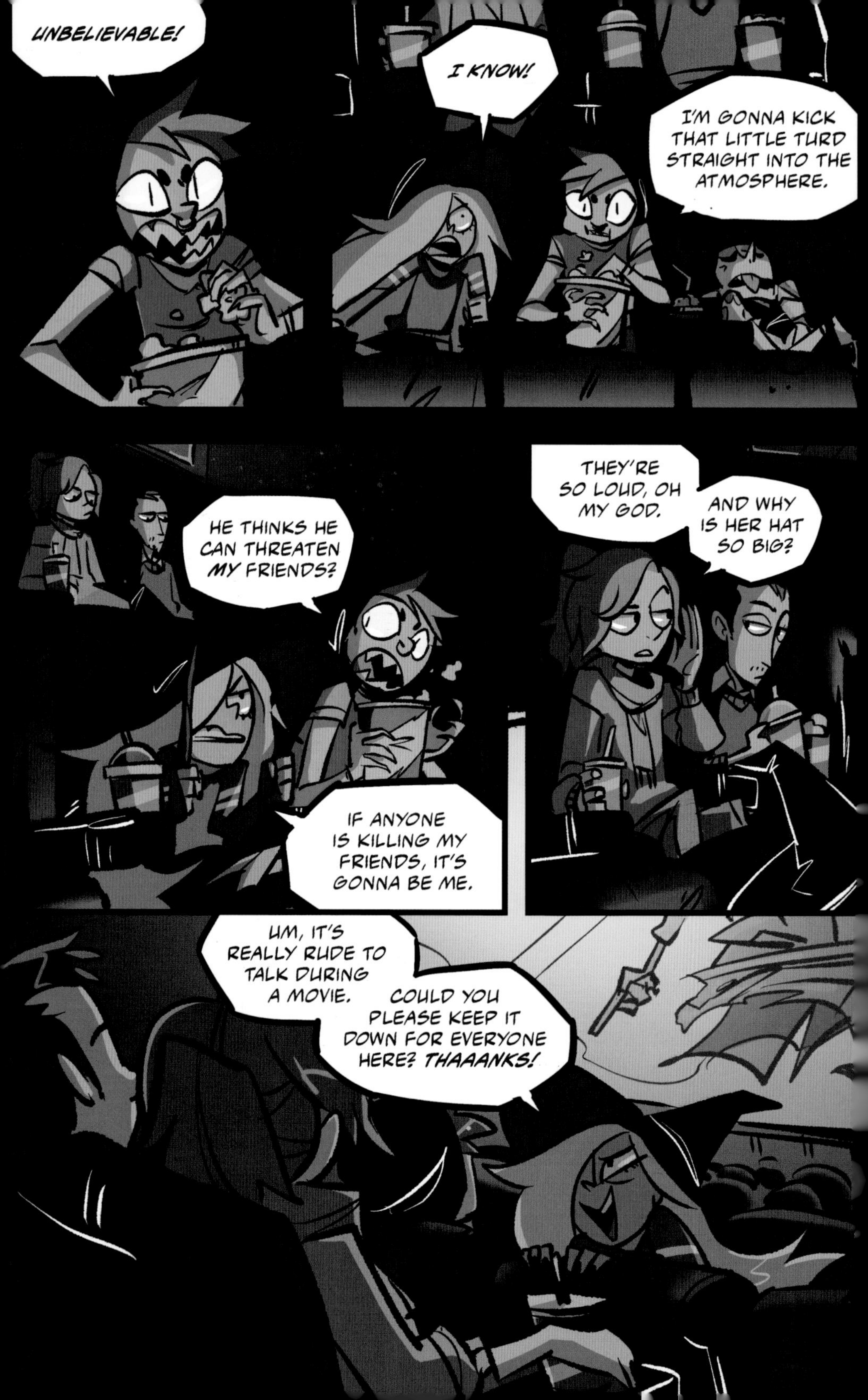
UNBELIEVABLE!
I KNOW!
I'M GONNA KICK THAT LITTLE TURD STRAIGHT INTO THE ATMOSPHERE.
HE THINKS HE CAN THREATEN MY FRIENDS?
IF ANYONE IS KILLING MY FRIENDS, IT'S GONNA BE ME.
THEY'RE SO LOUD, OH MY GOD.
AND WHY IS HER HAT SO BIG?
UM, IT'S REALLY RUDE TO TALK DURING A MOVIE.
COULD YOU PLEASE KEEP IT DOWN FOR EVERYONE HERE? THAAANKS!

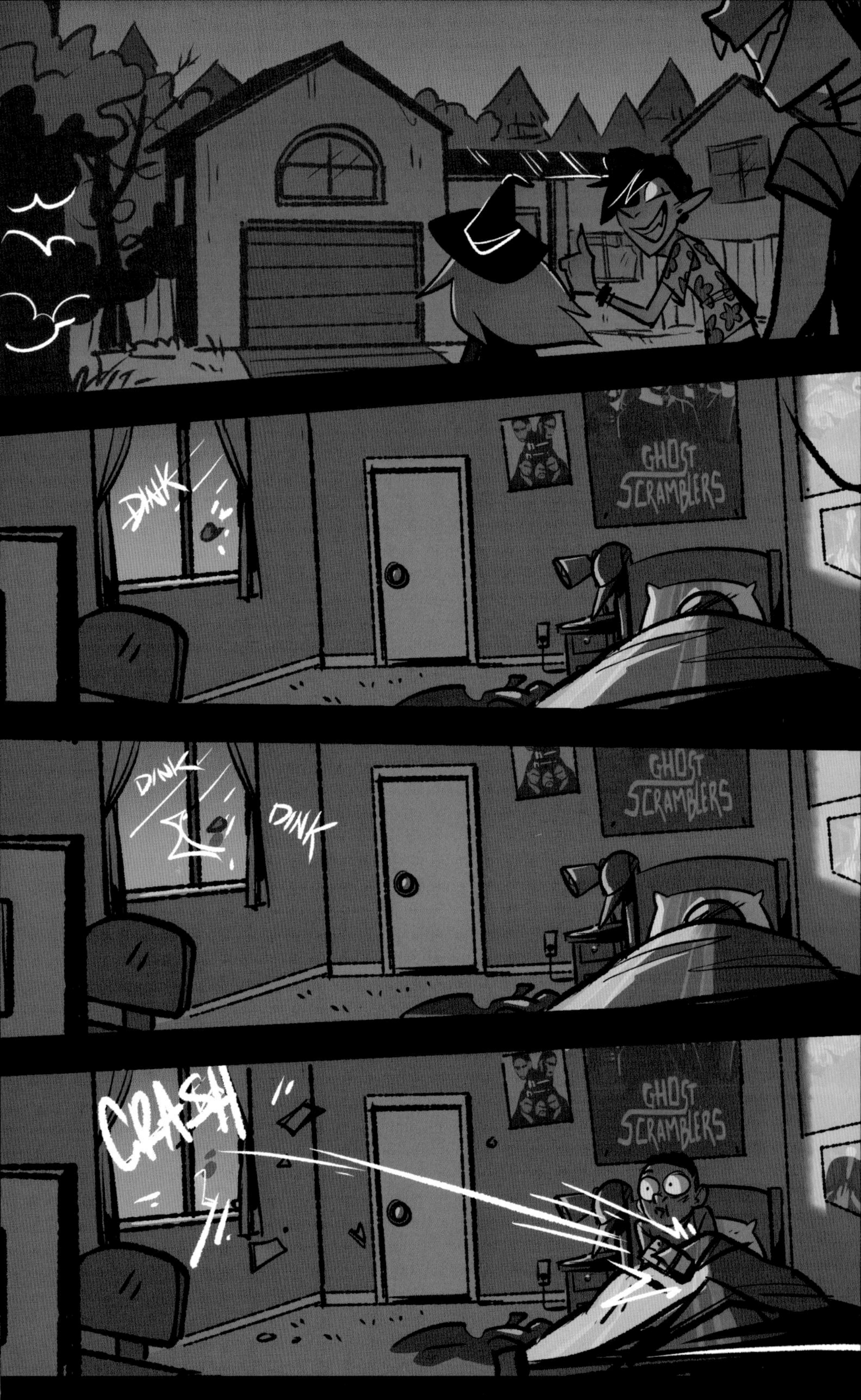

DINK
GHOST SCRAMBLERS
DINK
DINK
GHOST SCRAMBLERS
CRASH
GHOST SCRAMBLERS

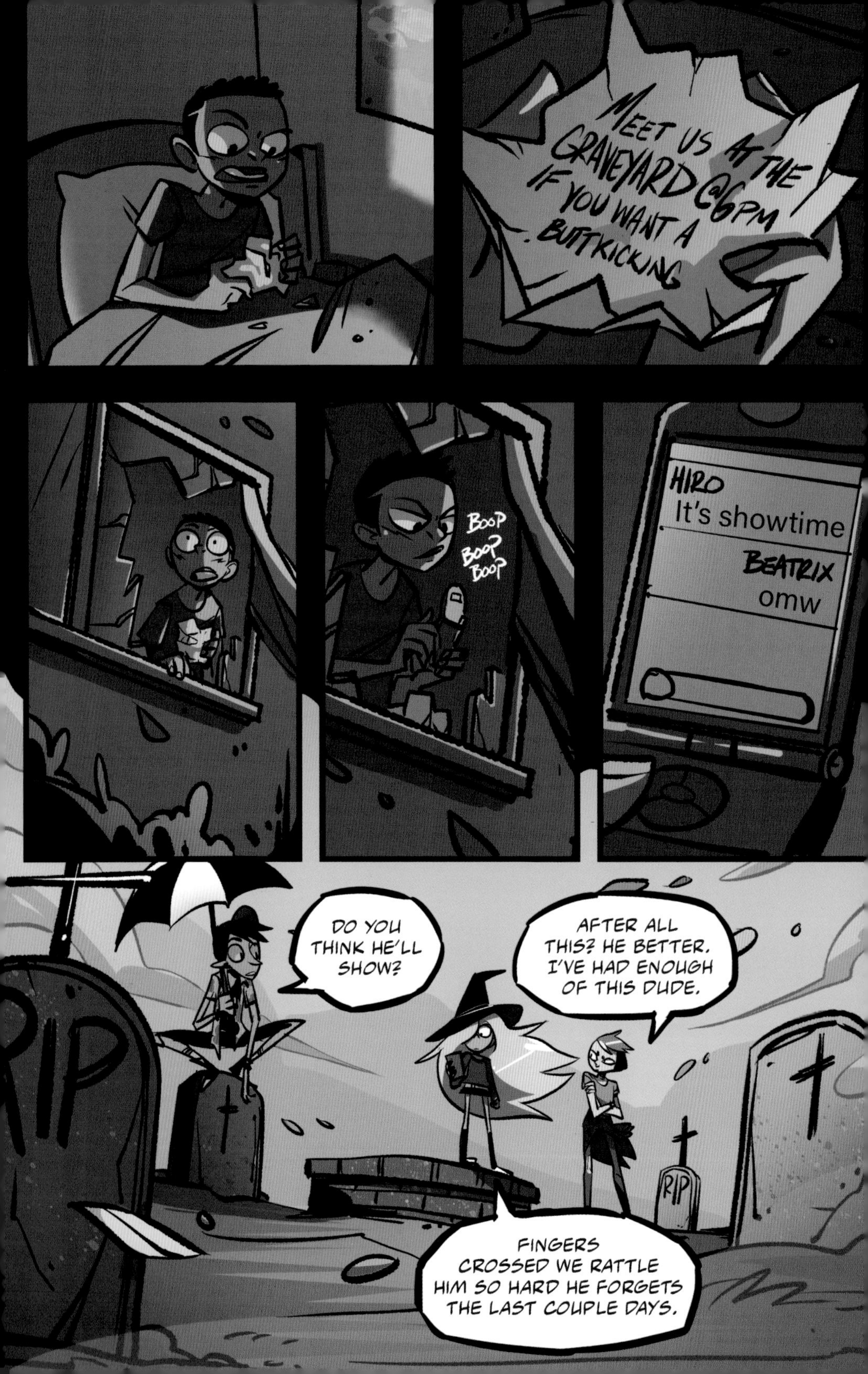

MEET US AT THE GRAVEYARD @6PM IF YOU WANT A BUTTKICKING
BOOP BOOP BOOP
HIRO
It's showtime
BEATRIX
omw
DO YOU THINK HE'LL SHOW?
AFTER ALL THIS? HE BETTER. I'VE HAD ENOUGH OF THIS DUDE.
FINGERS CROSSED WE RATTLE HIM SO HARD HE FORGETS THE LAST COUPLE DAYS.
RIP
RIP

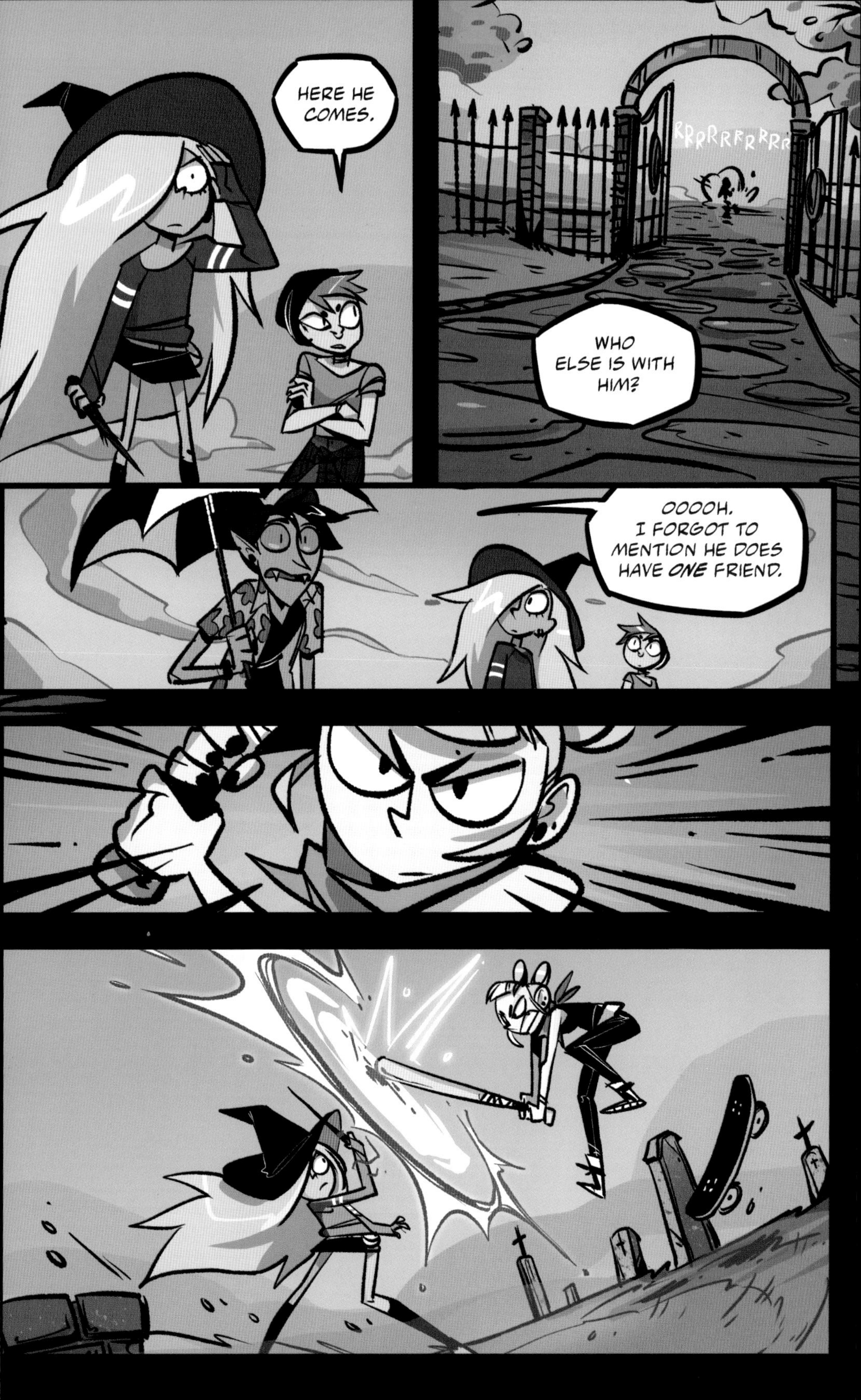
HERE HE COMES.
RRRRRRRRRRR
WHO ELSE IS WITH HIM?
OOOOH. I FORGOT TO MENTION HE DOES HAVE *ONE* FRIEND.

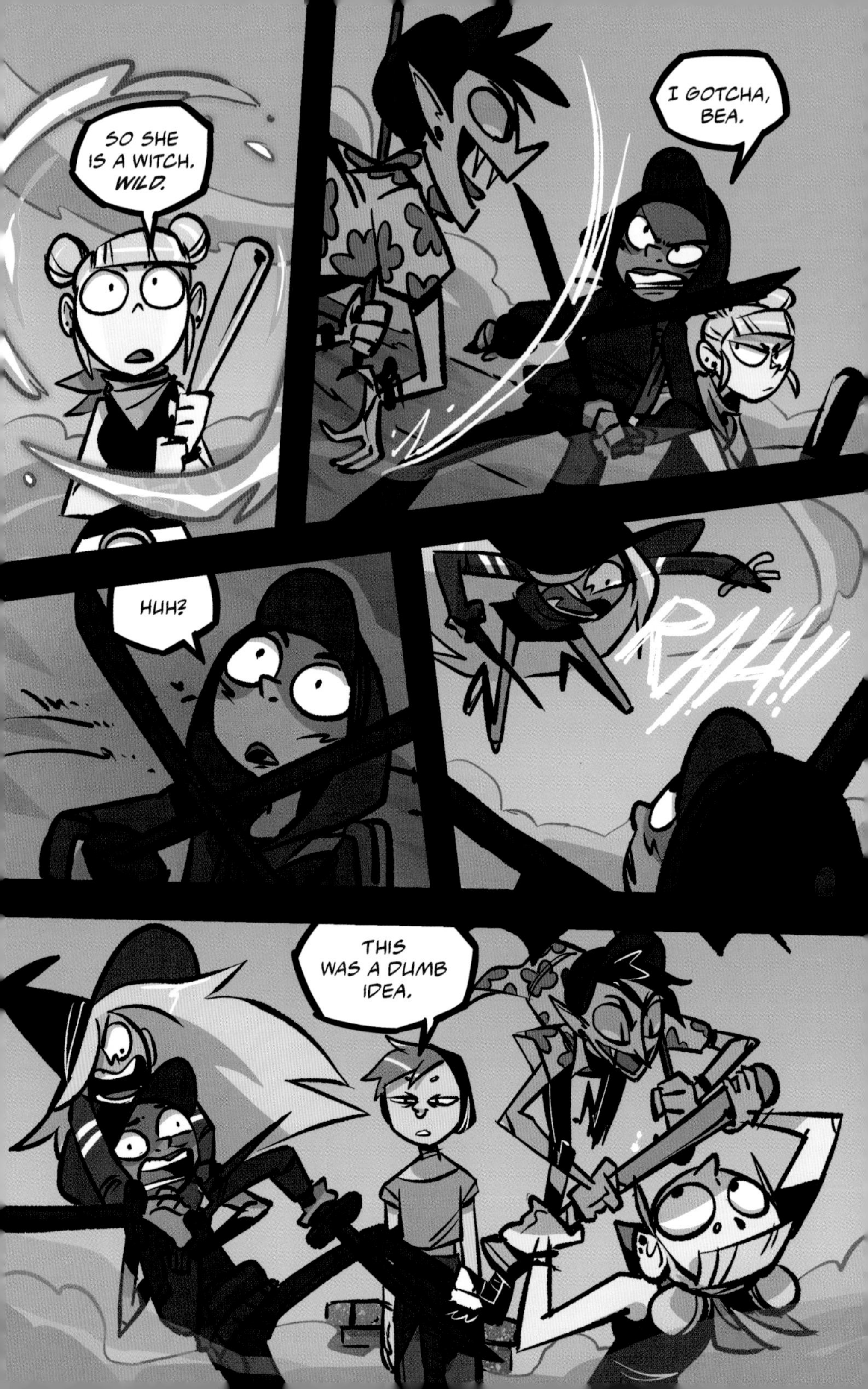
SO SHE IS A WITCH. WILD.
I GOTCHA, BEA.
HUH?
RAH!!
THIS WAS A DUMB IDEA.

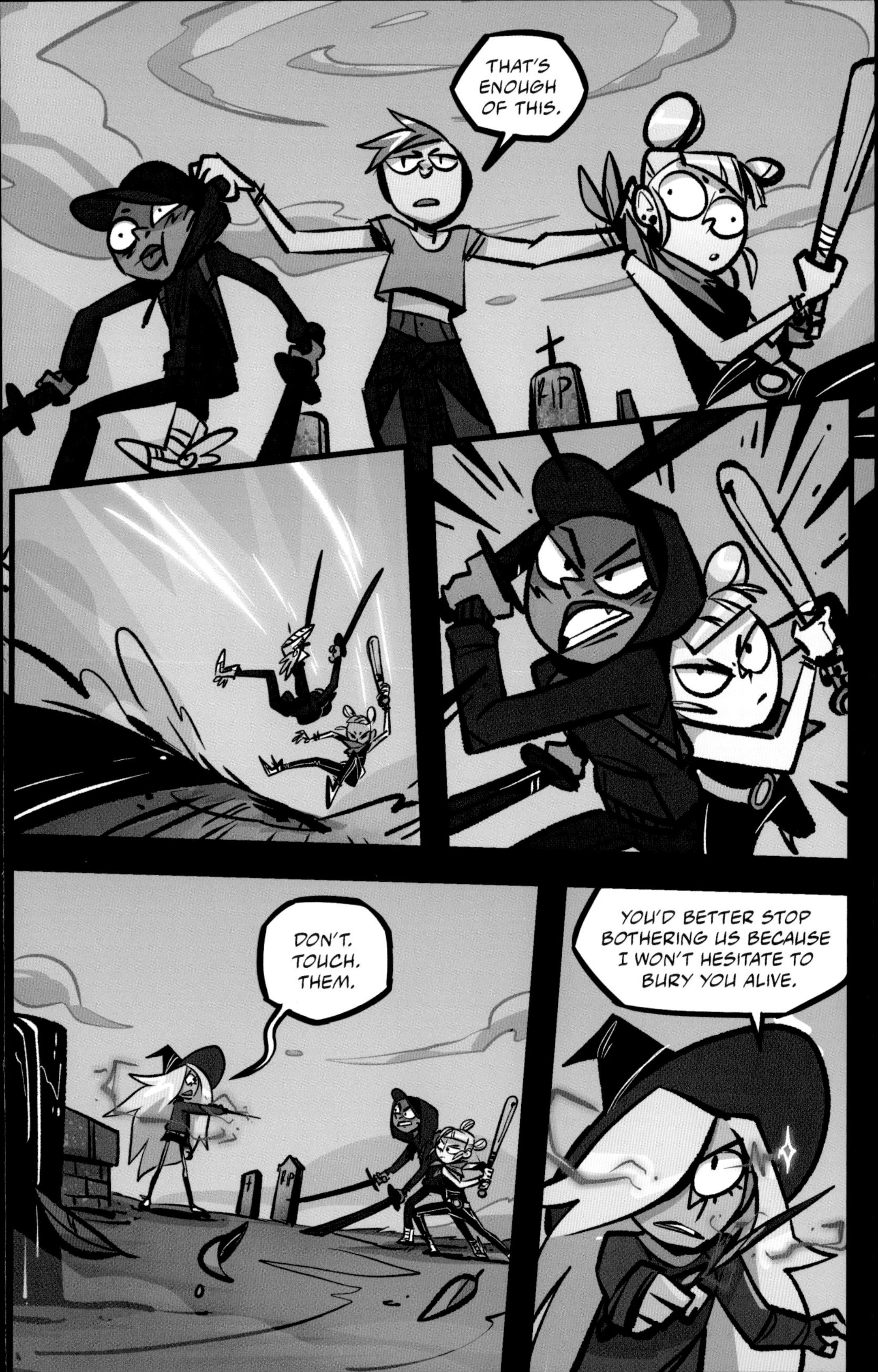
THAT'S ENOUGH OF THIS.
RIP
DON'T. TOUCH. THEM.
YOU'D BETTER STOP BOTHERING US BECAUSE I WON'T HESITATE TO BURY YOU ALIVE.

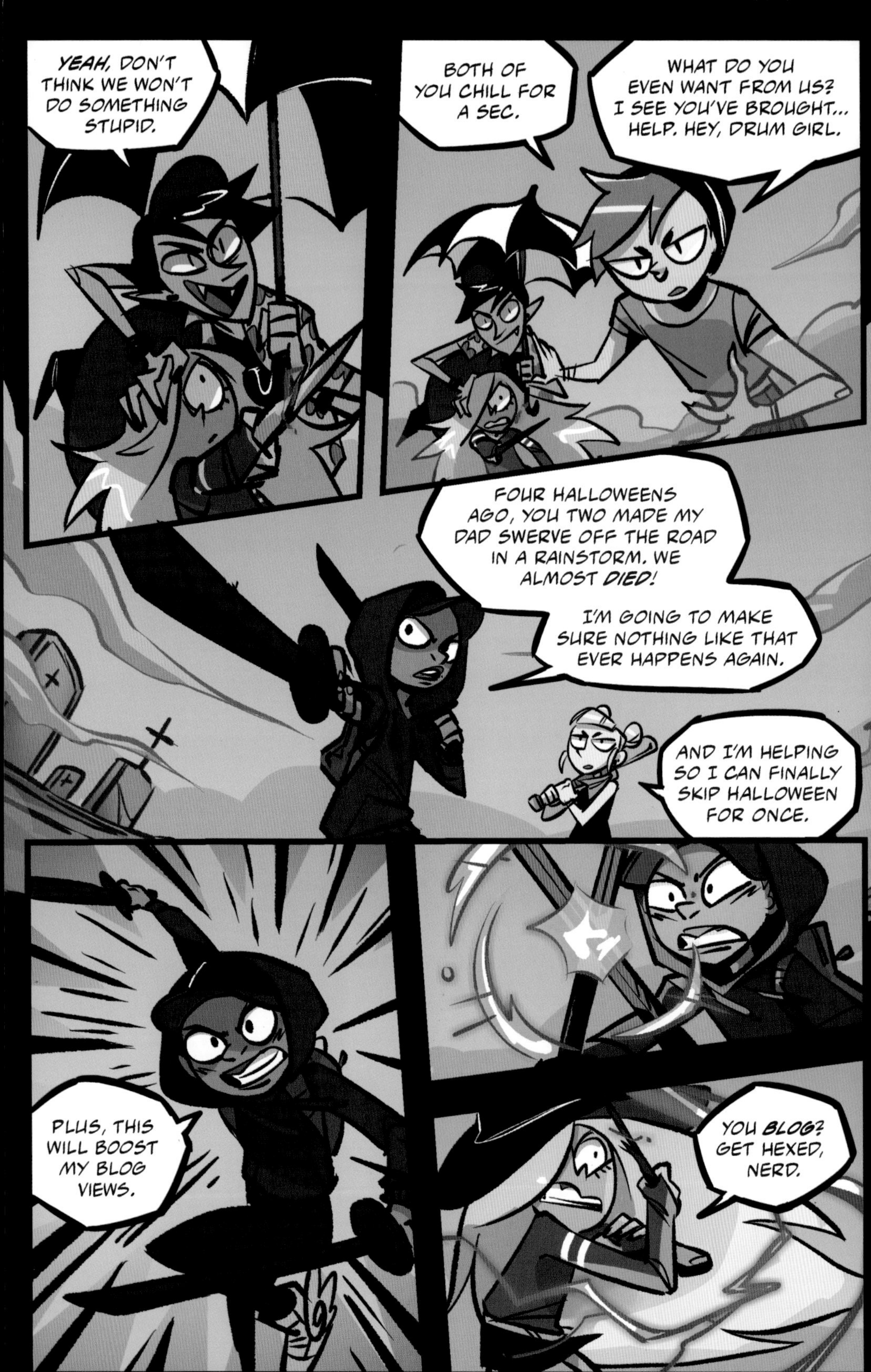
YEAH, DON'T THINK WE WON'T DO SOMETHING STUPID.
BOTH OF YOU CHILL FOR A SEC.
WHAT DO YOU EVEN WANT FROM US? I SEE YOU'VE BROUGHT... HELP. HEY, DRUM GIRL.
FOUR HALLOWEENS AGO, YOU TWO MADE MY DAD SWERVE OFF THE ROAD IN A RAINSTORM. WE ALMOST DIED!
I'M GOING TO MAKE SURE NOTHING LIKE THAT EVER HAPPENS AGAIN.
AND I'M HELPING SO I CAN FINALLY SKIP HALLOWEEN FOR ONCE.
PLUS, THIS WILL BOOST MY BLOG VIEWS.
YOU BLOG? GET HEXED, NERD.

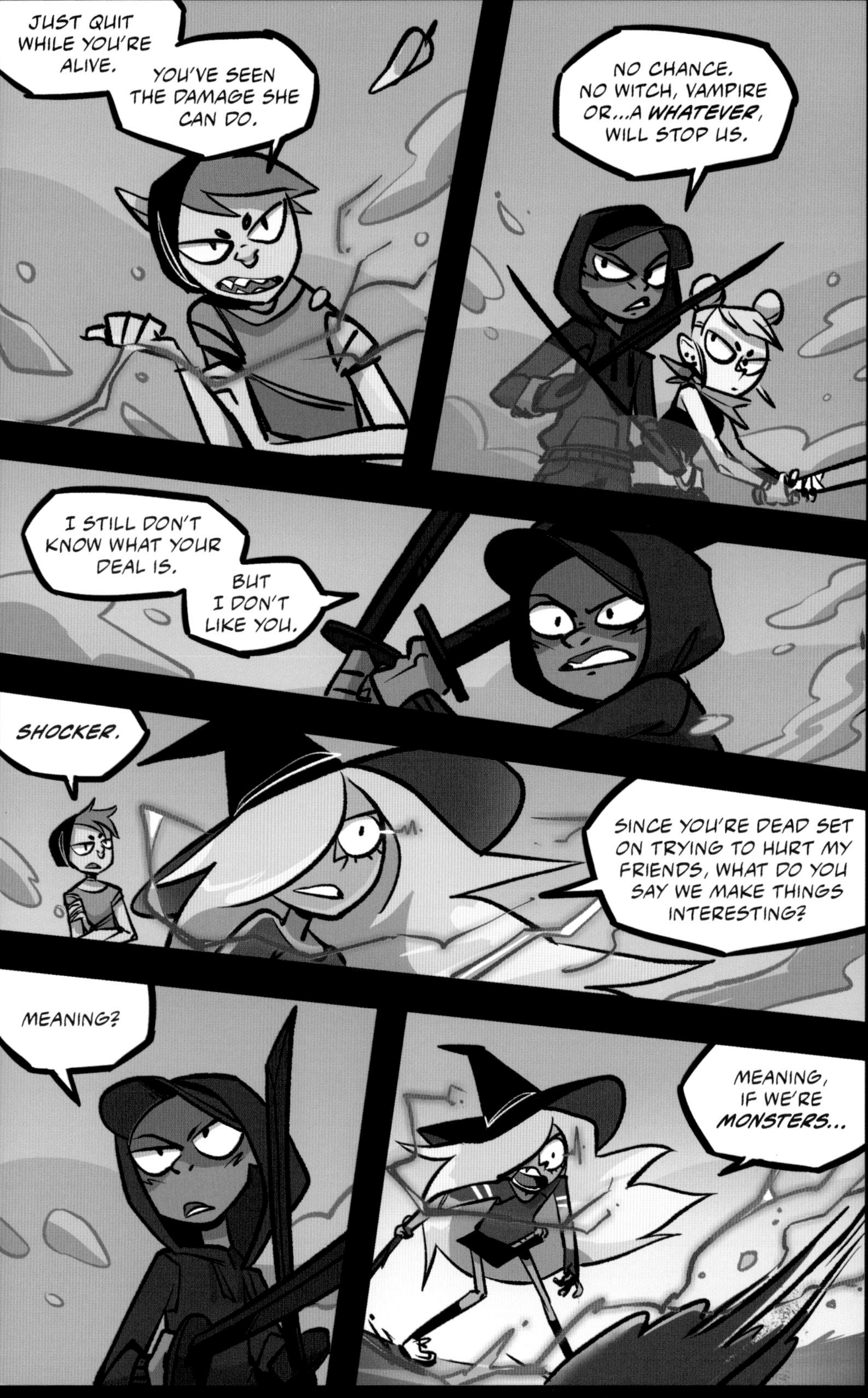
JUST QUIT WHILE YOU'RE ALIVE.
YOU'VE SEEN THE DAMAGE SHE CAN DO.
NO CHANCE. NO WITCH, VAMPIRE OR...A *WHATEVER*, WILL STOP US.
I STILL DON'T KNOW WHAT YOUR DEAL IS.
BUT I DON'T LIKE YOU.
*SHOCKER.*
SINCE YOU'RE DEAD SET ON TRYING TO HURT MY FRIENDS, WHAT DO YOU SAY WE MAKE THINGS INTERESTING?
MEANING?
MEANING, IF WE'RE *MONSTERS...*

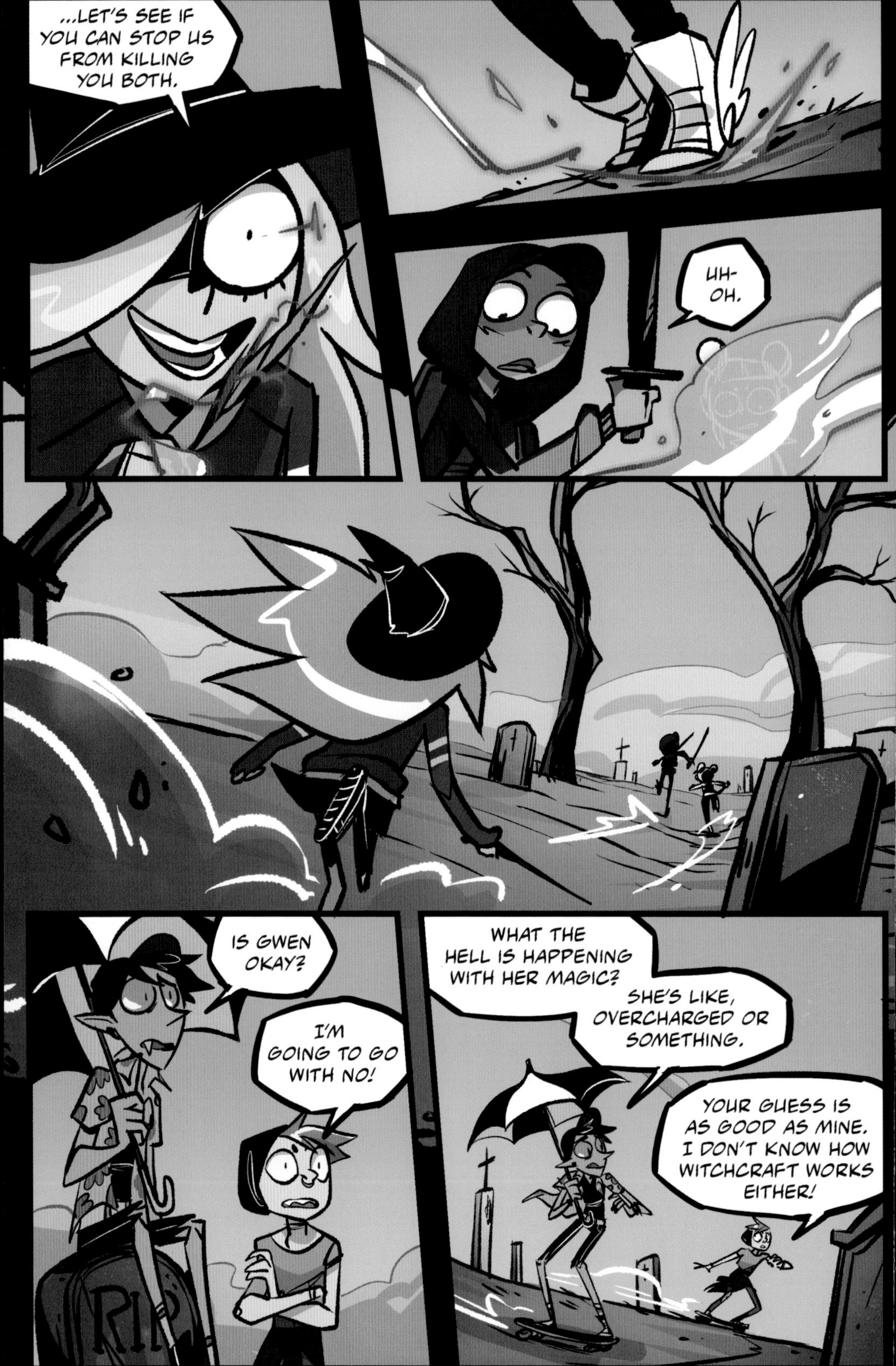
...LET'S SEE IF YOU CAN STOP US FROM KILLING YOU BOTH.
UH-OH.
IS GWEN OKAY?
I'M GOING TO GO WITH NO!
WHAT THE HELL IS HAPPENING WITH HER MAGIC?
SHE'S LIKE, OVERCHARGED OR SOMETHING.
YOUR GUESS IS AS GOOD AS MINE. I DON'T KNOW HOW WITCHCRAFT WORKS EITHER!
RIP

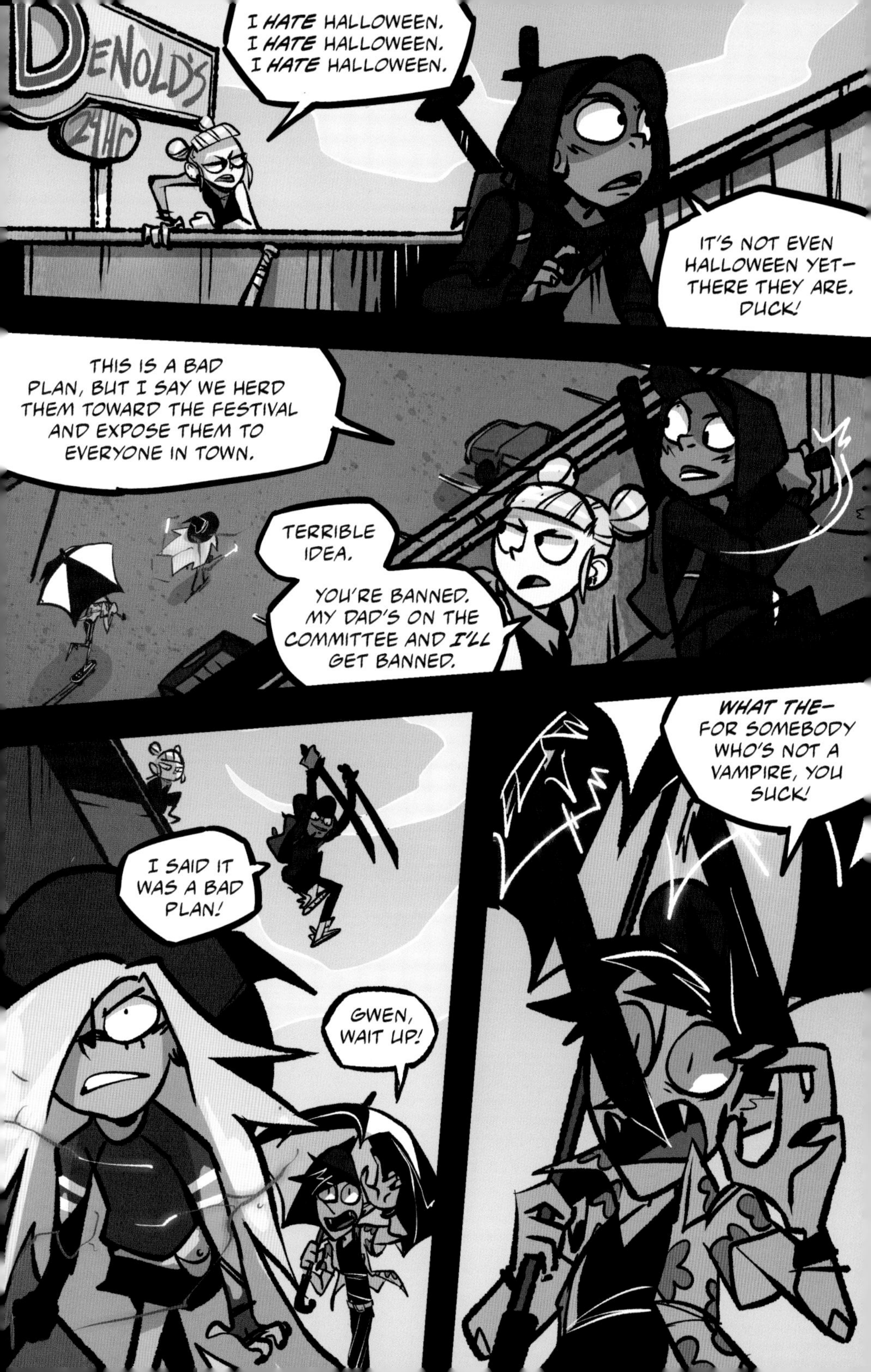
DENOLD'S
24 HR
I *HATE* HALLOWEEN.
I *HATE* HALLOWEEN.
I *HATE* HALLOWEEN.
IT'S NOT EVEN HALLOWEEN YET—THERE THEY ARE. DUCK!
THIS IS A BAD PLAN, BUT I SAY WE HERD THEM TOWARD THE FESTIVAL AND EXPOSE THEM TO EVERYONE IN TOWN.
TERRIBLE IDEA.
YOU'RE BANNED. MY DAD'S ON THE COMMITTEE AND *I'LL* GET BANNED.
I SAID IT WAS A BAD PLAN!
GWEN, WAIT UP!
*WHAT THE—*
FOR SOMEBODY WHO'S NOT A VAMPIRE, YOU SUCK!

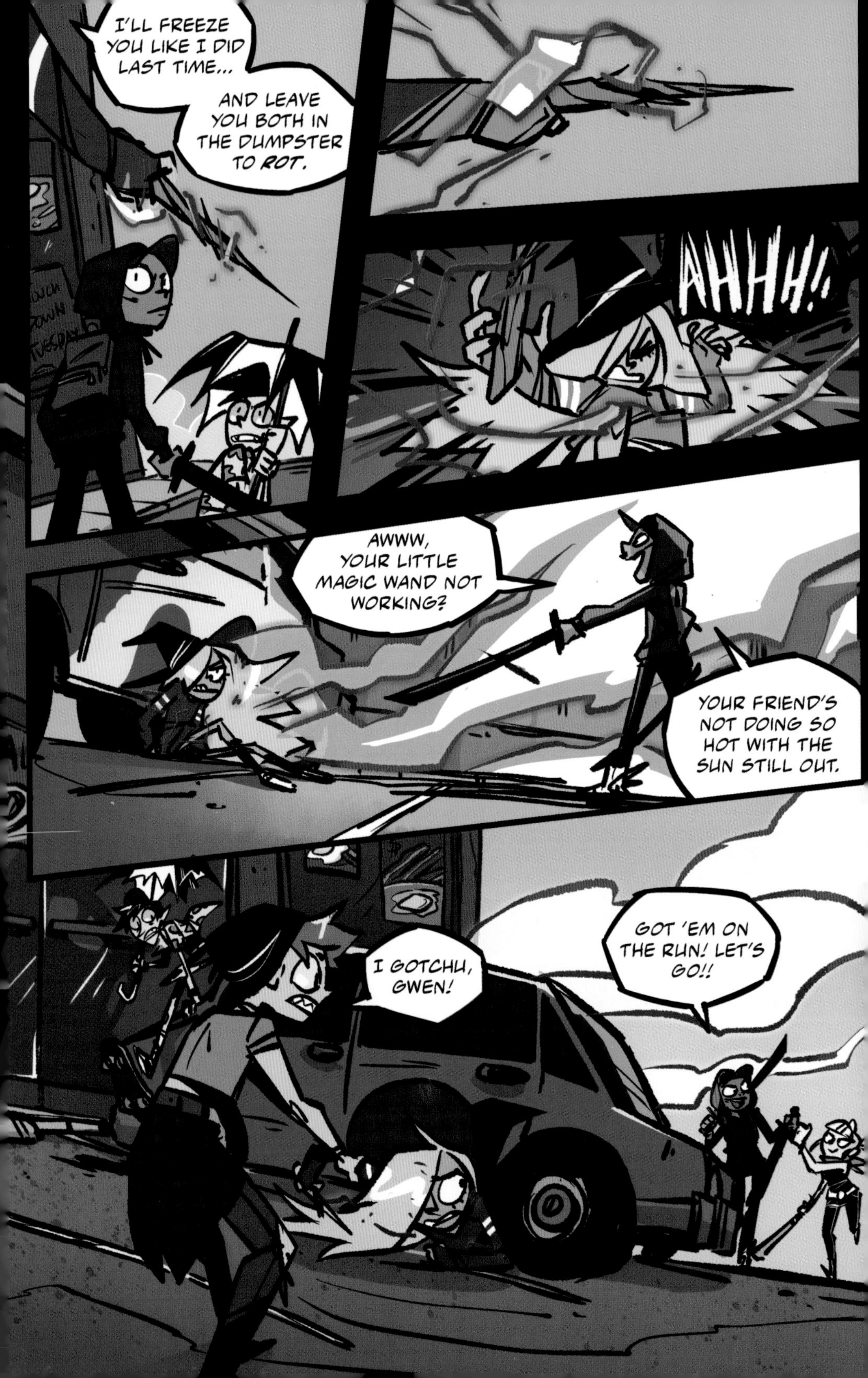
I'LL FREEZE YOU LIKE I DID LAST TIME...
AND LEAVE YOU BOTH IN THE DUMPSTER TO *ROT*.
AHHH!!
AWWW, YOUR LITTLE MAGIC WAND NOT WORKING?
YOUR FRIEND'S NOT DOING SO HOT WITH THE SUN STILL OUT.
I GOTCHU, GWEN!
GOT 'EM ON THE RUN! LET'S GO!!

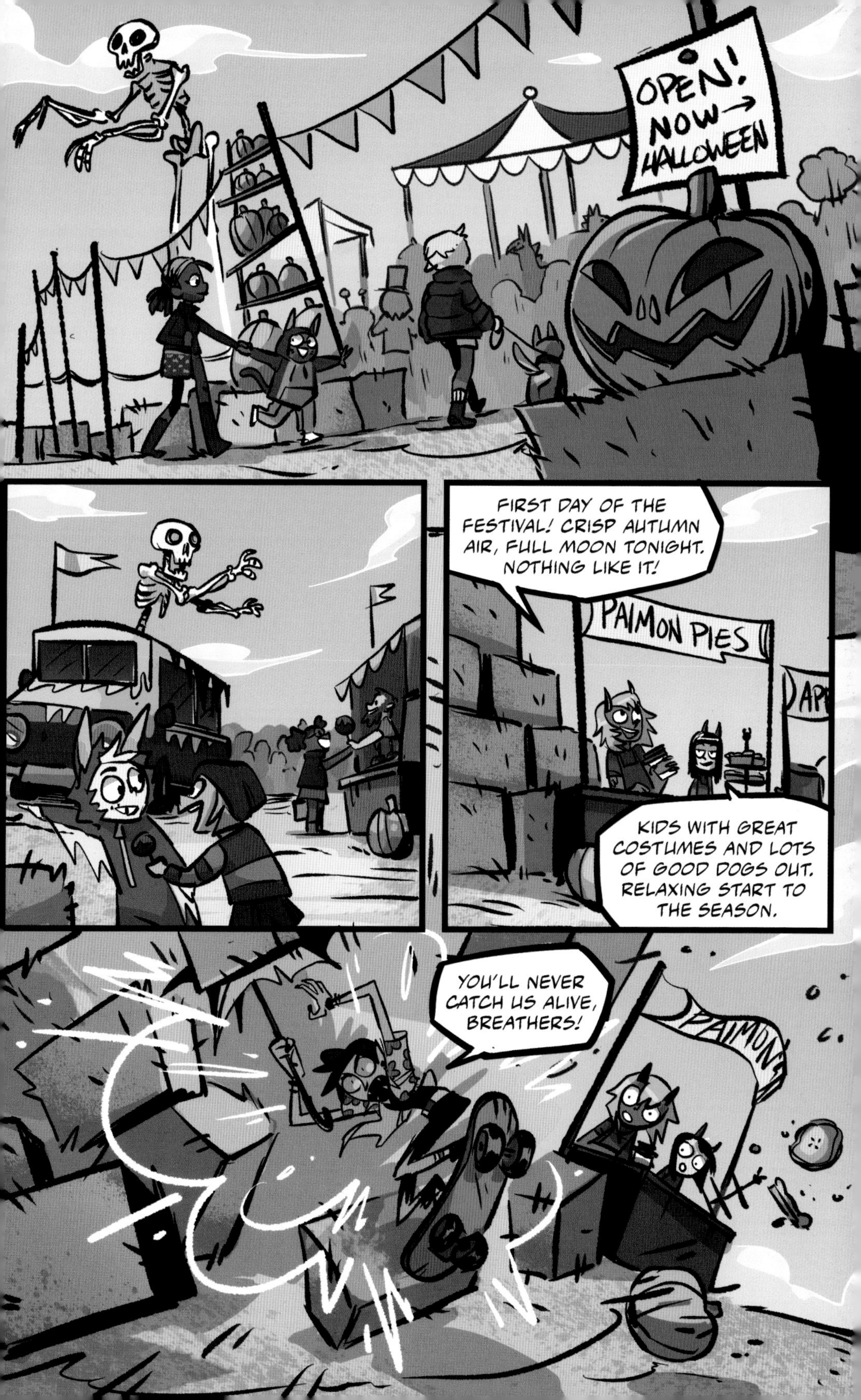
OPEN! NOW → HALLOWEEN
FIRST DAY OF THE FESTIVAL! CRISP AUTUMN AIR, FULL MOON TONIGHT. NOTHING LIKE IT!
PAIMON PIES
KIDS WITH GREAT COSTUMES AND LOTS OF GOOD DOGS OUT. RELAXING START TO THE SEASON.
YOU'LL NEVER CATCH US ALIVE, BREATHERS!
PAIMON

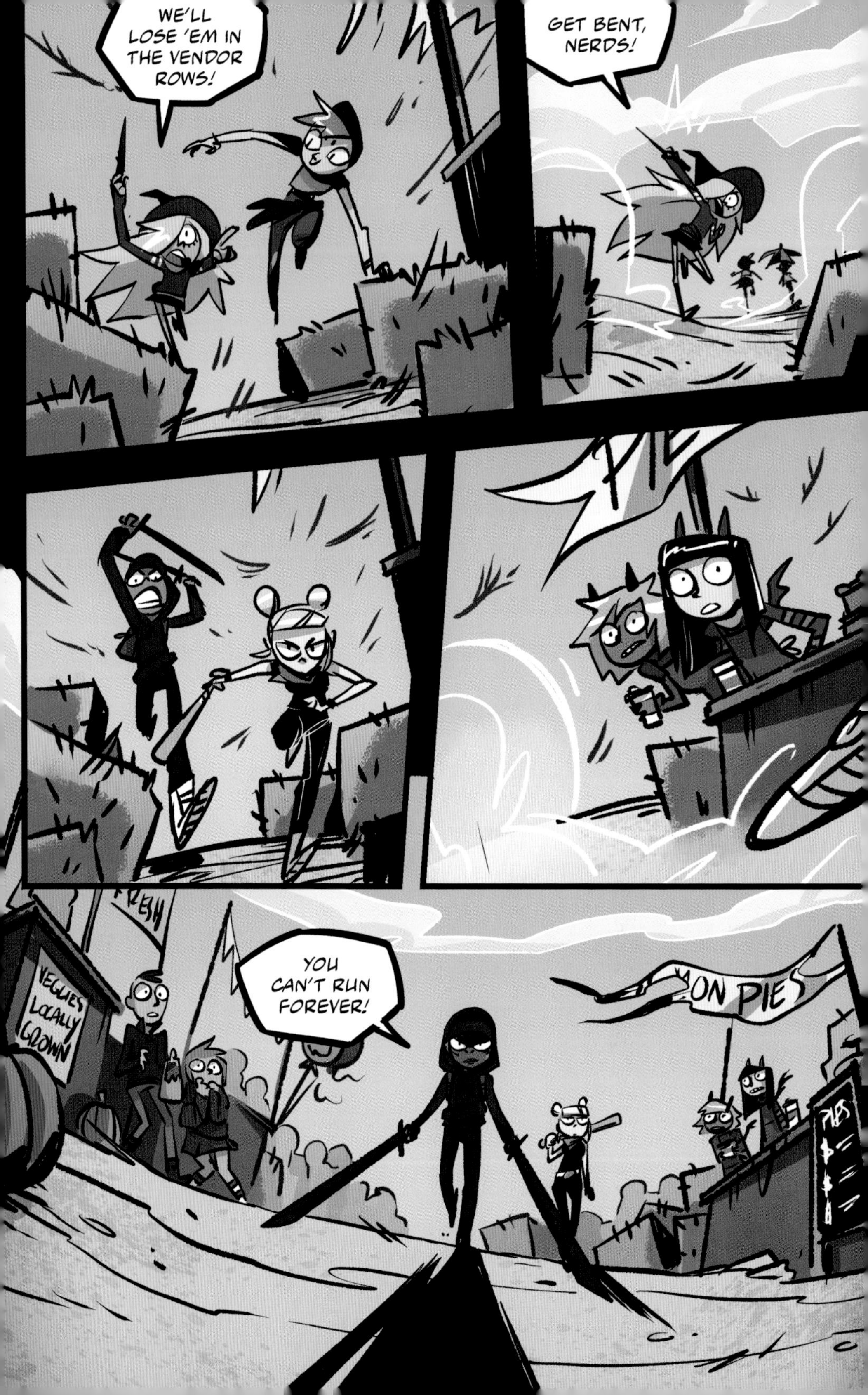
WE'LL LOSE 'EM IN THE VENDOR ROWS!
GET BENT, NERDS!
PIES
FRESH
VEGGIES LOCALLY GROWN
YOU CAN'T RUN FOREVER!
ON PIES
PIES $ $

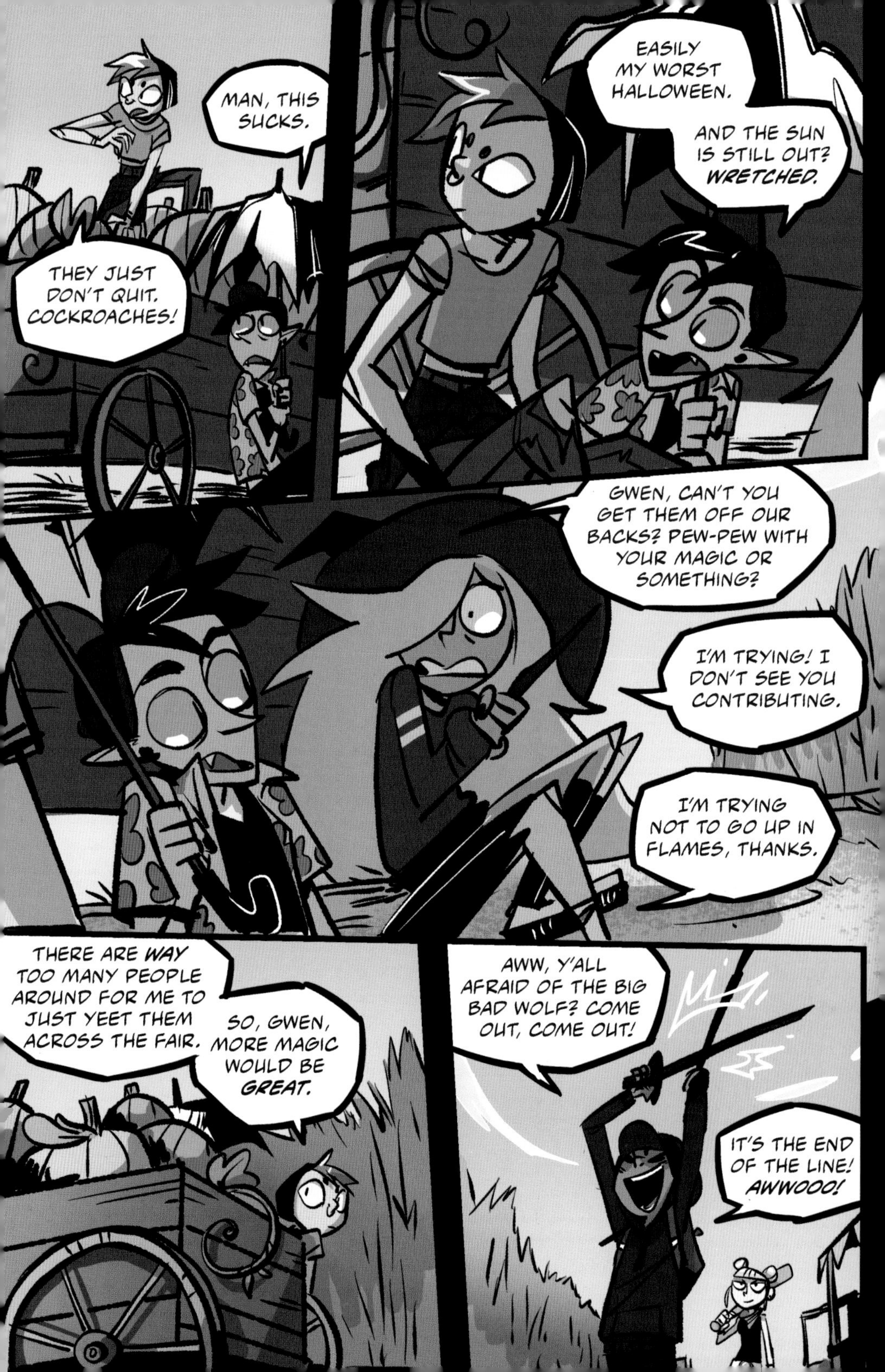

MAN, THIS SUCKS.
THEY JUST DON'T QUIT. COCKROACHES!
EASILY MY WORST HALLOWEEN.
AND THE SUN IS STILL OUT? *WRETCHED.*
GWEN, CAN'T YOU GET THEM OFF OUR BACKS? PEW-PEW WITH YOUR MAGIC OR SOMETHING?
I'M TRYING! I DON'T SEE YOU CONTRIBUTING.
I'M TRYING NOT TO GO UP IN FLAMES, THANKS.
THERE ARE *WAY* TOO MANY PEOPLE AROUND FOR ME TO JUST YEET THEM ACROSS THE FAIR.
SO, GWEN, MORE MAGIC WOULD BE *GREAT.*
AWW, Y'ALL AFRAID OF THE BIG BAD WOLF? COME OUT, COME OUT!
IT'S THE END OF THE LINE! *AWWOOO!*

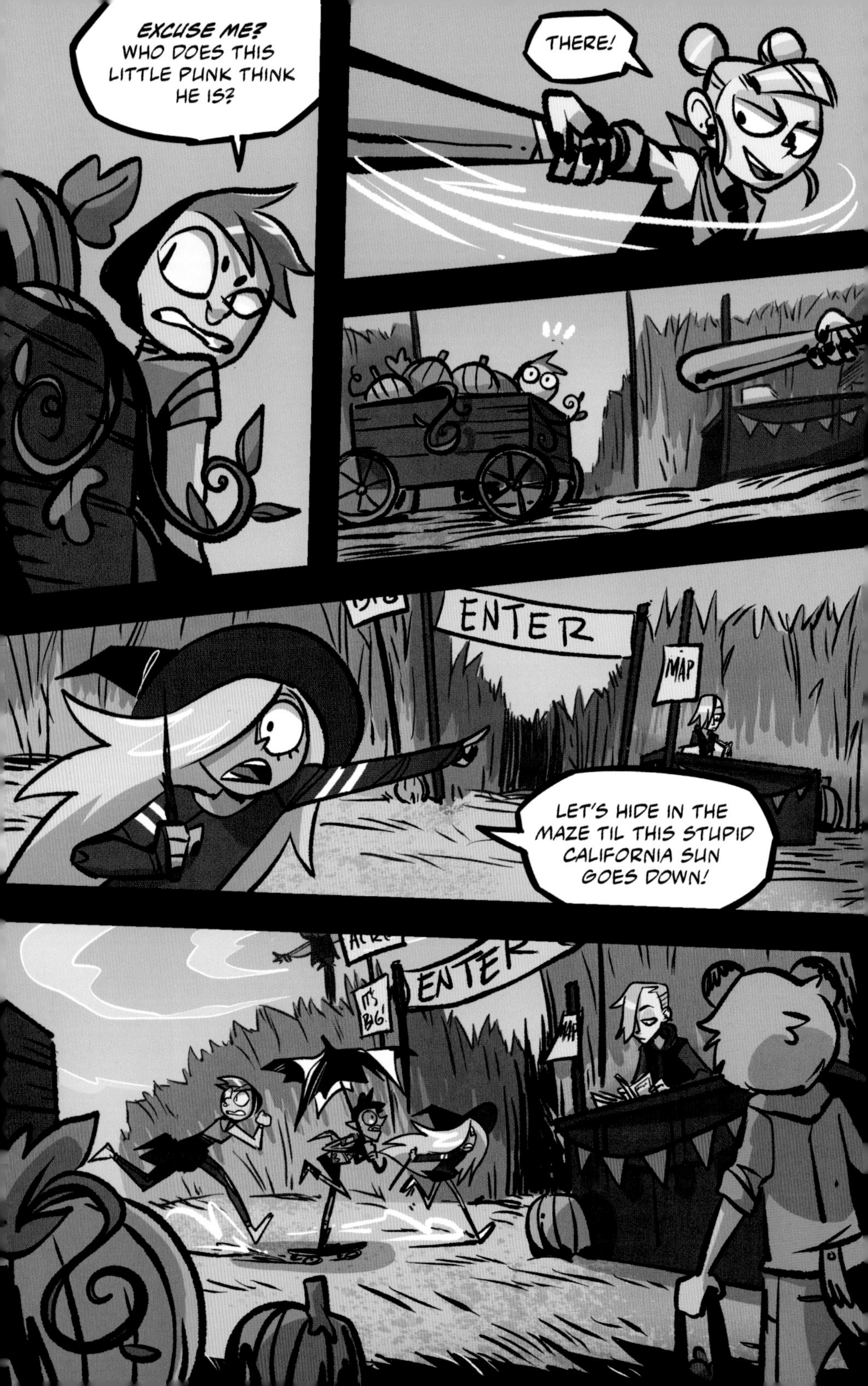
EXCUSE ME? WHO DOES THIS LITTLE PUNK THINK HE IS?
THERE!
ENTER
MAP
LET'S HIDE IN THE MAZE TIL THIS STUPID CALIFORNIA SUN GOES DOWN!
ENTER
IT'S BIG!

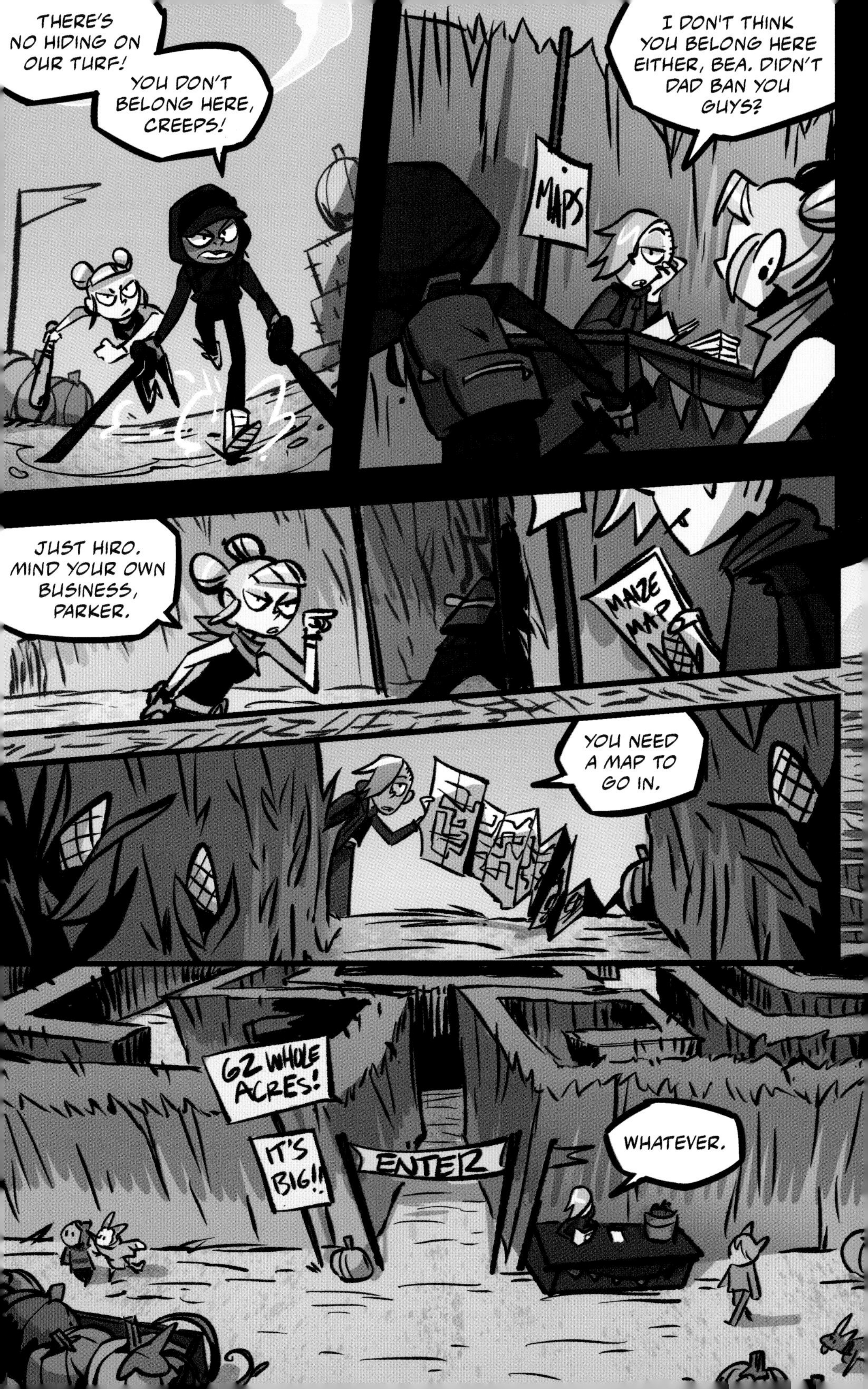
THERE'S NO HIDING ON OUR TURF!
YOU DON'T BELONG HERE, CREEPS!
I DON'T THINK YOU BELONG HERE EITHER, BEA. DIDN'T DAD BAN YOU GUYS?
MAPS
JUST HIRO. MIND YOUR OWN BUSINESS, PARKER.
MAIZE MAP
YOU NEED A MAP TO GO IN.
62 WHOLE ACRES!
IT'S BIG!!
ENTER
WHATEVER.

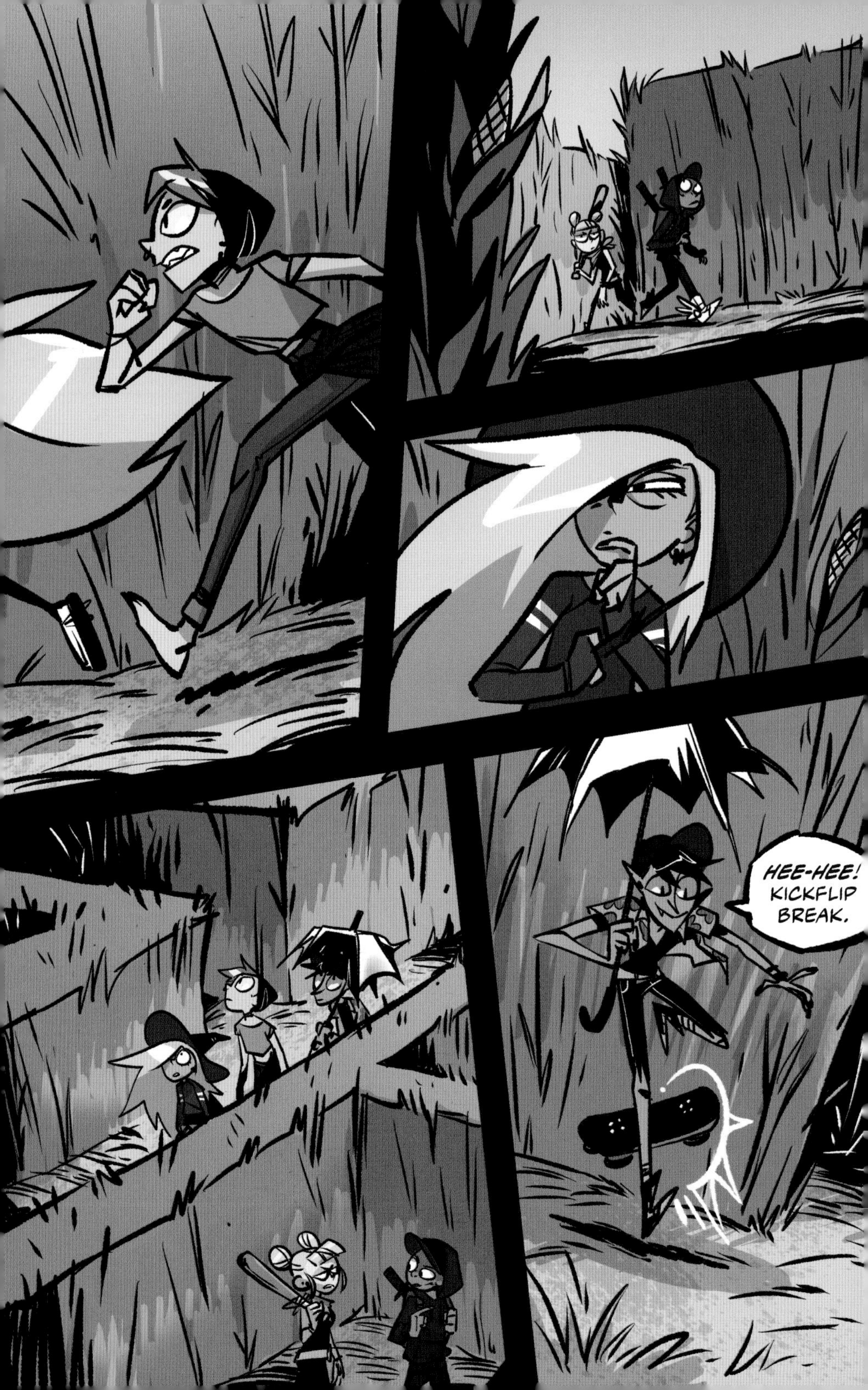
HEE-HEE! KICKFLIP BREAK.

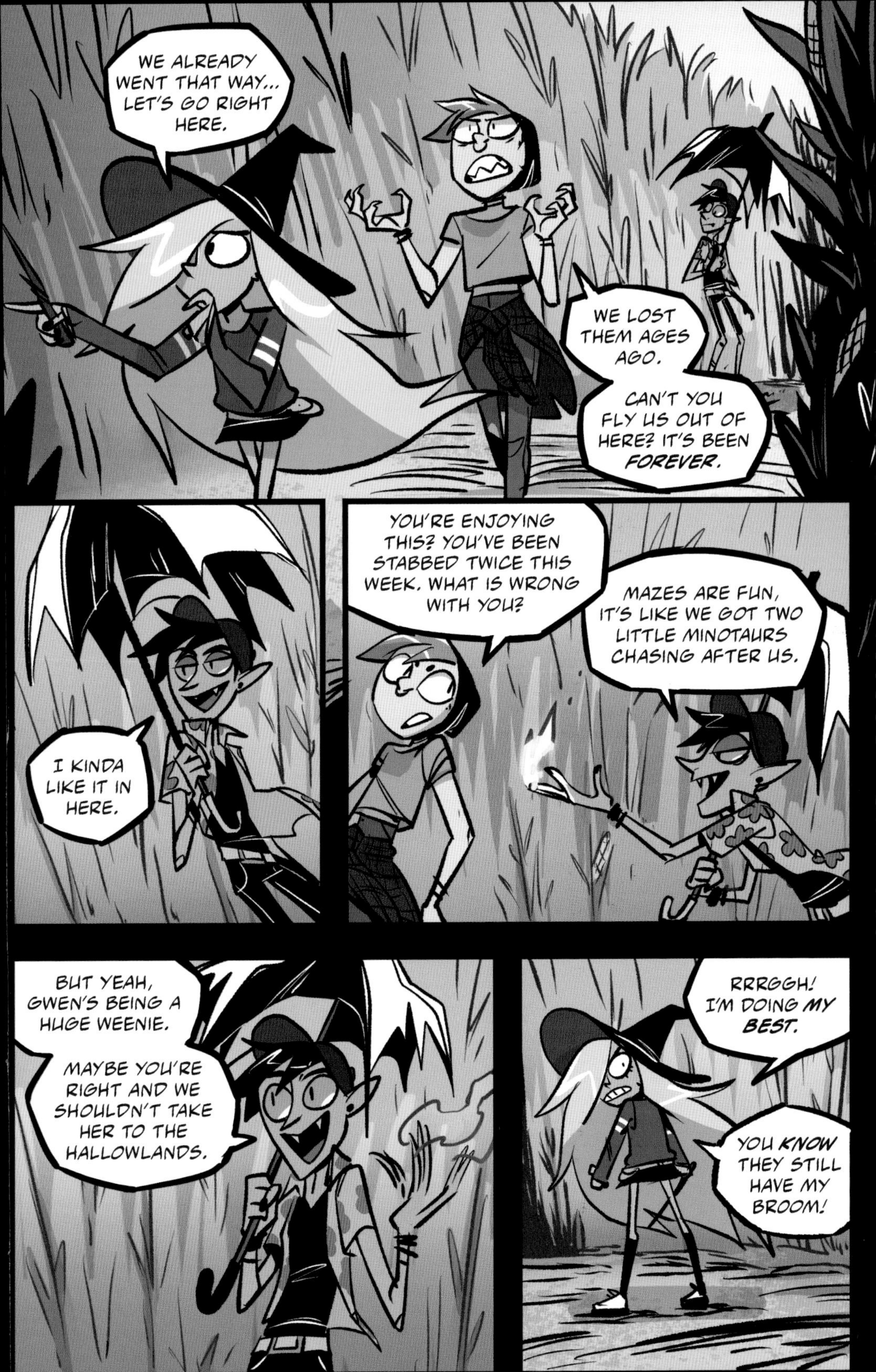
WE ALREADY WENT THAT WAY... LET'S GO RIGHT HERE.
WE LOST THEM AGES AGO.
CAN'T YOU FLY US OUT OF HERE? IT'S BEEN *FOREVER*.
I KINDA LIKE IT IN HERE.
YOU'RE ENJOYING THIS? YOU'VE BEEN STABBED TWICE THIS WEEK. WHAT IS WRONG WITH YOU?
MAZES ARE FUN, IT'S LIKE WE GOT TWO LITTLE MINOTAURS CHASING AFTER US.
BUT YEAH, GWEN'S BEING A HUGE WEENIE.
MAYBE YOU'RE RIGHT AND WE SHOULDN'T TAKE HER TO THE HALLOWLANDS.
RRRGGH! I'M DOING *MY BEST*.
YOU *KNOW* THEY STILL HAVE MY BROOM!

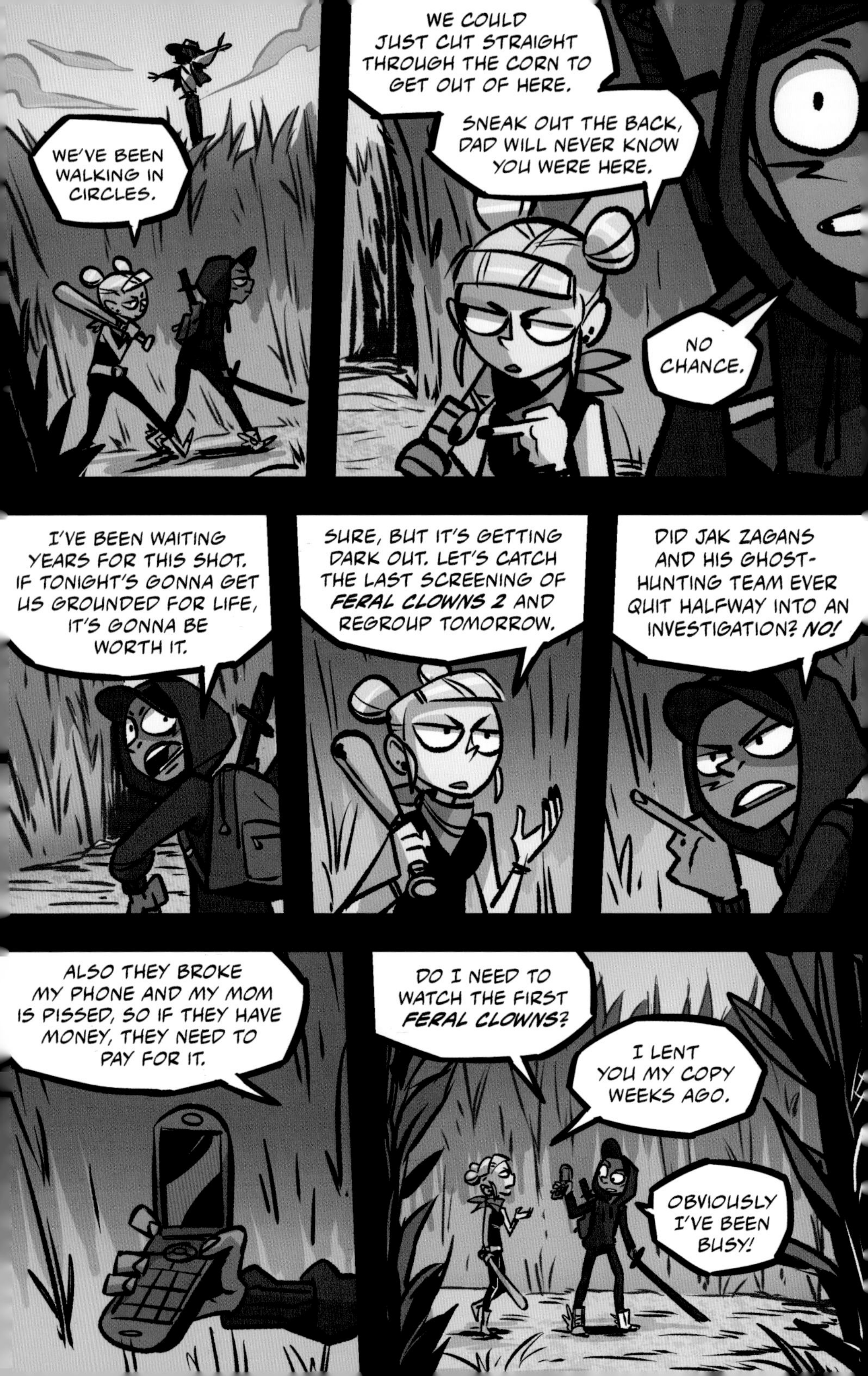
WE'VE BEEN WALKING IN CIRCLES.
WE COULD JUST CUT STRAIGHT THROUGH THE CORN TO GET OUT OF HERE.
SNEAK OUT THE BACK, DAD WILL NEVER KNOW YOU WERE HERE.
NO CHANCE.
I'VE BEEN WAITING YEARS FOR THIS SHOT. IF TONIGHT'S GONNA GET US GROUNDED FOR LIFE, IT'S GONNA BE WORTH IT.
SURE, BUT IT'S GETTING DARK OUT. LET'S CATCH THE LAST SCREENING OF FERAL CLOWNS 2 AND REGROUP TOMORROW.
DID JAK ZAGANS AND HIS GHOST-HUNTING TEAM EVER QUIT HALFWAY INTO AN INVESTIGATION? NO!
ALSO THEY BROKE MY PHONE AND MY MOM IS PISSED, SO IF THEY HAVE MONEY, THEY NEED TO PAY FOR IT.
DO I NEED TO WATCH THE FIRST FERAL CLOWNS?
I LENT YOU MY COPY WEEKS AGO.
OBVIOUSLY I'VE BEEN BUSY!

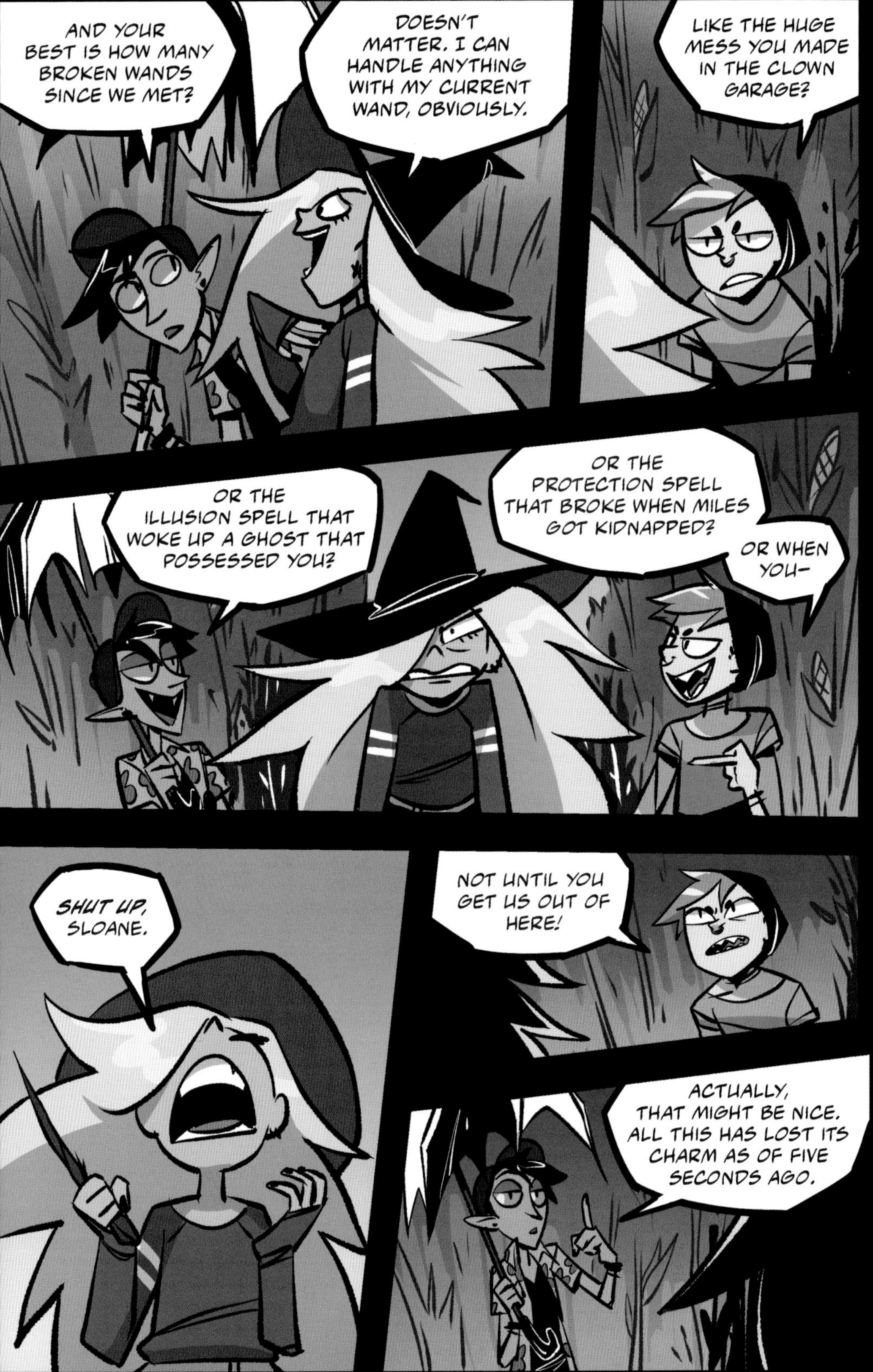
AND YOUR BEST IS HOW MANY BROKEN WANDS SINCE WE MET?
DOESN'T MATTER. I CAN HANDLE ANYTHING WITH MY CURRENT WAND, OBVIOUSLY.
LIKE THE HUGE MESS YOU MADE IN THE CLOWN GARAGE?
OR THE ILLUSION SPELL THAT WOKE UP A GHOST THAT POSSESSED YOU?
OR THE PROTECTION SPELL THAT BROKE WHEN MILES GOT KIDNAPPED?
OR WHEN YOU—
SHUT UP, SLOANE.
NOT UNTIL YOU GET US OUT OF HERE!
ACTUALLY, THAT MIGHT BE NICE. ALL THIS HAS LOST ITS CHARM AS OF FIVE SECONDS AGO.

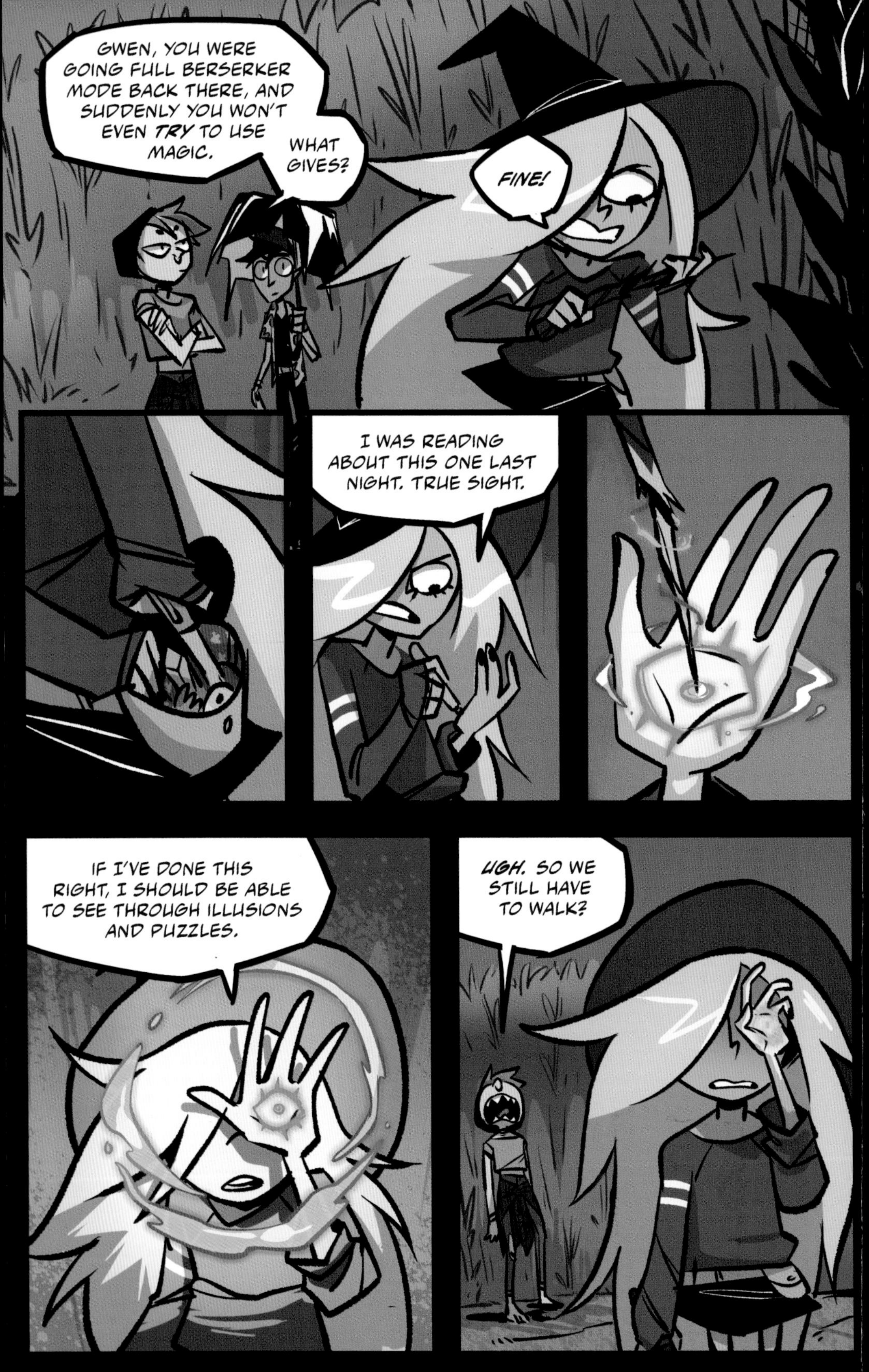
GWEN, YOU WERE GOING FULL BERSERKER MODE BACK THERE, AND SUDDENLY YOU WON'T EVEN *TRY* TO USE MAGIC.
WHAT GIVES?
*FINE!*
I WAS READING ABOUT THIS ONE LAST NIGHT. TRUE SIGHT.
IF I'VE DONE THIS RIGHT, I SHOULD BE ABLE TO SEE THROUGH ILLUSIONS AND PUZZLES.
*UGH.* SO WE STILL HAVE TO WALK?

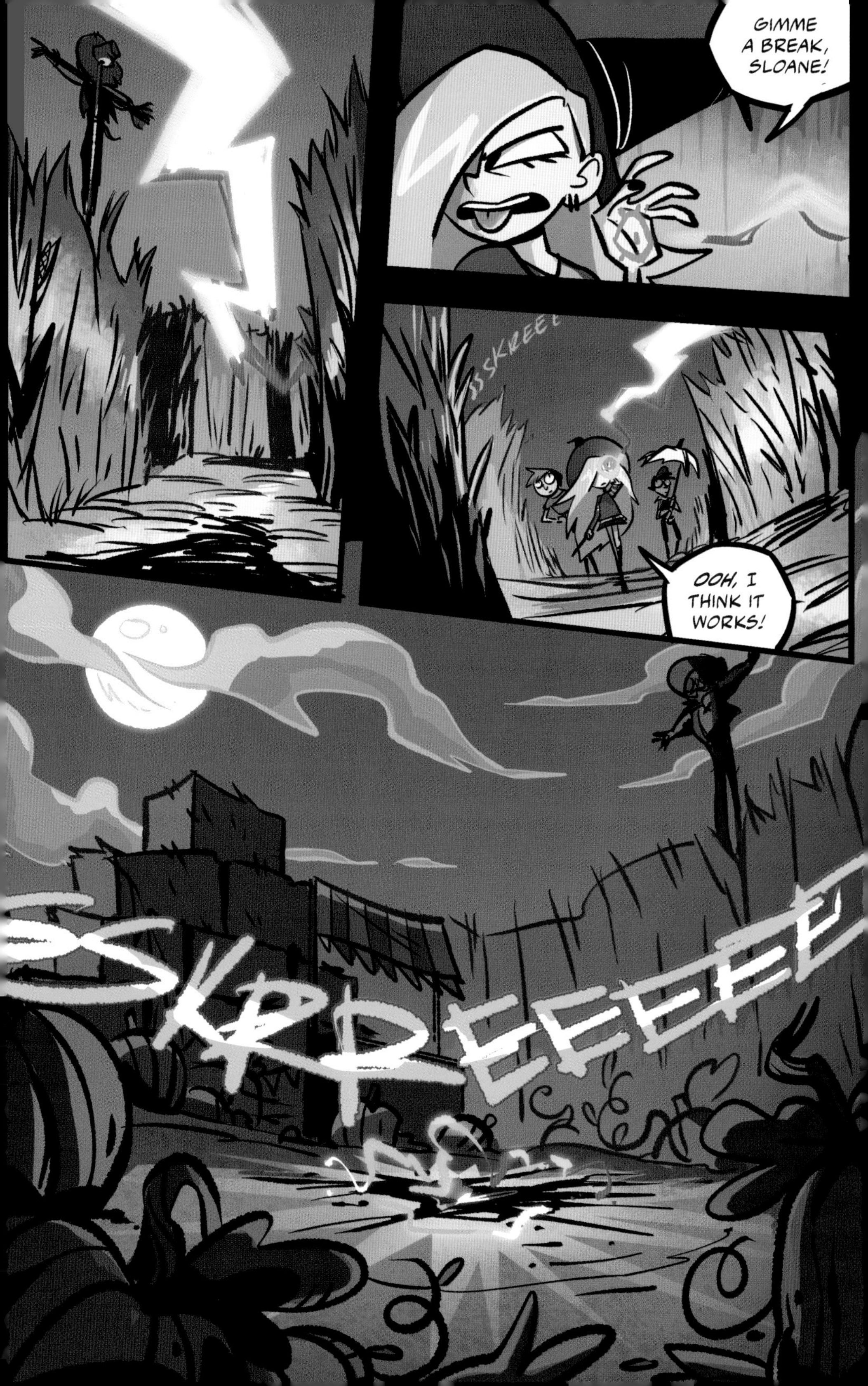
GIMME A BREAK, SLOANE!
SSSKREEE
OOH, I THINK IT WORKS!
SKRREEEEEE

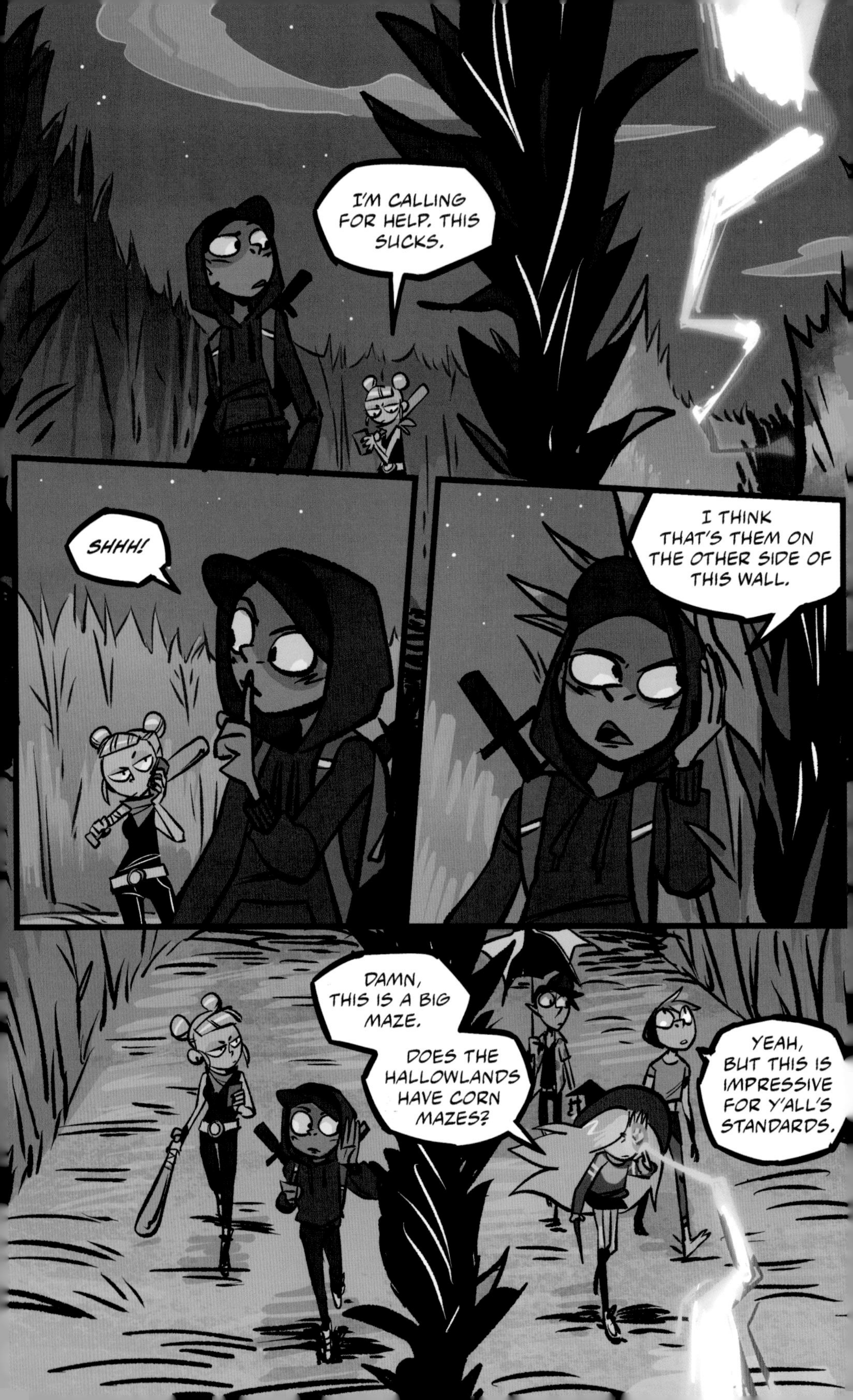
I'M CALLING FOR HELP. THIS SUCKS.
SHHH!
I THINK THAT'S THEM ON THE OTHER SIDE OF THIS WALL.
DAMN, THIS IS A BIG MAZE.
DOES THE HALLOWLANDS HAVE CORN MAZES?
YEAH, BUT THIS IS IMPRESSIVE FOR Y'ALL'S STANDARDS.

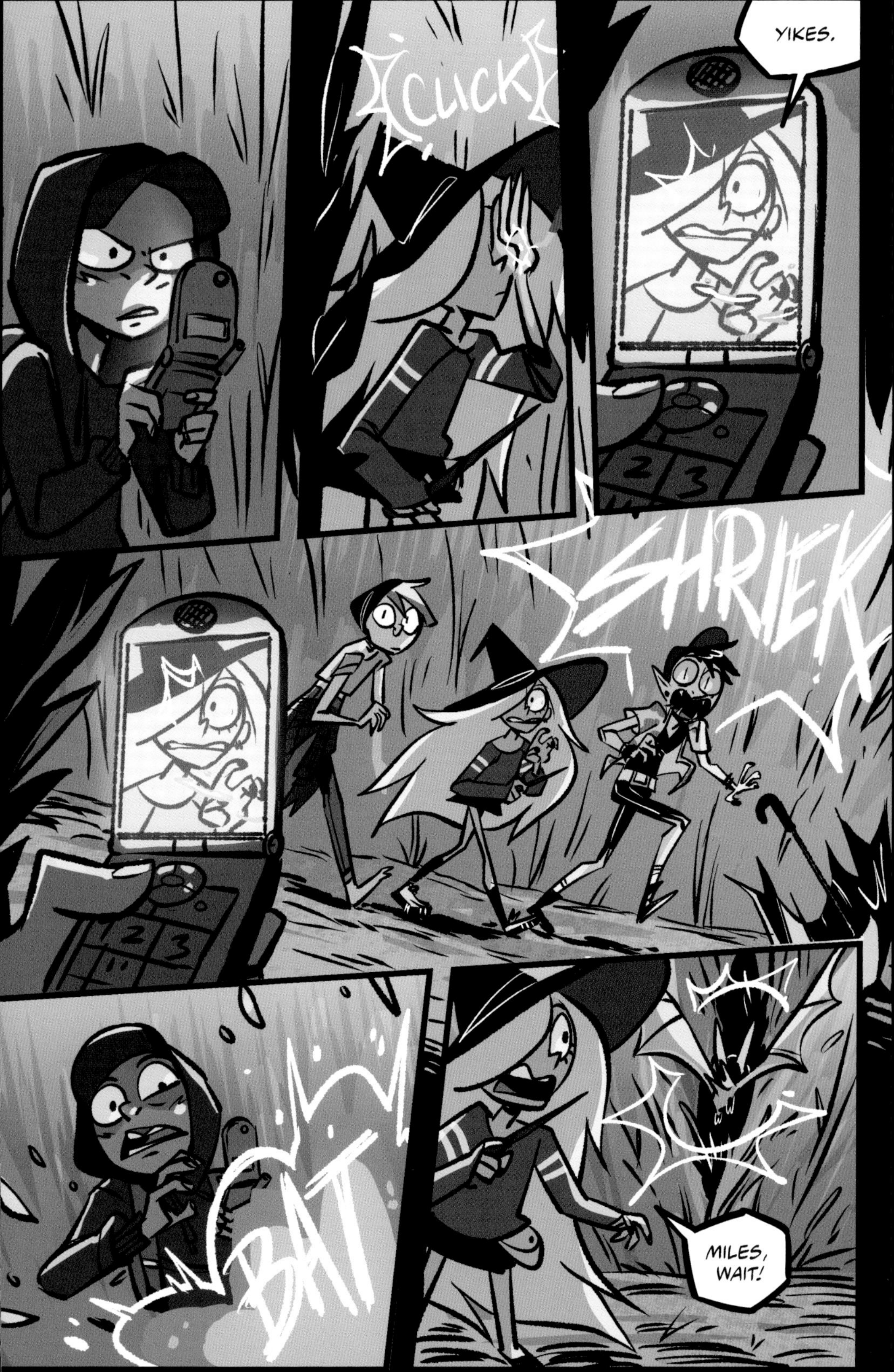
CLICK
YIKES.
SHRIEK
BAT
MILES, WAIT!

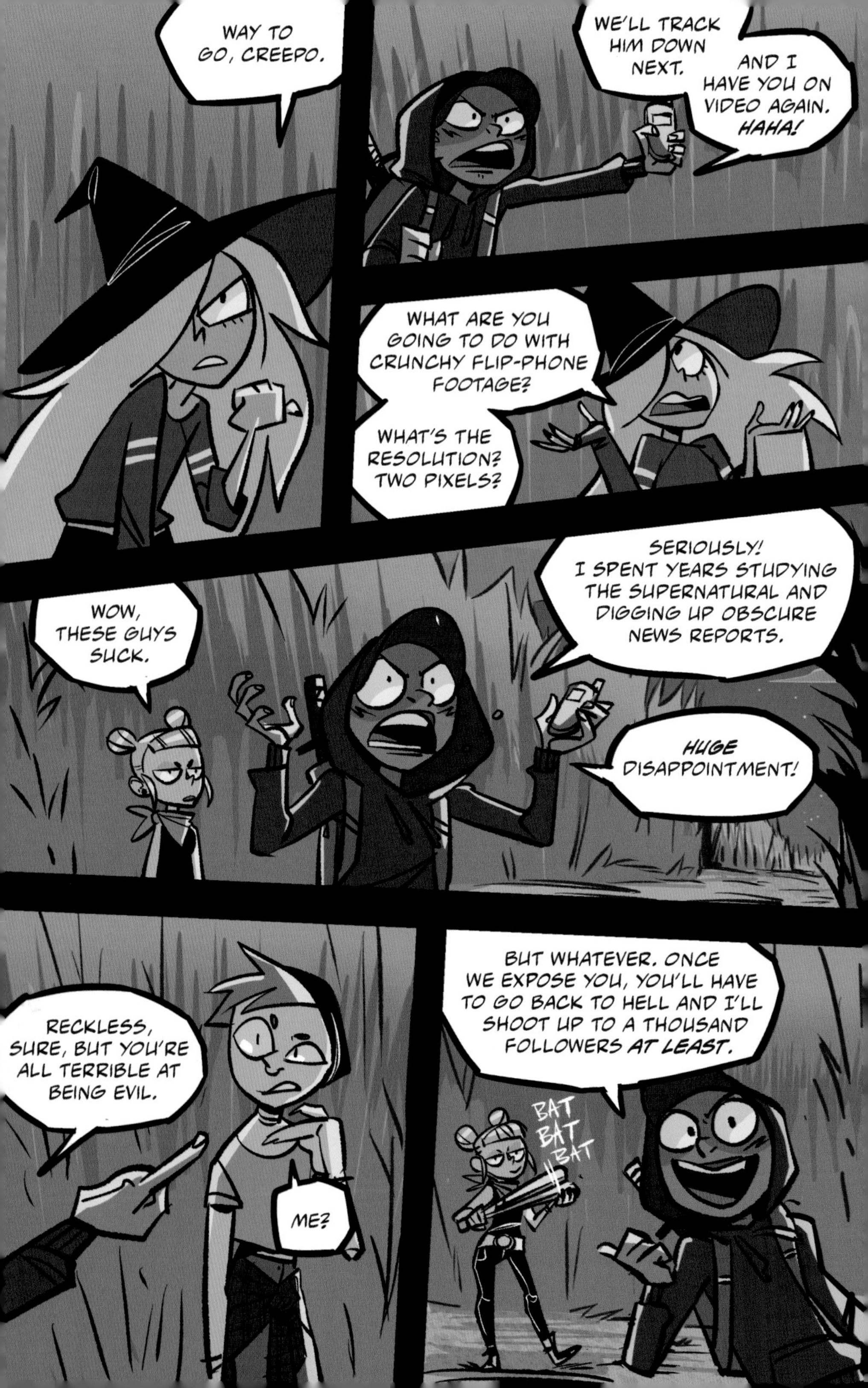

WAY TO GO, CREEPO.
WE'LL TRACK HIM DOWN NEXT.
AND I HAVE YOU ON VIDEO AGAIN. HAHA!
WHAT ARE YOU GOING TO DO WITH CRUNCHY FLIP-PHONE FOOTAGE?
WHAT'S THE RESOLUTION? TWO PIXELS?
WOW, THESE GUYS SUCK.
SERIOUSLY! I SPENT YEARS STUDYING THE SUPERNATURAL AND DIGGING UP OBSCURE NEWS REPORTS.
HUGE DISAPPOINTMENT!
RECKLESS, SURE, BUT YOU'RE ALL TERRIBLE AT BEING EVIL.
ME?
BUT WHATEVER. ONCE WE EXPOSE YOU, YOU'LL HAVE TO GO BACK TO HELL AND I'LL SHOOT UP TO A THOUSAND FOLLOWERS AT LEAST.
BAT BAT BAT

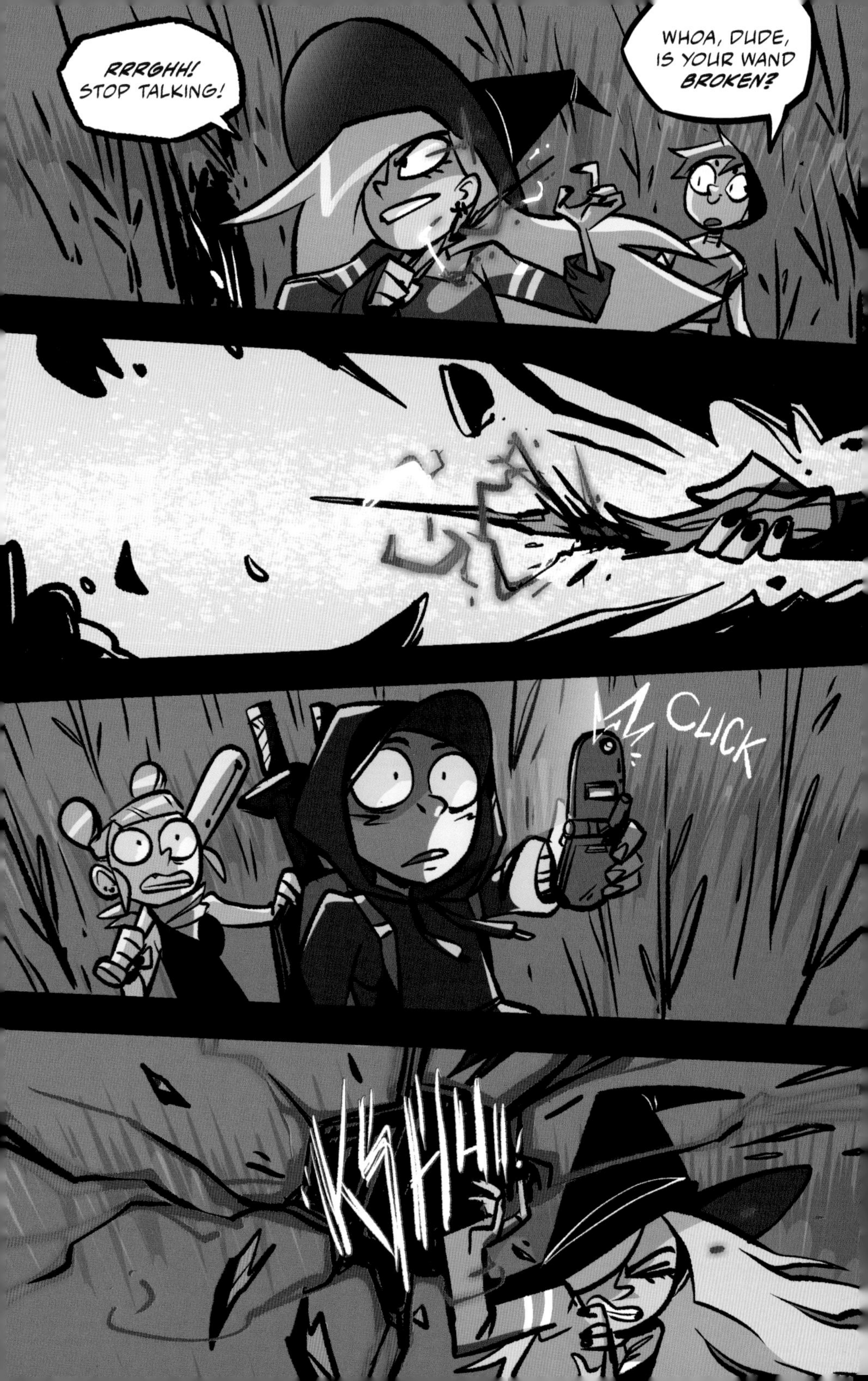
RRRGHH! STOP TALKING!
WHOA, DUDE, IS YOUR WAND BROKEN?
CLICK

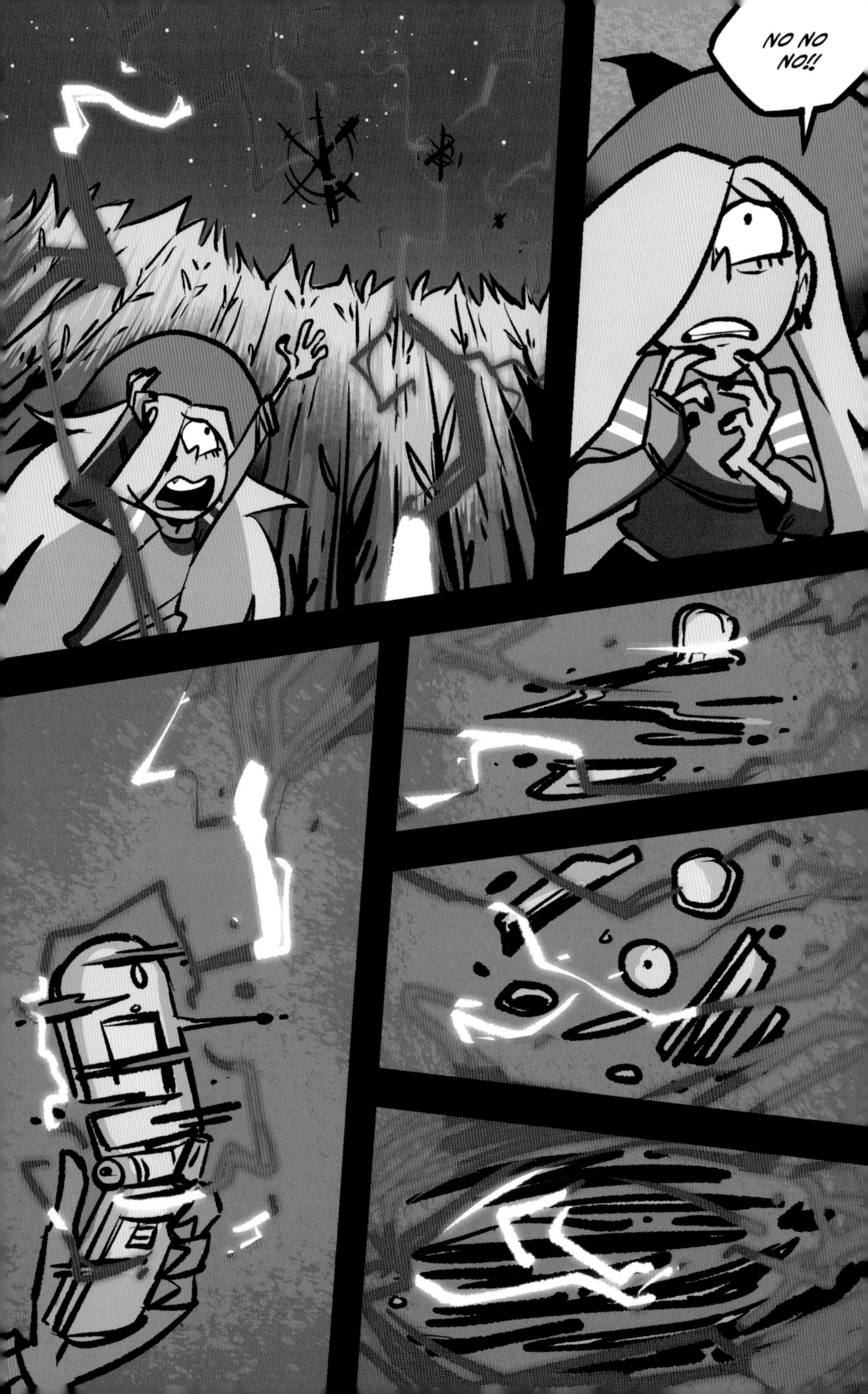
NO NO NO!!

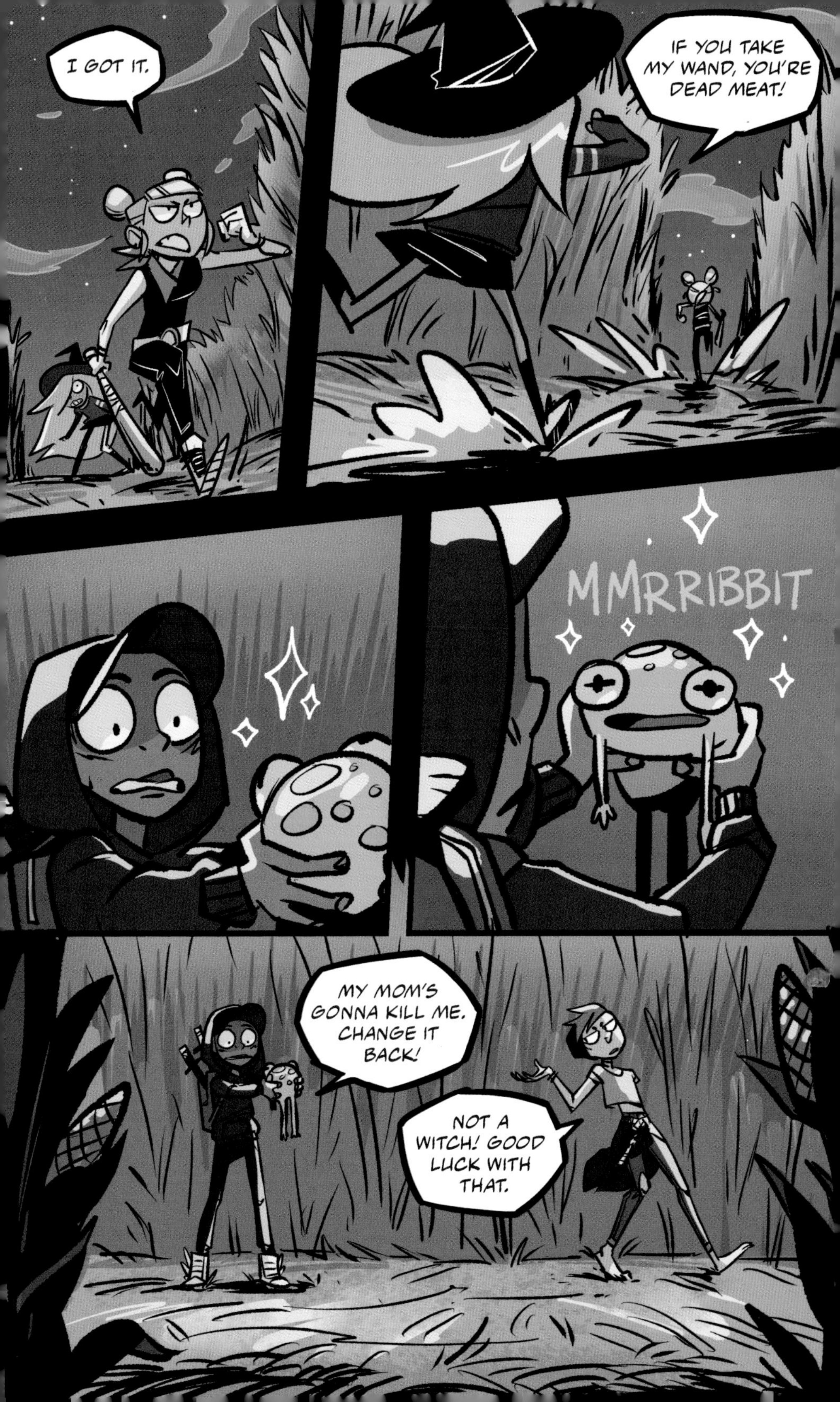
I GOT IT.
IF YOU TAKE MY WAND, YOU'RE DEAD MEAT!
MMRRIBBIT
MY MOM'S GONNA KILL ME. CHANGE IT BACK!
NOT A WITCH! GOOD LUCK WITH THAT.

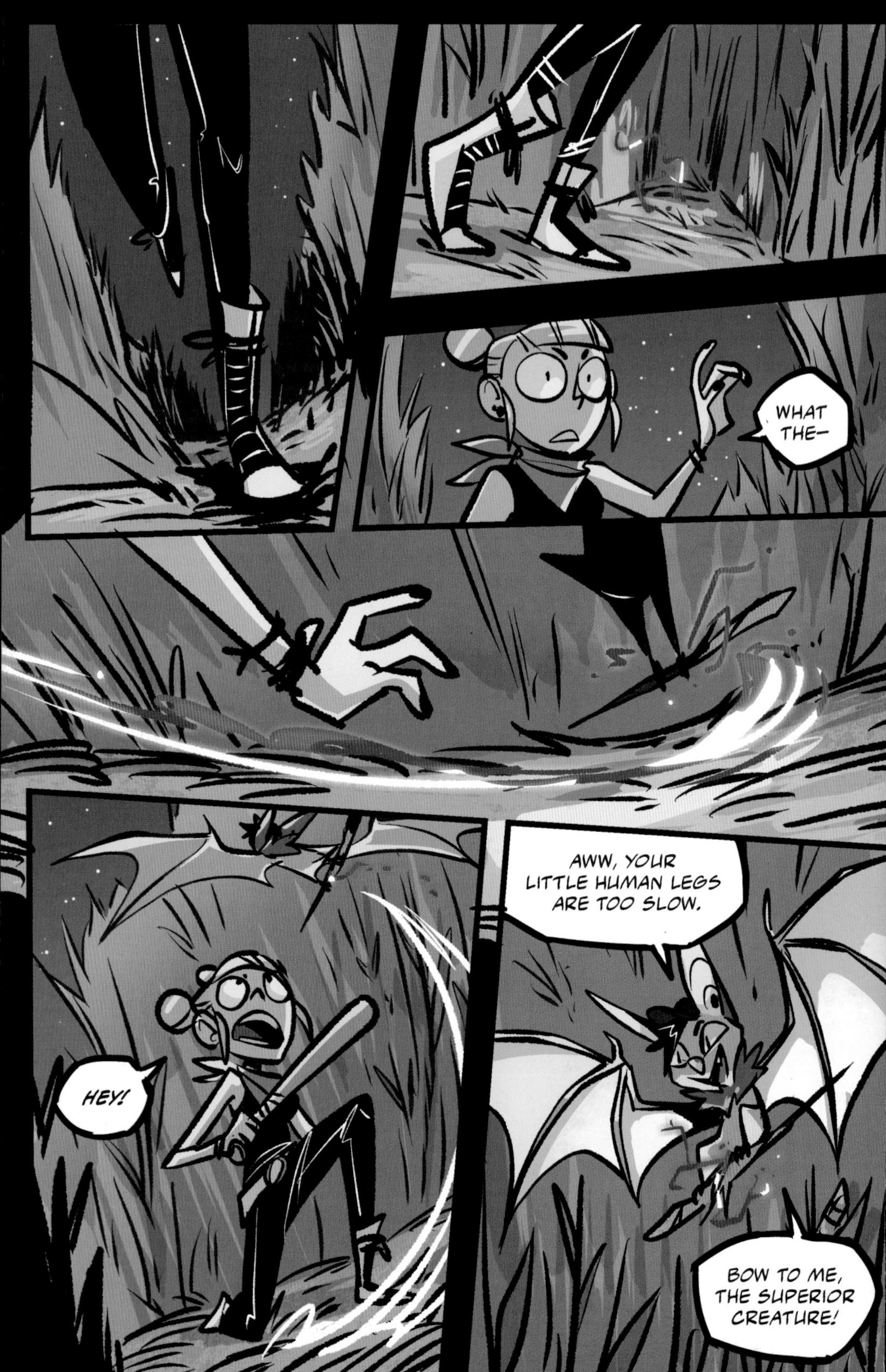
WHAT THE—
HEY!
AWW, YOUR LITTLE HUMAN LEGS ARE TOO SLOW.
BOW TO ME, THE SUPERIOR CREATURE!

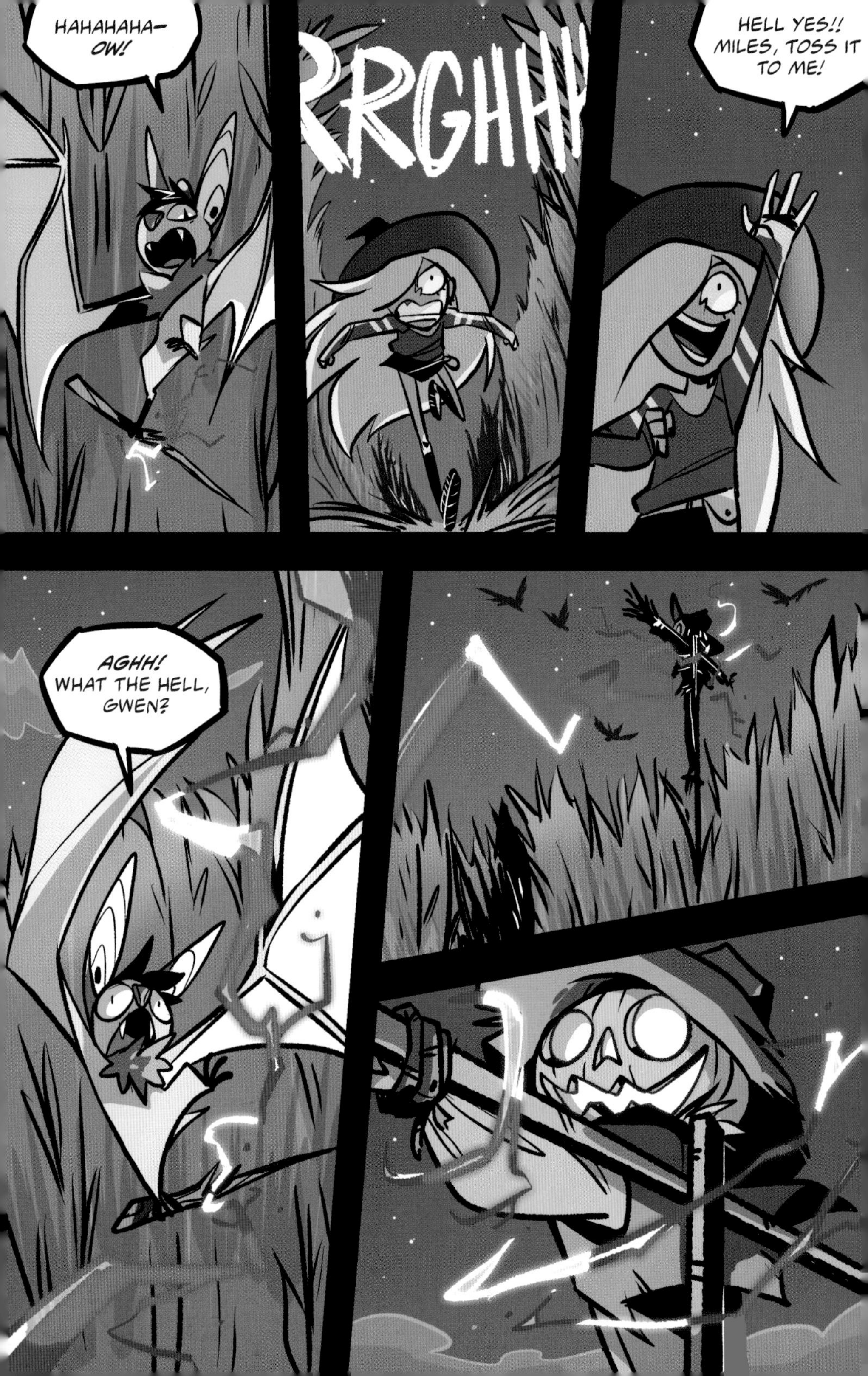
HAHAHAHA-
OW!
RRGHH
HELL YES!! MILES, TOSS IT TO ME!
AGHH! WHAT THE HELL, GWEN?

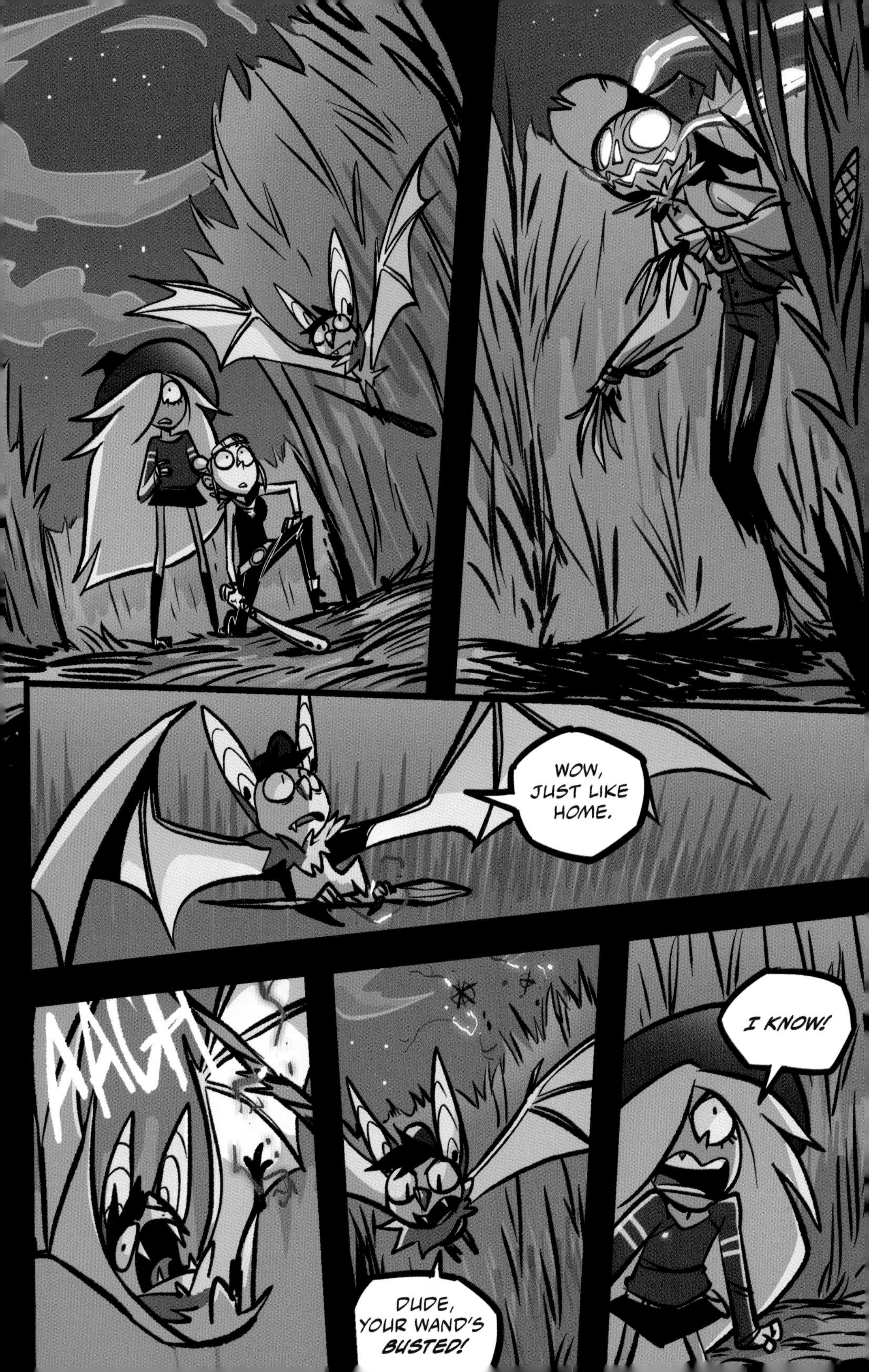
WOW, JUST LIKE HOME.
AAGH!
DUDE, YOUR WAND'S *BUSTED!*
*I KNOW!*

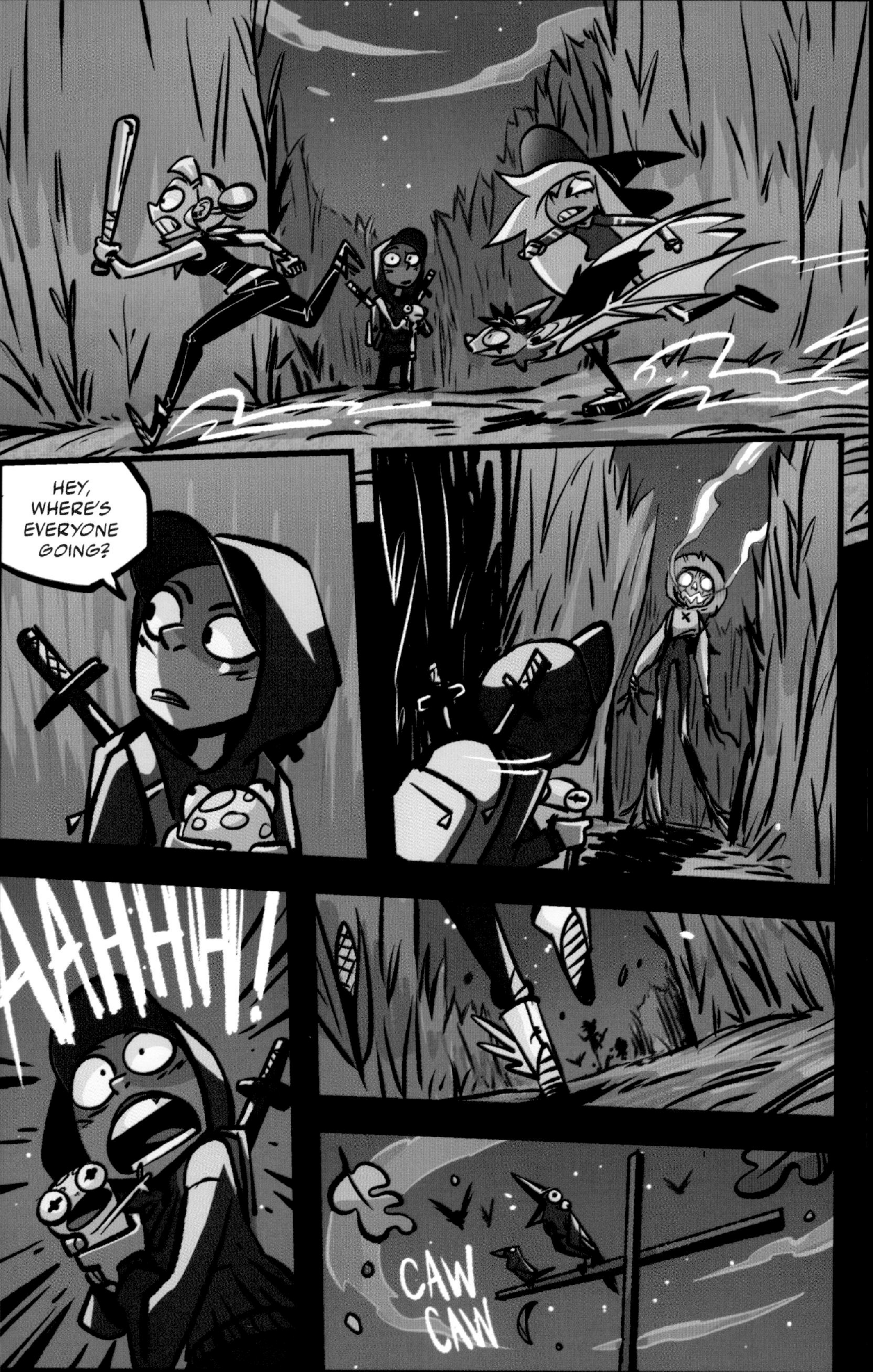
HEY, WHERE'S EVERYONE GOING?
AAHHH!
CAW CAW

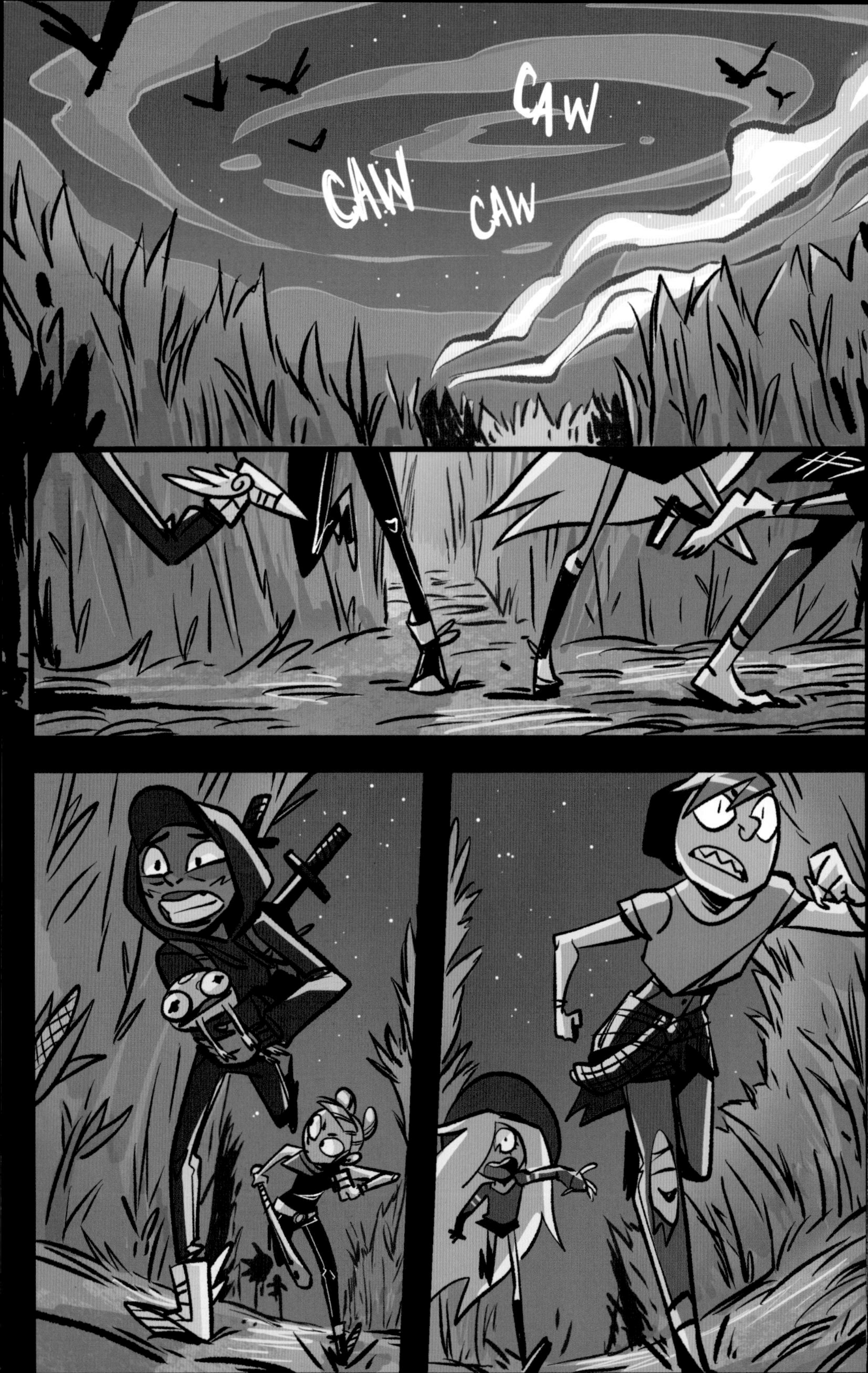
CAW
CAW
CAW

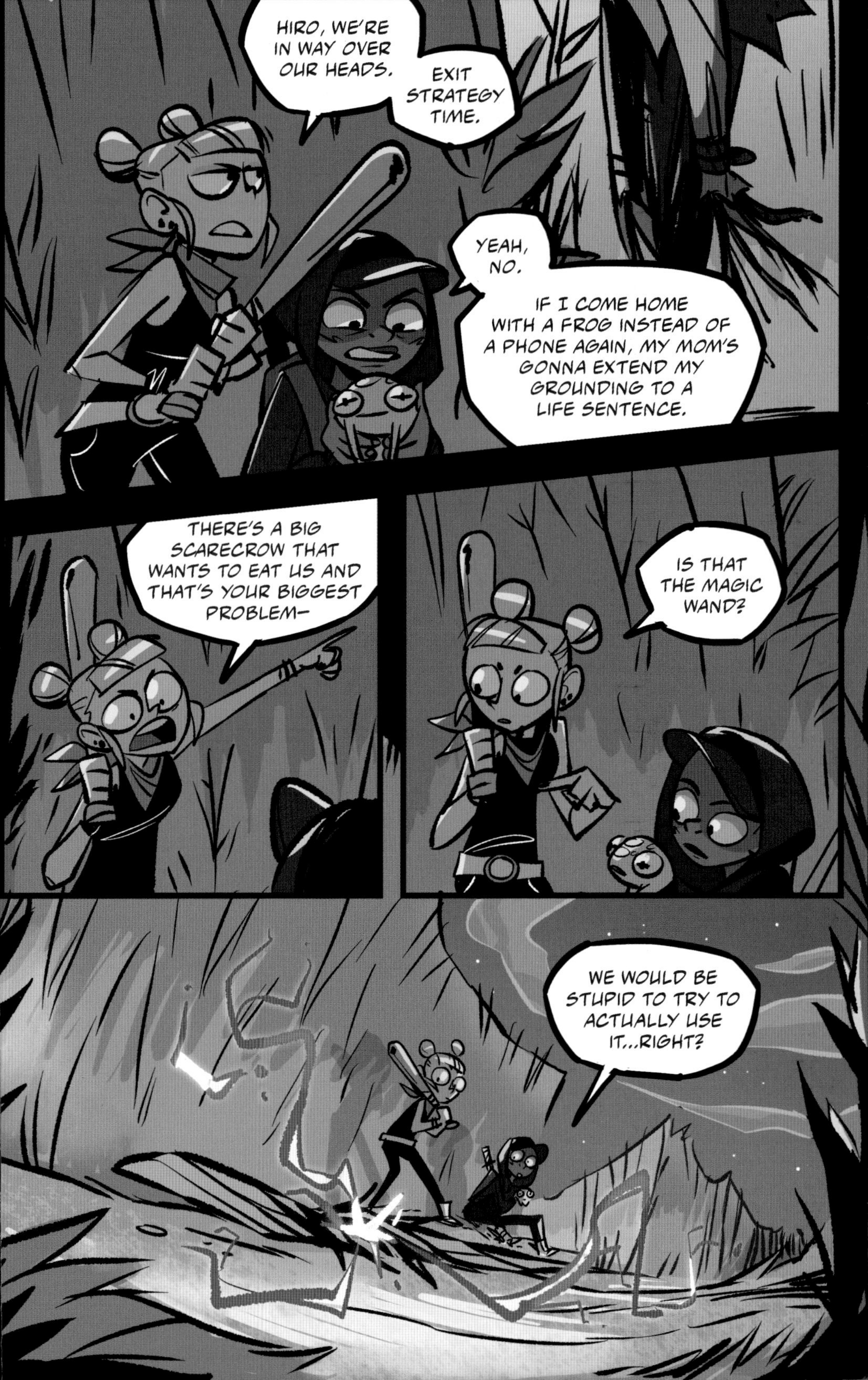
HIRO, WE'RE IN WAY OVER OUR HEADS.
EXIT STRATEGY TIME.
YEAH, NO.
IF I COME HOME WITH A FROG INSTEAD OF A PHONE AGAIN, MY MOM'S GONNA EXTEND MY GROUNDING TO A LIFE SENTENCE.
THERE'S A BIG SCARECROW THAT WANTS TO EAT US AND THAT'S YOUR BIGGEST PROBLEM—
IS THAT THE MAGIC WAND?
WE WOULD BE STUPID TO TRY TO ACTUALLY USE IT...RIGHT?

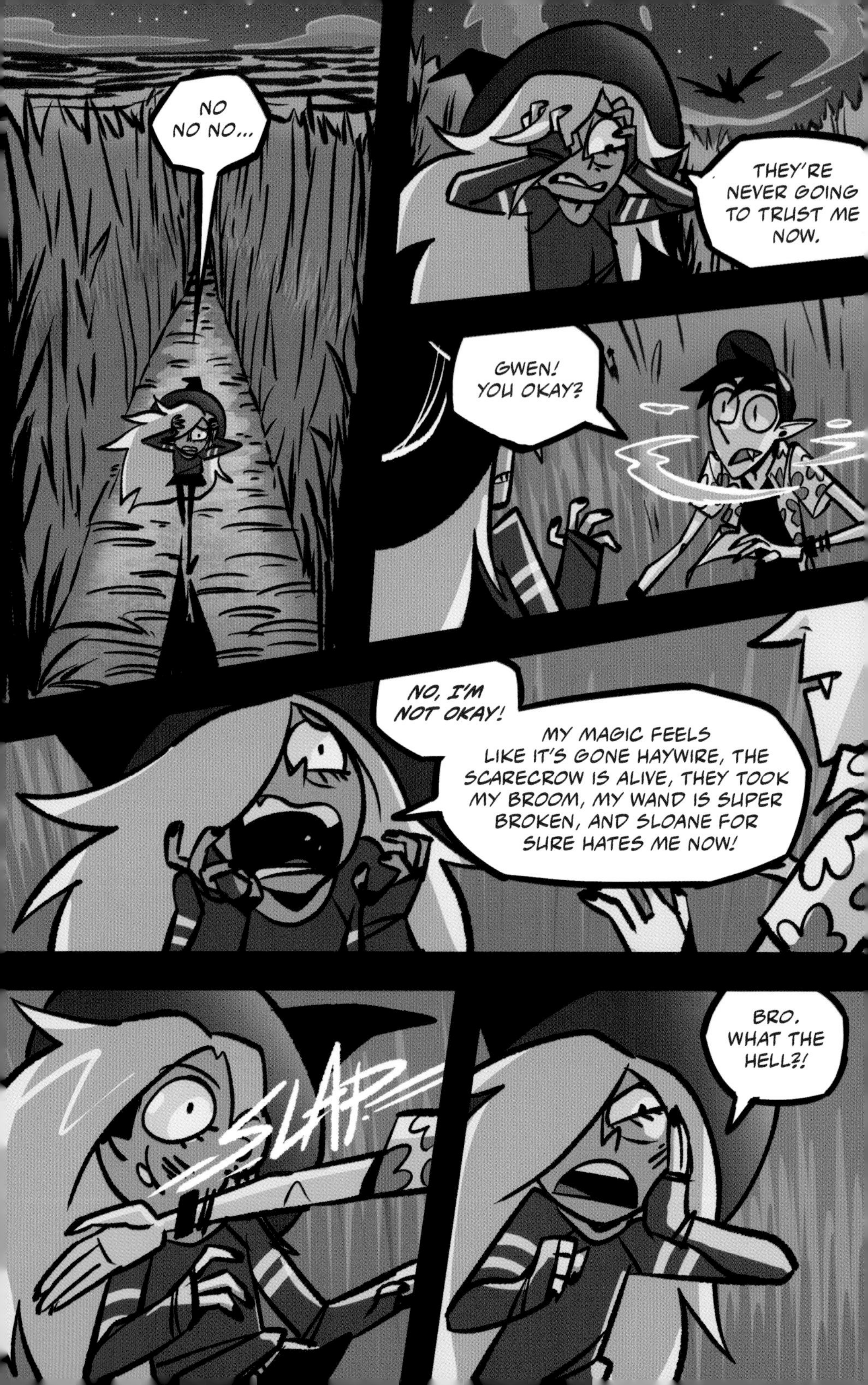
NO NO NO...
THEY'RE NEVER GOING TO TRUST ME NOW.
GWEN! YOU OKAY?
NO, I'M NOT OKAY!
MY MAGIC FEELS LIKE IT'S GONE HAYWIRE, THE SCARECROW IS ALIVE, THEY TOOK MY BROOM, MY WAND IS SUPER BROKEN, AND SLOANE FOR SURE HATES ME NOW!
SLAP
BRO. WHAT THE HELL?!

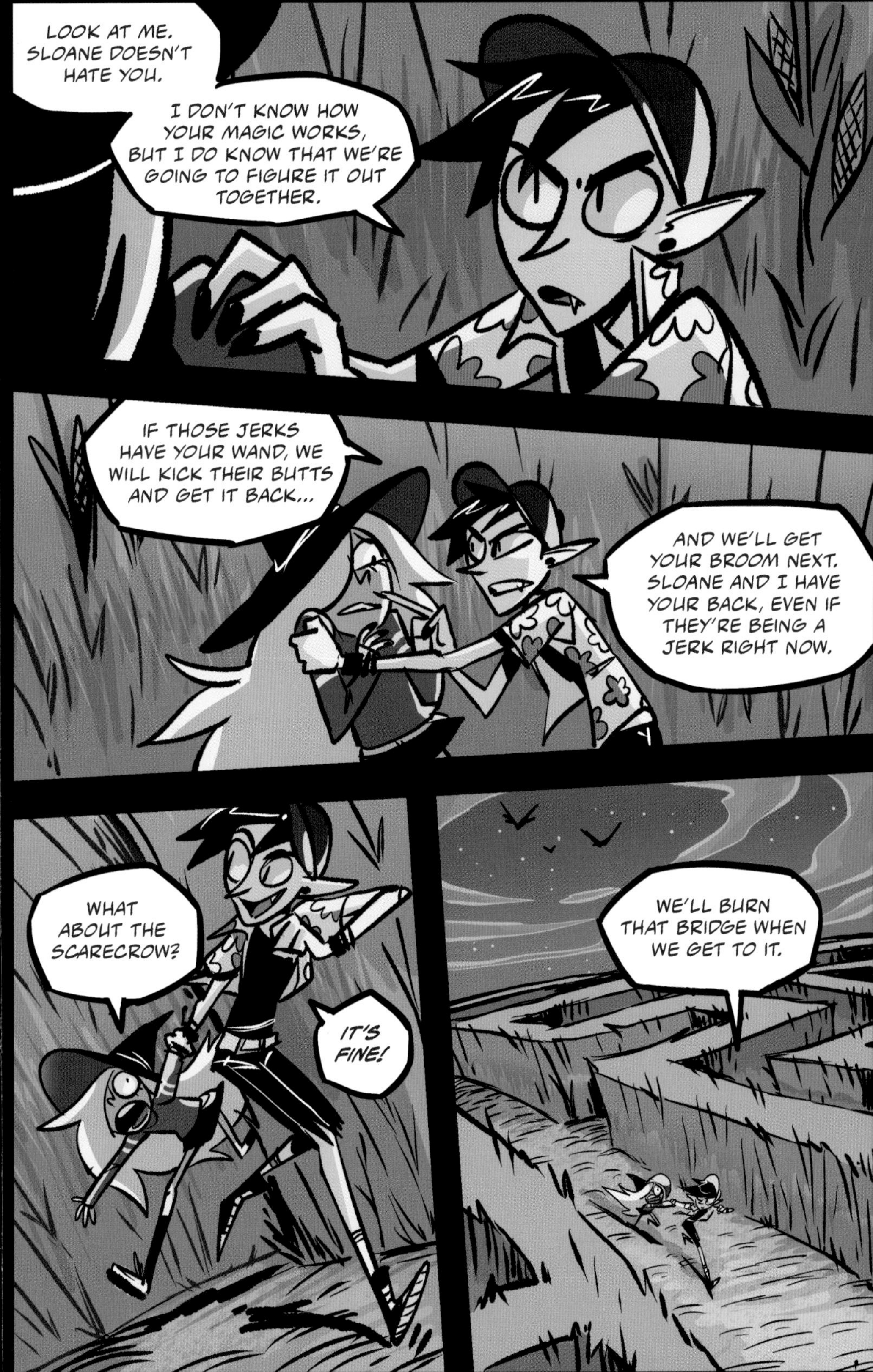
LOOK AT ME. SLOANE DOESN'T HATE YOU.
I DON'T KNOW HOW YOUR MAGIC WORKS, BUT I DO KNOW THAT WE'RE GOING TO FIGURE IT OUT TOGETHER.
IF THOSE JERKS HAVE YOUR WAND, WE WILL KICK THEIR BUTTS AND GET IT BACK...
AND WE'LL GET YOUR BROOM NEXT. SLOANE AND I HAVE YOUR BACK, EVEN IF THEY'RE BEING A JERK RIGHT NOW.
WHAT ABOUT THE SCARECROW?
IT'S FINE!
WE'LL BURN THAT BRIDGE WHEN WE GET TO IT.

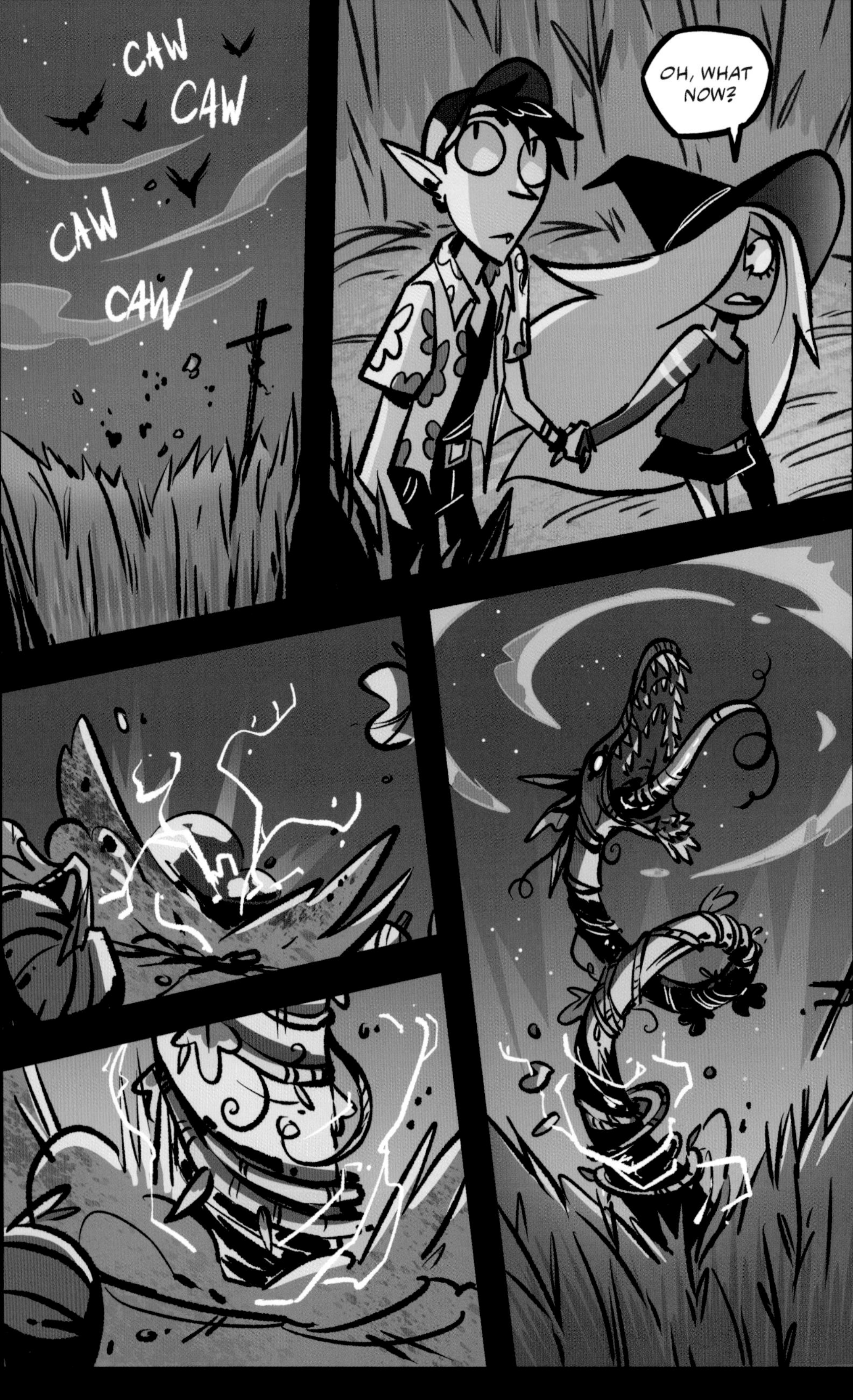
CAW
CAW
CAW
CAW
OH, WHAT NOW?

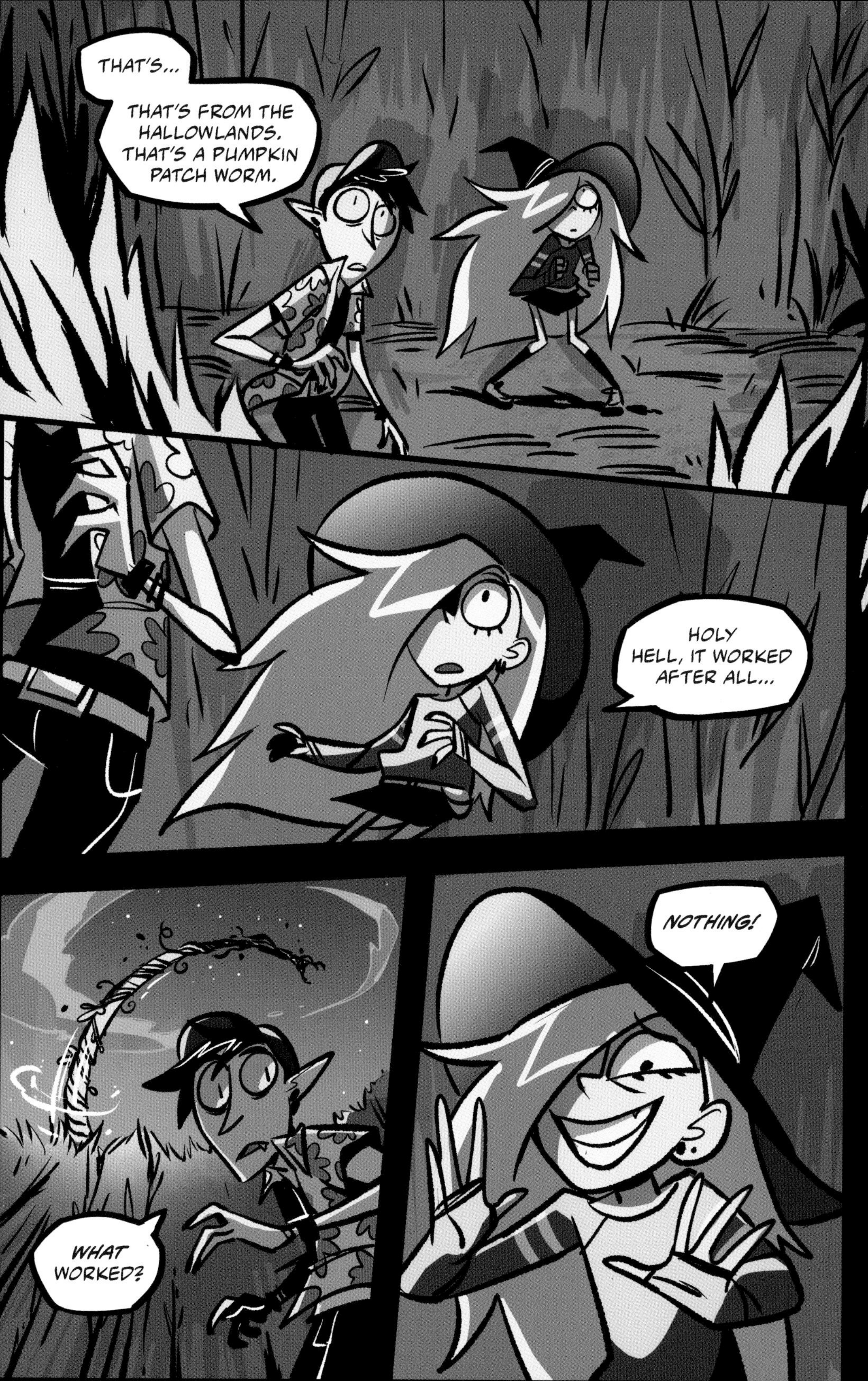
THAT'S...
THAT'S FROM THE HALLOWLANDS. THAT'S A PUMPKIN PATCH WORM.
HOLY HELL, IT WORKED AFTER ALL...
WHAT WORKED?
NOTHING!

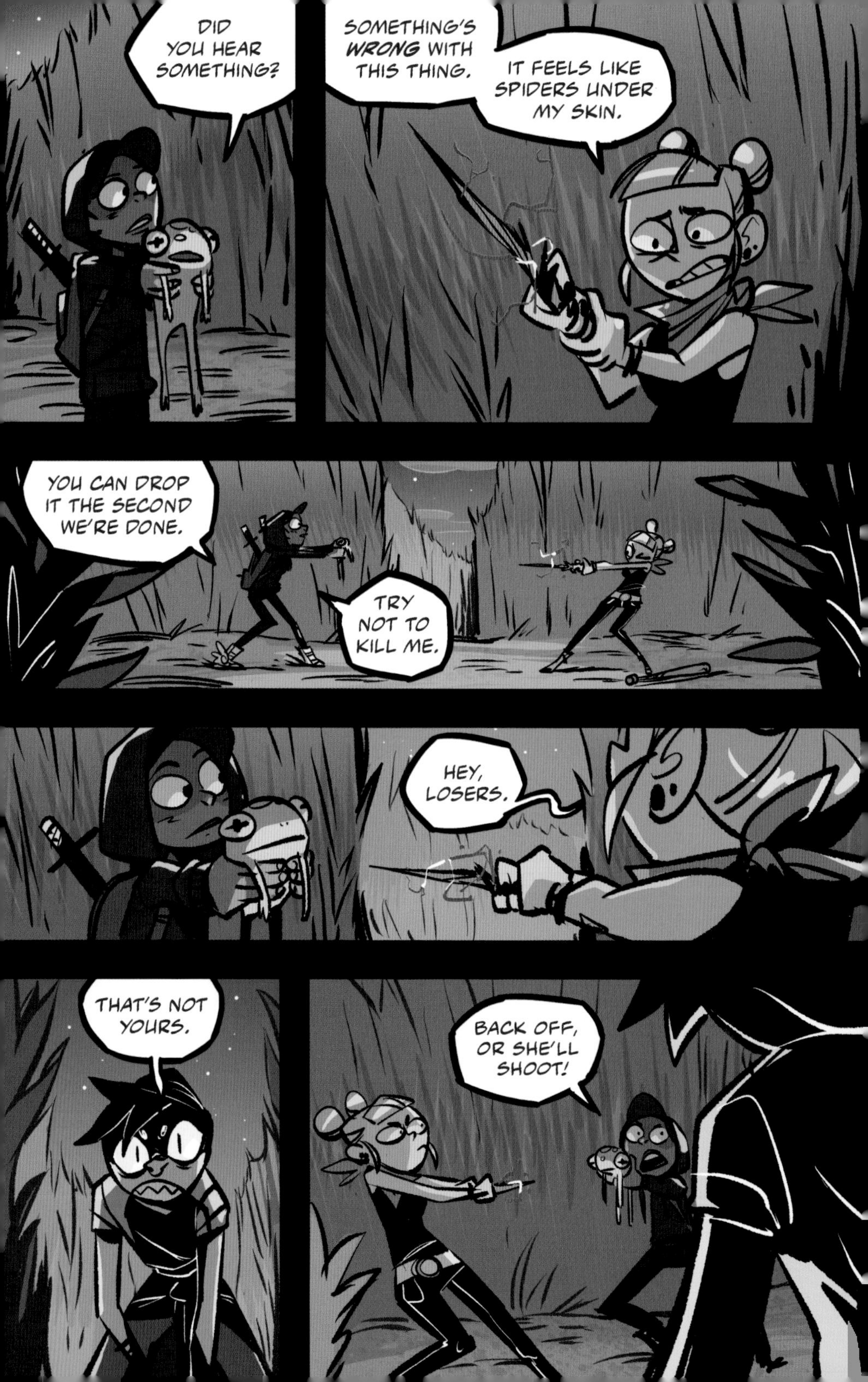
DID YOU HEAR SOMETHING?
SOMETHING'S *WRONG* WITH THIS THING.
IT FEELS LIKE SPIDERS UNDER MY SKIN.
YOU CAN DROP IT THE SECOND WE'RE DONE.
TRY NOT TO KILL ME.
HEY, LOSERS.
THAT'S NOT YOURS.
BACK OFF, OR SHE'LL SHOOT!

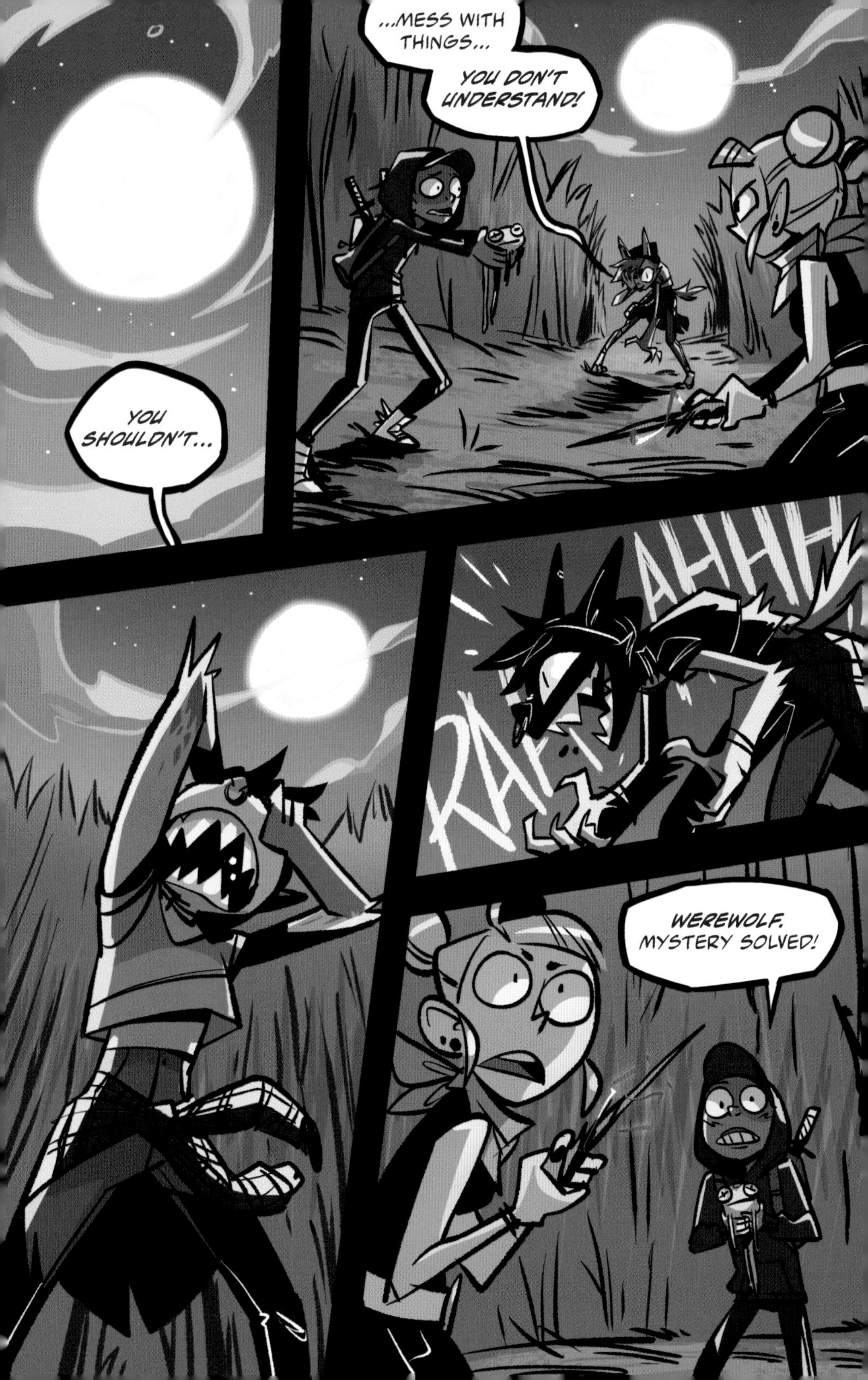
YOU SHOULDN'T...
...MESS WITH THINGS...
YOU DON'T UNDERSTAND!
RAHHHH
WEREWOLF. MYSTERY SOLVED!

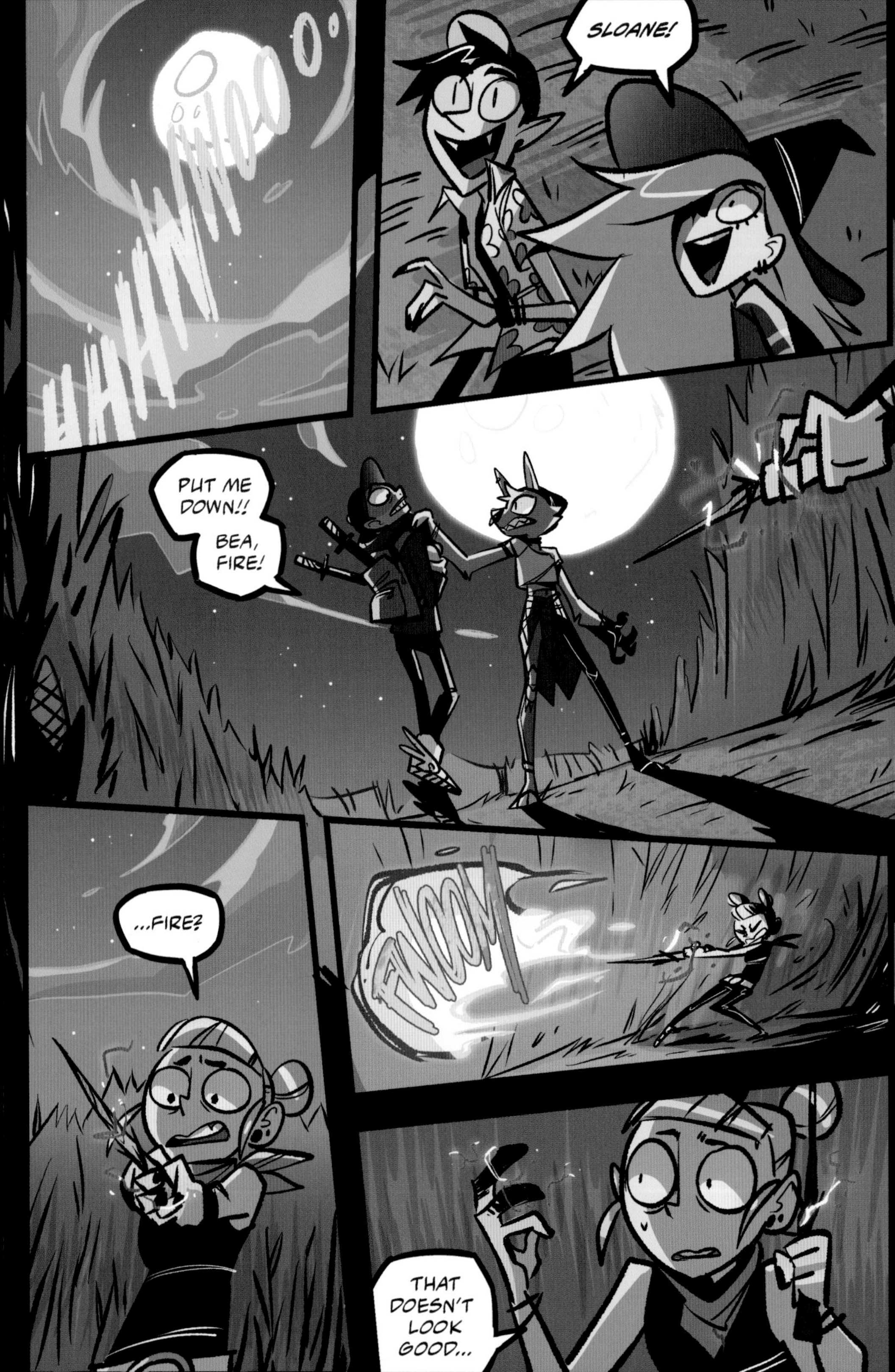

AHHWHOOO
SLOANE!
PUT ME DOWN!!
BEA, FIRE!
...FIRE?
FWOOM
THAT DOESN'T LOOK GOOD...

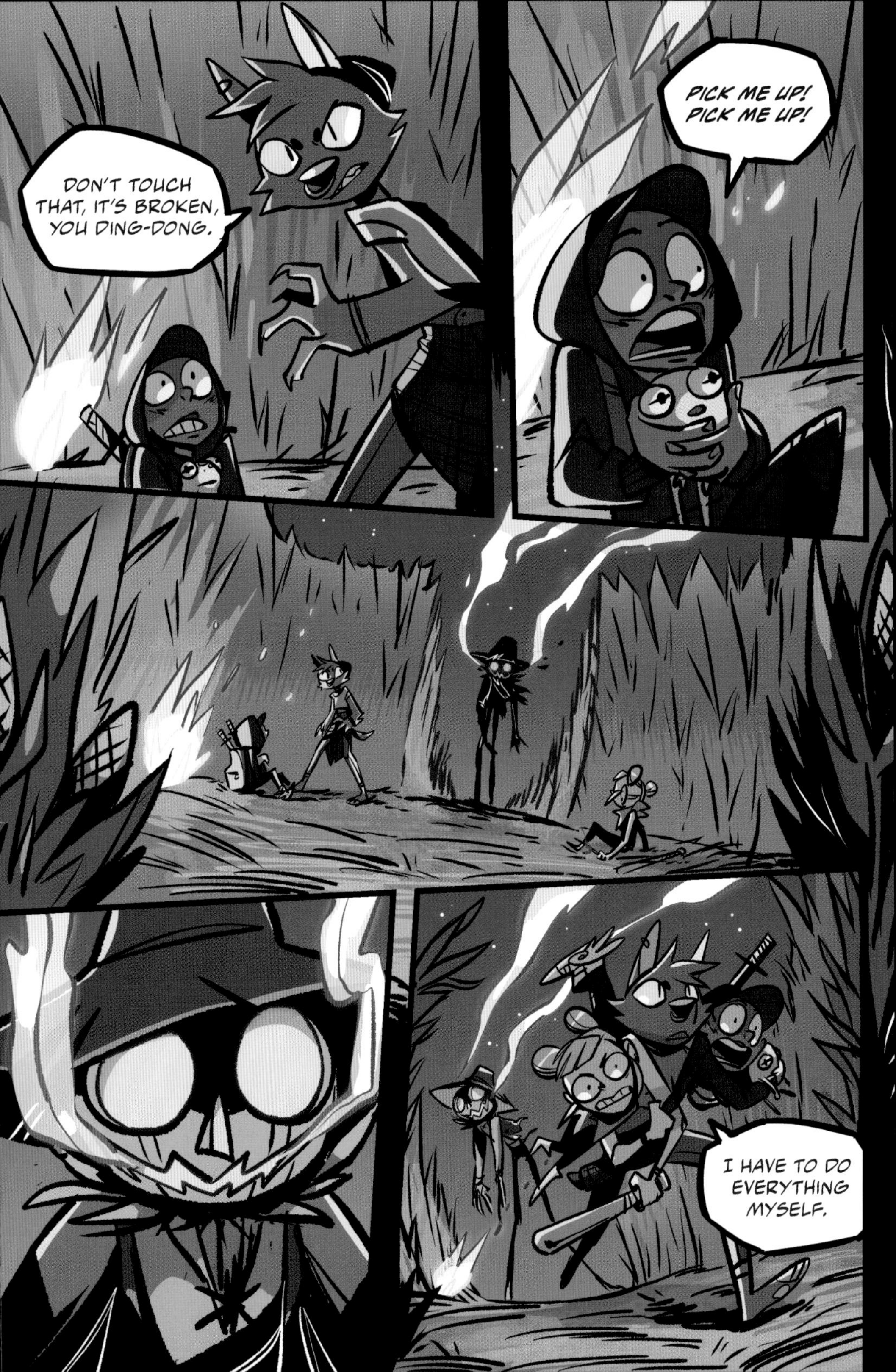
DON'T TOUCH THAT, IT'S BROKEN, YOU DING-DONG.
PICK ME UP! PICK ME UP!
I HAVE TO DO EVERYTHING MYSELF.

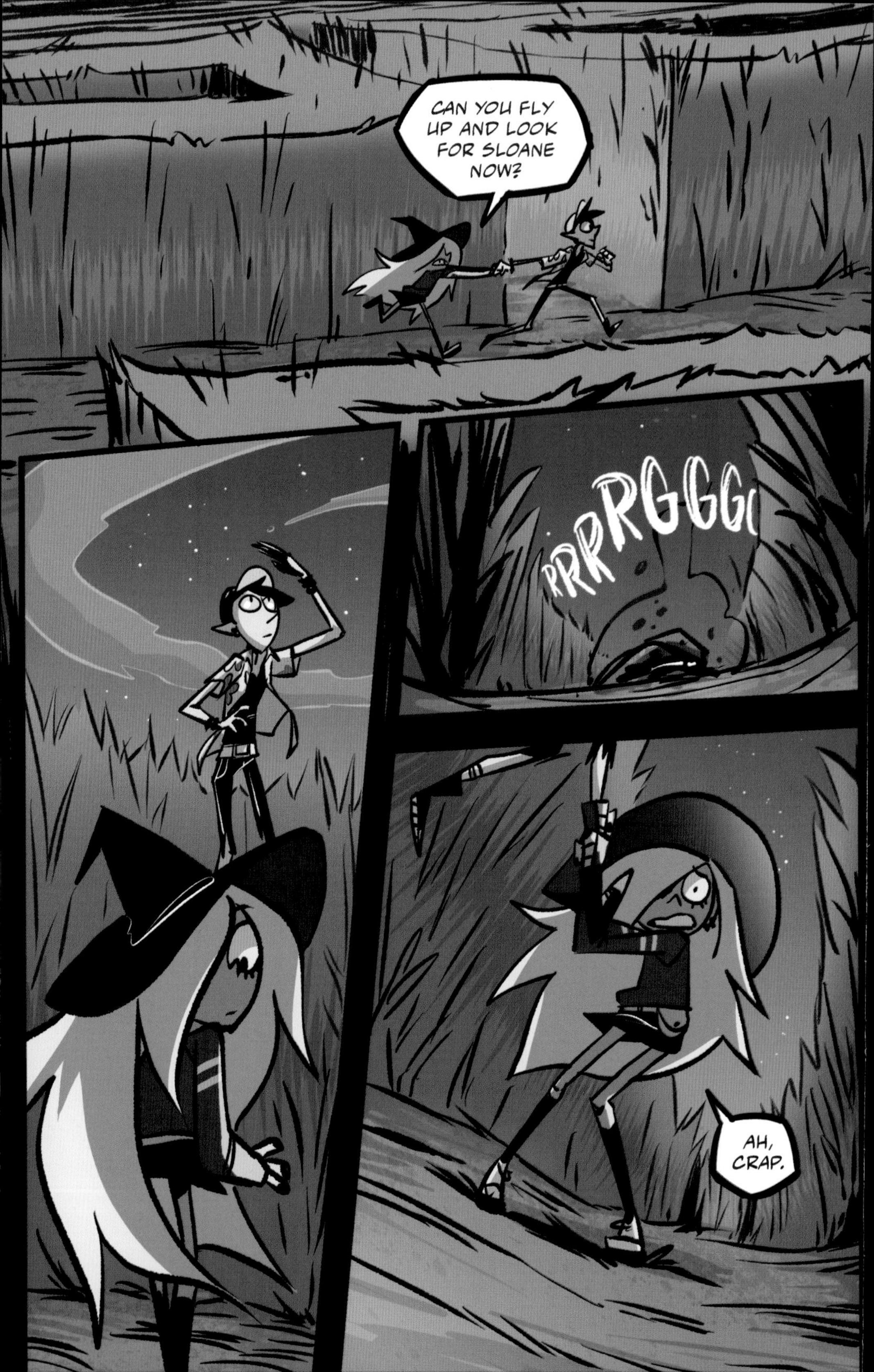
CAN YOU FLY UP AND LOOK FOR SLOANE NOW?
RRRRGGG
AH, CRAP.

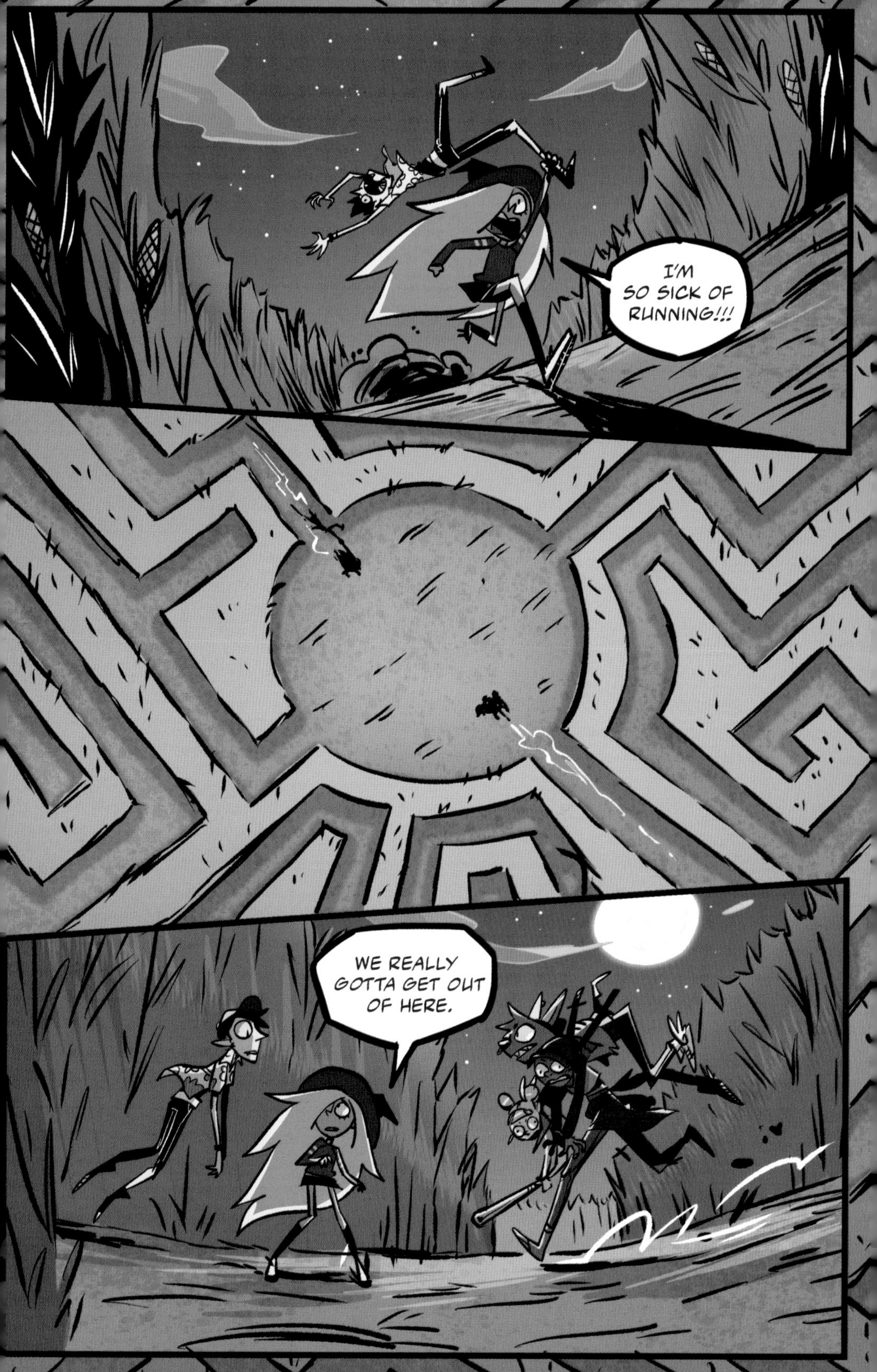
I'M SO SICK OF RUNNING!!!
WE REALLY GOTTA GET OUT OF HERE.

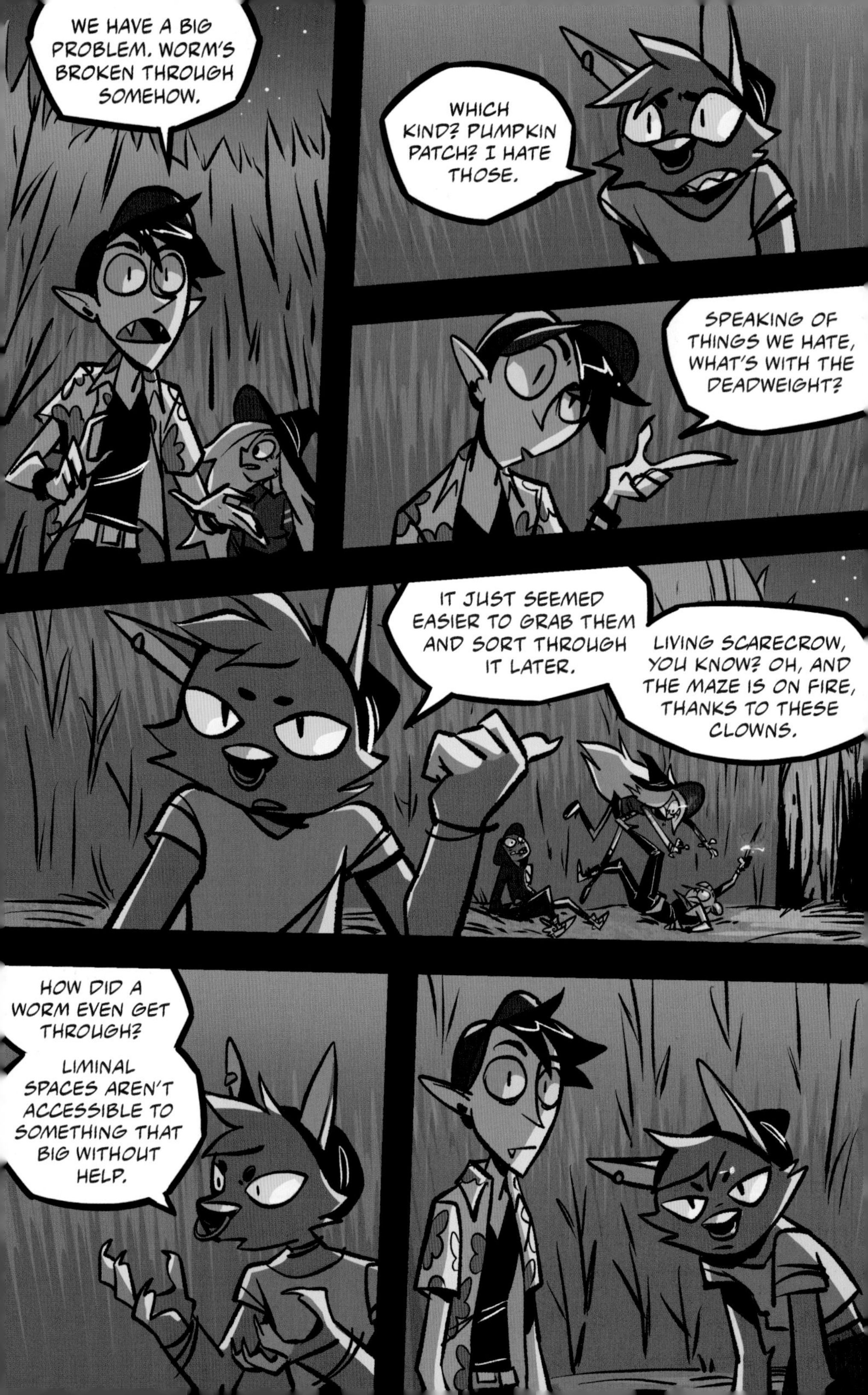
WE HAVE A BIG PROBLEM. WORM'S BROKEN THROUGH SOMEHOW.
WHICH KIND? PUMPKIN PATCH? I HATE THOSE.
SPEAKING OF THINGS WE HATE, WHAT'S WITH THE DEADWEIGHT?
IT JUST SEEMED EASIER TO GRAB THEM AND SORT THROUGH IT LATER.
LIVING SCARECROW, YOU KNOW? OH, AND THE MAZE IS ON FIRE, THANKS TO THESE CLOWNS.
HOW DID A WORM EVEN GET THROUGH?
LIMINAL SPACES AREN'T ACCESSIBLE TO SOMETHING THAT BIG WITHOUT HELP.

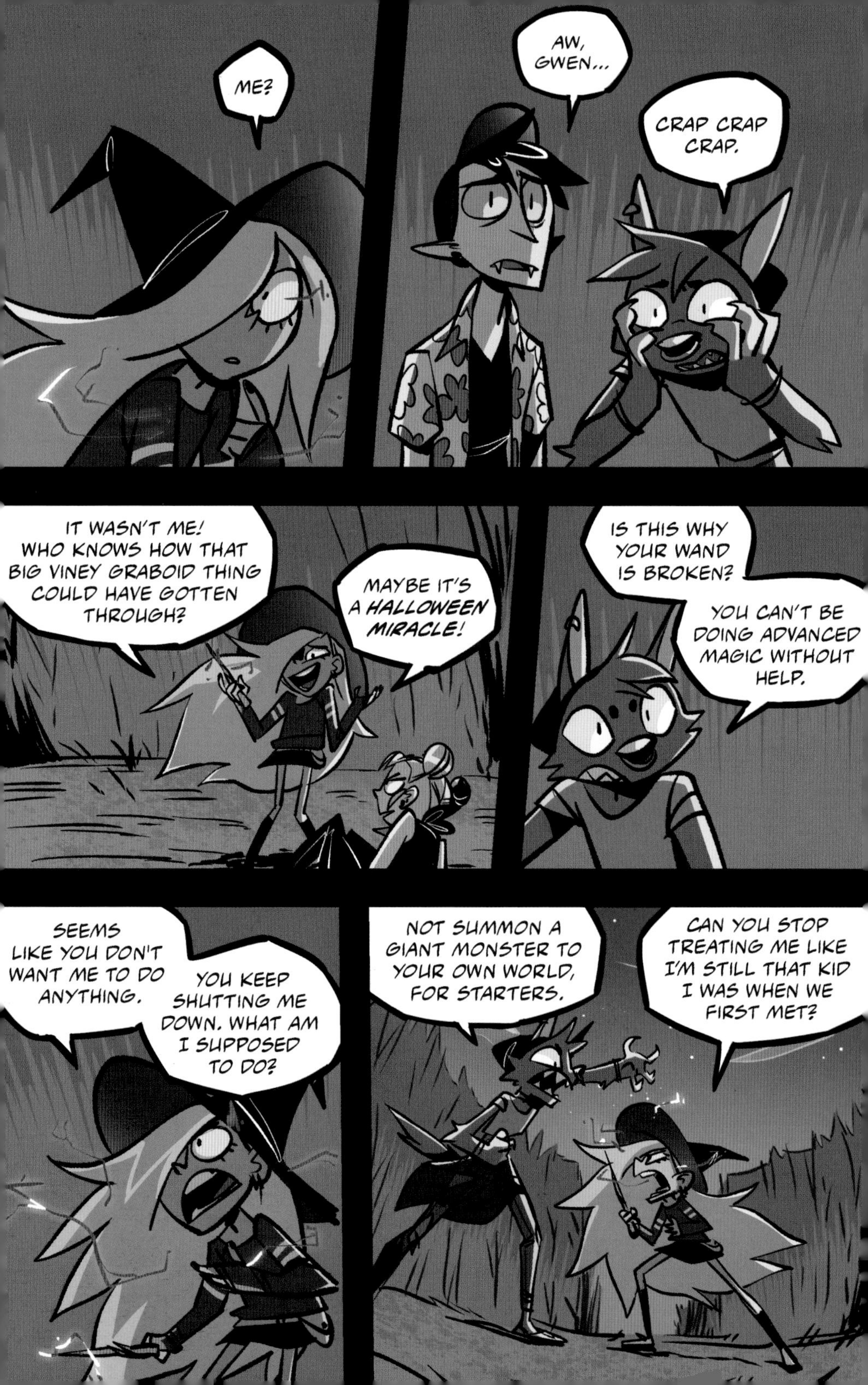
ME?
AW, GWEN...
CRAP CRAP CRAP.
IT WASN'T ME! WHO KNOWS HOW THAT BIG VINEY GRABOID THING COULD HAVE GOTTEN THROUGH?
MAYBE IT'S A *HALLOWEEN MIRACLE!*
IS THIS WHY YOUR WAND IS BROKEN?
YOU CAN'T BE DOING ADVANCED MAGIC WITHOUT HELP.
SEEMS LIKE YOU DON'T WANT ME TO DO ANYTHING.
YOU KEEP SHUTTING ME DOWN. WHAT AM I SUPPOSED TO DO?
NOT SUMMON A GIANT MONSTER TO YOUR OWN WORLD, FOR STARTERS.
CAN YOU STOP TREATING ME LIKE I'M STILL THAT KID I WAS WHEN WE FIRST MET?

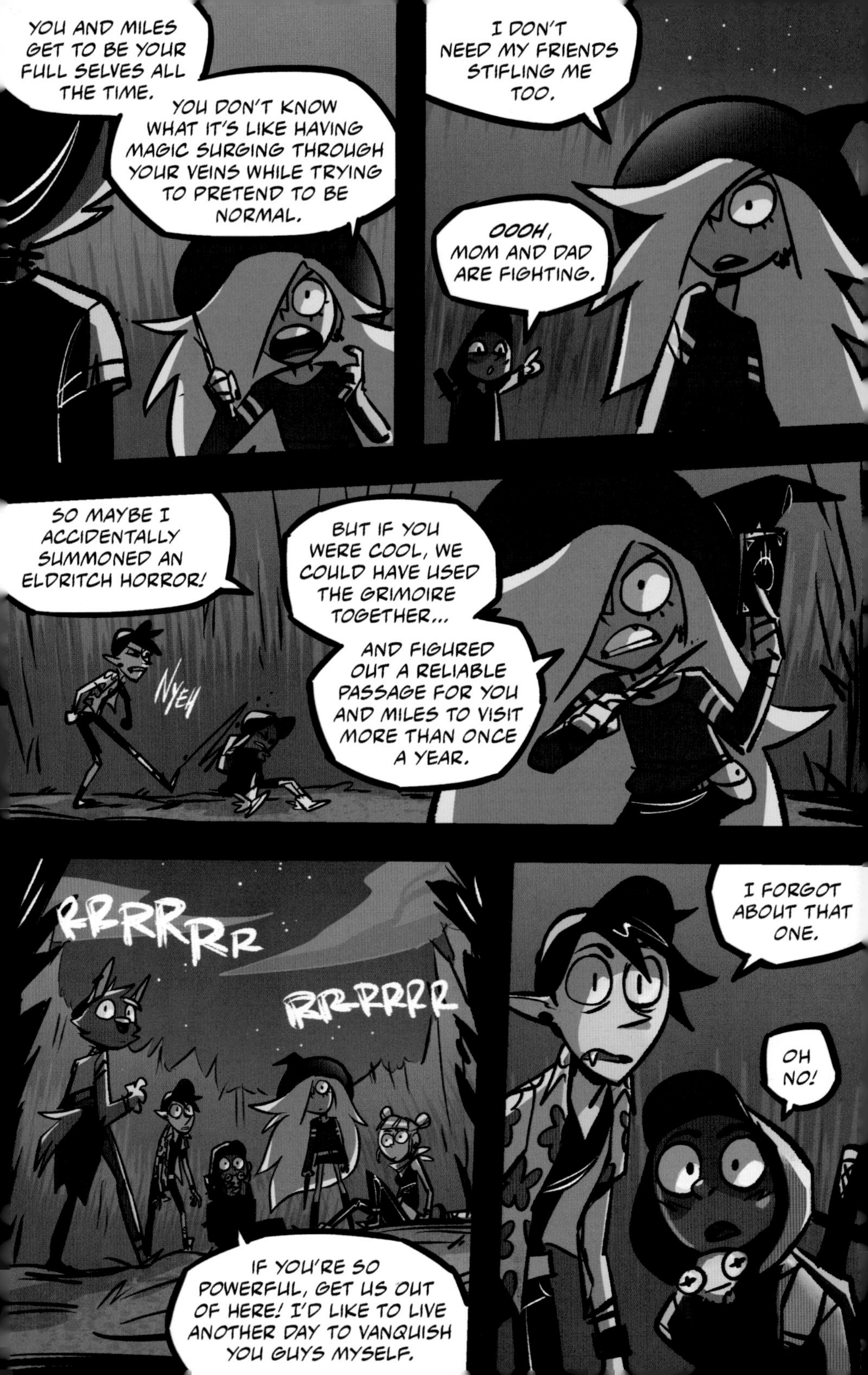
YOU AND MILES GET TO BE YOUR FULL SELVES ALL THE TIME.
YOU DON'T KNOW WHAT IT'S LIKE HAVING MAGIC SURGING THROUGH YOUR VEINS WHILE TRYING TO PRETEND TO BE NORMAL.
I DON'T NEED MY FRIENDS STIFLING ME TOO.
OOOH, MOM AND DAD ARE FIGHTING.
SO MAYBE I ACCIDENTALLY SUMMONED AN ELDRITCH HORROR!
NYEH
BUT IF YOU WERE COOL, WE COULD HAVE USED THE GRIMOIRE TOGETHER...
AND FIGURED OUT A RELIABLE PASSAGE FOR YOU AND MILES TO VISIT MORE THAN ONCE A YEAR.
RRRRRR
RRRRRR
IF YOU'RE SO POWERFUL, GET US OUT OF HERE! I'D LIKE TO LIVE ANOTHER DAY TO VANQUISH YOU GUYS MYSELF.
I FORGOT ABOUT THAT ONE.
OH NO!

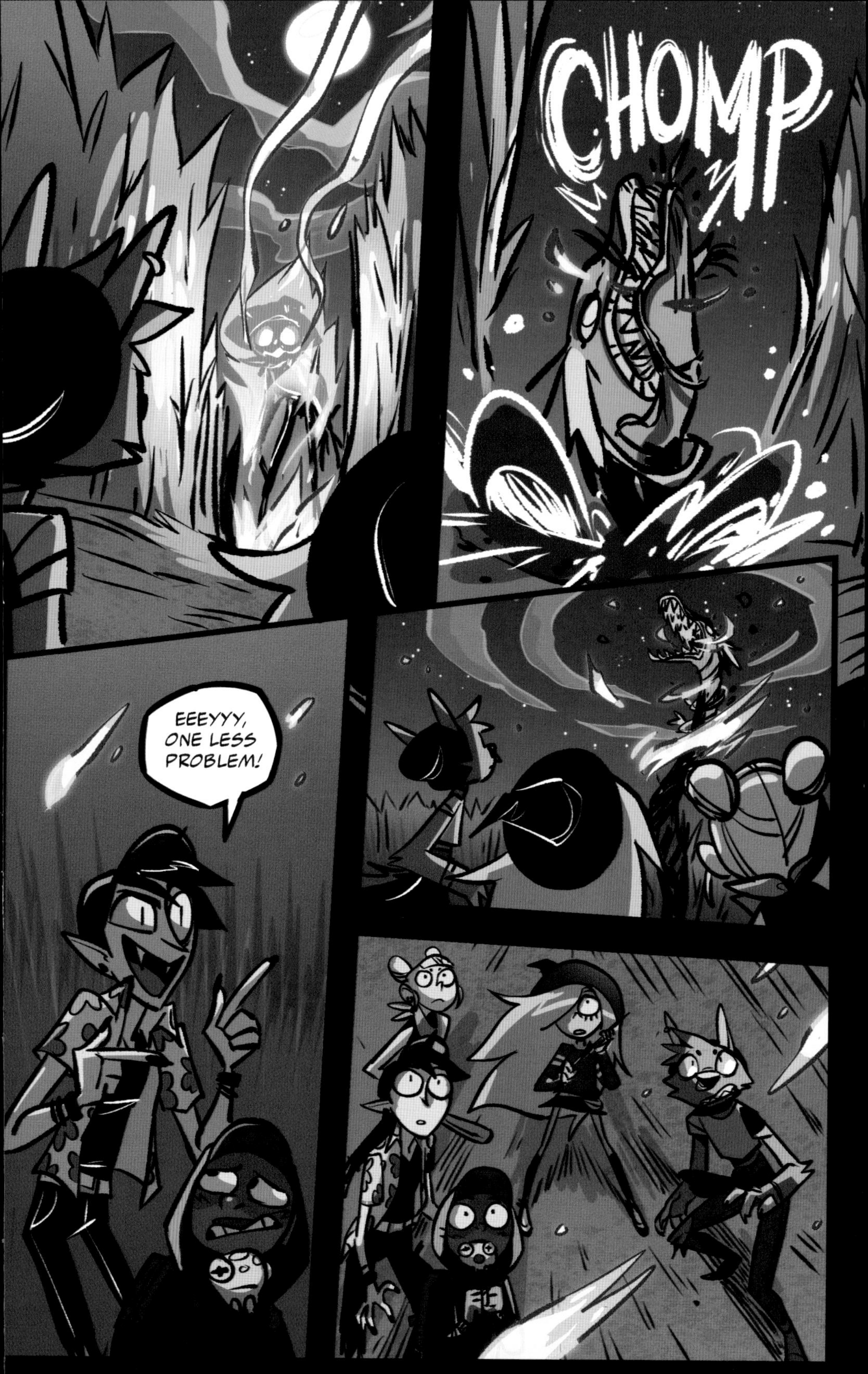
CHOMP
EEEYYY, ONE LESS PROBLEM!

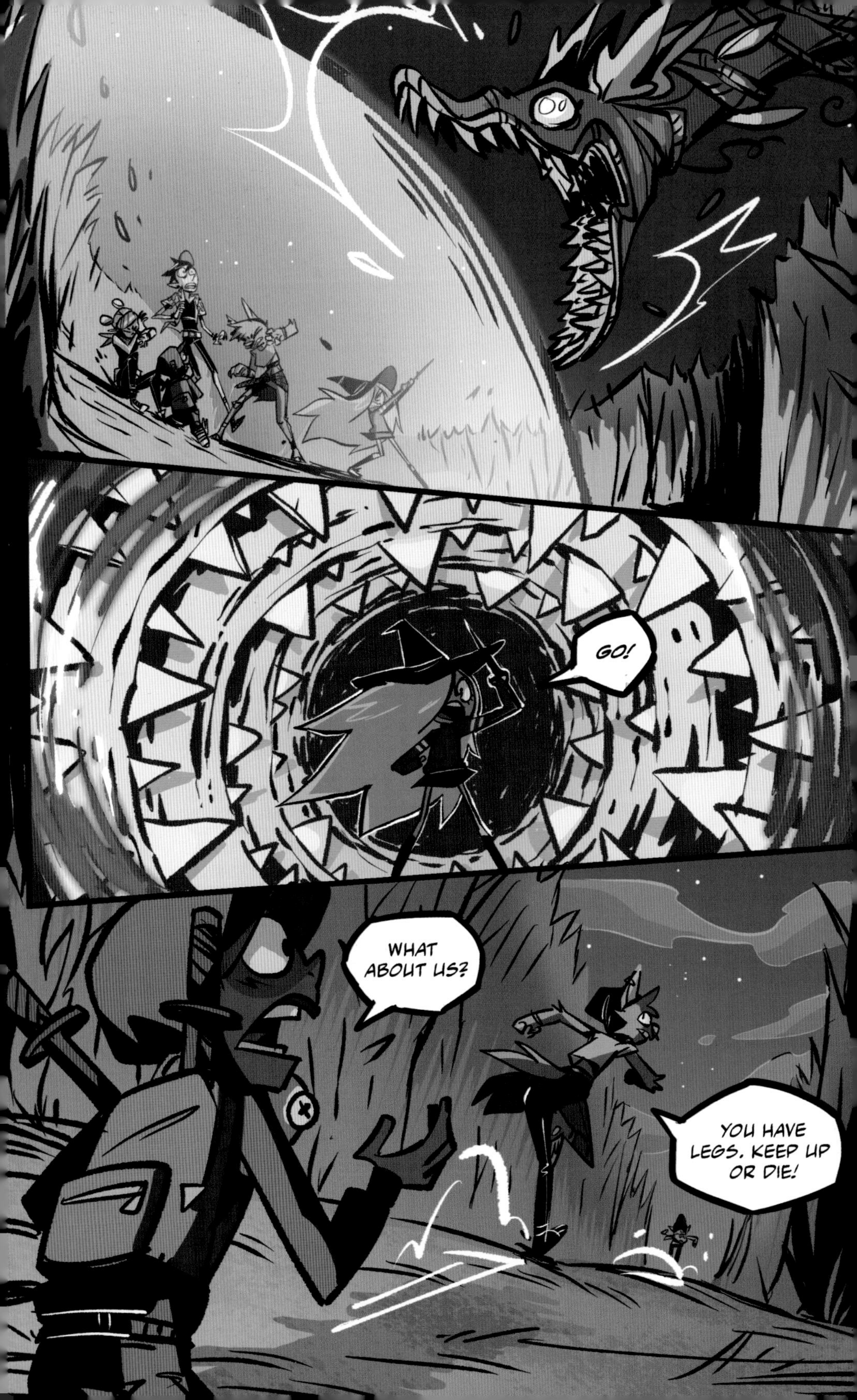
GO!
WHAT ABOUT US?
YOU HAVE LEGS. KEEP UP OR DIE!

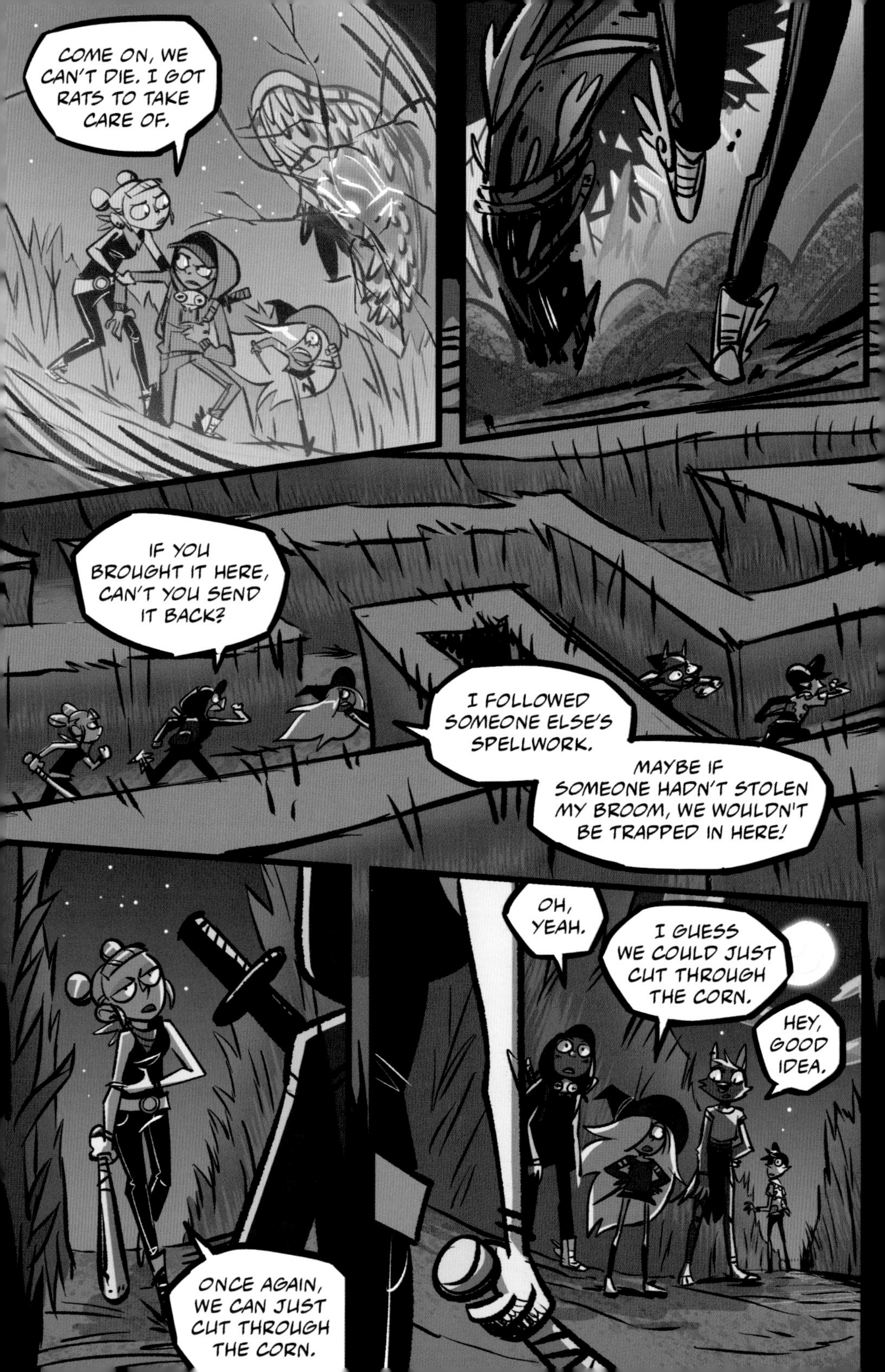
COME ON, WE CAN'T DIE. I GOT RATS TO TAKE CARE OF.
IF YOU BROUGHT IT HERE, CAN'T YOU SEND IT BACK?
I FOLLOWED SOMEONE ELSE'S SPELLWORK.
MAYBE IF SOMEONE HADN'T STOLEN MY BROOM, WE WOULDN'T BE TRAPPED IN HERE!
ONCE AGAIN, WE CAN JUST CUT THROUGH THE CORN.
OH, YEAH.
I GUESS WE COULD JUST CUT THROUGH THE CORN.
HEY, GOOD IDEA.

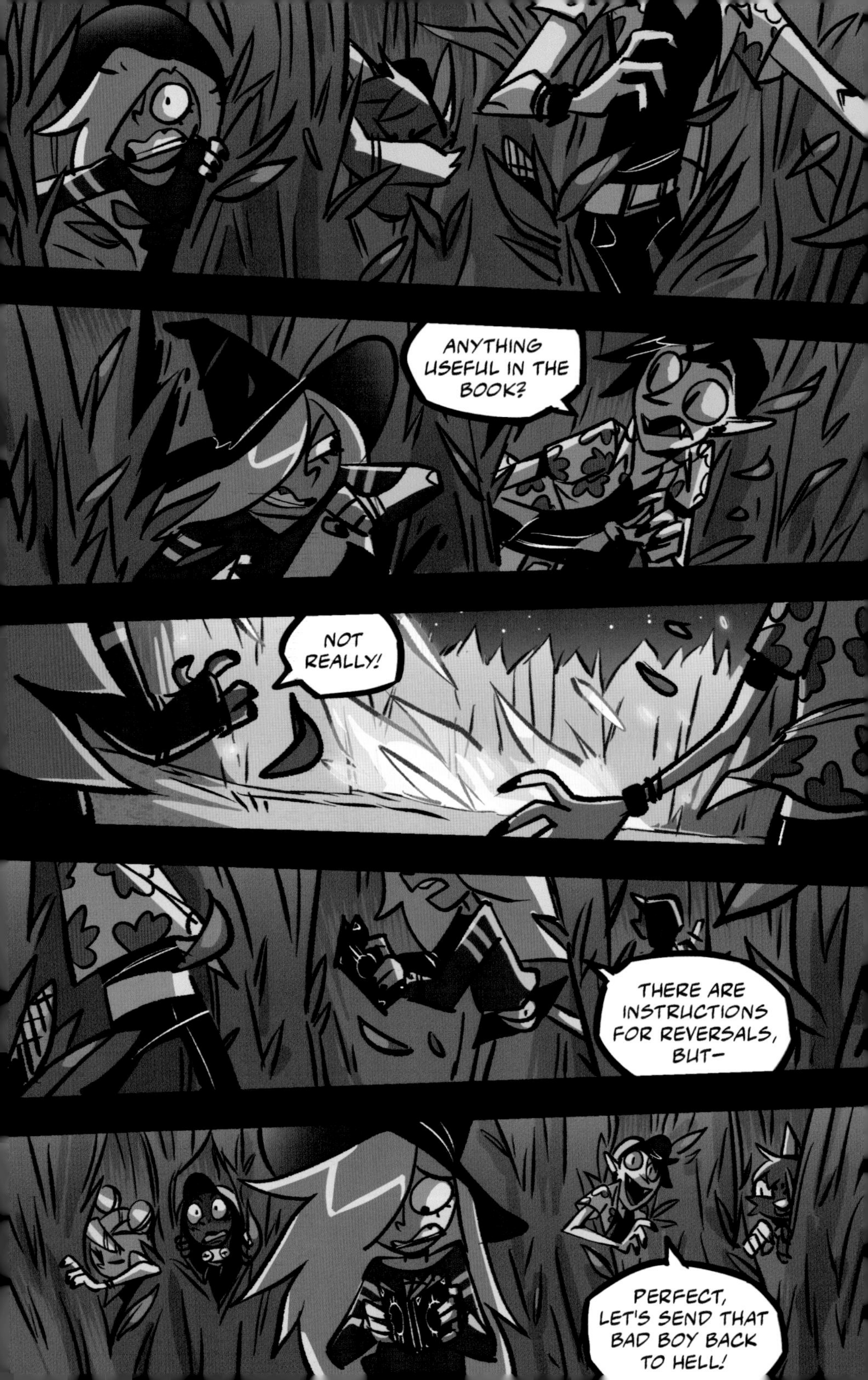
ANYTHING USEFUL IN THE BOOK?
NOT REALLY!
THERE ARE INSTRUCTIONS FOR REVERSALS, BUT—
PERFECT, LET'S SEND THAT BAD BOY BACK TO HELL!

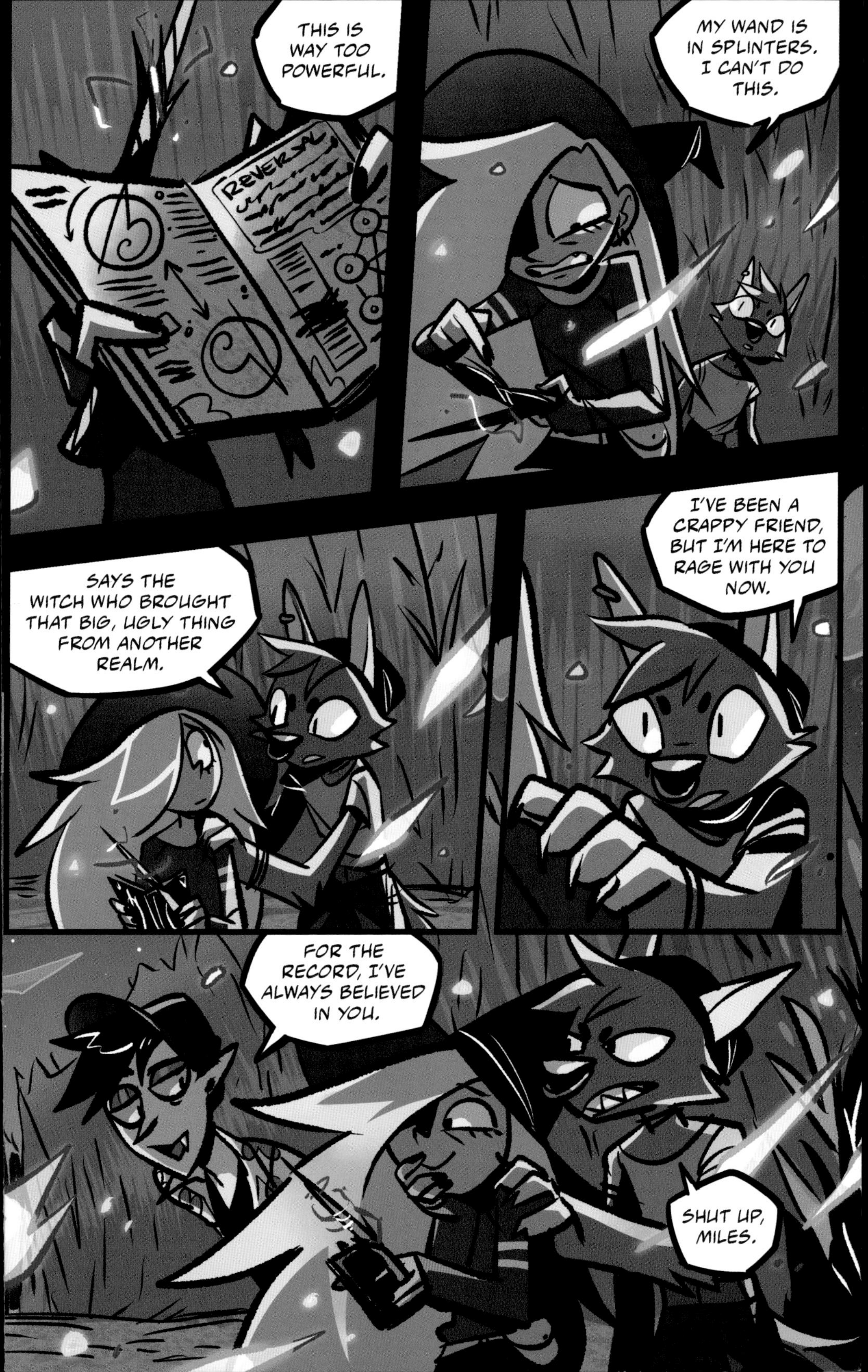
THIS IS WAY TOO POWERFUL.
REVERSAL
MY WAND IS IN SPLINTERS. I CAN'T DO THIS.
SAYS THE WITCH WHO BROUGHT THAT BIG, UGLY THING FROM ANOTHER REALM.
I'VE BEEN A CRAPPY FRIEND, BUT I'M HERE TO RAGE WITH YOU NOW.
FOR THE RECORD, I'VE ALWAYS BELIEVED IN YOU.
SHUT UP, MILES.

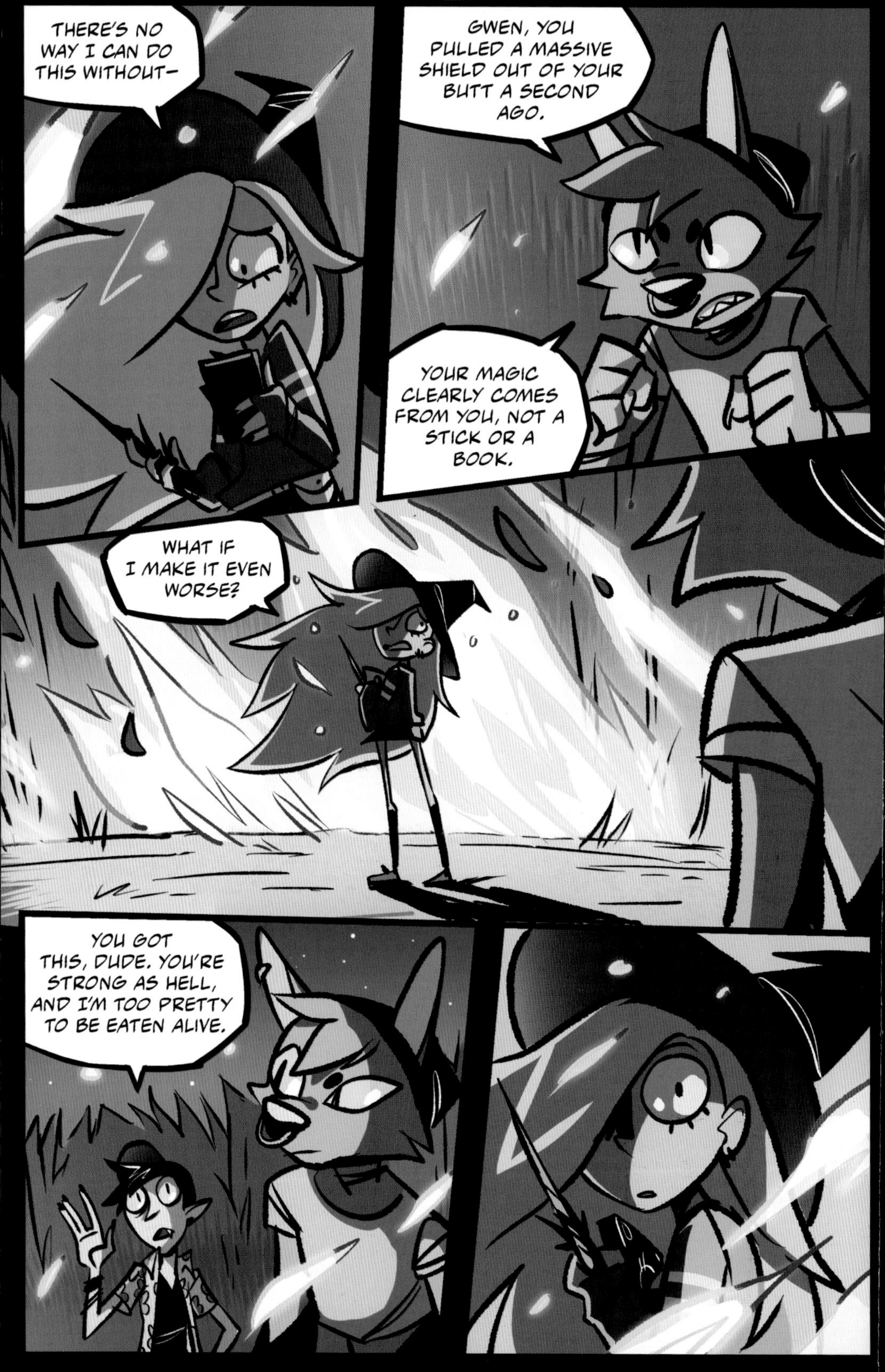
THERE'S NO WAY I CAN DO THIS WITHOUT–
GWEN, YOU PULLED A MASSIVE SHIELD OUT OF YOUR BUTT A SECOND AGO.
YOUR MAGIC CLEARLY COMES FROM YOU, NOT A STICK OR A BOOK.
WHAT IF I MAKE IT EVEN WORSE?
YOU GOT THIS, DUDE. YOU'RE STRONG AS HELL, AND I'M TOO PRETTY TO BE EATEN ALIVE.

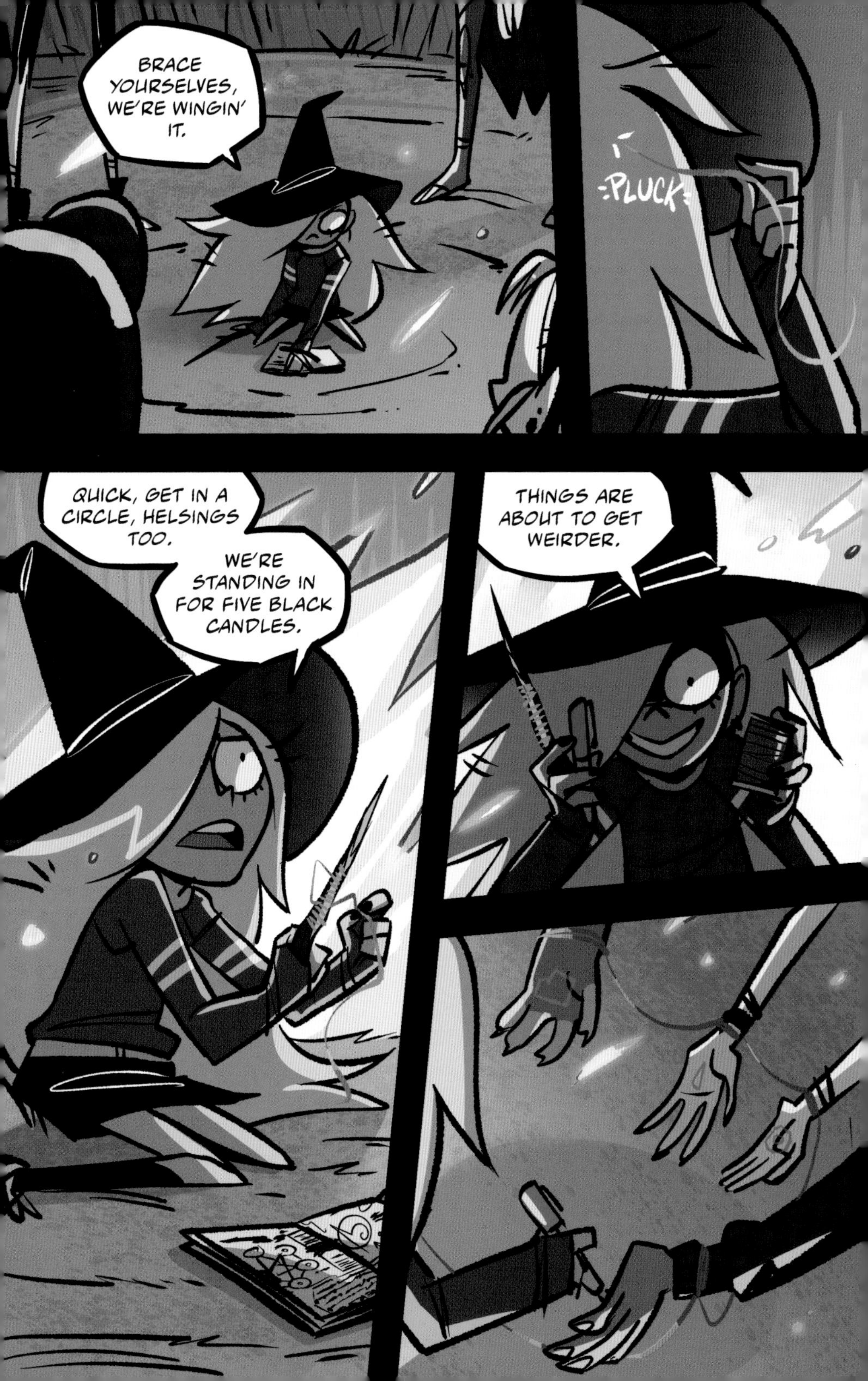
BRACE YOURSELVES, WE'RE WINGIN' IT.
=PLUCK=
QUICK, GET IN A CIRCLE, HELSINGS TOO.
WE'RE STANDING IN FOR FIVE BLACK CANDLES.
THINGS ARE ABOUT TO GET WEIRDER.

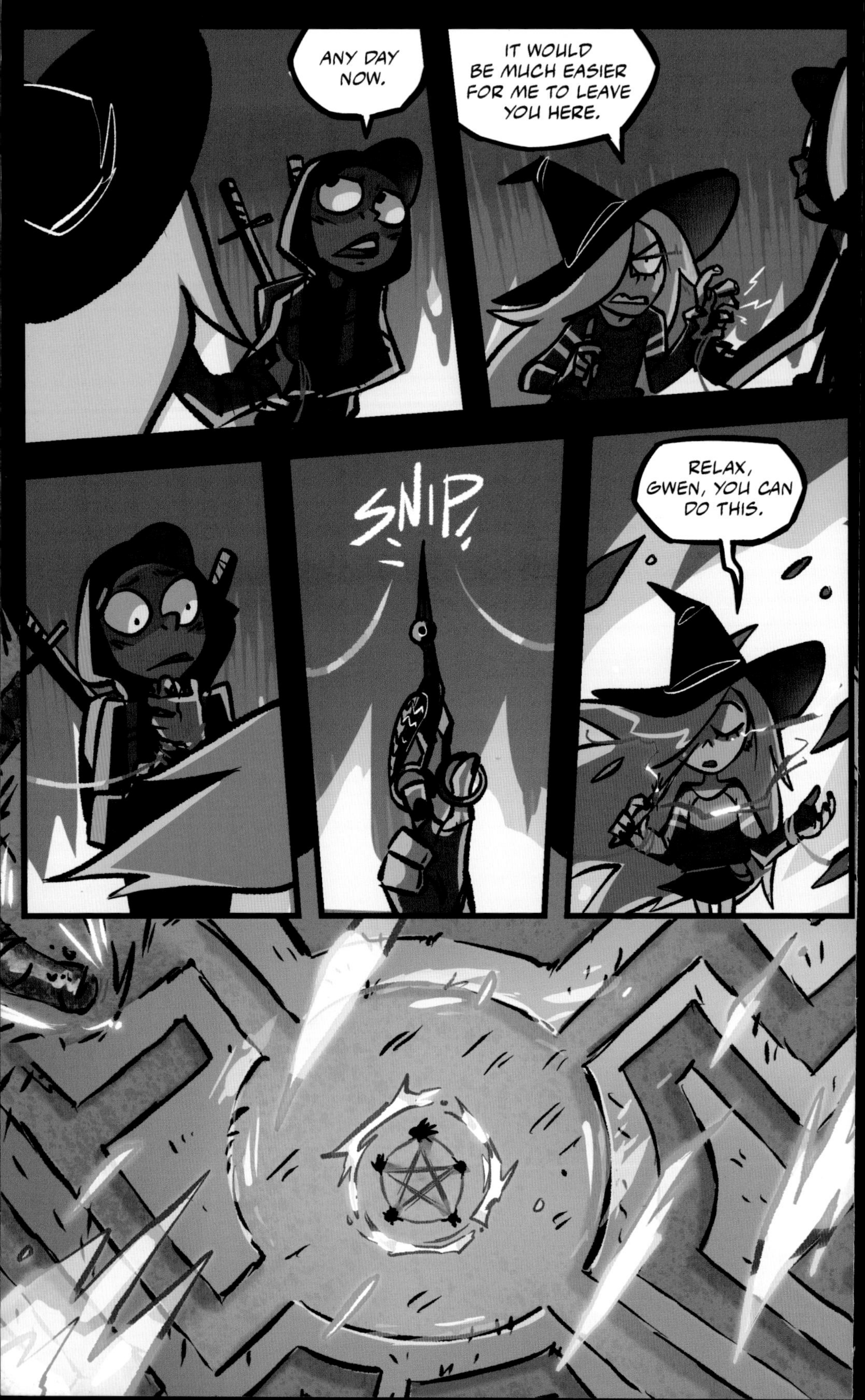
ANY DAY NOW.
IT WOULD BE MUCH EASIER FOR ME TO LEAVE YOU HERE.
SNIP
RELAX, GWEN, YOU CAN DO THIS.

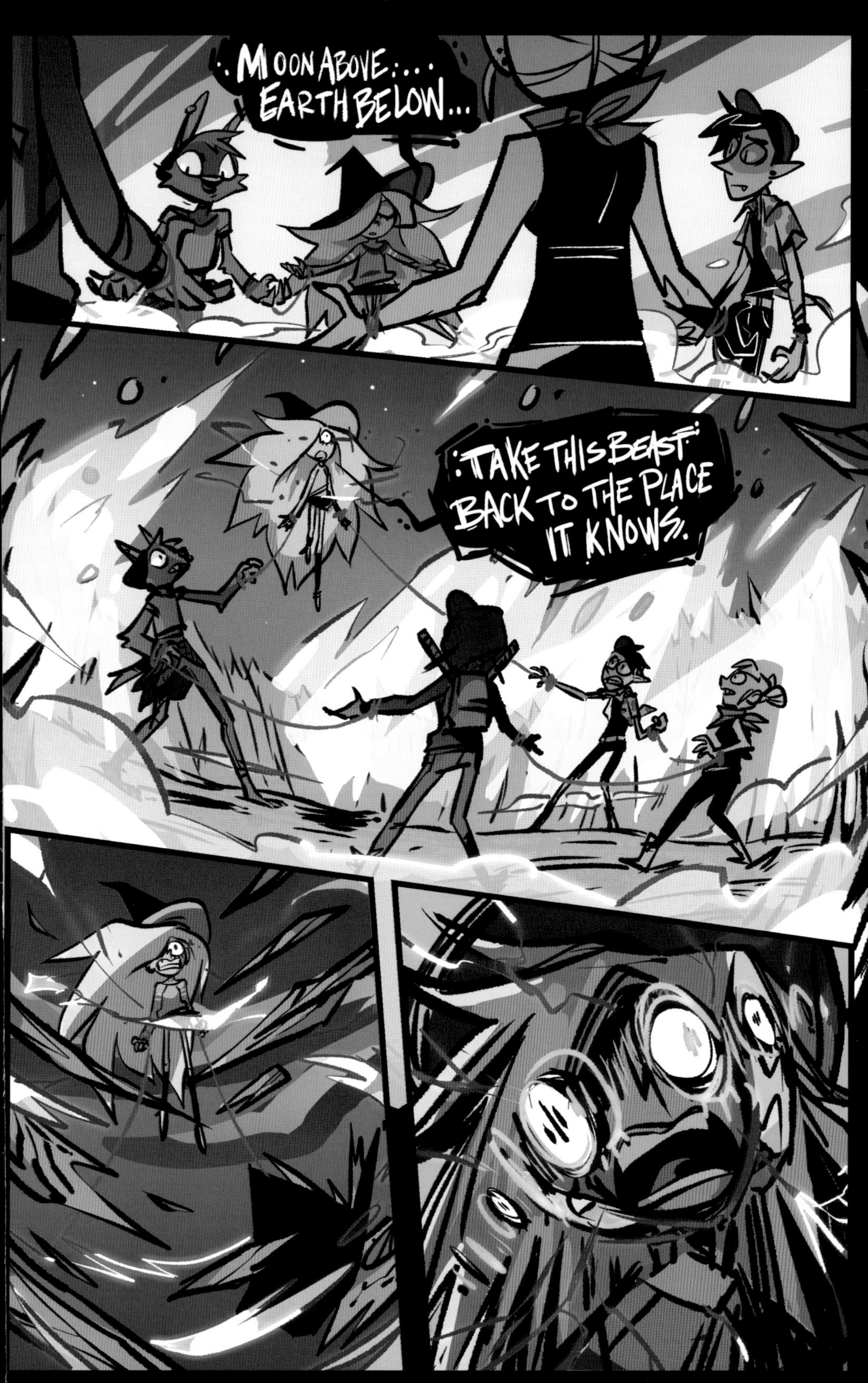
MOON ABOVE... EARTH BELOW...
TAKE THIS BEAST BACK TO THE PLACE IT KNOWS.

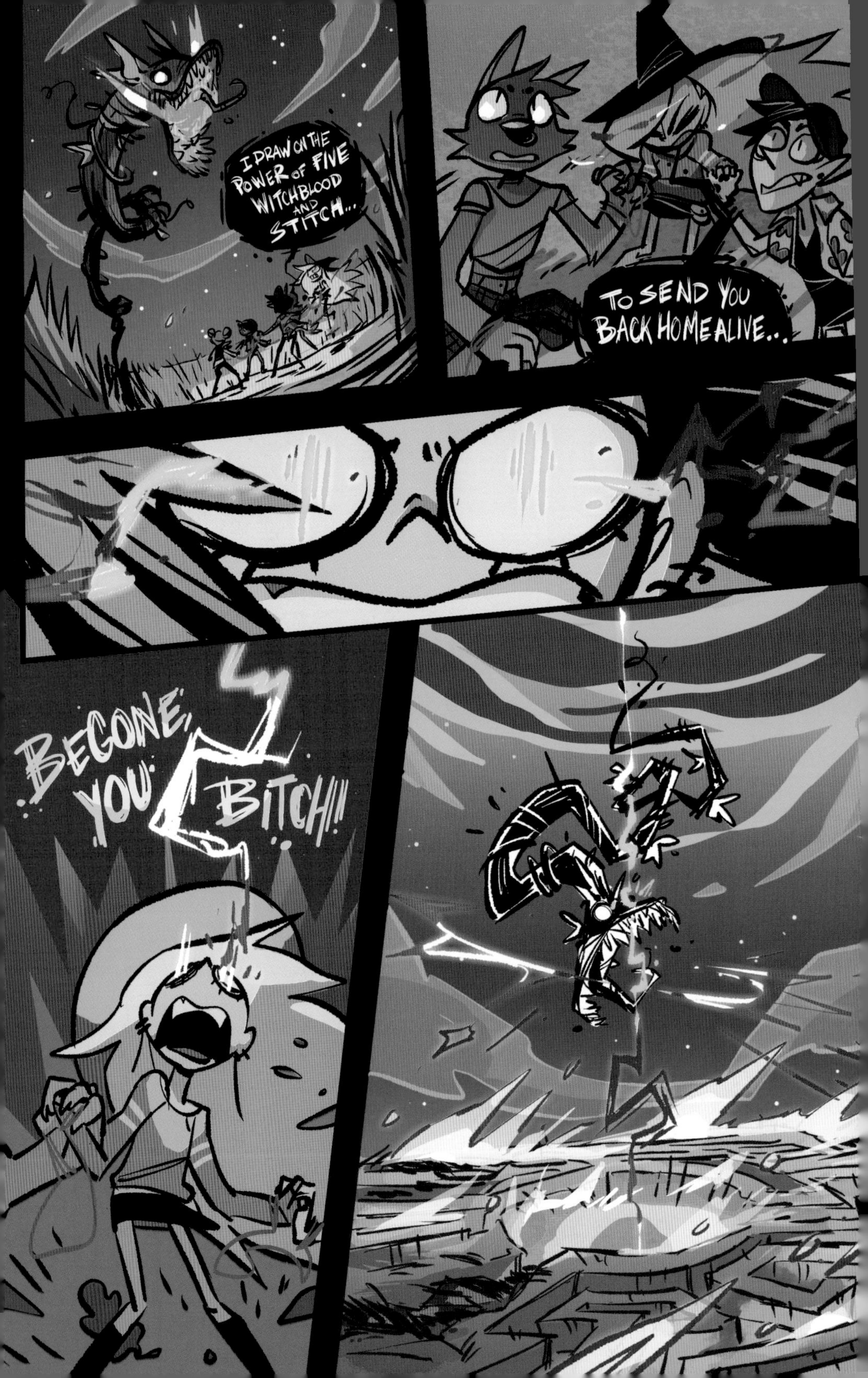
I DRAW ON THE POWER OF FIVE WITCHBLOOD AND STITCH...
TO SEND YOU BACK HOME ALIVE...
BEGONE, YOU BITCH!!!

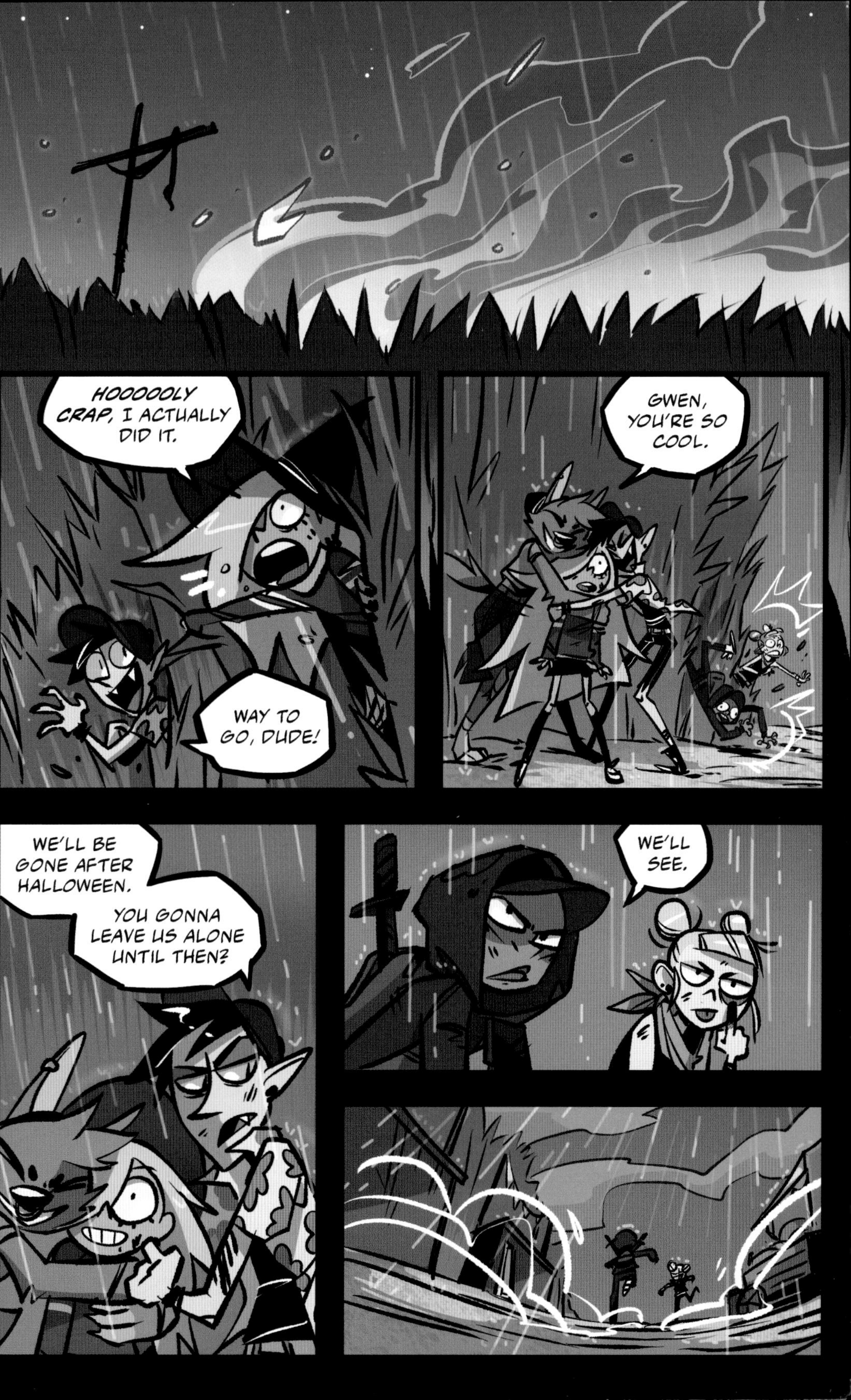
HOOOOOLY CRAP, I ACTUALLY DID IT.
WAY TO GO, DUDE!
GWEN, YOU'RE SO COOL.
WE'LL BE GONE AFTER HALLOWEEN.
YOU GONNA LEAVE US ALONE UNTIL THEN?
WE'LL SEE.

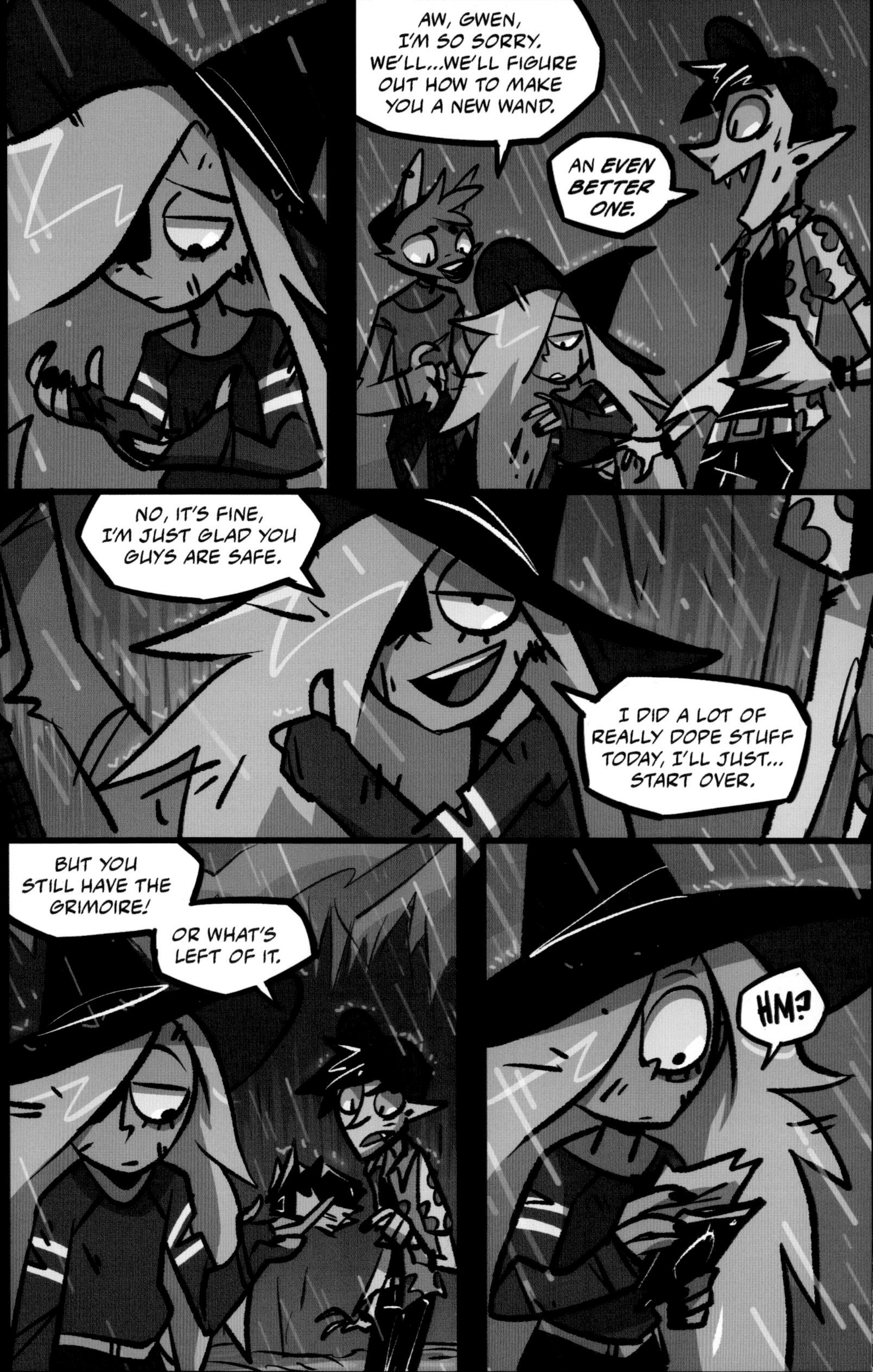
AW, GWEN, I'M SO SORRY. WE'LL...WE'LL FIGURE OUT HOW TO MAKE YOU A NEW WAND.
AN *EVEN* BETTER ONE.
NO, IT'S FINE, I'M JUST GLAD YOU GUYS ARE SAFE.
I DID A LOT OF REALLY DOPE STUFF TODAY, I'LL JUST... START OVER.
BUT YOU STILL HAVE THE GRIMOIRE!
OR WHAT'S LEFT OF IT.
HM?

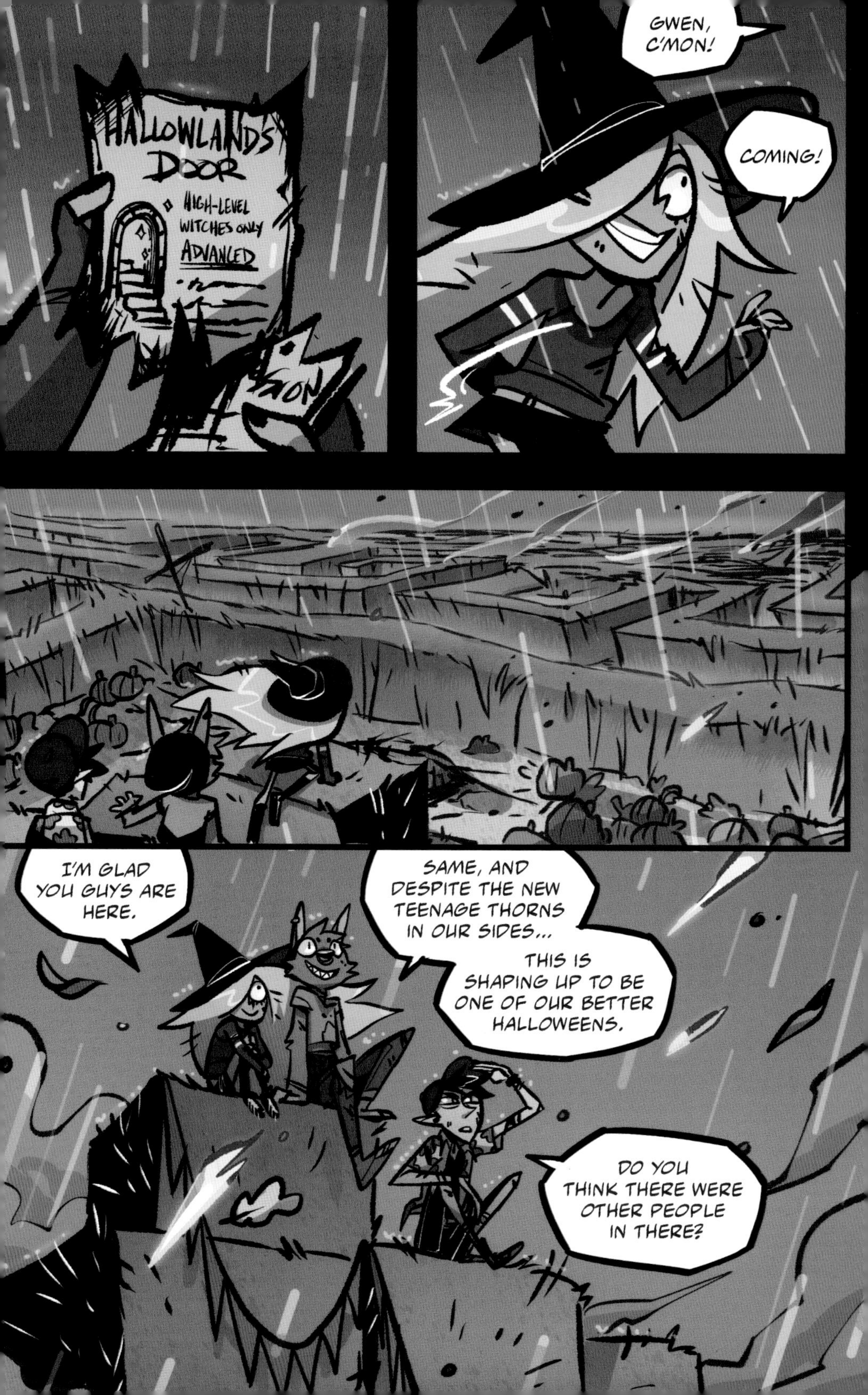
HALLOWLANDS DOOR
HIGH-LEVEL WITCHES ONLY
ADVANCED
GWEN, C'MON!
COMING!
I'M GLAD YOU GUYS ARE HERE.
SAME, AND DESPITE THE NEW TEENAGE THORNS IN OUR SIDES...
THIS IS SHAPING UP TO BE ONE OF OUR BETTER HALLOWEENS.
DO YOU THINK THERE WERE OTHER PEOPLE IN THERE?

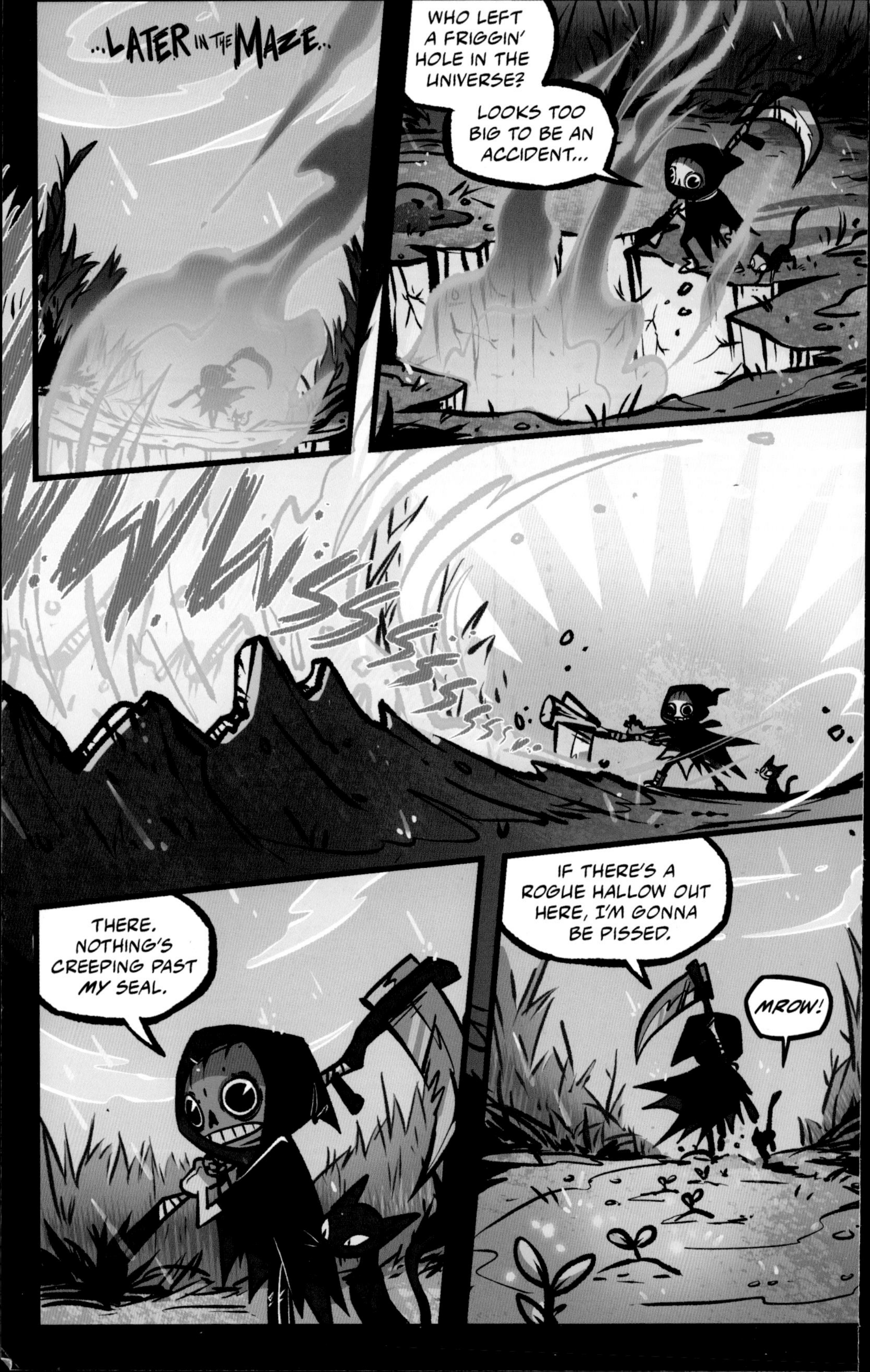
...LATER IN THE MAZE...
WHO LEFT A FRIGGIN' HOLE IN THE UNIVERSE?
LOOKS TOO BIG TO BE AN ACCIDENT...
WWWWSSSSSSSSS
THERE. NOTHING'S CREEPING PAST MY SEAL.
IF THERE'S A ROGUE HALLOW OUT HERE, I'M GONNA BE PISSED.
MROW!